ROUGH BEAST

ROUGH BEAST

A NOVEL BY

GARY GOSHGARIAN

DONALD I. FINE, INC.
New York

For Kathleen, again, and
Nathan and David—not so rough.

Copyright © 1995 by Gary Goshgarian

Library of Congress Catalogue Card Number: 95-060937

ISBN: 1-55611-464-8

Manufactured in the United States of America

10   9   8   7   6   5   4   3   2   1

Designed by Irving Perkins Associates

And what rough beast, its hour come round at last,
Slouches towards Bethlehem to be born?

—William Butler Yeats
"The Second Coming"

AUTHOR'S NOTE

A special thanks goes out to the following people for providing me with medical and other technical information: Jerry Yukovitch, Allen Katz, Eliot Spector, Charles Ellis, Frederic C. Blanc, Dr. Mauricio Fava and Dr. Douglas Geenans. If there are any technical inaccuracies, they are all mine.

Also, there is no town of Carleton or Coburn in Masschusetts or Argyle-on-the-Hudson in New York. Nor, to my knowledge, was there any research project such as the one described in this story.

PROLOGUE

Ten years ago.

Joe Samborsky was not certain that the howl came from him or the house. But it jolted him out of his doze.

For a moment he blinked around the living room from the wing chair. Everything was still. No movement, no sound but the rain on the windows. Nothing out of place. The reading lamp beside him was still on, but the fire was now a bed of ash and unburnt log ends. His magazine had slipped to the floor. On the table still sat the half-glass of water and his vial of nitroglycerin. He flicked the cap and popped a pill under his tongue. In a minute the hot bulb in his chest would cool.

Probably a dream, he told himself—the tail end of some nightmare soundtrack played on the inside of his skull. Except the howl still resonated in his consciousness.

He hoisted himself out of the chair and shuffled to the staircase. The master bedroom at the top right was dark. The stillness of the house magnified the creaking of the stairs as he climbed. He muttered a prayer it wasn't Anna in the grip of a stroke or cardiac arrest, but the moment he stepped into the bedroom he could hear the soft grating of her breath. Thank God, she lay peacefully asleep.

He headed down.

Sophie. Maybe her time had come. According to Dr. Beth, she wasn't due for another two weeks. But vets had been wrong before.

The clock in the kitchen said 2:20. He slid the bolt on the cellar door. If she was delivering, he'd wake up Anna. It was possible Sophie just

1

yowled in her sleep, dream-running from that randy mongrel up the road.

Joe flicked the switch. The cellar was strangely quiet. No clicking of her nails as she crossed the floor. No red-and-white spaniel smiling up at him. Not even a whimper as the light roused her from sleep. What if she had already delivered and was down there quietly nursing her pups? Anna would be furious if he discovered them without her. She was ritualistic about important events. Also, Sophie was technically Anna's dog, her constant companion before the bypass that sent Joe into retirement.

He would have gone back up for her except for the strange hush from below. Perhaps he was still a little charged from that howl, but it was so quiet down there. As if the cellar were holding its breath.

Another thing, the air had a damp acrid quality—the way it did before they had the ditches dug. If there was water on the floor from the rain, he'd give those construction guys hell. Six months ago he had shelled out $1,800 to have four drainage ditches dug out back to stop storm flooding. Because they were at the bottom of a hill, the cellar flooded after a major downpour, filling the place with an awful smell. If there was water on the floor, he would raise his own stink.

He clutched his nitros and started down. If Sophie had delivered, he'd tell Anna how he just woke up himself. She'd never know he peeked.

Halfway down, Joe Samborsky heard a queer animal sound that sent a shard of ice through his heart.

"I'm coming, girl," he said. "It's all right."

Joe rounded the bottom stair toward the furnace where Sophie's basket sat with the bright red goosedown pillow, the one Anna bought when Sophie had conceived, the one from the Orvis catalogue—a hugh cushiony mitt that could accommodate a Saint Bernard, Joe had said. Anna fussed that if Sophie had a large litter, she'd need a big bed. Joe mumbled something about spoiling the old girl, but he wrote a check for $92.48. Two weeks later Sophie got her bright red corduroy, hand-stitched genuine goosedown nursing nest.

It was the odor that hit him first. Butchershop smells.

Sophie lay on her side a few feet from the workbench. Sophie's time had come, all right, but she never made it to her basket.

In that instant before realization, it looked as if she had dragged the bright red pillow from the wicker to the middle of the cement floor, deciding there wasn't enough room in the basket for her and her pups. Her left hind leg was frozen in the air, as if asking Joe for a belly rub.

But it wasn't her pillow. Sophie lay on the bloodied heap of her insides that had come from a rupture in her stomach. Her eyes were open, blood was pooling under her mouth, her tongue hung out.

But what made Joe cry out were the three white things feeding on Sophie's innards. They looked like huge pupa with domed heads and claws. Two were in a tug of war with a length of Sophie's intestines, the third was busy within the carcass. When it heard Joe, its head snapped up, a shiny organ clenched in its teeth. It snarled, estimating Joe with slitted eyes that assuredly did not belong to any puppy in creation. Nor did its reptile claws and scaly hide.

Inside Joe's chest the bulb flared white hot, sending a filament down his arm. One of them now shuffled toward him with its back raised, hunched to spring. Joe's body slammed backward into the support pole. The pain never registered. Nor the fact that the nitros dropped out of his hand. As he clutched his chest, Anna came thumping down the stairs, calling his name. Joe tried to tell her to stay up, for God's sake . . . Go back, damn it. But the words wouldn't come.

For a brutal moment before his heart valve burst, all Joe Samborsky heard was the gnarling of those things at Sophie's remains.

Then his wife Anna screamed as if pieces of her throat were coming loose.

CHAPTER

1

The one thing Terry Hazzard remembered about that strange morning was how the woman who came to buy her house seemed more interested in Terry's moving out than in her moving in.

Her name was Claire Manning, a tense, cheerless woman. She was the sixth party to see the place in a week but the only party to come without the realtor. For some odd reason she wanted to inspect the place on her own.

According to Beverly Otis, their agent, the woman had driven by the other day and "it was love at first sight." Beverly was full of such hype: *A seller's market; money's no object; name your price.* Theirs was $380,000, which the third party had offered and which Terry was happy to accept, except for Beverly's insistence that this Manning woman had come by to bid. "The way she carried on," Beverly had said, "I think she'd kill for it."

She pulled up the driveway in a modest blue sedan a little after eight. An hour early. Terry didn't want to show the place until Calvin was off to work and Matty at school. Calvin was gone, but her twelve-year-old Matty was still inside. And he was in one of his black moods. The kind that triggered fifty-megaton headaches.

Except for her stern expression, Mrs. Manning was quite handsome. She looked to be in her late fifties, had stylishly coiffed champagne hair and was smartly dressed in a beige designer pants suit, white silk blouse and several twenty-two-carat gold chains—in fact, too smartly for house shopping. She also looked incongruous beside the Ford Escort. More the Mercedes or Jaguar type, Terry thought.

Through oversized red-tint lenses she said, "I'm sorry about the time, but I have to leave town shortly." A faint birthmark made a stain under her right eye.

"No problem," Terry said, and led her up the driveway.

"It's just the kind of place we're looking for." There was a forced brightness in her tone.

"Have you been looking long?"

"No," she said, but didn't elaborate.

"Are you from out of state?"

"Yes." Another expectant pause, then as an afterthought she added, "Virginia."

A diamond the size of a small olive lit up her ring finger. A good sign, Terry thought. Beverly was hoping she'd top the price at four hundred thousand—which amazed Terry, given that they had bought the place just ten years earlier for $72,000. Terry had to wonder why so fancy a woman was even interested in buying her house. After all, eight-room colonials were common fare in Boston suburbs. And Carleton was not Weston or Dover. Maybe she liked trees. They bordered five hundred acres of dense conservation land —Magog Woods.

"My husband's taking a new teaching job in New York state," Terry said to keep things going.

"How nice." Her smile was like a rictus. And beneath the ceramic exterior she seemed distracted.

"Is your husband coming by?" Terry asked.

The question brought her head around. "My husband?" The birthmark flared. The woman looked startled.

"You said just the kind of place we're looking for."

"Yes, of course," she said, her face relaxing. "No, he's not coming by." And she looked away.

As the woman paused to take in the landscaping, Terry felt a sudden ambivalence. While she was glad to be starting anew, she worried if they could ever find as nice a place, even on Calvin's increased salary. From a real-estate point of view, theirs was a middle-class dream house—a twenty-year-old central-entrance colonial with eight rooms, two fireplaces, a large modern kitchen, a spacious family room, and surrounded by a sweeping lawn and flower gardens spread over an acre lot. Six months ago they put in a twenty-by-forty-foot swimming pool that was Calvin's idea—a yearning since a childhood of poverty.

But what made the place exceptional was Magog Woods. It created the illusion of quintessential rural living though Carleton was just ten miles west of Boston. Who could ask for more, and on an English professor's salary?

And yet, she was relieved to be leaving. The memories of two stillbirths in the last three years were hauntingly bound to the place. The first was far enough back for time to have dulled the sting. But the second, last November 11, to be exact, still gnawed at her. She was nearly eight months into term when the staining began. While taking a shower on the morning of the tenth, she started hemorrhaging; before she had passed out, Calvin rushed her to Emerson emergency. Two days later she was sent home without a baby. For the second time in three years she had stripped a nursery—shelves stuffed with animals, pictures, mobiles, Matty's repainted crib, even the wallpaper she had hung herself. She had not entered the room since. Like the first, that fetus was severely deformed.

Six months had passed, yet she was still beset by the hundred painful reminders triggered by the merest detail—the slant of the sunlight through the window, the musty odors of spring-damp woods, the hum of the shower.

Calvin said she was being irrational. Lots of women had miscarriages but they didn't scapegoat their homes. Terry knew that. Yet she felt as if they were sharing the place with an unseen malevolence, like that house in that *Amityville Horror* movie. No midnight screams from the cellar or rats in the walls or footsteps on the roof. Nothing so dramatic. Nor the occasional bouts of murky water, funny odors, or horticultural blight. It was the more subtle signs: what was happening to them as a family. As if the internal rules had been altered; their son Matty's extreme, even violent, mood swings, Calvin's sexual alienation, and those awful miscarriages. Even these migraines. Until recently she never got headaches. Were she given to such beliefs, which she was not, she would swear their house was cursed.

Then out of the blue came Calvin's job offer—and, with it, release, escape. . . .

"Mrs. Manning," Terry said when they reached the front door, "my son is inside. I'd appreciate it if you didn't mention the reason you're here."

The woman took off her glasses to read Terry's face. Her eyes were marbles of blue ice. "I don't quite follow."

"Well, it's just he's not too keen on moving . . . you know, leaving his friends and all. He's quite attached to the place."

The truth was, Terry feared another scene. Last week when they broke the news about Calvin's new job, Matty had a full-blown temper tantrum. He locked himself in his room, pounding and swearing that it wasn't fair, that they couldn't make him move. When it was over, Terry discovered that he had punched a fist-sized hole in the wall.

The woman glared at her as if to say she wasn't out here in her DKNY suit, Ferragamo pumps and pricey chains to be jerked around by some wishy-washy suburban hausfrau. "I understand, but you *are* thinking of selling." It was less a question than a statement.

"Yes, of course."

"And when exactly are you planning to move?"

"Sometime over the summer."

"The summer is three months long. Could you be more definite?"

She was all business. Well, it could take them months to find a place up there. "The earliest we could be out would be July 15." The same date she quoted to others.

The birthmark darkened like litmus. "Mrs. Otis said you wanted to finalize as soon as possible."

"That's true, but we're not planning on moving for two months." Matty's Little League went to the first week in July. Even the fifteenth would be pushing it.

"There must be a misunderstanding. We expect to be in by June 1."

"June 1? That's only three weeks." Either Beverly had misstated things or this woman was confused. "My son doesn't get out of school until the seventeenth." She struggled for a moment. "I mean, the absolute earliest would be July 1."

There was an uneasy glint in the woman's eyes, but she tossed her head and it was gone. "Well, I'm sure we can work it out." She glanced at her watch and walked to the front door.

Work what out? Terry wondered. There was no way they could

move in three weeks. And why bring up a date before she's even stepped inside?

Terry pulled open the screen door and wondered how Calvin must have felt when he first laid eyes on the place—like Moses glimpsing the promised land.

They had been living in a four-room flat in a congested and depressed part of Watertown, a place that had grown cramped once Matty was born. For over a year they had looked in Carleton and neighboring towns. Then, coincidentally, Beverly Otis called. Calvin came out on his own, took one look and offered the widow her asking price before she came to her senses or before anybody else topped his bid.

"The steal of the century," Beverly had proclaimed. By the time he brought Terry out, it was a done deal. He had bought the Samborsky place for a song, unaware, of course, of the history of the Samborskys in that house.

Terry led the way in, her head pounding.

Matty was on his knees in the back closet when they entered the kitchen. "Mom, where's my glove? I can't find it." He had Little League practice after school.

"Look under your bed?" said Terry, and introduced Mrs. Manning as a fellow environmental campaigner.

He gave a perfunctory wave, then bounded up stairs. He was dressed in jeans and a long-sleeve turtleneck. He looked too warm for the day. Terry had given up pushing him to wear one of the beautiful polo shirts she had spent a fortune on. She'd settle on him just being civilized. The legendary teenage miserableness had struck early.

Terry opened the cupboards and drawers, pointing out their spaciousness and the energy-efficient appliances. The woman looked around in a mechanical kind of way. She was more interested in the article under the refrigerator magnet: Terry's own op-ed piece in the *Patriot Chronicle* last month, the one in which she urged county residents to take a stand in forcing one of the area's worst polluters to clean up waterways fouled by years of illegal dumping.

She wished she had thought of removing it. No way to sell your house. "Unfortunately," she said, feeling the need to explain, "Carleton is a tad complacent about such things." The fact was that most Carletonites wouldn't fess up to a problem unless they found the *Exxon Valdez* in their swimming pools.

The woman walked to the sink. She fingered the purifier attached to the faucet. "Have you had water problems?"

"Not to speak of. Comes out a little murky once in a while."

"It was pretty bad in the shower this morning," Matty said, coming back into the kitchen and stuffing his glove into his handpack.

Terry gave him a look. "Because of all the rain the last few days."

The woman looked concerned and turned on the water, watching it stream into the sink. It ran clear.

"We get bottled water anyway. Everybody does these days."

"Gotta go," Matty said, and stuffed a wedge of toast in his mouth. He had not touched the grapefruit or the bowl of yogurt and muesli. Were the woman not there, Terry would have made a fuss, but she didn't want to risk a scene.

"Eat this on the way." She stuffed a banana in his backpack. "And feed the cat, please."

He ignored her.

"Hey," she sang out pleasantly, "Daisy needs to be fed."

He brushed past her. "Fuck you." The words were barely audible, but Terry felt as if she had been punched. "What?"

"I said you feed her, I'm late."

Terry gaped at him. That's *not* what he had said. And the realization jagged through her. He had his foul moods, even temper tantrums, but never had he spoken to her like this.

She took a deep breath to regain control. Mrs. Manning, still at the sink, gave them the quick eye, then turned to the backyard.

Terry's face burned. "Matthew!" she said as he opened the back door. "Feed the cat."

He stopped and looked back at her, eyes dilated, challenging her. For a moment the room faded to a blur, as if they were locked in a tunnel vision. He's going to explode, she thought. He's going to have another fit right in front of this woman.

But he didn't. Instead, he stomped back into the kitchen and dumped a can of fish into the cat's bowl.

Terry felt the press of tears but fought it back, making an awkward grimace to Mrs. Manning as if to say her young son had gotten up on the wrong side of the bed. The woman turned anxiously to the window again, watching a raccoon drinking from the open pool.

Matty opened the cellar door and plunked down the bowl. "She outside?" he said.

Ordinarily the cat would be right there, eager to get at the chow.

"No." Terry peered down the stairs. In the muted light she saw the cat crouched at the bottom stair—poised, her ears flat back, her eyes large. When Matty called her, she shot away.

"That's odd," Terry said, trying to deflect attention to the cat.

"Maybe it's me," said Mrs. Manning.

"But she's not shy. Quite the contrary."

Mrs. Manning glanced down the stairs. "She looks frightened."

"Probably the raccoons," Terry said, grateful for new footing. "Last week a big male chased her onto the garage roof." She could see the cat hissing at her from the shadows below.

"Bet it's rabies," Matty said.

"Rabies?" Mrs. Manning said.

Damn, Terry thought. He's doing it on purpose. "Matty, she doesn't have rabies." But she made a mental note to call the vet.

"That's what the papers said."

He was trying to drive the woman away. To kill the sale.

She took in a lungful of air. "Oh, there was some report of a few wild animals having the disease," she said, "but that was in the western part of the state, Pittsfield or someplace. A dog and a couple of skunks tested positive, but that's eighty miles away."

"The papers said strange animal behavior in Magog Woods."

Terry's face flushed. She imagined the woman's report to her husband. Nice home, lovely landscaping, big brand-new pool, woods full of rabid raccoons. Drawing out the syllables she said, "Matthew, you're going to be late."

He read the anger in her face, but before he was out the back door, he flashed a secret grin. She could feel its heat on her face.

"Is there something I should know?" Mrs. Manning's expression looked like cement hardening.

"Noo," Terry said. "Some frisky raccoons, a few dead squirrels, no big deal. And," she added, "they *all* tested negative. I can assure you, there haven't been any reports of rabies anywhere near here."

Which was true, but she didn't tell the woman how officials were baffled by the condition of the carcasses. They had been ravaged.

During the next fifteen minutes, as she led Mrs. Manning through the rooms, Terry became certain that the woman was simply going through the motions. Whatever interest she'd shown outside had faded to perfunctory responses. Not the responses of a woman "who'd kill for it." No questions about closet space or insulation, no comments about the large crack in the ceiling of the family room. Nor any sign that the woman was digesting any of the details about plumbing and electricity that Terry rattled off. She also had no interest in seeing the cellar. (Probably afraid Daisy would spring on her, foaming at the mouth.) Had she not specified the new heating system, Terry was sure the woman would never have asked. She had written the place off and was just following through to be polite. Way to go, Matty!

It wasn't until they were upstairs that Mrs. Manning displayed the slightest interest. She asked about the room with the closed door. Terry's stomach made a fist as she opened it. She explained their eventual plans for a guest room. But as she moved to close the door, Mrs. Manning pushed her way in. Her eyes caught the hot air balloons and goofy cats Terry had painted on the ceiling.

"Looks like a nursery," the woman said. "Are you having a baby?"

"I was," Terry said. "I lost it."

"I'm sorry to hear that," she said, and walked to the rear window. Then as if to clear the air, she said, "Is the pool new?"

"Yes, last fall."

For some reason, the woman was interested. "Must have been a project putting it in."

"Yes." The house was perched on a hill with mature growth all around. "They had to cut a lot of trees for the bulldozers and all. It was a real circus."

Something dark moved across Mrs. Manning's expression. "I can imagine."

"Do you have children?" Terry asked.

"No."

"Is the pool a problem for you?"

The woman turned sharply. "Should it be?" That strange intensity was back in her eyes.

"No, I mean, some people find it a liability."

"Not at all," she said, flashing her facsimile smile. Then she stepped out.

Terry closed the door, feeling puzzled, as if something else had just been exchanged. She showed the other guest room and bath. Mrs. Manning gave cursory glances, checked her watch, then followed Terry into the office, which, because of the huge twin skylights, was the brightest room in the house. Terry pushed open a window and warm air flooded in.

Mrs. Manning peered out. "So very quiet."

"We almost never see cars on the street."

Boston was only ten miles away, but they could have been living in Aroostook County, Maine. Because of the woods, their neighborhood felt sealed off. The only hint of civilization was the barking of the Starkeys' German shepherd on Hutchinson. Some days the tranquility was so stark that Terry craved the din of the outside world. A few weeks ago a DPW crew was down the street working on some kind of feasibility study for a town sewer. Instead of annoyance, the drilling and jackhammering were a relief from the constipated hush. When one of the workers, a big blond guy, later dropped by to fill his thermos, Terry was so grateful for the company, she had to restrain her gabbiness so as not to give the wrong impression.

Mrs. Manning scanned the two desks—Calvin's neat piles of student papers and Terry's stacked with bills.

"What do you do?" Mrs. Manning asked.

It was a question she hated, because simple motherhood never seemed valid. For seven years she had taught art at Carleton High until Matty started grade school. Once they moved, she intended to find another job, maybe with a newspaper; and the NYPI Office of Personnel had promised to help place her. She glanced at the desk photo of Matty in his number 11 Devil Dogs shirt. "Just raising my son."

"And your husband is a professor of English."

"How did you know?"

The birthmark again flared. "Well, you must have mentioned it," she said. "I'm not psychic."

"Of course." She had mentioned his new teaching job, but had she specified college? Or English? It didn't matter. Her headache was making her feel faint, and all she wanted was to get this over with so she could lie down. The woman was weird and unpleasant.

She led the way to Matty's room. "I must caution you, he's entered his Ooga-Booga phase."

"Beg pardon?"

"Technical jargon," she said opening the door.

The walls were plastered with posters for horror movies. Between those for *Pet Sematary* and *Child's Play* was a large picture of Freddy Krueger with his flame-rutted face and five-blade slasher claw. (It covered the hole Matty had punched in the wall.) On the opposite wall were some of Matty's own drawings—werewolves, full hairy faces with bloody mouths and bright green eyes. And with Matty's likeness. Of all the pictures in the room, these bothered Terry the most—the ones Matty had apparently projected of himself.

"We're hoping his next stage is Monet," Terry said, "but it'll probably be Hieronymous Bosch."

The woman was not amused. She checked her watch, her jaw was set to go. The visit had been a waste of time. The house was not for her.

Before leaving, Terry's eye caught the aquarium bubbling on the bureau. One of the fish was missing. Yesterday when she was vacuuming, there were two golden fantails, now there was one. The female was gone. Matty would have mentioned it if it had died. The big male was fixed at the bottom by himself. Poor guy, Terry thought, lost your woman. Maybe Daisy had pawed her out. But cats didn't really do that, did they? Besides, she hasn't been out of the cellar for a week.

Terry took a pinch of flaked shrimp from the can. Condolences, she thought, and flicked her fingers above the surface.

Suddenly the fish shot up from the bottom right out of the water and sunk its teeth into the tip of her finger. Terry let out a yelp, more out of shock than pain. The fish was fixed on her finger, flapping in the air.

"God," Terry cried. She plunged her hand back into the tank, hoping it would swim away. But it didn't. She pulled her hand out again but it held fast, flapping in the air. Though she couldn't feel much pain, blood was mingling with the water. This was ridiculous, she thought. There was a box of Kleenex on Matty's desk. "Could you hand me a few of those?" But when she looked over her shoulder, Mrs. Manning seemed in shock.

"He's stuck," Terry said, grinning foolishly. "I'm fine; I just don't want to drip blood on the carpet."

Mrs. Manning pulled out a wad of tissues.

"Hold them under," Terry said. The woman hesitated for a moment, then held the tissues at arm's length, looking as if she feared the fish would fly off Terry's finger at her.

With her free hand Terry grabbed hold of the body. She didn't want to kill it or give a yank for fear of tearing off a chunk of her finger. Taking care not to crush the rim of its mouth, she pinched it until she worked her finger free. Inside she could see needle-like teeth and a bloody bit of her flesh. She dropped it back into the tank and it shot to the coral arch at the bottom. With the shadows it seemed to be staring at her as its tiny mouth worked away. It was eating a piece of her finger.

She pressed her finger into the tissue, staring dumbly at the fish. "I didn't think they had teeth."

She spoke to herself because Mrs. Manning was on her way down the stairs, wiping her face and hand on a handkerchief as if she'd been sprayed with acid.

Terry followed her out the front door and down the driveway. The incident had clearly upset her. "Sorry about that," she said. "I'm really fine."

No doubt, it was the last she would see of her. Before bombing back home, she'd probably make a pit stop at the Emerson emergency room for a rabies shot.

Mrs. Manning got in the car and closed the door.

"I'm really fine," Terry repeated through the closed window. "It's nothing."

The woman started the car. Not even a goodbye?

Through the window Terry saw her scribble something on a slip of paper. Then the window rolled down.

"My number is on the back," she said, handing it to Terry.

There was an out-of-state number on the back. She turned it over. It was a check made out to Calvin and Terry Hazzard: $300,000.

"What's this?"

"A fifty-percent deposit."

"You've got to be kidding," Terry muttered.

"Hardly," she said without humor. "I'll make the formal arrangement with Mrs. Otis and set up a convenient time to pass papers if the amount is sufficient."

"Six hundred thousand dollars?" Terry felt dazed.

"Yes, but it comes with the stipulation that you vacate by June 1. I'm sorry, but it's impossible to be more flexible. Perhaps," she added, "you can rent a place until your son is out of school."

Terry nodded dumbly, trying to put it all together. She wanted to say $600,000 was ridiculous, nearly twice its value. But she caught herself and took a deep breath to regain control. "I have to talk it over with my husband first," she said. "It's only three weeks."

"I understand. I'll contact you tomorrow."

"That's too soon."

The woman clearly didn't like that but said, "All right, Wednesday," and cranked up her window, her manner void of any pleasure expected of the occasion.

She drove down the driveway and into the street, leaving Terry staring at the check and wondering what the hell had just happened.

Ten minutes later Claire Manning had the Escort up to seventy in the fast lane of Route 2 heading east toward Boston. From her carry-on bag she pulled out a portable phone and made three calls. The first to Beverly Otis to tell her that by noon Wednesday she wanted the purchase-and-sale agreement signed and the lawyer lined up for the title-transfer by the week's end. Beverly promised to take care of the necessary details and would have it all wrapped up as desired. As soon as papers were passed, as agreed, Beverly would receive a $20,000 cash bonus above her six percent fee.

The second call was to BlueSky Charter at Logan Airport, where her Learjet was fueled and waiting to take her to Dulles International near Washington, D.C. She informed her pilot that, given the light traffic, she would reach Logan by ten-fifteen, leaving plenty of time to drop the car off at Budget. The flight would take only an hour, which meant no problem making the twelve-thirty luncheon. She was already dressed.

The third call was to her husband.

She felt a small ripple of excitement as she punched the numbers. She had never before dialed the White House.

After two transfers she heard her husband's voice.

"I'm on my way," she said.

"How did it go?"

"The good news," she said, "is that we're almost home."

There was a pause. "And the bad?"

"I'll tell you in person."

"Claire, I'm in the antechamber of the Oval Office."

"All the more reason."

"Well, how bad is it?"

"Nothing that can't be fixed."

"You're sure."

"I'm sure."

"Fine. It's what I want to hear," he said. "Don't be late. We're having lunch with the president and secretary of defense at twelve-thirty."

"When was the last time I let you down?"

"Good point."

CHAPTER

2

Calvin Hazzard looked out his office window to the grungy strip of stores along the trolley tracks and thought about the view from the lush green bluff over the Hudson River. Then he walked down the hall to the office of the English department chair and turned in his resignation.

Before this, he had never thought of living anywhere else but in Boston. More than half his adult life had been spent here. He had gone to Northeastern University and Harvard, and for the last dozen years had taught at Middlesex State College, in the heart of the city. Yet after two decades he had grown weary of urban life: of the concrete and steel, the congestion, the bumper-to-bumper commute, and, of course, the soaring street violence that was rapidly diminishing the quality of life. Every week the student newspaper published a list of robberies and muggings on campus. Two years ago a student was murdered on the way to her car.

While it was never an option, he had for years harbored a yearning for a simpler, greener world—maybe someplace in Vermont or Maine, taking his job at a picturesque little college with a horizon of mountains instead of Vito's Onion-and-Steak Subs. Then two weeks ago the Fed-Expressed letter arrived, and now he was thinking of living out the rest of his life in Argyle-on-the-Hudson, New York, a flossy little town distinguished by its postcardy views, secluded summer estates and a small, handsome technical college.

"New York Polytechnic Institute," said Charlie Cobb, looking at Calvin's letter. "Isn't that where you gave a paper?"

"The same place." Last month, on an unexpected invitation, he had delivered a paper on Hemingway to members of its English department.

Cobb squinted at the address. "Argyle-on-the-Hudson?" he drew out the syllables as if it were a town in Uzbekistan. "What's it near?"

"Clover Junction."

Cobb snorted. "That's what I thought." Charlie lived in Back Bay, two trolley stops from campus. He once said he'd rather be mugged than live in the country. "Better you than me."

His voice was cut by police sirens Dopplering by. Calvin had become so inured to the city sounds that he barely noticed. What in Argyle-on-the-Hudson were birdsong and chapel bells.

Cobb's eyebrow arched quizzically. "I just don't get it."

Calvin nodded at the window. "What, that I could leave all this?" The Middlesex campus, which squatted on Columbus Avenue just beyond Mass. Ave., consisted of tightly packed white brick cubes that had as much collegiate charm as a turpentine factory.

"Okay, it's not Harvard Yard, but you're a tenured full professor at a respectable university in the heart of Boston." He kicked a stack of cardboard boxes beside his desk. It was full of applications from people responding to a department ad for a Romantics scholar. "One opening and three hundred applications. There are people in here who'd give an arm for your job."

He was right, of course. Boston was the academic Gold Coast, with more institutions of higher learning within a ten-mile radius than anywhere else in the world, and a quarter-million college students who kept the city young and smart. Though Middlesex State was a lackluster place, with a Papa Gino's in the student union, a ghetto at its flanks, and trolley tracks bisecting the campus, it still lay at the heart of America's cultural map.

"You're leaving Mecca for the goddamn boonies."

"That wouldn't be my wording, but something like that." And Calvin had a flash of New York Poly's campus—a splendid array of Gothic buildings, oak trees and rolling greens perched above the Hudson River. The English department, located beside a sleepy duck pond, was a solidly built structure of gray stone and brick, festooned with ivy and looking like it grew naturally out of the site. The campus looked like Oxford University in miniature. It also had a wonderful gym with a machine for every muscle.

"Look, if it's sylvan remoteness you want, move to Acton or Boxford, or some other hole in the woods," Cobb said. "No doubt they offered a higher salary."

"If they offered less, I'd be paying *them*."

Charlie laughed. It was a department joke that you were rolling if you made your age in thousands. Calvin was thirty-seven and salaried at $36,225, which not only reflected the fact that English professors were universally an underpaid breed, but as a state institution Middlesex paid according to civil service scales. Were it not for the meager annuities from his writing text, Terry would still be teaching high school. As it was, they had to borrow to build the pool.

"You going to tell me how much?"

"Sure you want to know?"

"Just curious how much I'm losing you by."

"An endowed professorship at a hundred grand plus walking money and the two courses of my choice per year."

Charlie Cobb stared at Calvin for a long moment without expression. Then he said, "What the Christ was your paper?"

"*A Farewell to Arms* as early cyberpunk."

"Cut the shit."

Calvin grinned. "Nothing special—a recap of his war years." In fact, it was a patch job of past publications. "I was in the right place at the right time."

"But an endowed chair and a hundred grand? That's remarkable. Remarkable," Charlie repeated, his eyebrows arching in dismay.

Enough dismay to raise a blister of resentment in Calvin, but he bit back a defensive impulse because they were both thinking the same thing.

Calvin was a popular teacher who enjoyed the classroom, but he was not much of a scholar, nor did he endeavor to be. In his twelve years he had published a mere nine papers on twentieth-century American fiction, some travel articles in the popular press, a small university-press book developed from his doctoral thesis on Hemingway to help win his tenure, and a freshman composition text to pay the mortgage. Not the kind of credentials to solicit an endowed chair. Nor were Hemingway scholars in high demand these days. Nobel Prizes notwithstanding, white macho men who posed on the carcasses of endangered species and lamented castration to women were not in.

Also, Calvin Hazzard did not cut a professorial image. He was broad and hard, handsome in a thuggy kind of way, with a head full of dark ringlets and an open manner. His dress was trendy—not an elbow patch or Harris tweed in his wardrobe. As Terry said, he looked more like a health-club trainer who put on a sport coat and tie to attend the opening of a new spa.

Calvin was himself surprised by so kingly an offer, but what the hell! *Carpe* the *diem* while you can.

"You know, of course," Cobb continued, "there's no way I can come remotely close with a counteroffer."

Calvin slapped his chest. "I'm shocked."

"Bullshit, but I wish I could," he said. "Was this something you've been working on for a while? I mean, I didn't see it advertised in the job bulletins."

"It wasn't. They came after me, as difficult as that might be to accept."

"Hell, I didn't mean it that way."

"Yes, you did. How did just-plain Calvin Hazzard pull down such a deal? I'm not sure, but I'm taking it." Then he added, "The idyllic setting notwithstanding, their remoteness is not a draw, I'm told. Nor the fact that they graduate physicists and engineers." He explained it the way Priest had: that until recently the English department was just a service shop—a few nuts-and-bolts comp and lit courses. Then suddenly the board of directors decided that scientists and engineers needed to be humanized. "So they pumped in some dough to beef up the curriculum and recruit staff."

Charlie said, "You're a goddamn peace dividend."

"Me and the Hubble telescope."

"So, for a hundred grand you're going to teach Hemingway to engineers?"

"For a hundred grand I'd teach Hemingway to chipmunks."

Cobb made a snorty laugh. "They must have one hefty endowment."

"Priest said something about an anonymous benefactor with a love of literature and deep pockets."

"And we get Papa Gino."

"Yeah, but those coupons add up."

Cobb nodded. "In a few years we can have the Veggie Special Chair." He stood up and threw his hand across the desk. "Well, my friend, I'm green with envy."

"Expect you'd die of fresh air."

"There's that," Charlie said. "You know, you're leaving me short for the fall schedule with this. It's not the way it's usually done," he said, thinking out loud. "Deliver a paper in April, get bought away in May. Hell, maybe I can scrape up a couple TA replacements. The students will squawk, but it'll save us a few bucks in the long run."

"And you wonder why I'm leaving."

"None of us is here because we want to be," Charlie said. "How does Terry feel about it?"

"She's happy for the change," he said. "We're a little apprehensive about Matty leaving his school and friends. But in the long run I think it'll be good for all of us."

Out the window the clouds moved across the quad. More than the honor and money . . . Calvin saw the move as a way to jump-start their marriage. Terry had not been the same since the last miscarriage. After the initial shock, she had slipped into a state of sullen anxiety. She had badly wanted the baby—another boy, tests had revealed—and had prepared both the house and her soul for it. They had even picked a name. Because it had happened so late in term, the loss was particularly hard—and one that produced a lot of foolish bickering. Worse, its toll was taken of Matty, who apparently dealt with their tension by turning inward, secreting himself in his room or tree house. But it wasn't just Matty's brooding or growing alienation that bothered them. During the last few months he had experienced disturbing fits of anger—unexpected outbursts of rage that Calvin was certain had roots in the tension between him and Terry.

As Calvin watched the trolley squeal to a halt below, he made a silent prayer that their new green world would heal them.

Calvin left Charlie Cobb a little before ten and headed for his second class without stopping at his office. At twelve-twenty he was through for the day. Ordinarily he'd go back to the office and grade papers and hold student conferences. But he had to pick Matty up at school and take him to Little League practice on the other side of town. He also had to stop off at the Registry of Deeds to photostat the deed for their house because their original was destroyed when a bad storm in March flooded their cellar.

Although it was just three hours before the rush hour, the ride to the registry, just across the Charles River, took him forty minutes. Somewhere along the line there was a breakdown that brought the city to a halt as if there had been a nuclear alert. It was one of Boston's oldest traditions, and not one he'd be able to miss.

The Middlesex County Registry of Deeds was a huge red brick Gothic-revival structure designed with turn-of-the-century optimism. The second floor was a human counterpart to the traffic jam. A huge open room with endless rows of standup slant desks at which people were busy taking notes from the large tomes of deeds that filled the shelves in side rooms and the upstairs gallery.

The procedure would have been painless were it not for the lunch-hour mob doing title searches. Calvin waited at least fifteen minutes for the next available computer, then, entering his name and address, found the bound volume number his deed was registered in. In one side aisle he found Book 13664 and carried it to a slant desk.

There it was on page 486. On the top written in large, emboldened Gothic type were the words: "Know all Men that we Calvin Hazzard and Teresa Krueger Hazzard, Husband and Wife both of Carleton, Middlesex County, Massachusetts . . ." The quaintness of wording echoed a bygone era. But looking at their signatures, he felt a twinge of nostalgia. When that ink was still wet, they were ten years younger, still in their twenties and just starting out. Matty was just two, and life was green with promise.

He put a marker in the pages and headed for the copy machines. There were five pages in all, most of which consisted of the finely printed gobbledygook spelling out grantor covenants. There was also a page detailing the size, orientation and boundaries of the property with simple schematic diagrams. At the bottom of one was the footnote reference to Plot 5, with a volume and page number. Apparently the property had been part of a larger parcel that had included some of the conservation land of Magog Woods before it was subdivided into the plan that was sold to the Samborskys. "For title, see deed from J.B. Wick, dates September 30, 1968, recorded with said Deeds in Book 9238, Page 235."

That meant nothing to him. A cipher of ancient history.

But a thought rose up in his mind from a place all but forgotten.

His eyes dropped to the line at the top of the third page: "I, Anna I. Samborsky as sole tenant of Carleton . . . grant to . . . said land being on the Southerly side of Jason Road as shown in Lot 6 . . . in full consideration of $72,000.00."

Seventy-two thousand dollars. The woman had all but given the house away. When he had signed the purchase and sale agreement, he remembered asking Beverly Otis why the low price.

She had shrugged and said there was a minor liability because the land had at one time been used for commercial storage. Besides, the woman was a grieving old widow whose husband and dog had died the same day. She had wanted out, and fast.

minor liability

"Don't look a gift horse in the mouth."

It's nothing, she had said.

Nothing, he had told himself.

Still nothing, he thought, and left.

CHAPTER

3

Matty was small for his age, so he was easy to beat up.

They had done it before, and he hadn't squealed. It was never anything bad, just a few slaps and sucker punches, an occasional knuckle haircut—a "noogie," as it was known—one of Bobby Gorawlski's specialties. Another was the "pink belly"—whacking his gut with fingers while other kids pinned him down. Never any blood or telltale signs. The worst part was the humiliation—especially the time Bobby pushed him down into dog mess in front of Gina Whitehead. Everybody hooted hysterically, including Gina.

Matty had not forgotten the sting of that. Not for a minute.

School was out and Matty headed up the long incline of Hutchinson Road. Little League practice was scheduled for three-thirty at the Robert Gregory field about three miles the other side of Carleton. He was wearing his number 11 red Devil Dogs T-shirt, but he had no desire to practice ball today. And he had forgotten that his father was to pick him up at three.

About half a block from the wood he heard Gina call. "Maatty."

At first he ignored it.

"You deaf or something?"

He turned around. Gina Whitehead was pumping toward him on her bike. She lived around the corner from him. Although they had known each other since babyhood, they had an on-again, off-again friendship. Some days they were like brother and sister. Other days, cat and dog.

"I thought you had Little League." She always wore outfits a little too old for her. Today it was yellow tights, a green tank top under an

25

open pink shirt. A yellow barrette at the back of her head held up her blonde hair like a plume. She looked like a startled parrot.

"It's been canceled."

"How come?"

"Coach got sick."

"Well, you could get your bike."

"Naw, that's okay."

"We can go to the pond and look for frogs. Come on."

"Uuh-uh."

"They're just coming out of hibernation."

"Some other time."

"How come?"

"Cuz I don't want to."

"How come you're such a spoilsport?"

"I don't feel like riding." Matty looked at the high wall of trees—five hundred acres of Magog Woods. Deep woods. Black woods. He felt the trees pull at him. He wanted to be in there, alone, running through them.

Gina put her foot on the pedal, getting ready to go. "I think all the kids are right about you."

"What do you mean?"

"Just that you're wicked weird."

His face flushed.

"Everybody says so," she said, then pedaled off.

Wicked weird. What does she know?

He watched her disappear down the road, then cut into the trees. Evergreens rose around him like giant fingers. He moved within, away from the houses and the cars, where the air was cool and moist.

The raw breath of winter had not fully departed. In a month the place would be a green cathedral. He loved the woods, the heavy, sullen air, the dark, the solitude, the sweet, musty odors of matted pine needles and wet earth, of things decaying and being born.

On any other day he would have headed straight for TopTree—the elaborate tree house he and his father had built high in a massive oak.

TopTree was Matty's secret place, his private sanctuary, now nearly hidden by the thick head and surrounding saplings. Over the years they put on a roof and sides and curtained windows, brought up an air mattress, some toys, including Daisy Too, a big stuffed cat in gray corduroy that his grandmother had made. Ordinarily he would have headed up there, stretched out, read his muscle magazines, looked for raccoons and possums, played with Daisy if she happened by. (His dad had constructed a pulley basket for bringing her up.) Not today.

No. Today his blood was humming again. It had happened twice before. But never with such intensity.

He wondered if maybe this was part of the changes his mother had said all boys went through—"the onslaught of puberty," she had called it. He didn't understand and was a little scared, but he liked the changes. He felt stronger, more alive. Ready to bust out.

It began in his fingers—a funny, hot, fluidy sensation that spread up his arms and into his neck and down his loins. Like a transfusion of hot blood.

He broke into a run. It felt wonderful—his legs moving him along as if any second he would take flight. He cut south away from Top-Tree, half giddy with the desire to take off his clothes, to go naked through the trees, to jump over the bushes and fallen limbs, to feel the cool, dirty squish between his toes. To shimmy up the bark of a high oak. With antelope strides he cleared hummocks and fallen trunks fueled by the strange music ringing in his veins.

"Hey, it's Mat the Rat."

The voice stopped him cold.

Ahead, three figures emerged from the shadow of a huge boulder known as Druid Rock.

Bobby Gorawlski, Michael Rizzo and Jackie Stoneburner.

Bobby grinned at him like a malevolent Cheshire cat. The others snickered, then Jackie began the familiar chant. "Mat and Gina sitting in a tree, K-I-S-S-I-N-G. First comes love, then comes marriage, then comes Junior in a baby carriage. Mat and Gina sitting in a tree, K-I-S-S-I-N-G . . ."

Bobby took over. "Mat and Gina sitting in a tree, P-I-S-S-I-N-G."

They dissolved in laughter.

Bobby G. was also in the sixth grade but had twenty-five pounds and four inches on Matty. "You some kind of asshole, or something?" he said.

"No."

"Then how come you're sneaking up on us like that, dork?"

"I wasn't sneaking—"

But before he could finish, Bobby pushed him with both hands.

Matty flew backward and hit the ground so hard that the expense of air caused his nose to leak.

"Fucking *gross*," Jackie squealed. "He blew snots all over his face."

They clutched their stomachs and gagged and roared.

Matty wiped his face on his sleeve. That weird, hot tingling in his arms and hands was back. So were the sounds in his head—a strange rabble, like muffled shouting through a fog.

He started to get up when Bobby pushed him back with his foot. The wet from yesterday's rain soaked through his pants.

There was something in Bobby's hand he was cupping. A cigarette, but it was all twisted at the end.

Jackie caught Matty eyeing it. "Hey, isn't his father a cop?"

"Nah, he's only a teacher."

"He better be," Bobby warned. "You say anything and your ass is grass."

Matty wondered how his ass would be grass if he told. He didn't get it, but he sort of liked the phrase.

"Little wimp'd probably shit his pants and run home to tell his mommy."

"Just because you're smoking a cigarette?" Matty said.

"You don't even know what it is, do you, dickhead?"

"He hasn't even got a dick," Bobby said. "Even his girlfriend said so."

"What girlfriend?" Matty asked.

"Gina," Bobby answered. "She said it got frostbite and broke off."

They roared again, and Matty felt his face fill up. "She didn't say that."

"Oh, yeah? Just ask her." Bobby held the roach under his nose. "She said lots of things."

"Yeah, like you got hair coming out of your ears," Michael said. "Why do you think he wears turtlenecks all the time? To hide you're a friggin' monkey."

Matty had heard that before and felt the edge of their words. But he was also taken by the ritual with the funny cigarette.

Bobby lit it, inhaled, and for a long moment held his breath. It was strange. Matty never saw anybody smoke like that before. Then in a burst Bobby let his breath out. "Awesome," he said to the others. He handed it to Michael.

"Yeah, you don't even know what it is," Michael said.

"I know what it is." Matty tried to sound savvy.

"What is it, then?"

"Yeah, what is it, dork?" said Michael. When Matty didn't answer, he announced, "It's a pot joint," handing it to Bobby.

"A pot joint," Matty said. "I knew that."

"A joint," Jackie corrected.

"You didn't know, I could tell," Bobby said, releasing a faint cloud. "Ever hear of marijuana? Huh? Well, that's what we're smoking. Drugs. Nothing for a pussy like you." He passed it to Jackie. Matty watched Jackie suck it to a blush.

Bobby Gorawlski was *the* power kid at Butler: the one who always did cool things that got him into trouble, who swore like the big guys, who talked back to the teachers, who wore his hair long on top and shaved on the sides and with a braided rattail, who drank beer from his older brother's supply. He had fired a real gun and seen nine Arnold Schwarzenegger movies. (Matty's parents didn't let him see any of the real good stuff. "Too violent for little boys," his mom said. It wasn't fair. She was making him into a wimp.) Rumor also had it that Jackie had seen an X-rated movie showing naked men and women doing IT.

"He probably doesn't even know how to smoke it," Jackie said. One of his incisors was not fully grown yet, giving him an unfinished look.

Matty watched him take a long drag, hold his breath and pass it to Michael, then back to Bobby. Such a strange ritual: inhaling and holding your breath until your face turned red and eyes popped out, then the explosion of smoke followed by a groan of "wicked awesome." It looked dumb.

Matty had heard of drugs mostly from television reports of police busts. His parents and teachers also warned about the dangers. On the telephone pole at the corner of Hutchinson and Jason there was a sign: A DRUG-FREE SCHOOL ZONE. But Matty wasn't too sure what form drugs took. On TV they looked like flour wrapped in plastic bags—not these twisted cigarettes without filters.

Michael whispered something in Bobby's ear.

"No friggin' way!" Bobby squealed.

Michael then whispered something else that made Bobby grin. "Oh, yeah."

While Matty lay on his backside, the three went into a huddle. When they broke, Michael held his joint to Matty. "If you're no pussy, try it."

"I don't want to," Matty said. He started to get up, but Bobby pushed him down again with his foot.

The sound in Matty's head was creating a pressure against his temples. They had to stop teasing him. They had to, because he was getting angry. His whole body was becoming angry.

"No, pussy. You're gonna try it." Bobby held the thing just inches from Matty's nose. Matty took it.

"Come on, pussy. Try it. Afraid it'll stunt your growth?"

More giggles.

More red fog roaring.

"You're already a midget."

"Yeah, maybe you'll turn into a bug."

"No," Bobby said, "it's *Honey, I Shrunk the Wimp.*"

While they yowled and slapped hands for their wit, Matty just stared at the joint. He raised it to his nose. It had a sweet, tarry smell. He felt a little scared because of his parents' warnings. And because of the way he felt.

"You're letting it burn down," yelled Michael.

He could feel their eyes on him. He couldn't look like a pussy. Maybe a small drag to look good.

That's what he'd do, one quick drag. He brought the joint up to his mouth, noting how wet the end was. He pinched it the way Bobby did, inhaled, and clamped down on the smoke.

But something went wrong—the smoke got sucked into the wrong place. Suddenly he was lost in a fit of coughing. Desperate for breath, he pulled himself to his knees, unaware that he had dropped the cigarette and that they were screaming "asshole" at him because it had fallen in a small puddle of mud. All Matty could do was lean against a tree and cough until the awful tickle in his throat would let him catch air.

When, at last, his breath came, he straightened up and turned around. Tears were streaming down his face from the coughing.

Bobby's abrupt blow to the side of his head did not register pain until Matty went down and Bobby had pounced on him, his knees straddling his chest. Matty looked up to see an open palm come down again against the side of his cheek. He tried to block it but Michael and Jackie were on his arms. Again the hand came down, then backhanded the other side of his face. Through the pain his first thought was how for the next two weeks he'd go to school with a huge black eye and everybody would know who got him.

Matty cried out from the pain, but when he opened his mouth Jackie stuffed it with a fistful of dead leaves.

What happened next, Matty would only vaguely recall through a blood haze. All that registered was an eruption someplace at the core of his brain. An eruption that made his body shudder. He heard himself make a sound he didn't recognize. A deep-throated, growling sound.

The next moment he tore his arms free, sending Michael and Jackie rolling backward. Matty clawed at Bobby, his fingers yearning for flesh but only catching the loose fabric of the sweatshirt. With a sharp snap, he pulled Bobby to him. Their foreheads cracked and Bobby let out a yelp. In an instant Matty was on his feet. He lifted Bobby up by the front of his shirt until his feet dangled, then dropped him. The next moment Matty was on him, clawing his face and neck and growling. All he would recall of the moment was the urge to sink his teeth into the doughy flesh of Bobby's face and tear it off.

Bobby was colorless with fright. "Help me," he screamed.

Matty flashed his head around at the other two. The noise in his head was a roar.

The others were stunned. "We were just joking," Michael said. "Let him go. Please."

Jackie picked up a heavy stick, holding it in front of him like a lance. "Let him up, Matty, c'mon." He was crying. Bobby was crying. "You let him up or else."

"He's bleeding," Michael said.

Bobby's face was gashed down each cheek. He was holding his hands in front of him and blubbering.

Matty got up and in one move his hand went through the stick. The boy looked in disbelief at the two halves in his hands then back at Matty.

Bobby pulled himself to his feet. Slowly they backed away, not taking their eyes off Matty.

Before they bolted, in a ragged voice Matty whispered, "Say anything, and your ass is grass."

CHAPTER

4

Fifteen hundred miles due south, Jerry Mars was dressed for Nature.

His silver spandex swimsuit and matching top were slashed with blues and pinks that color-coordinated with his mask and fins. Reef perfect. A man alive in Nature had Nature alive in him, Jerry believed.

The beach was nearly empty. The only people within a hundred feet were the old man, his daughter and his granddaughter. Nobody was in the water. The morning rain had held back the crowd.

Jerry yawned and made a wide stretch. The sun was back out and the bank of storm clouds was receding over the sea. Time to get wet.

He removed a tube of Number 30 sunscreen from his tote bag and slathered his arms and shoulders, face and legs. The Caribbean sun was deceptive, especially in the cool of the water. Handsome as it was, a tan wasn't worth the price of premature aging or risks of melanoma. Jerry was very particular about his health.

He picked up his snorkeling equipment and walked down the sand. The old gent with the white hair was on his knees making a sandcastle with the little girl. The mother was sitting in a short beach chair reading the New York *Times*. The man's back was reddish brown and beaded with perspiration. He looked ready for a dip. Fins and mask sat nearby.

Jerry walked by the man, smearing spit on the glass face plate to prevent fogging. He slipped on his fins, adjusted the mask and snorkel, then dove into the blue-green surf.

In a matter of minutes he was out to the little island that put

Trunk Bay on half the postcards in the Virgin Islands. Below were little markers with arrows—an underwater trail through the coral reef. Jacques Cousteau by the numbers. All assignments should be like this one, he thought, and snorkeled to the far side of the islet, which made a rough oval about the size of a football field.

Few sights compared with this coral reef. The place was a miniature Grand Canyon under warm, opalescent water and furnished in polychrome formations in domes, plates, thickets, fans and populated with damsels and grunts, red squirrel fish and filefish, French angels and parrots, and millions of tiny silver herring looking like pelting rain. He spotted two spiny lobsters poking out from a coral cavity. (That's what he'd order for dinner, he decided. To celebrate.) He had hoped to see sharks, but the people back at the dive shop said they never came into the bay. You had to go to the outer reefs. Would have been perfect.

But Jerry was not too disappointed. Everywhere he looked, something was eating something else. Halfway around the island he spotted a patch of spiny black sea urchins. With a rock he smashed one and watched as dozens of fish appeared from nowhere, drawn by a cloud of guts. He crushed five others, making a spreading plume of viscera, and in an instant there was a feeding frenzy. Normally docile parrots and wrasses were suddenly in tugs of war over the scraps, flashing before his eyes like antic rainbows. Amazing how vicious the reef really was beneath all the cosmetics. (Mother Nature was surely a widow.) And highly efficient. No such thing as a fish dying of old age. The reef was a perfect recycling mechanism, kept in balance by predation and fear. Maybe that explained why fish had lidless moon eyes. Living in a state of constant alarm, ready to eat or be eaten at any moment.

Jungle eyes. What he called them back in Vietnam. The look he loved.

Jerry swam around for another twenty minutes until he noticed the old man making his way along the rocks, the orange snorkel like a carrot leading him on. Morning exercise, and right on schedule.

Jerry moved to the shore rocks and stood up so that he was half out of the water.

"Hello there," he shouted.

The man, who was maybe twenty feet away, raised his mask out of the water and waved. He was wearing a long-sleeved T-shirt. Smart, in this sun.

"Want to see something?"

The man stared at him. It was clear he wanted to snorkel on.

"One heck of an eel down here," Jerry shouted, pointing below. He spread his arms. "A real monster." And waved the man over.

Slowly the man turned and floated to the shallow rock nearby. He steadied himself, then pulled off his mask and snorkel.

Jerry clicked his finger at the man. "Now I got it."

"Beg pardon?"

"I noticed you were back on the beach," he said. "For an hour I racked my brain wondering where I'd seen you before. It just hit me. You're Stefan Karsky. Excuse me, *Doctor* Stefan Karsky."

When the man smiled, his eyebrows arched into a chevron. "Do I know you?"

"Your reputation precedes you, doctor." Jerry held out his hand. "Jerry Mars. Just like the planet," he said. "The original, nobody could pronounce."

Karsky took Jerry's hand. The familiar realization flickered across Karsky's eyes when he noticed that Jerry had no index finger. "And how do you know me, Mr. Mars?"

"Jerry, please. Your picture in the papers."

"Got a hell of a memory. I don't think I've been in the papers for years."

Jerry tapped the side of his head with his finger. "I can remember faces, but I couldn't tell you what I had for breakfast." Jerry noticed the thick middle fill the man's shirt.

Karsky smiled politely. "Well, I'm flattered. And what do you do for a living?"

"Nothing as fancy as microbiology," said Jerry. "Wastes and disposals."

"I see." Karsky nodded. "Here on vacation?"

"Business, actually."

"Conference?"

"You got it."

"Couldn't pick a better spot."

"I'll say. And yourself?"

"A little of each. We've got a place on the island, and I do some research at the marine labs on St. Thomas."

"Then you can probably tell me if we're in danger."

"Beg pardon."

"That eel. Spooked the devil out of me. Aren't they poisonous?"

Karsky shook his head. "None that I know of. Green morays can give you a nasty bite, though."

"Wasn't a moray." Jerry made a circle with his fingers. "Thin and very long."

"Could have been a sea snake, but—"

"Yikes, aren't they deadly?"

"There are dozens of species, but only a few are venomous. Was it reddish brown with a black tail?"

"Uuh-uh. White and yellow stripes."

Karsky's eyebrows arched again. "You sure?"

"Absolutely. Bright white and yellow, like . . . I don't know what . . . a braided rope."

"*H. ornatus*," Karsky muttered.

"Come again?"

"*Hydrophis ornatus*. The scientific name of a species I'm studying."

"What a coincidence, but are we safe?"

"Yes, of course. They're venomous but very timid."

"That's a relief."

"The question is, what's it doing in shallow reef rocks. I've only found them in deep seagrass. Sixty feet and more. They never come in."

"Well, you can check for yourself." Jerry slipped on his mask and dipped his face in the water. "He's right under those rocks, not too far from the marker."

"I'd like to." Karsky put his mask back on. When he noticed Jerry hesitate, he said, "You're going to show me, aren't you?"

Jerry looked at Karsky. "It's a deadly one, right?"

Karsky raised his mask. "If it's *H. ornatus*, the venom is quite toxic for humans, but they aren't the least bit aggressive. In fact, quite the contrary. Besides, they have tiny mouths, and their teeth face inward."

Jerry nodded. "If you say so," and slowly fitted his mask.

"How do you actually catch them?"

"A noose."

"A noose," Jerry said. "How about that?"

Then he took a deep breath and kicked down to the marker some twelve feet below.

Painted number 11, it was actually a huge, smooth block of cement that once had served as a mooring. Jerry anchored himself to it until Karsky kicked next to him, then pointed into the dark crevice among a nearby pile of boulders. He had no intention of getting closer.

While Karsky poked his head in for a look, Jerry fanned the sand for the inflation tube. He had buried it yesterday along with the length of white and yellow PVC cord that fastened to the cement block a dozen feet behind him. He then exposed a separate length of cord. He tapped Karsky to show him. Karsky backed out of the crevice and held up the cord to his mask. With a precise flourish Jerry slipped the flattened tube around Karsky's middle right over the T-shirt and locked the pulley clip. He yanked the CO_2 cartridge release, and before Karsky could register on what was happening, Jerry shot up the full length of the cord with the inflated tube embracing his rib cage like a fat boa constrictor. His feet spread, and from underneath Jerry kicked up and pulled off Karsky's fins.

The man was too stunned to comprehend his circumstance. With the four-foot cord still locked in his hand, he gaped dumbly at Jerry, who grinned and made a moving S with his arm. *Nature strikes back,* but the joke was lost on Karsky.

Because the inflation tube had fixed so high on Karsky's chest, his mask would not allow a clear view of what held him. But he could see that he was bound in suspension between the sand and the watery ceiling a mere body-length above his head. Then, like the snap of a magician's finger, he began to kick and squirm for his life. It would be brief. For a sixty-eight-year-old man thirty pounds overweight, about two minutes.

This was the fun part. While Karsky thrashed on his noose, Jerry swam predatory circles around him, taking it all in. The first minute Karsky burned up trying to work the tube off his chest, trying to snap off the nonnegotiable steel clip, fighting the cord that was tested for 2,000 pounds.

When he could no longer hold his breath, Jerry flashed the man a wave, pointed to his watch and raised his sole index finger. One minute, and counting. He then shot to the surface.

Nobody else was in the water. Because they were hidden behind the island, he swam a short distance to check the beach. On shore the granddaughter still played in the sand while her mother was lost in the news.

When Jerry returned, Karsky was dancing on his rope in full panic. From the surface he could see him trying to get his teeth into the inflated tube. Even if he could get a grip—which he couldn't—he had no bite left. Besides, the material was the stuff auto airbags were made of—he'd have to have razorblades for teeth.

Which reminded Jerry what a shame that sharks never entered the bay. What an occasion for a feeding frenzy. He had seen films of common reef sharks gone berserk over a bucket of fish mash. Imagine a live human being up close and personal—just a couple of slashes to let the word out and the place would be a red whirlpool of sleek bodies and flashing teeth. The perfect cover.

(For a moment he had flashes of that time in Nam when he and a buddy paid fifty dollars to watch a pack of dogs take apart a naked VC informant. It was in the cellar of the Dixie Sport's Club, a private night spot for connoisseurs on the north side of Saigon. All that was left was a faceless head and a messy ribcage. Saved on bullets.)

While it seemed like an hour, in real time maybe only a hundred seconds had passed. And below, Karsky was nearly gone. In a last desperate burst, he pulled himself down the rope arm-over-arm to the bottom, hoping to slash the tube on a sharp edge. But years of sea stress had rounded smooth the cement block and boulders. And yesterday Jerry had cleared the area of any shells and sharp-edged rocks. All Karsky managed to do was stir up a cloud of sand. And without fins his buoyancy quickly defeated him. In seconds his final fling at salvation was over, and he bobbed back up, arms out and twitching like a man practicing flight.

From the surface Jerry watched as the last air from Karsky's lungs floated up like a string of silver mushroom caps—little pockets of screams expanding as they reached the surface, breaking silently. Jerry let them stream across his facemask, tickling his neck and shoulders. What a pity, in water they carried no sound.

Then Jerry shot down to watch Stefan Karsky die—to catch the last splendid moments. He positioned himself just inches from Karsky's mask. A surge of recognition and a hand went up to grab Jerry. But there was no strength in it. His diaphragm shuddered for air that would not come. The snorkel sank loosely in his teeth, making an absurd grin around the bit. A few lazy bubbles trickled from the corners of his mouth. His arms began to curl into his chest. Though the mask was still in place, it was half-flooded. A froth of mucus had filled the nose cavity. But what especially caught Jerry's attention was Karsky's eyes. They seemed to fill his facemask. Stop-action terror—the look was like catnip to Jerry.

Jerry had watched many people die up close, first in Vietnam, then in his stateside trade. He was certain he could detect the exact moment of death—not in the final heartbeat or the last breath or when he heard the rattle. No. He could catch it in the eyes in that split moment when they passed from light to eternal sightlessness. It was like trying to catch the green flash of a tropical sunset. Conditions had to be just right, and you couldn't blink or you'd miss it. Like the green flash, it was elusive but just as rewarding.

Jerry pressed his mask close until it nearly touched Karsky's. He held the man's face in his hands and watched life flit from the eyes. The green flash.

Jerry corkscrewed to the surface, heart pounding as if he had just made love. The water was still clear of bathers but a few more people had arrived at the beach. He had perhaps fifteen, twenty minutes before bathers came out. He gulped air, then kicked back down.

The dead man made pop-eyes at him. Like a fish. With a knife he exploded the tube and removed it from the body. He raised the man's shirt and examined the skin. No bruises or abrasions. The inflation tube had embraced him like a pillow; and without fins, the man could never get enough kick to leave pressure marks. Stefan Karsky had drowned with no signs of foul play, as the newspaper would report.

Jerry fitted a fin back on Karsky's left foot, straightened out the legs and back, and set the orange snorkel so that he appeared to be watching the fish. He pushed the body into deeper water and dropped the other fin nearby. Passed out trying to free-dive for his other fin.

On the surface Jerry pulled off his mask. The sun was on his face. Someplace from the thick green hills he picked up a waft of exotic flora. It was the place of elemental nature.

The headlines would read: NOTED NEW ENGLAND SCIENTIST ACCIDENTALLY DROWNS OFF ST. JOHN, V.I.

Before Jerry put the mask back on, he checked his reflection in the faceplate. He adjusted the strap of his tanktop. Somewhere he had read that color meant danger—the gaudier the fish, the deadlier. *J. ornatus*. Reef capo, he thought as he finned back to shore.

CHAPTER

5

By midafternoon Terry's headache had blessedly faded. So had some of the sting from Matty's words. (She would speak to him tonight, calmly but firmly, making it clear that such behavior was totally unacceptable.) The two-hour nap had helped. So did the $300,000 check. Every so often she'd hold it under the light to check the decimal point. It just seemed too good to be true.

She still had not been able to reach Calvin with the news, but she contacted Beverly Otis, who could barely contain herself.

"What did I tell you, money was no object," she screamed into the phone. The six-percent commission was directly proportional to her decibel level.

"What did you say the asking price was?" Terry asked.

"The truth," Beverly said. "Three hundred and eighty. It's unheard of, you got almost twice. I mean, what can I say? She knew what she wanted."

It still didn't make sense. "Did you know?"

"I knew she wanted it. I just didn't know how much." Then she asked, "So when do you want to close? She's out of town today but she'll be back tomorrow after."

"I haven't even reached Calvin yet."

"Of course. My God, is he gonna flip out. But, you know, hon, I don't have to tell you this is nothing you want to let hang too long. I mean, well, it's unheard of, twice the market and all."

"I understand." It was the three-week deadline that they had to work out.

"Look, I'll find you something for a few weeks. If worse comes to worse, you can have my place and I'll take a hotel."

When Terry got off the phone, she went outside to walk about, as if enacting a ritual of departure. The midday sun was warm, and the smell of newly mown grass spiced the air. She strolled across the lawn nearly giddy with delight. She could almost feel the check, like a bird-heart beating in her breast pocket. In a day or two the New Century FOR SALE sign would be slashed by a proud red SOLD stripe. And they would have over a half-million dollars cash to start life over. Amazing.

Still, she felt some guilt because the Mannings were going to buy a house with a sick dogwood in the middle of their lawn. Matty's tree. They had planted it when he was born. Every Christmas, Easter and Halloween he would decorate it. But something was wrong. Here it was midspring—it should be fat with buds. Instead, the winter casings turned to black dust in her fingers. And strange shoots were growing out of the bark of the trunk and limbs like an infestation of parasites.

With cutters she snipped off a thick branch. The cross-section was a three-quarter circle of gray dry wood, one-quarter green. The branch was seventy-five percent dead. The same with others she sampled. How could that be?

She went around in back. Because of all the rain she hadn't been out for days. Every spring she took pleasure in exploring the area for new growth just as it happened—like catching nature in a privy moment. Like clockwork it always began with the crocuses. Last year she had planted a strip of bulbs near the pool. There was little growth, but flowerless—just long, slender blades, no sweet little cups of lavender and pink. The same with the tulips. She had put in 150 Holland bulbs. Again, all the energy had gone into wide, flabby leaves. Half the plants lacked buds, the other half were the size of olives. The same with the forsythia bushes—undersized flowers, and only half-alive.

She stood in the middle of the yard turning over the possibilities —too much rain, too little sun, too cold a winter? No, none of that. Last week's was the first real precipitation all season. They got plenty of sun, and the winter was mild. It shouldn't bother her because in a few weeks, it wouldn't be theirs anymore. Still, she felt like a stranger in her own backyard. Nothing was growing right. Nothing was doing what it was supposed to do. The place was a horticultural sick ward—everything either diseased or dying. Nature seemed out of whack.

And yet, the grass was a lush emerald mat.

Then it hit her: Calvin's chemicals. Of course. Since the day they moved in, he was determined to turn the yard into a showplace lawn —the obsession of a man who, raised in an urban tenement, had never known a lawn of his own. By himself he had torn up all the old grass, relandscaped the yard and planted some industrial-strength seed. His dream was a thick, weed-free carpet that connected him to the vast network of green middle-class America. And for his flawless turf he had layered the place with lime, pesticides, herbicides and fertilizers. God knew how many hundreds of pounds he had spread over the ground—ten years' worth—neutralizing the ancient habits of nature for some Platonic ideal of yardgrass. Now they had an obscenely green lawn that spread around flowerless beds and a graveyard dogwood.

The sound of the telephone snapped her out of the moment.

"No, he's not here. Didn't you pick him up?"

"He wasn't at school, and Tojian said he never showed up. And none of the kids has laid eyes on him since school let out."

It was five-thirty and Matty had been out for three hours. He never skipped Little League practice. *Calm down*, she told herself. He's probably at a friend's. But he would have called by now. He always did. Maybe they got wrapped up in Nintendo and lost track of time. Sure. But for three hours? He hadn't done things with friends for weeks.

Suddenly her mind was a flood of hot thoughts—the kind that lay just below every mother's consciousness. What if he'd gotten hit by a car and was unconscious or worse in some emergency room? Twelve-year-old boys didn't carry IDs, and his name wasn't in any of the books in his backpack. How would anybody know to contact her? Or, what if some pervert had coaxed him into his car on the way to the field? (For all their warnings about strangers, how much cunning would it take to fool a boy of twelve?) Or what if he was lying in some hole in the middle of Magog with a broken leg?

"Why didn't you call me earlier, Calvin?"

"Because I've been driving all over town looking for him. I checked the other fields in case he got his schedule mixed up. I also checked the center."

Maybe he was at Christopher's. Or Gina's. "Never mind," she said. "I'll call around."

"Terry, don't panic. He's probably at Jackie Stoneblacker's."

Jackie Stoneburner. How much Calvin knew. He and Matty hated each other. "Keep looking," she said, "then call me."

She slammed down the phone while Calvin was still talking. If he wasn't at any of his friends' houses, she'd call the police.

God, don't let this be happening.

But another voice told her to hold on, not to lose it. He had simply forgotten about practice. He was probably riding around the pond with some kids. Or in his tree house. If she couldn't find him by phone, she'd head into the woods.

She went out to the garage. Matty's bike was up against the wall.

She ran back inside and called Christopher's, Evan's, Gina's, and Jesse's houses. No Matty. No idea where he was. She called his teacher. She had seen him leave school at the usual time but that was all she knew.

By the time she got off the phone, Terry was frantic. He wouldn't be out this late without calling. It wasn't like him. He always called . . .

The tree house.

She was halfway out the door when the phone rang.

Dear God, please let it be "Hi, mom."

"Mrs. Hazzard?"

"Yes?"

"Betty Gorawlski."

For a moment, the name meant absolutely nothing to her, as if the woman had uttered a foreign phrase. "Yes?"

"I'm calling about your son."

"Is he all right?"

"Well, that's what I'm calling about."

"What happened? Is he hurt?"

There was a long, maddening pause.

"He attacked my son."

Terry heard the words but couldn't process them. "Attacked . . . ?"

"Bobby and his friends were walking through Magog when Matty jumped them."

"Jumped them?"

"Yes. And he did a real good job, because Bobby's face and neck are covered with scratch marks. The doctor thinks there'll be scars."

"No . . . oh, God . . . I don't know what to say. I'm sorry. I don't know where Matty is . . ."

"Well, I'm sorry to hit you with this, but we're pretty upset. I think you'd better have a serious talk with him. I also suggest you consider getting some help, because, according to the boys, he was out of control."

"Out of control?" What did that mean? "Yes, okay . . . thank you."

"You know," said Betty before she hung up, "there's a rumor that some of the kids at Butler are experimenting with drugs."

The word bloomed in her mind.

"I'm not saying Matty is one of them, but from the sound of his behavior, it's possible he was on something. The boys said he went at them like some kind of wild animal."

She hung up the phone and turned around.

Matty was standing behind her. He was covered with filth and blood.

"I said *what happened*?"

"Nothing happened."

"Nothing happened? You've been gone for three hours, you come home with your face a mess and covered with mud, your shirt torn and you tell me *nothing happened*? Will you please stay still?"

There were welts on his left cheek. His right eye was puffy, and a purple shiner was blooming under it.

"I'm all right."

Terry grabbed him by the shoulders and spun him around. "Damn it, Matthew, tell me what happened. Right now."

His eyes were red, maybe from crying. The pupils were dilated, from anxiety, fear? The bruises didn't appear bad but a bone could be chipped, and there could be abrasions on the eyeball. She would call Mitch Tojian, their pediatrician, but he was still at practice.

She pulled Matty to the sink, wet a towel and dabbed away some of the dirt on his cheekbones. Those little bastards, she thought. Bobby, Michael and Jackie. The Butler bullyboys.

To be sure, she'd take him to Emerson.

"I had a little accident." He fought against her grip. He was strong for his age, but at times she was amazed at how strong. It was almost like trying to restrain a grown man.

"Let me look at it," she snapped. "What kind of an accident?"

He refused to answer.

They had roughed him up before, according to Gina. But he would never tell, as if upholding a prepubescent code of *omertà*. This time she wouldn't allow it. "If you don't tell me the truth . . ." she began, but suddenly went blank.

What, go to your room? No Nintendo or TV tonight? Threaten to tell Calvin? Nice options. Maybe you could give him a spanking for not telling how he got beaten up.

". . . I'm going to get really upset. Who did this to you?"

"Mom, it was nothing."

"No, it isn't nothing. It was Bobby Gorawlski and Michael and Jackie Stoneburner, right?"

Silence.

"Did they start it? Just tell me *that*."

"They were walking in the woods when Matty jumped them."

He tugged to get away. He smelled of damp mud and perspiration. Such an adult odor, she thought.

"I have to go to the bathroom."

She sighed and let him go.

He poured himself a glass of bottled spring water from the refrigerator. His uniform shirt was ripped down the back; he would need a new one. The white turtleneck under it was muddied, as was the back of his pants. His hair was a mess, and the rim of his left ear was caked with blood. He couldn't have started it. It was that Gorawlski kid. He was twice Matty's size and a thug—the school menace. Every kid at Butler was afraid of him.

Suddenly Terry felt furious at Betty Gorawlski and her self-righteous certitude that Matty was to blame—that he was "out of control," that maybe he was "on something." The idiot woman had scared her half to death. They had had a fight, and Matty had won. Simple as that. But to think that because her fat little hood son got his face scratched, she threw the drug demon at her. The bitch. Terry had a mind to call back and blast her about the purple egg swelling under Matty's eye. The little thug could have blinded her boy.

Still . . . "Bobby Gorawlski's mother called," she said, struggling to conceal her fury.

Silence.

"She said you attacked him and some other boys, and that you scratched his face."

Matty's expression did not change.

"Tell me about it."

He put the glass in the sink and started walking out of the kitchen.

"Matthew Hazzard, I'm talking to you."

"I wanna take a shower." His voice was hoarse. How it had changed over the last few months, she thought.

"Please just tell me who started it, Matty."

Nothing.

Damn it, it was one thing to have a code of honor, it was another to lapse into total incommunicado. Well, she finally told herself, it was just one of those things boys do growing up—they get into tussles. This one just happened to draw blood and welts, but nothing critical. Hearing her son's slanted account of the incident, Betty Gorawlski had simply overreacted. In a sense, Terry couldn't blame her, what with his face scratched. (Still no need to cry *drugs*.) She would just chalk it in her boys-will-be-boys column.

"All right, tell me where you've been the last two and a half hours."

"Taking a walk."

"Can you at least tell me *where*?"

"The woods."

He started upstairs.

"When you come down, I'm going to have you checked just in case."

Matty's head snapped back as if spring-released. "What?"

"We're just going to the clinic to have you looked at, to make sure . . ."

"*NO!* I am not going to the doctor's."

His extreme reaction startled Terry. His eyes were all pupils. He looked . . . terrified.

"You could get an infection."

"No. I'm not going. I'm fine."

"They'll just check to see nothing's wrong."

He pounded his hip with his fist. "NO! I'm telling you, nothing's wrong." She could see him fight back the tears.

"But, Matty, there might be some damage to your eye or cheekbone."

"There's no damage."

"Then there's nothing to be afraid of." If Tojian weren't coaching today, Matty would go to him. Tojian was patient and kind, never distracted or rushed. It was he who persuaded Matty to sign up for Little League. They were pals. He could handle this.

"No."

"All they'll do is put some medication on the bruise—"

"NO!"

He pounded the banister and rushed upstairs.

"Lots of soap," she shouted pathetically behind him.

The pressure in Terry's head was now so great, she feared a stroke. She flopped down in a chair thinking about going after him when the telephone rang again.

It was Calvin. "I've been everywhere. I can't find him."

"He's home."

"Is he all right?"

"He had a fight, his face is bruised but he's okay . . . I guess."

"A fight?"

"I don't know what happened exactly. I don't want to talk. Just come home."

While she waited for Calvin, Terry sat at the kitchen table with a cup of tea and listened to the water rushing through the pipes to Matty's shower. It sounded like voices whispering just below the threshold of consciousness.

She sipped her tea, hoping to settle the anxiety rumbling in her soul.

"From the sound of his behavior, he might have been on something. The boys said he went at them like some kind of a wild animal."

By the time Calvin arrived, she decided she would call the doctor.

Calvin got home a little before six. "Where is he?"

"Taking a shower." Terry was at the kitchen table with a cup of tea, holding her head.

Another killer headache. He wished she'd get that checked. She got them daily now. It was probably migraines but he still wished she'd see a doctor. "What happened?"

Terry looked up at him through tired eyes. "I think he's all right," she began. "I guess he had a fight with some kids in the woods."

"Who?"

"Bobby, Jackie Stoneburner and Michael whatever his last name is."

"Is he all right?"

She nodded. "Some scrapes and bruises." She took a sip from the teacup.

Her manner suggested that there was more. "But . . . ?"

"No, I think he's going to be fine. I wanted to take him to Emerson for a checkup but he got hysterical."

He studied her a moment. "You're holding something back."

She looked away for a second, then back at him. "Betty Gorawlski called, Bobby's mother. She claimed that Matty attacked them, and Bobby got his face messed up. He may even have a scar. I guess Matty scratched him."

"Good! The little shit's had it coming."

"It's nothing to celebrate. She said he went at them like a . . . a wild animal, that he was completely out of control."

"Says who?"

"The kids."

"Three against one, I would have gone wild too."

"That's not what she meant. She meant wild like on drugs."

"Drugs? He's not on drugs, for God's sake. He's twelve years old." But he felt the conviction drain from his words the moment he uttered them. How did he know Matty wasn't on drugs? How did he know what was going around? Drugs had been found in Carleton High, why not the elementary schools? It happened elsewhere. Butler wasn't immune. Nor was his son, goaded by peers to try a little something the way they dared each other to jump off trees and snow-tube down steep hills or swim too far in Spy Pond.

Suddenly Calvin felt a rush of guilt. Maybe this was his punishment for not spending more time with Matty, for being too busy with his writing . . . He left the kitchen and headed upstairs. As he approached the top steps, Matty ran out of the bathroom and into his room, clutching the towel to himself.

"Hey, buddy," Calvin said, but the boy closed the door behind him. Had the door been fitted with a lock, Calvin was certain it would have been bolted in his face.

Matty was no more modest than the next twelve-year-old, especially in front of his dad. Probably embarrassment over the bruises. Even so young, Matty had enormous pride.

"Matty, are you okay?"

No reply.

On the wall outside his door hung a large colored photo Terry had taken of him when he was three. He was sitting at the kitchen table naked except for the empty milk cup on his head, his fat little round face grinning proudly over the milk moustache under his nose. He looked like a cherub being raised by clowns. Suddenly Calvin felt a sadness. His little boy had passed from a chubby tot smelling of milk to a boy, angled out and hardened with muscle— almost as if he had missed the process. Conveniently he had absented himself from his only child, leaving for Terry the full weight of parenting so that he could write precious articles on subjects nobody cared about. For the first time since Matty's birth, Calvin became acutely aware that he had been a pretty lousy father.

He tapped on the door. "Can I come in?"

He turned the handle. He pushed it open no more than a few inches when Matty yelled, "NO. DON'T COME IN!"

The next instant Matty flew across the room and body-slammed the door shut.

The impact against the jamb was like a gunshot.

Terry called from below, "What happened? Is everything all right?"

For a moment Calvin did not respond, he was so stunned by the violence of Matty's reaction. He just stood staring at the closed door, only inches from his face. He turned toward the stairs and Terry below. He nodded to say it was nothing.

"Just leave him be," Terry whispered.

He nodded again, words frozen.

In the split instant while the door was ajar, he had glimpsed something—something that was too fast for his eyes but which had nonetheless registered subliminally. Like a reluctant dream it left an after-image just beyond reach—one that had cut to the quick of his subconscious, leaving him with a feeling that he had glimpsed something . . . something terribly out of place. (Later, he would tell himself that it was the bright purple shiner that he had picked up in that flash moment. And yet for the rest of the night he would feel unsettled, as if his deeper mind had in that brief moment recorded something very, very wrong.)

From below Terry tried to read his manner. "What is it?"

"Nothing."

A few moments later the light strip under Matty's door went black. He had gone to bed for the night.

"Six hundred thousand dollars?" Calvin bounded out of the bathroom pulling up his pajama bottoms. "What?"

Terry was standing beside the bed with the check in her hand.

"Tell me you're not kidding."

"I'm not," Terry said, handing him the woman's check. "A deposit of half, the other half on signing."

"My God," said Calvin, gaping at the script: *Three Hundred Thousand————— and 00/100.* "There *is* a God," Calvin whispered. "What did you tell her?"

"That I'd talk it over with you and let her know in two days."

Two days? Anything could happen in two days. He started for the phone. "You have her number?"

"Calvin, she's not going to change her mind overnight. Besides, we have her deposit."

Calvin was beaming. If it were earlier, they could go out and celebrate. "Look, there's a bottle of Taittinger in the cellar left over from Christmas. Twenty minutes in the freezer and it'll be chilled. What do you say we light a fire, snuggle up around the check and get goofy?"

But Terry wasn't in the mood. Betty Gorawlski's call had deflated her spontaneity, even though she agreed that Matty was too sensible to experiment with drugs and that Betty was getting back for Matty rousting her son and his goons.

Calvin, however, was reeling with excitement. He had never seen such a large check in his life. Never even visualized one. "She couldn't know much about real estate," he said.

Terry pulled back the blanket and slipped into bed. "Well, there is one catch. She wants us out in three weeks."

"Three weeks? For this kind of money, we can be out in three days."

"And just where are we going to live? And what about Matty? He's got school until the end of June, and Little League until July 7. We haven't even thought about finding a place in Argyle yet. We can't be out by then."

"He wouldn't have to miss a day. I'll call Priest to find us a storage company. We can move everything out except for essentials, find an apartment for a couple months. If not, we can stay in a hotel and fly up there on weekends until we find something. It'll be inconvenient for a while but so what?" With a lunatic grin he flapped the check in the air. "*And* we can afford it."

He didn't know anything about Argyle-on-the-Hudson, but the cost of housing had to be less than Greater Boston, which ranked third in the nation. He could fly up there on a weekend and buy a place with the deposit alone. "Terry, this is your basic once-in-a-lifetime kind of thing. Even if it means living out of Motel 6 for a month, we'll be rich."

Terry settled on her pillow and closed her eyes. "Let's talk about it tomorrow."

"Okay." He kissed the check and laid it on the night table. Before getting into bed, he flexed his biceps in the wall mirror. "The biggest biceps in the English department," he said.

"There's an accomplishment," Terry said with a flat voice. "And Helen is second," thinking of the department secretary.

Calvin smiled, and in the mirror his biceps bulged. His neck was thick, his chest broad, his deltoids bulbous. Except for a small tire of permafat, he had the body of an athlete half his age. It was all the years of jogging, StairMaster and pumping chrome at the university gym. He pinched his beer-wings and swore that had he been a survivor of a concentration camp, he'd have come out bone and beer-wing. Biology, he told himself. He had beer-wing genes.

He climbed into bed and switched off the light. In a few moments he felt Terry snuggle up against him. It was the lovemaking cue, one that Calvin never let go unacknowledged. He had dated several women before Terry, including a few students. By comparison Terry's libido fell midrange. She liked sex the way she liked Thai food: occasionally, and one-chili mild. Rarely did she express a craving that matched his own appetite, nor did she order the three-pepper blowtorch special. When conditions were just right and Terry was in the mood, their lovemaking was fine. It wasn't that he wished her a flaming Jezebel—just a tad more wicked.

They kissed and caressed each other for several minutes until, breathing heavily, Terry went to the bathroom to turn on the light. When she emerged, she was naked. In the yellow glow her long legs looked gilded, and her tight, athletic bottom looked like halves of a nectarine. Ordinarily just the thought of that bottom would make Calvin tumescent. But not tonight. For some reason, perhaps the draining excitement over the Manning offer, Calvin could not become aroused, even as Terry pressed into him, moving rhythmically against his groin, her thigh over his, her hand caressing him.

"You okay?" she asked after a few moments.

"Guess I'm distracted."

"But it's the fourth time this month."

Which was true. Last week it had happened, and twice before that. But except for where it counted, he was fully primed. He had gotten into bed feeling elated about the sudden windfall and the prospect of their new life up the Hudson, his stomach fluttering with anticipation. But, damn it, below the waist he felt dead.

Terry gave herself a quick rub. "Mmm, I'm so fired . . ."

"Thought I was too."

Terry pulled back the cover and took the limp length of flesh between her fingers. "Come on, guy."

He didn't get it . . . until recently he had been priapic. Where the hell did the fire go all of a sudden?

A chilling thought. *Maybe I've got some kind of blockage.* He shook the thought away and gave her a squeeze. "Like I said, there's a God and He loves balance."

She laughed softly. "Then I shouldn't take it personally."

"It's Mammon killed the beast," he said.

"So I'm rubbing myself all over your body while you're calculating profits. I feel like I'm shacked up with Scrooge McDuck."

"Tomorrow, I promise."

She smiled. "This is a switch."

He got up and went into the bathroom. In the mirror he looked down at himself. Maybe it was stress he wasn't even aware of—the distracting excitement of the last week weeks. (Maybe he should check with a urologist.)

He gave one last look in the mirror and thought how, this upset aside, life was finally turning around for them. Then he turned, flicked off the lights, got into bed and went to sleep on that hopeful thought.

CHAPTER

6

Dr. Stefan Karsky stood tall beside the understated BiOmega sign. His arms draped around the shoulders of a man and woman in white smocks. The man was pudgy and wore a full beard. A third man stood a little behind the woman looking at something off to the side. The woman, rather elegant, looked a few years younger than Karsky. Apparently he had said something funny, because she had turned toward him and was laughing. The fat man was laughing too, his eyes disappearing in slits.

Jerry Mars had to admit that Karsky looked quite dapper in his shirt and tie. More like a politician than a microbiologist. His face had that same healthy tan he wore yesterday in the water, and those big white teeth flashed brightly in the sunlight. He seemed a tad thinner, and his hair looked darker. But those hooded eyes were unmistakable—as if they were forever stuck in the middle of a blink. Also unmistakable was that expansive boyish smile he had worn while they chatted. Such an affable smile.

Jerry smiled back at Dr. Stefan Karsky, and with a black felt-tipped pen slashed an X through his face. He then tucked the photo back into his briefcase and took a sip from his soda water.

The plane touched down at JFK as scheduled at 4:47. Because he had only carry-on luggage, Jerry was in a cab and out of the airport within fifteen minutes.

He checked into the Carlyle Hotel an hour later. (That it was JFK's favorite hotel in New York somehow amused him.) At eight-fifteen, from a phone booth at another hotel, he dialed the number they had given him. It was to another public phone with a Washington, D.C., area code.

Somebody who called himself Roman answered. "I saw the notice in the morning paper. You do good work."

"I try."

Jerry had never met Roman. In fact, he was certain Roman—if that was his real name—never met any of the people he brokered. His function was to match operatives with clients. For that, Roman got twenty percent of Jerry's take. It kept everything smooth and anonymous. Jerry had no idea why he was paid so much to kill Dr. Stefan Karsky. He asked no questions and they told no lies. Important was the fact that they paid well: $30,000 net was the most Jerry had ever been offered for a clip. It was a stipend up there with what wiseguys pulled for big political jobs. And the transactions were conducted anonymously. The money, minus Roman's fee, was automatically wired to an account in the Bank of Bahamas for which only Jerry knew the withdrawal-access code.

Jerry jotted down the next assignment Roman recited. Only bare details were ever given. Again, this was to look like an accident. Jerry reminded Roman that such assignments had to be custom-tailored to each circumstance. You just couldn't push somebody off a building and walk away. You had to study the person's habits, look for the proper moment, plan ahead. It called for special stagecraft. He asked for a fifteen percent increase. Roman was silent for a moment, then grunted his concession. Next time Jerry would ask for twenty.

Several questions were in Jerry's mind, but asking was not politic. Roman told him all he needed to know for the job. But maybe he'd do a little probing on his own when he got there. It couldn't hurt, and it might even be useful. It was clear that these weren't revenge hits. The level was too high, which meant that what he was hired to kill was not people but information they carried—the kind that could be highly profitable in side-sales. And who would ever know with this kind of anonymity? To Roman, Jerry Mars was an eleven-digit number in Grand Bahama.

Jerry looked again at the next face in the photo. Beyond the name, the only identification that Roman yielded was another aging BiOmega scientist. The address: Sandwich, Massachusetts. Cape Cod.

Good. Least they have lobsters with claws.

CHAPTER

7

"Have a good sleep?"

"Uh-huh."

"Feel better?"

"Yup."

"Good," Terry said. "Sure look a lot better."

Matty nodded, then wolfed down his bowl of Count Choculas. Terry had stocked a cabinet full of health-store granola and muesli, and all he liked was those brown sugar pellets in the shape of vampires. While he ate he studied the offer for a pair of googly eyeglasses on the back.

He did look a lot better than he had last night. In fact, remarkably so. The purple crescent under his eye had faded to a mere shadow. The puffiness was gone, and the cheek welts were faint red traces. And all in a mere fifteen hours. Either Terry's anxiety had exaggerated the extent of the bruises, or his pubescent recovery powers were in high gear.

Still, Terry was determined to have Dr. Tojian examine him. While there was a remote possibility of cheekbone fracture, what especially pestered her mind was the possibility he had experimented with drugs.

Betty Gorawlski's alarm aside, the front page of today's Boston *Globe* reported that the use of cocaine, marijuana and LSD among young people was on the rise, according to a University of Michigan study. The greatest increase was in children under fourteen. The story said that while drug abuse had dropped among inner-city youths, it was on the rise in the suburbs. Terry wondered grimly whether Matty's violent resistance to a medical checkup stemmed from his fear of detection.

"The water's pretty bad still," he said.

"I know. It's probably all the rain." For some reason, every time they got heavy rains, the water turned color. It had been doing that ever since they had moved in ten years ago. Town officials said it had something to do with the water tables not being able to absorb excessive downpours. She wished she had asked the DPW guys about it when they were around. It seemed to be getting worse. This morning it looked like tea.

"Kind of smells funny, too."

She hadn't noticed. But, then, Matty had an acute sense of smell. In fact, he was an habitual sniffer, investigating the world nose-first —the cereal, his baseball glove, magazines, shoes, his clothes. Everything had to meet olfactory approval. What raked her mind was the thought of cocaine. Wasn't sniffing a sign of usage?

"You know that woman who came yesterday?"

"Yeah."

"Well, she made an offer to buy our house."

The change in him was immediate. He slammed down his glass. "I don't want to move. I told you that." The rage was back. "I'm not going to go to some stupid town in New York."

"But Dad got a great job . . ."

"I don't give a damn," he said, pushing up from the table. He made a step to leave when the phone rang.

"Would you please answer it?"

"No."

"Matthew!"

He gave her a defiant look. "No."

"Damn it, Matty, do as I say."

For a long moment he glowered at her through menacing eyes. *Fuck you* eyes. He muttered something under his breath, then picked up the phone.

She could tell by the sudden change in his voice that it was Dr. Tojian. As arranged. Before bed last night, she had called to explain the situation and Tojian had agreed to call Matty before he left for school and ask him to come to the office later that day for a replacement team shirt before Friday's game. His old one was ruined in the fight. If Matty complied, he would take matters from there.

Matty complied. "Yeah, sure," he said into the phone. When he hung up he told her that Dr. Tojian wanted him to pick up a new shirt.

"You can take your bike," Terry said pleasantly.

He nodded.

Before he left, Terry said, "Matty, I don't want you near those kids. If they tease you or try to pick a fight, you walk away or tell the teacher. Okay?"

He slipped on his backpack without response. The silent treatment.

"Matty!"

"What?"

"Promise me, no fighting."

He nodded. Then, in a soft voice: "I don't want to move."

"We'll talk about that later. Hug?" She held open her arms. Matty put a stiff arm around her.

"Did you feed Daisy?"

"Can't you do it?"

"Not unless you want to split your allowance with me," she said, and smiled.

Matty put his bookbag down and got a can of cat food from the cabinet. He opened the cellar door and dumped the food into the red bowl. "Daisy? Daisy?" He made kissing sounds. "She out?"

"Not that I know of."

Matty bounded down the stairs, calling for the cat, while Terry went upstairs to bring down a basket of laundry. She was pleased that Tojian's ruse had worked. But the hard part was how he was going to convince Matty to submit to an exam, especially a blood test. Not that Matty was afraid of needles. He prided himself on his toughness against pain. But if he had taken something, he might suspect detection. Terry was counting on Mitch's artfulness with kids.

She carried the basket downstairs. As she headed to the table by the washing machine, she glanced at Matty. He was on all fours, staring under the large worktable.

"Find her?" she asked.

He didn't answer.

She put the basket down and began to sort the whites from the coloreds when she heard a low whining sound. She turned to see Matty, poised . . .

"Is she all right?"

Matty said nothing.

"Matty?"

Still nothing. He was frozen in that weird position on the floor, his eyes wide and fixed someplace under the table.

She squatted beside him. "Matty, damn it, *answer* me."

Suddenly from underneath, the cat made a loud hiss, then bolted out from the back and ran under Calvin's SolarFlex bench. Her tail was flat, her ears back and her eyes wide. She hunched under the easel, looking at Matty and making a loud, lugubrious groan. The next moment she had shot up the stairs.

"What's her problem?" Terry began, but stopped short.

Matty's eyes were trained on the top of the stairs, his mouth slightly open. He looked . . . what? Entranced? At first she thought he was playacting, doing one of his movie-creeps impressions. But then she noticed his eyes. They were large and glassy, his light brown irises all pupils. He was breathing out of his mouth—no, more like panting.

"Matthew?" she said.

At that same moment she heard the screen door slap shut as Daisy pushed her way out. And the spell was broken.

Matty got to his feet and ran up the stairs. In a moment, the back door slammed again and he was gone, leaving Terry in the cellar trembling in the realization that her twelve-year-old son looked stoned.

For the rest of the morning Terry wondered grimly if Matty had used the cat as a pretext to go down and take something. But that didn't explain Daisy's strange fright . . .

By ten o'clock she was so distraught that she called Mrs. De-Laura, Matty's teacher, to ask if he seemed all right. Her first comment was on the faint purple mark under his eye, no doubt speculating on child abuse. Terry told her about the fight, the reason, in fact, for her concern. Mrs. DeLaura said that might explain his state that morning: he seemed "a little jiggy." She also said that while she had Terry on the phone she wanted to tell her that Matty had been acting rather . . . well, belligerent lately. That he would fly off the handle at the slightest provocation. She wasn't sure what his problem was but he was losing his ability to control his anger.

Jiggy, belligerent. Wasn't that what crack did to kids? She couldn't wait until Mitch Tojian examined him. But did blood tests tell if somebody was on drugs? Maybe urine tests.

To clear her mind Terry showered and got dressed, made herself some tea from bottled water and went out into the backyard with the morning paper.

By midmorning she felt more settled in the thought that if Matty had experimented with drugs, at least they would know in a couple of days and put an end to it.

It was a glorious warm spring day. White puffy clouds tumbled across the blue sky. The grass blazed with preternatural greenness. She could hear cardinals chirping in the trees. And from someplace she heard the chattering of squirrels.

She settled in a lawn chair in the middle of the yard and spread the paper out on the table. It occurred to her how all the turmoil with Matty had pushed Mrs. Manning from her mind. That all seemed like weeks ago. After her tea she would give Beverly a call. Then she'd have to call Claire Manning, still uncertain if they were making the right decision. It was all happening too fast. Maybe she'd ask for a few days' extension.

She drank her tea and went through the paper. The headlines were particularly depressing. There was another oil spill, this time off the coast of Maine. The beaches were threatened, and lobstermen and environmentalists were outraged. "President urges immediate global ban on ozone-depleting chemicals." The "eco-president," the media had dubbed him. Another story reported the recent appointment of some big honcho scientist to head up the newly commissioned Federal Biotechnology Agency. How remote she felt from the world of politics and science. The White House and its doings were as far from her little patch of the world as was the ozone layer.

A rustling behind her. She looked around.

From the wall of trees a raccoon burst onto the lawn. Then another right behind it in pursuit. A big frisky male, maybe the one that had spooked Daisy. It was strange to see them in the daytime. And running so fast. Usually they were tentative as they approached, hoping for a piece of toast or lettuce. Terry loved watching them, not just because it made her feel close to nature but because they were so graceful in their movements, especially their upper bodies and black little hands, so precise and delicate, and the way they placed them on the ground like ballet dancers. But not today. This was hot pursuit. The fires of spring. *The fires of spring.* She tried to recall the source poem while watching the raccoons cavort.

From the distance they appeared like Disney characters in bandito faces and bushy ringtails trundling in tandem across the grass. As they got closer she could hear a hissing noise. Then amazingly the female shot up the trunk of the maple tree like a squirrel, ran across the heavier branches with the male right behind her in obedience to some ancient internal rules. The kind we all danced to, she thought. Maybe she was about to witness their mating. That would be something.

But when the female reached the end of the branch, she froze, with nowhere to go but down. She regarded the seven-foot drop, then leapt to the ground before the male could reach her. It was a clumsy jump for her short legs, and before she got to her feet the male flew through the air onto her hindquarters. There were some raucous noises Terry didn't think possible for raccoons. In a lightning swipe of a claw, the male pulled up her tail, dug his claws into her sides and clamped his jaws on the nape of her neck as a pink flash spiked itself into her rear.

Was *this* normal raccoon mating behavior? It looked so . . . brutal. She had thought raccoons such gentle creatures, like big cartoon cats with hands.

The female let out a squeal as the male drove her, held her clamped in his teeth. The female—the whites of her eyeballs exposed, her little mouth gaping in pain—struggled to pull herself free, emitting a high-pitched scream. When the male finished, he rolled her onto her back and bit into her lower abdomen, ripping through the soft white undersides with his teeth. Terry let out a cry and threw her tea mug at him, but it all happened too fast. By the time she got near, the female lay dying on her back, her front paws scratching air, a bloody fissure in her belly.

The male spun around and for a long moment regarded Terry while churning its tail like a cat about to spring. Terry swished the newspaper at it, but instead of backing away, the animal moved toward her on its hind legs, actually shuffling while rearing up as it got closer, claws fanning at her, its organ poking out of bloody fur as if he wanted her for seconds.

She backed until she was behind the lawn furniture. The raccoon stopped. Fully upright, it regarded her, then sauntered back to the carcass and tore out a hunk of meat.

Terry stomped toward the animal, again rattling the paper, trying not to think what she'd do if it suddenly sprang at her. The raccoon looked up, its pointy face wet with blood.

She stopped cold when a phrase bulleted through her brain: *strange animal behavior*. And right behind that: *rabies. But would rabies explain this obscenity? And didn't rabies mean foaming at the mouth?*

She looked around for something, a stick, a rake—anything to defend herself. There was nothing within reach. If the animal suddenly charged her . . . she tried not to think of what those claws and teeth could do to her. She could scramble onto the table—but so could the raccoon.

She inched backward so as not to draw it to her. She had moved some six feet when the creature suddenly flew at the ruined female and buried its face in the carcass and with its teeth tore free the intestines. The teeth that nature had designed for bugs and frogs— not flesh of its mate. For a moment it struck Terry that, whatever the cause, the raccoon was suffering some horrendous short circuit of instincts, a confusion of its insectivorous nature with that of some ancient precursory carnivore. But that thought shaded into a more chilling realization. This did not happen to be a confusion of instincts. This wasn't cannibalism. The male was eviscerating his mate, not out of hunger, but because he wanted to.

Terry ran back to the table, picked up her chair and threw it. The chair hit the ground clumsily and fell about a foot short of the carcass, sending the male into the woods. She waited, but it was gone.

Terry now moved to where the female lay spread on the lush grass. Its eyes and mouth were frozen open, the front paws were black little fists, the hind legs made a V in the air, and its viscera spilled out of the hole in its belly.

"My God!" Terry whispered.

This was not supposed to occur in the animal kingdom. Rape and murder.

The rules were out of joint.

CHAPTER

8

Terry ran inside and called the Carleton Health Department, where a woman named Helen Burdick identified herself as the animal inspector. In a guarded tone the woman said she recognized Terry's name from her editorials in the *Patriot Chronicle*.

"It might be rabies-related, ma'am, and it might not be. No way of telling from this end. It's doubtful, though."

"I'm telling you, he went at her like Jack the Ripper."

"I understand that," Burdick said. "But occasionally animals do such things. Have breakdowns, just flip out like people. What we call an anomaly—"

"This was more than an *anomaly*."

"Well, I once saw a mother duck peck to death one of her ducklings, but it wasn't rabid or suffering any known syndrome. These things happen."

"Mrs. Burdick, I'm not the expert that you are, but for ten years I have lived at the edge of Magog Woods, and for ten years I have become familiar with raccoons to the point of recognizing individual family members, including the female spread out on my lawn and the male who ravaged her. This is not familiar raccoon activity nor anything we can chalk up to an anomaly. It was monstrous behavior —and barring demonic possession, my best guess is rabies."

"Well, ma'am, it would be a first, since there hasn't been a case of rabies in Middlesex County in seventy-seven years."

The smugness in her voice made Terry want to smash the phone against the wall. No doubt the woman chalked her up as some kind of shrub-hugging rabble-rouser, dashing off an outraged editorial for every little environmental infraction in town. "How do we test for certain?"

"If the male's still hanging around, I could call the police."

"What for?"

"Shoot it," she said. "Only way is to test the brain tissue."

Terry looked out the window. The male was nowhere in sight. But in the sunlight the female lay on the lawn like a gaping wound. "What about the female?" Terry asked. "Can't you test the carcass, where she was bitten?"

"Not really. The virus shows up in the saliva, but you'd need large gobs of the stuff that didn't dilute. And from what you said, it sounds like he left quite a mess. Suppose we could test if the female was rabid, on the out chance that if the male's diseased, his mate would be too. Like AIDS."

"But she didn't look rabid."

"You mean, she wasn't foaming at the mouth."

"Yes," Terry said, and in her mind that vicious strip of video replayed itself. "Just terrified."

In a labored manner, as if addressing a slow child, Burdick explained that mouth-foaming aggressiveness was only one symptom of the disease—in fact, a late stage of its progress. A rabid animal might not exhibit any clear behavior. There was also the so-called "dumb rabies," where affected animals appeared dopey, passive, or unusually friendly. The female could still have been a carrier but in the early stage. What distressed Terry was that Matty passed through Magog Woods each day—shortcuts to and from school. He explored them for wild flowers and toads. His tree house was deep inside. He practically lived in the woods.

"Can't you send somebody out?"

"Nope. Maybe in a couple days I can get out there. But then we have the problem of decomposition. Screws up the test results. Unless, of course, you care to refrigerate the carcass."

Great suggestion, Terry thought, and imagined explaining to Calvin and Matty why there was an eviscerated raccoon in the fridge.

" 'Course, you can do it yourself."

"Do what?"

"Cut off the head, pack it in ice, and bring it in."

Bitch!

With a note of cheery sadism in her voice, the woman added, "A raccoon's neck isn't too thick. All you need is an ordinary garden spade or a shovel with a good edge. I don't recommend an axe because the head has to be intact. And if you swing and miss, it could mess up the brain. If you do it, I suggest you get to it soon because I'm leaving for the state lab at eleven-thirty. One more thing. Use rubber gloves."

Terry hung up. She called Calvin and told him, but he was on his way to class and wouldn't be free until late that afternoon. She called the police, but the sergeant regretted he couldn't spare anyone to deliver the carcass. She even called the state labs in Jamaica Plain, but the head of epidemiology said they didn't make house calls. The procedure was just as the animal inspector had advised: remove the head, pack it in ice and deliver it herself.

She went back outside, worried that the male might spring at her from the woods. But there was no sign of him. She went back to the house, doubled up some plastic trashbags and filled them with ice. Then, fighting the egg of nausea rising in her throat, she got the garden spade and a small rake. The blade was a little dull, so she honed it with the file she used on Matty's ice skates.

She forced herself not to look at the torso. The animal's head was back, its mouth in a frozen gape, the lower jaw poking at the sky. Gently she wedged the spade into the exposed fleece of the throat, thinking that this had to be the most sickening act of her life. For a moment she feared she could not go through with it. But she knew she had no choice. She couldn't use her foot for fear that blood would geyser onto her. She got a lawn chair, placed it over the carcass, then stood on the chair and with a hammer drove the blade down, concentrating on the end of the spade handle and the hammer.

The first blow was weak because she feared that some residual reflex would make the body jerk and she knew *that* would send her off. Gratefully, there was none, and on the third blow she felt the blade guillotine with a sickening crack through the neck bones. Still on the chair, she took the rake and worked the tines under the head. She swallowed hard and with a clean movement deposited it into the bag and tied a twist around it.

Before she left for town hall, she buried the remains of the raccoon in a shady patch just inside the woods behind their pool pump. Though she could not see the male, she felt it watching her, the way one might feel she was being watched while walking through a strange, deserted house.

The health department was on the second floor of the Carleton town hall in the center. Helen Burdick was taking a call, so Terry wandered to a bulletin board in the small waiting area. There were notices about town office employees, softball games, a six kilometer race and an Earth Day rally scheduled for May 1.

But what caught her eye was a small map of the carcinogenic hot spots in the state. Also, a bar graph highlighting the total cancer deaths and illnesses for the last ten years. Various kinds of cancers were footnoted, including child leukemia, melanoma, mesothelioma, pancreatic cancer, liver cancer, lung cancer. The town of Coburn was listed as having the highest incidence of the state—nearly five times the state average, and twice that of Plymouth, site of the state's sole nuclear power plant. The child leukemia rate alone was six times that of the state. Even though Coburn was nearly a dozen miles from Carleton and was serviced by a different water supply, the figures appalled Terry. There were mothers like herself in those stricken towns—mothers who went out of their way to make sure their kids ate the right foods and took their vitamins, who struggled against the press of the junk-food culture to minimize the intake of salt, fats, cholesterol, and chemical preservatives; who were neurotic about scouring their homes free of asbestos; who judiciously tested for radon and lead paint; who brought them to doctors and dentists on a regular basis. Mothers like herself who woke up one morning to discover that some unknown pollutants had given their babies leukemia.

Terry's head pounded like a jackhammer. As if there wasn't enough anxiety in her life, now she had to worry about Carleton being a carcinogenic hot spot.

"Mrs. Hazzard."

Terry turned to see a large woman, about thirty-five, dressed in bib overalls and a blue workshirt. She had a wide, ruddy face that wore no makeup, and her brown hair was pulled back in a tight knot. She looked like an Amish thug.

"Didn't think you'd actually show, ma'am." Her disappointment was palpable.

The "ma'am" rubbed Terry wrong, but she took a deep breath to put it away. She rested the weighted bottom of the trash bag on the floor. The head was buried under two store-bought bags of ice cubes. She held out the neck of the Hefty, but the woman didn't take it.

"Been a change of plans, I'm afraid. I'm just too pressed too make it to the lab today. Probably not until Friday, if then."

Terry felt she'd been dismissed. "And just what do I do with this?"

The woman tipped her head to say it wasn't her problem. "Can run it over yourself—they're open until four-thirty. Or pop it in your refrigerator until I get a window. And before you ask, we don't have one."

The little victory grin made Terry's blood boil. There was no way she could take it herself. In an hour she had to pick up Matty from school to run him over to Dr. Tojian's. "I can't accept that," Terry said.

The woman gave a shrug. "Suit yourself." She started away.

"Are you happy with your job, Ms. Burdick?"

That stopped her. She turned around. "Beg pardon?"

"I ask because I'm wondering how the town would react if it knew that its animal inspector resisted testing the ravaged remains of a raccoon suspected of a rabid attack."

"Are you threatening me?"

"Yes. And here's more: I've got a twelve-year-old son who likes to walk through the woods. Were I to learn that rabid animals are running around, or, God forbid, were he to get bitten by one because you were too fucking negligent in your job, there's no telling what kind of anomaly I'd commit on you."

Helen Burdick's face went tight. Suddenly she was aware of the lobby full of staffers and townfolks frozen in fascination. The receptionist looked like a still life, only her eyes shifting from Terry to Burdick.

The effect was immediate. Ms. Burdick wiped her mouth and made a sheepish grin to the small audience. "Suppose I can get over this afternoon." She took the bag and went to the desk and muttered something to the secretary, who left. A few moments later she returned with an Igloo ice chest. "Results should be ready in two days," she said, stuffing the bag inside.

Terry stood still, watching her pack the bag in the cooler.

"Any other problems?"

Burdick's voice was audible, so it was probably intended for the lobby rather than Terry. Nonetheless it took her by surprise. "Any other problems?"

Yeah, my stomach is a hot fist and the front of my brain is about to explode; the backyard is suffering horticultural dysfunction; my husband no longer gets it up for me; the cat's acting weird; one goldfish is missing, the other is the piscatorial equivalent of Jeffrey Dahmer; and my son might be on drugs. Outside of that, things are just ducky, Helen.

"Is there anyone I can talk to about lawn chemicals?" Terry explained about the flowers and the dogwood.

"Our tree man is out. But I'd say it's the last year's drought. Wiped out lots of dogwoods. The flowers—I'd guess it's all the rain we've had. Most of the energy goes into the leaves instead of the blooms."

"My concern is that something might have gotten into the ground water, it's been running milky and sometimes smells."

"That's odd, we've gotten no other complaints. Then again, you have one of the few private wells in town."

Ironically, having their own well was a feature that particularly delighted Terry, presumably there was no fear of contamination from others.

"Of course, you can get that tested, too. But I doubt it's fertilizers unless you put it down a foot thick."

The cancer map flicked on in Terry's head.

"Might be the heavy rain," she continued. "Causes wells to back up."

Terry nodded and started to go. "One of the benefits of conversion, I suppose."

"Beg pardon?"

"When we convert to Quabbin."

The woman stared at her blankly.

"The reservoir."

"What about it?"

"Isn't Carleton converting?"

"No."

"Then what was the feasibility study all about?"

"What feasibility study?"

Suddenly Terry felt stupid. "For three weeks they've been drilling holes in the streets. Jason, Woodside, Hutchinson."

"Who has?"

"Some men in yellow trucks. I don't know, the Department of Public Works. They said something about trying to determine the size of the granite ledge or something."

"Mrs. Hazzard, we're a relatively small town with only a handful of administrators, and we all know each other's business and budget lines. A feasibility study like you're describing is not something out of petty cash. Nor can Carleton afford to even think about converting to Quabbin. Besides, we've got perfectly good wells."

"That's what the man said."

Burdick nodded with satisfaction, wide-eyed, insinuating Terry was making this up too. "Do you remember what the machines looked like?"

"I don't know, big, tall, pounding things."

The woman went over to the reception desk, picked up the phone and punched four numbers.

"Russ, know of any DPW crew that's been taking core samples at the west end? Jason near Magog? A resident reports a truck's been tapping streets for the last three weeks. Said the guy claimed they were doing a feasibility study on water lines to Quabbin." She laughed, then mumbled a few "uh-huhs," laughed some more at his comments, then hung up. "Nothing on the books—not the town, state, or the feds, ma'am. And nobody drills streets without a permit."

Gotcha, her face said.

"Maybe you can explain that to the taxpayers who ride the asphalt patches each day."

"Come again."

"Why the streets were torn up and town administrators are the last to know." Terry smiled sweetly and left.

CHAPTER

9

"Dr. Stefan Karsky, a professor of microbiology at Harvard University and former associate of the Center for Disease Control in Atlanta, died in a drowning accident on the island of St. John of the Virgin Islands. A resident of Magnolia, he was 68.

"Born in Poland, Dr. Karsky moved to this country with his family in 1949 following the Allied liberation of Eastern Europe. Three of Mr. Karsky's childhood years were spent in concentration camps at Treblinka and Dachau.

"Dr. Karsky graduated from Worcester Polytechnic Institute in 1953 with a bachelor's degree in chemistry and received a doctorate in biology from the University of Chicago in 1958. From 1960 until 1967 he taught microbiology at Stanford University. He joined the faculty at Harvard in 1973 following six years of research for the government.

"Dr. Karsky was a former trustee of St. Elizabeth's Hospital and president of the American Institute of Immunology from 1967 to 1970. He was also the author of numerous articles and books, including a seminal text, 'Principles of Immunology' published in 1978.

"On sabbatical leave since January, Dr. Karsky was working on the fourth revision of that book while using the marine research facilities of the University of the Virgin Islands in St. Thomas. His daughter and granddaughter were with him for a week's visit."

The photograph they had run of Karsky was recent. But to Jack Perry's eyes he hadn't lost his boyish good looks in the nearly twenty-five years since those days when they were quartered in a squat, windowless cinder-block bunker off the beaten path where the only clue to the secrets within read BIOMEGA—NO TRESPASSING. What today sat innocently on the obit page as "research for the government."

"St. Thomas police Inspector Colin Conway said that Dr. Karsky had drowned in a 'freak accident' while snorkeling in Trunk Bay on the island of St. John. According to Inspector Conway, Dr. Karsky apparently blacked out while swimming in thirty feet of water. His body was discovered by other snorkelers. Ironically some of Dr. Karsky's research on human immunology centered on the biology of poisonous sea snakes. He was an avid scuba diver who was quite familiar with the waters of the Virgin Islands. According to authorities, the water and weather conditions were calm at the time of his death. Dr. Karsky was planning to return to Harvard in June to resume his research and teaching duties . . ."

Jack Perry closed the newspaper.

Freak accident? The phrase scratched at his mind like a claw.

CHAPTER

10

Morgan Chadwick Reese, president of the United States, flashed a florid grin at the gathering of distinguished guests from both houses of Congress, the cabinet, White House aides, members of the National Institute of Health and other human services departments, and the clutch of reporters who filled the rear of the White House Yellow Room. He took a sip of water as the voices subsided and began the induction ceremony.

"Ladies and gentlemen, we have gathered today to mark an historic moment in both science and government. From this day forth, the Commission on Biotechnology will represent a bridge between the American government and the burgeoning bio-tech industry. As you know, the research in the area of genetics has grown exponentially over the last decade. The human genome project has already developed into a vast enterprise involving hundreds of men and women, all dedicated to the betterment of the human condition through the understanding of responsible gene manipulation . . ."

Behind the president were four cherry armchairs. In them sat the vice-president, the head of the National Institute of Health, the newly appointed director of the Commission on Biotechnology and his wife.

"I have asked Dr. Julius Wick to assume the directorship of the commission; and I am very happy to say that Dr. Wick has accepted. Dr. Wick brings to the commission a sterling career as a scientist and administrator. Before serving as president of Walden Research in New York State, he spent years pioneering the science of gene transfer, which has opened medicine to wondrous discoveries that may one day lead to the successful prevention and treatment of the diseases that still afflict mankind."

Julius Wick stared at a spot on the carpet as the president continued the litany of praise. Beside him, his wife glowed with pride. The appointment was everything she had worked for.

". . . But a true science is more than long hours spent in a laboratory or under a desk lamp. The ultimate purpose of science is to serve human life. It can be said that Julius Wick is a man of science who has proved himself to be a genuine benefactor of us all."

Julius made a side-glance at his wife. His smile was tight and humble. She made a quick little nod. Out the window she could just make out the tip of the Washington Monument that blazed approval in the sunlight. They were part of all that now—the Mall, the halls of Congress, the Oval Office just down the hall, the Singer portrait of George Washington hanging on the wall behind them. And as the president spoke, the loose ends were being tidied up. . .

"On a personal note," continued President Reese, "I can say that Julius is a man of the highest personal and professional standards. He and I go back more years than I'd like to admit to . . . Not only were we classmates at Princeton but, as fortune would have it, we worked together for the Department of Defense in the early seventies. Though he was just a few years out of graduate school, he had already established a reputation for brilliant research and as a man dedicated to the highest standards of professionalism . . ."

When the president concluded his introduction, he stepped aside so that the new director could give a few words of thanks. Julius Wick moved to the microphone.

At sixty-six, Wick was still an impressive-looking man. Though he was not a big man, slightly less than six feet and of medium build, he projected authority and intelligence. His face was long and angular, setting off deeply-set brown eyes. His look was steady and keen, but what gave him a rather jarring appearance were his eyebrows. They were thick black brushes that stood in contrast to his hair, which resembled silver wool and which grew halfway back on his skull and thick about the ears. With a high-bridged, aquiline nose, it was an impressive face, one not easily forgotten.

"Thank you, Mr. President," he began. "There's an old saying that behind every man stands a good woman. It's a bit dated today, but you should know that I would not be here today were it not for my wife. For three decades she has stood, not only by my side, but ahead of me." He raised his hand to her. "Claire?"

The audience applauded politely as Claire Manning Wick smiled and accepted the tribute.

While her husband delivered a brief acceptance speech, she settled back and scanned the frieze of distinguished faces—the White House chief of staff, presidential advisers, cabinet officers, aides, senators and congresspeople, CEOs, icons of the Academy of Science.

Her eye fixed on the Seal of the President that emblazoned the podium. Hanging just above the seal was Julius's shiny red face. With profound satisfaction she felt her body relax into the realization of the moment—how they had made it all the way to this august chamber and the high office to which they had been appointed. How startling it was to think of the distance they had traveled from the inauspicious beginnings twenty-odd years ago in that crude little laboratory of BiOmega. How far behind them all that was now. Everything was in its place, and ahead only endless blue skies.

CHAPTER

Through the one-way glass partition Mitch Tojian watched Matty Hazzard enter the outer office.

"We could have used you yesterday," Mitch said, stepping out. He put his hand on Matty's shoulder. "The Giants trounced us."

Matty made a flat smile. He was a good looking boy, and even though he was wearing a loose turtleneck, Mitch could see he was well built.

"What was the score?"

"I stopped counting after ten."

"Pretty bad," Matty said. He examined the wall photos of the different teams Mitch had coached over the last three years— groups of boys and girls in their red and white uniforms, the big bold print across their chests. DEVIL DOGS.

Nearby were some black-and-whites of Ted Williams, Carl Yastrzemski and Willie Mays. Mitch tapped the photo of Williams caught in the middle of a mighty swing. "I don't even think he could have saved us, given all the errors. But it's a long season."

From behind the desk he pulled out a Louisville Slugger. Along the shank in black was Williams's signature.

"Did Ted Williams really sign it?"

"Uh-huh. And I was about your age." He handed the bat to Matty. "Go ahead."

Matty positioned himself with the bat, his sneakers nearly touching.

Mitch spread Matty's feet along the white eye-exam line on the floor. He showed him how to stand and to choke up; he moved his hands so that the bat was off his shoulder, his elbow parallel to the floor. When he had the stance just right, he told Matty to swing. At first Matty seemed a little self-conscious, but after a few minutes Mitch had him smashing imaginary hardballs out the window and into the next town. The kid had a strong swing.

"What position am I playing Friday?" Mitch had used him in the outfield for the last three games.

"What position would you like?"

Without hesitation Matty said, "Second."

"You got it."

"All *right*." Matty's smile lit up his face.

Mitch had known Matty since he was born, and while he had always thought of him as level-headed, he was still only twelve. His mother's fear was not unreasonable. Drugs had slithered into the elementary schools of even the best of Boston's suburbs.

"I know you're quick on your feet, but you've got to have sharp eyes. Half the scoring comes from steals and errors, you know."

"Uh-huh."

Mitch pointed to the eye chart against the far wall. He flicked a switch and the lights all went out except for a lamp above the chart. "Read me the first line."

Matty faced the chart with his toes on the line. He looked jumpy, nervous. After a moment he read the line. Mitch had him read the next and the next, all the way down to the fine print.

"Not bad," Mitch said, thinking, so far so good. Maybe if he didn't announce he was having an exam, Matty wouldn't resist. He sat the boy on a chair and said he wanted to take a look at his eyes. The boy sat.

"Where did you get the mouse under your eye?"

"Mouse?"

"The bruise."

"I fell."

Terry said he'd been in a fight. "When did it happen?"

"Yesterday."

It seemed too faded to be yesterday. "Healing nicely. Does it hurt?"

"No."

Matty eyed him. An examination was taking shape.

Mitch was keeping up the chatter for distraction. "Got a real big game next week with the Cardinals." Matty's pupils were dilated—mydriasis, a condition that could be caused by any number of factors . . . the surge of adrenalin from excitement or fear, or from drugs. Could also be a brain tumor.

With the ophthalmoscope he looked into Matty's eyes. Mitch was not an ophthalmologist, but his immediate impression was that there was something markedly unusual about the boy's ocular anatomy. The vascular tree of retinal vessels was swollen—a condition that could very well be caused by cocaine or amphetamines. But drugs could not explain the glistening, silvery nature of the pigment epitheliums. The back surface of his eye was much more reflective than normal—even for infants. It was startling.

Mitch kept his voice neutral. "Let's see what you can do with the lights down." He dimmed the chart light with a towel, casting a dull glow across the letters. Even with Mitch's glasses he could only make out the top two lines. The rest were a blur.

Matty rattled off the letters of the first three rows.

"Try the next to the last line."

"T-Z-V-E-C-L."

That was the twenty/twenty line. To Mitch the bottom line was a smudge.

"O-H-P-N-T-Z," Matty said in one breath. He had twenty/fifteen vision in the dark.

"You'll be good for night games," Mitch said good-naturedly, but he was perplexed. The boy had the night vision of a cat.

He flicked the lights on. "Speaking of night games, I'm splitting a season's ticket with some friends. Maybe one night you and your dad would like to keep the seats warm for us."

"Really?"

"Eighth-row boxes right behind first-base dugout. Great place for autographs."

"All right!" Matty said, then his voice fell. " 'Cept my dad doesn't like baseball all that much."

"Well, I'm sure he'd like to see a game."

"But he likes to work late."

"Well, maybe you and your mom can go."

Mitch kept Matty talking while he moved him from the scale to the height chart to the examination table. He listened to the boy's heart through the stethoscope, examined his ears and checked out his reflexes.

Finally catching on, Matty moved to the door. "Can I have the uniform?"

"Sure, but just a couple more things."

He handed him a cup and directed him to the toilet for a urine sample. The boy thought about it, then went inside. Meanwhile, Mitch recorded his findings in Matty's folder. The last time he was in was six months ago, the previous December. At that time, as with all the rest, Matty's weight and height were in the fiftieth percentile for his age group. According to the charts, he was on the same height line, but his weight had shot up to the ninety-ninth percentile. In fact, for his height and age, he was off the charts—a hundred and fifteen pounds of dense muscle mass.

When Matty returned, Mitch took the sample and put it in a jar. "How about you let me take a look at you?"

"What do you mean?" Matty suddenly looked frightened.

"Just pop off your shirt and pants. There's just us guys here."

"No, that's okay." He moved toward the door. The color in his face had drained. "I gotta go."

Terry had said he was adamant about not going to the Emerson clinic. But the change in him was odd. It wasn't doctors the boy was afraid of, it was being seen with his clothes off.

"Well, how about just your shirt?"

Matty looked hesitant. Maybe he was wondering how far Mitch would push it. First the shirt, then the pants. It crossed Mitch's mind that the boy might have been sexually molested.

"It'll take just a minute."

"Do I have to?"

"No, you don't have to." Mitch smiled. "But since you're here, it seems like a good idea to check you out."

The boy shook his head. "No, that's all right." He had his hand on the doorknob.

"Then let me just see how good your throwing arm is, okay?"

"You mean play catch?"

"No, but, you see that bar?" He pointed to a chrome pipe across the door jamb. "Think you can do a few chinups for me?"

"Guess so."

The bar was perhaps six and a half feet from the floor. Mitch was about to lift Matty to it when he leapt in place, caught the bar with his hands and began to chin himself. Mitch watched. When Matty got to twenty, Mitch stopped him. Matty dropped his left arm, hanging from his right. His face was red, but he did not seem tired.

"How about one hand only?"

Without a word, Matty pulled himself to the bar so that his chin cleared his fist. Then with the same deliberate motions, he lowered himself and repeated the cycle. Astonished, Mitch watched the boy pump himself up and down. Mitch stopped him at ten—all with one hand.

"Move over, Ted Williams," Mitch said, struggling to restrain himself. The boy was a phenomenon.

"Can I have my uniform now?" Matty asked.

"Sure, but just one more thing," Mitch said. He didn't know how much farther he could push it. He sat the boy down and wiped his finger with an alcohol pad. "Just going to take a little blood, okay?" He pulled out a small syringe.

"I don't want to."

"Any guy who can do ten one-handed chinups can't be afraid of a little needle."

"I'm not afraid."

"Then what's the problem?"

"How you going to take it?"

"From your arm."

Matty thought about it for a minute. "I guess. Then I've got to go."

"No problem," Mitch said.

Mitch pushed up the sleeve of Matty's shirt. No signs of needle marks. "I think the other arm will be better, actually." Before Matty knew it, Mitch pushed up that sleeve. Nothing there either. "Make a fist."

Matty's forearm swelled into a small ham. It looked like the arm of a boy five years his senior. Mitch tapped it until a blue, ropy vein pressed to the surface. Matty winced slightly when Mitch inserted the needle. While he drew out the blood, Mitch kept up a monologue about baseball, all the while studying the boy's face. If he were on drugs at the moment, his mannerisms didn't betray him. He was simply nervous about the exam.

When the blood was drawn, Matty asked for his uniform again.

"Sure," said Mitch. "I do this with all the boys on the team."

He opened the closet and pulled out a new red and white uniform in a plastic bag. Then some iron-on numerals.

"It might be a good idea to try them on," Mitch said.

"Naw, that's all right."

"If they don't fit, you won't be able to change at the game. And the rules say each player has to be in uniform."

Matty blinked. "I think they're my size."

"What size are you?"

Matty shrugged.

"I think you better try them on just in case," Mitch said. "If they're too small, you'll be uncomfortable. If they're too big, you'll be tripping on them. You can use the outer office, it's private."

Matty was reluctant but he took the uniform and headed out. Mitch heard the latch click locked. He felt mildly guilty as he went into his own office, turned off the light and stood behind the one-way glass panel. But curiosity had overwhelmed him.

Through it he could see Matty survey the room, the uniform in his hands. He double-checked the door and smoothed down the Venetian blinds so nobody outside could see in. He put the uniform on the table. Though Matty turned his back to Mitch as he slipped off his jersey, his musculature was apparent. His triceps were massive, and his deltoids were thick round caps. Extraordinary.

To put on his pants, Matty didn't bother to untie his sweats. Instead he sucked in his gut and yanked them down. But they caught the band of his underpants and pulled them to his knees. For a split instant Mitch thought it was the trick of the light. But then he was certain, and an electric chill cracked through his body.

Matty had the genitalia of a grown man.

CHAPTER

12

Age could not conceal her. She was heavier and grayer, but still poised. Her hair was rolled into a French twist. Although unapparent in the photograph, a pencil-line scar cut diagonally across her forehead, through her brow and eyelid as if she had once been gashed with a razor. Whatever the cause, it had miraculously missed her eye.

And that was what gave her away: her eyes. No matter what indecencies time inflicts on the flesh, the eyes, Jerry always said, preserve the individual to the grave. In black and white it was impossible to guess the exact color. He had bet bluish gray, but they were light green peridots with yellow sparks at the center.

"Dr. Maria Terranova?"

"Yes?" She held open the door.

"My name is Jerry Mars." Again he had dressed for the occasion. A red polo shirt, gray linen jacket, white slacks and Docksiders. Cape Cod gentry. "First of all, I'd like to say what a lovely home you have."

"Thank you."

It was a Victorian house with a slate mansard roof and fussy gingerbread details. Painted teal blue with white trim, it looked like a piece of Wedgwood china. On the front porch were large clay pots bursting with geraniums. The house sat staunchly on a bluff overlooking the Sandwich Harbor. In the distance white sailboats cut across the blue expanse of water warming in the high spring sun. The nearest house was over half a mile away. It was a secluded spot on a dirt road through scrub and oaks. A two-day stakeout told him that she was alone in the house.

He flicked up a business card. "I'm a private investigator," he said. "If I may come in, I'd like to talk with you." She looked at the card. "I promise to be brief."

"Talk about what?"

"Well, I'm very sorry," Jerry said, "but I'm afraid I'm the bearer of bad news."

The woman's face stiffened. "Yes?"

"It's about an old colleague of yours, Dr. Stefan Karsky?" Recognition shimmered across her face. "Well, he expired in a drowning accident a few days ago in the Virgin Islands."

"Stefan Karsky?"

"Yes. You were colleagues."

"I'm sorry, Mr. . . . ."

"Mars." Jerry smiled. "Like the planet."

". . . Mars, but I don't know anyone by that name."

"You don't?"

The woman's left eye twitched ever so slightly. "No, I don't."

"How odd," said Jerry. "Then how about the name Black Flag?"

" 'Black Flag?' "

"As in Project Black Flag?"

The woman's eye twitched again. She started to close the door, but Jerry's foot caught it.

"Of course, it's been . . . what, twenty-five years? Maybe you should take some time to remember." He pushed back his sleeve and glared at his watch.

"I'm sorry, I don't know what you are talking about," she said. "Would you please remove your foot?"

Jerry did not. "I believe it was the code name of a research project you and your colleagues worked on at BiOmega Laboratories."

"Who are you?"

"I was a recent acquaintance of Dr. Karsky," Jerry said. His mouth expanded into a slender grin. "In fact, I was with him when he died."

"You're with intelligence."

Intelligence. The word dropped like a pebble in a still pond. What do we have here? He had been anonymously hired to kill two retired microbiologists within a few days of each other, but not told why. Nor was he supposed to know why. More professional that way. But his curiosity was beginning to swell. Two scientists linked by some secret government project way in the past. And now, *intelligence*. One word, and new possibilities. Maybe he'd play along, ride out the ripples. See where they took him.

"Intelligence? In a manner of speaking. As I said, I'm a private investigator."

"Working for whom?"

"That's the private part."

"What do you want?"

"I'd like you to tell me all you know about Project Black Flag."

He had hit a nerve. She glanced behind him to see if he had brought company. The rented van was pulled alongside the house out of sight. "Just me." He smiled.

She studied his face, his sincere gray sport coat and Ralph Lauren shirt with the collar up, probably wondering who he was—CIA, FBI, DIA, none of the above. "I'm sorry, you've got the wrong person." She pushed the door against his foot, but it did not budge.

"Maybe this will help your memory." From his briefcase he pulled out a folder containing the eight-by-ten photograph. "Bi-Omega," he said, laying his strange index finger on the sign just over his shoulder. "Catchy name. I especially like how the O in Bio is spelled with the Greek letter omega." He slid his finger to the figure of the woman with Karsky's arm on her shoulder. "Now, if you ask me, this is you, Dr. Terranova," he said, as if selecting wallpaper.

She did not respond.

"And you know what it is?" he continued. "The eyes. Everything else can go on a person, but not the eyes." he grinned. "They're a dead giveaway."

"Why is his face crossed out?"

"He's dead, as I believe I mentioned."

She pushed hard against the door, but he shouldered his way inside.

"If you don't leave immediately, I'll call the police."

He closed the door and snapped the latch. "No, you won't." As he lowered the briefcase, the woman pulled a walking stick out of a large porcelain vase beside the door. Jerry caught it and twisted it out of her grip. The heft of the brassy knobbed end could have changed things. "Guess I don't blame you," he said, and tossed it back into the holder.

"You have no right—"

"But I am, so cut the shit." He pulled out the Glock 9 mm. "Show and tell time." He nudged her toward the living room.

"I don't know what you're after," she said, "but how does it make you feel about yourself pushing around an old woman with your gun?"

"I kind of like it." He backed her into a wing chair.

Beside her was a rolltop desk. And on it a half-empty bottle of Diet Coke, a letter and fountain pen and a box of personalized stationery. She was in the middle of writing a letter to someone named Angela.

He nodded at the Coke. "Stuff's bad for you, all the chemicals. Besides, caffeine's a diuretic, flushes out essential nutrients. When you're thirsty, you should drink water. Good for the bowels and a natural moisturizer for the skin."

She sat in stony silence.

"Dr. Terranova, I am working for important people who know for a fact that you and your colleagues were conducting a secret research project for the government. I want you to tell me the exact nature of that project."

"Ask your important people."

Jerry sighed. "There is nothing to lose. National security will not be compromised. Nor will you in any way be incriminated, if that's your problem. Not for something that took place a quarter of a century ago."

"Who are you working for?"

"Let's say I'm freelance."

"I have nothing to tell you or anybody else, you creep."

"I was hoping we could have a civilized chat where you told me things and I took notes. You know, like in a classroom. But no, you had to get insulting."

She made a move but before she could straighten her legs, Jerry was pressing the barrel of the gun into her nostril. The woman sucked in her breath with a squeal.

"You have two choices: A—you can die with Black Flag. Or, B—you can tell me what you did and live the rest of your life." For a glorious instant her eyes flared with green before night swarmed from the center.

"Get off me—"

"Talk."

"Go to hell."

Jerry froze against her. What the hell was she holding? He pulled her up by the elbow and marched her out of the room, down the hall and into the kitchen.

"Where are you taking me?"

"For a walk."

"I'm not going anywhere with you." She tried to pull her arm free.

Jerry spun her around and raised the gun to her forehead. "Lady, if I pull the trigger, your brains will be all over the kitchen floor. Is your secret really worth that?"

The woman was trembling. She closed her eyes for a moment. She was going to talk, Jerry told himself.

When she opened her eyes she said, "I'm afraid you'll have to pull the trigger."

"You'd rather die?"

He gave her several seconds but she didn't respond. "What the hell were you people doing back then?"

The woman closed her eyes, waiting for the blast to explode away the back of her head. Jerry rested the barrel of the gun against a spot between her eyes. He let a full thirty seconds pass, but she kept her eyes pressed tightly and never uttered a word. Whatever she was holding back was so important that she preferred death to its exposure. He lowered the gun, but his curiosity would not go away. What she held back here was some kind of very forbidden fruit, and forbidden fruit meant power. And money—much more money than Roman's people were paying him, and so far that was top dollar. If he knew what kind of forbidden fruit, he might be able to determine potential customers and fetch himself a bonanza. It crossed his mind to torture it out of her, but she'd probably just make a lot of noise as the bones crushed. "Okay, you win," he said.

She opened her eyes, her chest deflated.

Besides, Jerry thought as he opened the back door, there was the next face in the photo—the chubby one in the beard.

"Outside." He took her gently by the arm. She hesitated a moment. "Lady, I swear I am not going to hurt you."

"You force your way into my home and threaten me with a gun and you expect me to believe you?"

"A man's only as good as his word." He dropped the gun back into his briefcase. "I won't lay a finger on you."

She stepped outside. Jerry's rental van sat back in the driveway, the windows opened a few inches, the little side curtains closed.

He led her across a narrow boardwalk that cut through the dune grass and down to the beach. In either direction stretched a wide expanse of empty sand. The only movement, a few gulls and the sailboats far off shore. He took in a deep breath. In the back of his head he could hear the McGuire Sisters crooning lines from "Old Cape Cod."

He nodded for the woman to walk toward the right. She was eyeing the briefcase. He smiled and dropped it to the sand. "Have a nice walk," he said. "And don't forget, vitamin A and lots of water."

She turned and headed down the beach, picking up her pace as she got farther away, her blue flowered skirt lufting in the breeze.

"What were you people doing?" he said to himself. "Why do they want you dead?"

When she was perhaps a hundred feet down the beach, Jerry went up to the van. The woman stopped to see what he was doing. He opened up his hands to show he wasn't holding the gun. *Only as good as his word.* She stared at him for a moment, then continued walking.

Jerry slid back the door. "Time to go to work," he said.

A huge black pit bull jumped out. Jerry led the animal to the crest of the dunes and removed the muzzle. The animal's tongue lolled out between huge jaws. The dog made no sound, but his eyes were black with jungle.

Jerry steadied the animal by the chain collar.

He pointed at the woman down the beach and, with a slap to the rump, said, "Rufus, kill!"

CHAPTER

13

"What is happening to him?" Terry wiped her eyes.

"I'm not quite sure," said Mitch Tojian. "It appears to be an endocrine disorder."

"Meaning what?" Calvin asked.

He had canceled classes and came in with Terry before nine the next morning, right after Matty went to school.

The charts in Matty's folder were spread out on the doctor's desk. "Well, the abrupt percentile jump in his growth, his advanced musculature, the axillary hair, pubic hair, and the enlargement of his genitals—they all point to a condition of precocious puberty called Cushing's Syndrome. His system is experiencing hormonal imbalance."

Terry struggled to control herself. "But what's causing it? Why's it happening?"

"Without blood tests I can't tell you exactly," he said. "But it's not an uncommon syndrome. I've treated several patients with the condition. We'll know in a few days, but something is triggering an excessive production of growth hormones."

"Such as *what*?" Calvin asked. He was sitting beside Terry.

"In most cases it's a problem with the adrenal glands. It could also be the pituitary gland. I specified a full hormonal screening."

"The pituitary gland?" Terry said. "You mean he could have a brain tumor?"

"It's a possibility."

Terry put a hand to her mouth. "This isn't happening."

Calvin laid his hand on her arm. "But he can be treated," Calvin said.

"Cushing's Syndrome is treatable with medication." Without the lab results, that was as comforting a prognosis as he could offer.

Terry wiped her face with tissue and nodded. She noted the Norman Rockwell print over his desk—a picture of a little boy with his pants pulled down, grimacing as the doctor tested the hypo. Mitch got up and poured them each a cup of coffee.

"We used to think he was just modest," Terry said, "the way he would avoid us seeing him naked. He'd lock the door whenever he showered and wrap himself up in a bathrobe just going to his room. He didn't want us to know . . ."

"How long's he been covering himself?"

"I don't know, a few months," Terry said. "A few months ago he complained about how hairy he was, compared to the other kids. His legs and under his arms. He wasn't twelve yet, but Calvin's hairy." Her eyes filled again. "Now I know why he wears long-sleeved shirts and turtlenecks all the time."

"We thought it was a fad," Calvin added.

Mitch jotted down what they said. "For about how long?"

"I don't know," she said. "Ever since he started kindergarten, he's worn T-shirts, even in the dead of winter. His parka and a T-shirt. Never even wore any of his sweatshirts. Not until recently. I guess the last few months."

"Has he complained about hirsutism since the first time?"

"No," she said, and Calvin agreed.

"Any other complaints—headaches or pains in the limbs or joints?"

"Once in a while he gets headaches . . . probably anxiety."

Mitch nodded and noted it down.

Then she remembered something. "I don't know if it's related, but he once complained about tingling sensations in his arms and legs. He didn't say any more about it, and when he didn't bring it up again, I forgot about it."

"But no complaints about pains in the wrists or knees." Mitch was thinking about the possible fusion of the epithisis from too rapid growth, but she said no.

"Mitch," Terry said, "he's twelve years old. He's at the age when the dominant fear is being different. How do we tell him he's not a freak?"

"We empathize. We tell him he's got a problem that other kids have, and that we're in this with him to make him normal again."

Her voice began to break again. "Who knows what kind of psychological damage has been done?"

"We can deal with that too," he said. "On the phone you said something about drugs."

"Just that he's been acting strange lately." Terry filled in the details of Betty Gorawlski's call. She also described the way Matty looked yesterday before school, and how the cat seemed skittish around him, and how she saw him hiss back at her.

Mitch recorded what she said.

"He's on edge all the time," she continued. "Also, he's been having bad dreams. Sometimes he cries out in his sleep—terrible cries. And when I go to him, he says it's just a bad dream. But night after night? And when I ask him what it was about, he gets mad, says it's nothing."

"Which is another thing," Calvin cut in. "His anger. He flies off the handle at the slightest provocation."

"Such as . . . ?"

Terry answered. "The other day he had such a fit of rage that I was scared he wouldn't come out of it. I don't mean a little temper tantrum. I mean a violent fit. He locked himself in his room, turned over the bed and tore the place apart, swearing at the top of his lungs. Saying the most awful things. I think what frightened me most was his voice. It didn't sound like him. It was full of rage, and, well, growly . . ."

"And how long did it last?"

"Maybe half an hour. I was frantic. I was going to call you but I decided to let him get it out of his system. When he quieted down, I went to check him and he was asleep under the blankets. The room was a mess. He had found the Raggedy Andy doll I had made him when he was a baby. It was torn apart, shredded. The stuffing was all over the room. The thing is, he didn't remember any of it when he woke up. In fact, he was upset his room had been turned upside down. When I told him he had done it, he denied it. Then he got quiet and began putting things away. It's like living with two people, Matty and some dark negative of him." She shook her head. "Where did all the rage come from? He was such a sweet, happy kid."

"We can bring him back."

"Can we?"

"When we know more. Can you say how long he's shown such rage?"

"Not long. Just the last few weeks."

He had known Matty since infancy and had never noted or heard Terry complain of aggressive behavior or irritability. "It's not a chronic problem."

"This is why I'm worried about drugs—that he'd been taking them because he can't cope with the changes in his body."

"It's possible. The urine test results will be back with the blood tests. If he's on something, it'll show up. Can you think of anything else?"

Calvin shook his head. And Terry just stared at her hands for a long moment without reaction. Then in a voice so low that Tojian could barely hear her, she said, "What's happening to him?"

It was such moments that recalled for Mitch Tojian the dark backroom of pediatrics, the one behind the cut knees, the influenzas and the ear infections. And the door nobody wanted to open. In medical school an old professor once cautioned the class that pediatrics could be the sweetest of specialties, and the most hellish. It was telling parents that their children tested positive for the AIDS virus; it was following a child's demise from the spot on the lung to the last desperate dosage of morphine before the lymph nodes cannibalized themselves; it was looking into the big, trusting eyes staring up from the pillows asking you when they could go home and not knowing that the leukemia raging through their bloodstream would lay them waste in two months. Mitch had prayed he'd never let himself become so intimately involved, that he'd maintain the chilled professional distance, that self-protective zone. But it never worked. From the limited anatomical observations he had made— the signs of precocious puberty, the optical anomalies and night vision—and the description of Matty's fits and lack of recall, Mitch's guess was a structural defect in the pituitary gland or an impinging tumor.

"I can't give you a diagnosis, but something in his system is producing an excess of steroids and other hormones. Let's wait until the tests are back."

She nodded, and then from out of the blue: "Yesterday I saw a male raccoon rape and kill his mate."

"Come again?"

Terry told him the details. "It was anything but natural or normal. She didn't present as animals do. He just jumped her, dug his claws in her back to pin her down. Then he drove her like . . . like a machine, and when he finished, he tore her insides out with his teeth and claws . . ."

"She thinks there's a connection,"Calvin said, shrugging.

"I know it sounds weird," Terry continued, "but I'm wondering if maybe there's something in the chemicals we've put on the lawn, something that could have caused Matty's endocrine system to go haywire, like the raccoons."

"For God's sake," Calvin said, "it's not like I've sprayed the place with Agent Orange."

"I know I'm paranoid about pollution, but you've dumped hundreds of pounds of that stuff on the lawn over the years. Who knows what effect . . . ?"

Calvin shook his head.

"It's a legitimate concern," Mitch said. "But the kinds of lawn chemicals—fertilizers, lime, insecticide, what have you—they wouldn't affect the endocrine system in such gross ways either in Matty or the animals."

She nodded. "It's just that our water's discolored and smells. On some days our backyard has a funny odor. And half the flower garden is dead or dying."

"It's just the rain," Calvin said with a defensive edge in his voice.

"You have well water, I take it," Tojian said.

"Yes, and I brought a sample in for testing."

"Good idea," Tojian said. "And you think it's all connected somehow—the strange odors, discolored water, dead flowers, and Matty's condition?"

"It's just a gut instinct, but I feel as if the devil himself is coming out of the ground."

"Aren't we getting a little dramatic?" Calvin said.

"We'll know in a day or two." Then she said, "God, our life seems to be on hold for test results—water, rabies, Matty's blood."

Nobody said anything for a moment.

"Mitch, I'm scared."

"I know you are, Terry."

His mind shifted back six months to Emerson Hospital when, on another case, he had dropped in to visit Terry after her second miscarriage. Even after three days she was still reeling from loss. She had been only five weeks from term. Her obstetrician, Larry Rosenblum, a friend from medical school, filled him in on the details she would never know. Nor the grim fortune that she had lost it. The fetus was grossly deformed—unlike anything in Larry's medical experience. He had described it as looking like some kind of throwback creature, with deformed hands and feet and a strip of hair down its back. But what threw them was the face—a prognathous, snouty structure, its mouth was full of teeth. It was as if Terry and Calvin's genetic material were inexplicably scrambled with that of a lesser species. Somebody had made a stupid crack about Rosemary's Baby. They told the parents nothing and chalked it up to one more medical anomaly . . . "Call me when the water profile is back."

She nodded.

They got up to go. "How do we let him know we know?" Calvin asked.

Mitch put his hands on their shoulders as they started toward the door. "More than anybody else in the world, he trusts his mom and dad will be right there, that they will not make fun of him or think he's a freak. You tell him that you caught a glimpse of him in the shower or while he was sleep. But you also tell him that we all want to make him okay again and we will. He's got to believe that, or he'll resist treatment, that's vital. The key thing is trust."

"When do we tell him?"

"Probably best to wait until I call. I'll also want to see him again Monday."

"I don't look forward to that," Terry said.

"Except it will be a relief for him to know you both know."

Mitch wrote out a prescription for lithium to stabilize Matty's moods and L-dopa, which, among other effects, would reverse the hirsutism. Then he walked them through the waiting room to the outside. Several women sat with children. They looked up and smiled, then looked away quickly when they saw Terry's face.

It was a glorious spring morning. Someplace an insistent robin chirped. Mitch accompanied them to the car.

Before they got in, Terry said, "Mitch, promise you'll stay with us, even if it means specialists."

"Of course. Endocrinology is a secondary area of mine. Even so, I'll stay close."

He shook Calvin's hand and gave Terry a hug. "I'll call you as soon as the tests are in. Saturday, the latest."

Mitch stood there watching them drive away. As he turned back to his office, he saw a man in a black van start up and drive off. If it hadn't been a mere coincidence, he would have sworn he was following them.

CHAPTER

14

"Maria Terranova, microbiologist and professor of genetics at the Massachusetts Institute of Technology, was found dead Tuesday morning on the beach outside of her Sandwich, Cape Cod, home, the victim of an apparent canine attack. She was 63 and made her home in Cambridge and in Sandwich.

"A 1947 graduate of Radcliffe College, Ms. Terranova received her doctorate in biology from Oxford University as a Rhodes scholar and joined the MIT faculty in 1975. A specialist in genetics, Dr. Terranova was the author of numerous scientific articles and three books. Before joining the MIT faculty she conducted research in microbiology for the US Army and for private laboratories.

"Prints in the sand indicate that Dr. Terranova was attacked by a single large canine. Although there were reports of alleged dog-pack attacks on two deer on the North Shore recently, police are ruling out any connection. However, police are expanding their search for the dog to Barnstable and surrounding towns . . ."

Jack Perry raised to his face the newspaper with the account of Maria Terranova's death when Terry and Calvin came out. He watched them say goodbye to the doctor, then get into their car and pull away. Did he start his car too quickly? In his side mirror he saw the doctor watch him fall behind them, thought for a moment that maybe the doctor suspected something, then decided he was getting paranoid when he saw the doctor turn and head to his office without looking back.

The green Saab turned down Center Street, and Jack fell two cars behind. For the last four days he had been dogging the car, mostly the woman going about town on chores—the library, a market, the local video store, Butler Elementary. What stood out was the trip to the Carleton Health Department. That and this visit. The shingle said DR. MITCHELL TOJIAN, PEDIATRICIAN, yet their son wasn't with them. And the woman had come out crying.

The Saab headed up Hutchinson, past the school and over the hill to Jason. It turned up the long drive while Jack Perry continued to the turnaround at the end and parked behind the clutch of birches at the upper corner of the lawn. He didn't turn off the engine; he'd only be a minute. Just to sort out his thoughts.

It was a modest white colonial against thick woods. A low fieldstone wall ran the full width of the property enclosing a wide deep lawn that looked like a putting green. A bright yellow hose made a snake across the lawn. Along the front of the house were hemlocks, rhododendron, azaleas and stuff he didn't know the names of. A spreading dogwood sat in the middle of the lawn. Unlike the others in the neighborhood, it lacked bloom. A red brick walk led from the driveway to the front door, low antique lanterns discreetly lighting the way. A yellow plastic tree swing dangled from a side maple. High oaks and pines formed the backdrop.

A Norman Rockwell, he thought, plastered over dirty little secrets.

CHAPTER

15

Calvin's office phone rang like a premonition.

"Calvin, what can I say? It's fantastic. I mean, what a killing!" Beverly Otis's voice filled his head. "I've been in this business for eighteen years and I've never seen anything like this before. I mean, almost twice the price is incredible!"

"Given what we bought it for." He had to hold the phone away.

"I'll say. So, when we gonna close? I can have her here tomorrow at ten, and the lawyer, and we pass papers before lunch so you can take your wife out to celebrate. They're paying cash, so no need for bank officials and mortgage approvals. I mean, a piece of cake!"

"Well, that's not why I called you, Beverly."

"Oh?"

Calvin's eyes fixed on the eight-by-ten desk photo behind his telephone. It showed Terry and Matty sitting on the top step of the brick walk that led to the front door. Her arm was around his shoulders, and Matty was beaming at the camera. Calvin had taken the picture last spring. The grass blazed in the sun, and in the background the dogwood was in outrageous bloom, looking like a pink cloud against the dark backdrop of Magog. It could have been a realtor's promo shot.

"I need some information."

"Information. Okay, uh-huh. Shoot."

"Ten years ago we bought the place for $72,000."

"A giveaway even then."

"Yes. Your exact words were 'steal of the century.' "

"It was." She chuckled musically. "In fact, had I known then what I know now, I'd have bought it myself."

"That's my question."

"What?"

"Why so cheap?"

He could hear the flustering in her voice. "Huh? You want to know
. . . I don't quite follow."

"I'm concerned that I leaped without looking."

"Calvin, I think I'm missing something in this conversation."

He knew he wasn't putting it right. But he was blowing on a dull
red ember of guilt in the back of his conscience that had all but
extinguished. "Before I signed the purchase and sale, you'd said
something about the land once being used for commercial purposes." He still did not have it right. The words were off.

"Commercial purposes?" Beverly said. There was a long pause as
she put together what he was driving at. "Calvin, it's been over a
decade, so my memory isn't what it should be. But I think when you
signed the P and S, I made it clear that there might have been a
minor liability attached."

The ember flared. "Minor liability," he said like an echo.

"Remember? But it was nothing to get worked up about."

"Maybe you can refresh my memory."

"About what?"

"About the minor liability."

Another brief pause as Beverly regrouped. "Calvin, forgive me,
but why are we looking back? I mean in a few weeks you'll be off to
greener pastures—"

"Because I got the house for less than market value and I want to
know why?"

"All of a sudden after ten years? I mean, what's the problem?"

"We've got dying trees, flowers that won't flower, wild animals
that are acting loony." He could not get himself to add Matty to the
list.

"Is that it?" The relief in her voice was palpable. "I know how
Terry is about the environment and all. I've read her letters in the
paper. And I don't blame her, what with all the stuff going on. But
that could be anything. Some kind of disease or blight, or the winter
drought. Who knows? You should see my roses. My husband says
I've got a black thumb. Even before the Japanese beetles got to
them, they looked like Pearl Harbor."

"My concern is that the Samborskys or somebody else dumped something in the ground."

"Listen, Calvin, I really doubt there's any problem. I mean, your lawn is nice and green, right?"

"That does not tell me why the place went for a song."

There was another long pause. Then: "Calvin, this is a small town, and small towns have rumors. You came in cold from the outside and had no knowledge of what the mill can crank out around here."

"So you're saying the place was a commercial dump, and everybody knew, including the Samborskys, which explains the pricetag?"

"No, I'm saying that there were rumors about that end of the woods. But there was absolutely no evidence, believe me. You should know that. You had your backyard dug up for the pool, right? Find anything funny—barrels, odd structures, foundations—anything but God's good dirt?"

She was right. "No."

"There you are. Rumors."

"But they had to come from someplace."

Beverly chuckled. "The Greenpeace Fairy? Calvin, who knows where rumors come from? Maybe they affected the price, maybe not. And if they did, count yourself lucky."

"But didn't it surprise you what they were asking?"

"Sure, but in this business there are surprises every day." She tried to laugh him off. "Calvin, like I said when you bought it, don't look a gift horse in the mouth."

"Empty rumors?"

"Exactly." Her voice had resumed its satisfaction.

"Such as what?"

"Ridiculous things," she said, spinning them out. "That the place was haunted, that the woods had some Indian curse on it, that there were demon dogs running around. Numb-nutty things that just come out of the air . . . or maybe a bottle of Chivas. Who knows? But it was all nonsense, believe me."

"Did Mrs. Samborsky know its market value?"

"Who knows what she knew? She was a grieving old widow."

"But you were her agent. If you knew they were empty rumors, why didn't you push for a higher price?"

A gaping silence. "Calvin, what's the *point* of all this? I mean, like you're giving me the third degree."

"Because you sold the place for less than half the market value, maybe a third. She could have gotten two hundred thousand."

"Calvin, her husband had just died, and she was elderly and superstitious and was in a hurry to put things behind her. I mean, what can I say?"

"How long was it on the market before I bought it?"

"How could I remember how long?"

"You have records, and if you don't know, I could find out."

Another pause. "Eight months."

"Thought you said she was in a hurry."

"I don't know. I don't remember. Maybe she dropped the price."

"You have the folder."

"She started at ninety."

"Ninety? It was a steal at that price."

"What can I tell you? You had better taste than the rest."

"Or they knew something I didn't."

"Nobody knew anything," she said. "Look, Calvin, stop being so suspicious. Even if there was something there, all that chemical stuff breaks down anyway, no?"

"We can only hope."

There was another awkward silence. "Well, as soon as you and Terry make a decision on the offer, give a call, and we'll put together the P and S and get you some temporary housing, okay?"

"Yeah."

"But I think you better make a move fast, because she's not going to leave her offer in forever."

Mrs. Manning had given them until tomorrow.

"By the way, how's that big boy of yours? I saw his name in the paper the other day. On the Devil Dogs, my nephew Scott's on the Cardinals. God, they grow up so fast."

"Yeah."

"We'll talk tomorrow."

Calvin hung up. He felt clammy.

minor liability

His American Dream house. His own little West Egg. And like Gatsby, he jumped for the green light without thought.

She had mentioned the liability but he had never investigated. He had denied any risk. He came, he saw, he wrote a deposit, half-dazed by the bargain.

And he never told Terry. How could he? She was something of an alarmist regarding the environment. Every day there was a new doomsday piece magneted to their refrigerator about pesticides or the greenhouse effect or acid rain or the holes in the ozone layer or the disappearance of the tropical rain forest in Papua New Guinea or all the toxins in the food they ate. She would have had a SWAT team from the EPA in there before she let him buy.

find anything funny—barrels, odd structures in the ground, foundations, anything but God's good dirt?

None of that.

for a song.

God, if she knew.

CHAPTER

16

Jerry laid the photo of his BiOmega hits on the table. With his gloved hand he held up the canvas bag.

Rufus made a silent, shuddering motion with his mouth. Any other dog would have barked his brains out, but Rufus never barked. Jerry had trained it out of him with an electric prod. Barking, like the show of emotions, gave yourself away. Which was fatal in the face of an adversary. Mystery was all.

Rufus sat back, his body poised on his haunches as if posing for a photograph.

Jerry grinned. "Good boy." Control. Perfect control. And those eyes. They followed him to the cage door. "Protein," said Jerry. And from the bag he pulled out a live chicken by the feet. Instantly it started squawking and beating its wings. Rufus pressed his face against the bars, the white slash of those teeth. "Not yet," Jerry said. A little foreplay to sharpen the appetite.

Rufus's room was actually half of Jerry's garage divided by a steel grating from floor to ceiling. At one end was a gate that swung inward. Ordinarily Rufus had the run of the house except during such playtime. Jerry used the garage because he could hose the place out when Rufus was done. Not that Rufus left much.

He held the bird out so its wings beat freely while its head hung inches from the dog's face through the bars. Not a sound came from Rufus, not a muscle moved except the twitching of his upper lip over those teeth. From the bird a raucous squawking. Swan song for chickens.

His usual tosses were chickens and stray cats, a small turkey on Thanksgiving. Once when he toyed with the idea of pitting Rufus, he

103

snagged a lost mutt just to test his instinct. There was never any contest, but he dropped the idea because Rufus was too good for the pit. He was meant for bigger game. " 'What doesn't kill us makes us strong.' Right, boy? You, me, and old Fred Nietzsche." The dog backed up. "Rufus, heel!" The dog froze. Jerry unlatched the gate, stepped in and closed it behind him. The chicken banged its head against Jerry's leg as its wings tried to break away. He held the bird away from Rufus, his free hand palm up to signal restraint.

Rufus fought against invisible tethers, but he kept his place.

"That's my good boy." Rufus raised his face to his master, and Jerry fixed on his eyes and felt the heat of connectedness.

He walked to the middle of the floor with the chicken at arm's length. Eyes fixed on it, Rufus watched as Jerry carried it to the far side. The change made Rufus snap to all fours but Jerry caught him. "Heel!" And the dog dropped back down, half-growling, half-whimpering. Jerry made a slow teasing circuit of the arena with the bird, he stopped three feet from Rufus, dangling the chicken over his head. The wings flapped, Rufus squirmed but held his place. Jerry had trained him well.

When he cut back to the gate, Jerry said, "Rufus, steady." For a long moment he looked into the dog's eyes. Magnificent ferocity. The eyes Jerry loved. Jungle eyes.

Jungle eyes: Jerry had come to know those eyes more than twenty years ago in the steaming thick of Vietnam. Faking parental consent, he had joined the Marines at seventeen to see action. And he saw it. During his stint he had conducted 517 patrols, 262 ambushes, 29 sweep and clear operations around Da Nang. Some claimed that two years of jungle war had made Jerry a little crazy, addicted to his own adrenaline. That all the violence had deadened him. He knew better. It was just the opposite . . . like some mystical life quest had drawn him to the jungle for an awakening, a rebirth. Jerry never remembered feeling more alive than when he was in the bush under fire. His body had become a thing of raw nerve endings. His senses were supercharged. Unlike the terror that had gripped his buddies, Jerry felt he had been transported to a state of bliss. The greater the danger, the more he felt alive—and *wanted*. The worst people in the world were out there in the jungle, and they came shooting for *him*—Jerry Mars. He could imagine no greater honor than to be hunted, to be wanted by the baddest-ass killers there were.

It went the other way, too. Killing so exquisite an enemy was a privilege granted only the most cunning. He didn't mean remote-control stuff—dropping bombs or lobbing mortar shells or machine-gunning the bush. Real war was hand-to-hand combat. One-on-one. Rare in modern warfare, therefore all the more special. To Jerry Mars the supreme high was the terror in an enemy's eyes at the moment of his death—when he slashed the blade across the jugular or plunged the bayonet. For one brief moment the man he killed was the most special person in the world. He belonged to Jerry. He was all *his*, body and soul, engaged in a mystical ritual of exchange: life for life. There was no greater gift. And no greater pleasure than the look in his deathmate's eyes as life passed from him. Jerry would kill for those eyes. Jerry did. And it made him stronger than his fears of weakness. He would have killed without Vietnam. The war confirmed his calling. It was in the fabric of his being. Like Rufus.

"Beautiful," he said, and threw the bird toward the ceiling and slipped out the gate. Rufus let out a deep-throated whine but did not move. He turned his head to Jerry. "Good boy." He would not attack until Jerry gave the command.

The chicken flapped across the floor, tried to take flight, but got no more than a foot in the air before flopping to the ground again. Jerry watched it run in frantic circles at the far end. Rufus lowered his head and emitted a savage growl that sent the bird squawking against the grate, where it managed to lock its talons in the wire.

Jerry checked his watch. Three, two, one. He pressed the timer button. "Rufus, kill!"

Rufus shot across the cage, catching the bird in midair by the neck. Instantly his jaws snapped off the squawking. Three shakes and the bird's head was torn from its body. Jerry checked his watch. Zero to dead in 5.6 seconds. Chipped a full three-tenths off his record. "Good boy."

Jerry opened a bottle of Evian water and pressed against the cage to watch Rufus finish it off, shake it in his jaws like a stuffed doll. He snapped up the head. A few loud crunches and it was gone. No gourmet, Rufus. He ate everything but the wings. Of course, Jerry hadn't fed him since the day before yesterday. Keep his instincts as sharp as his appetite—something every trainer knew.

When Rufus was finished, Jerry opened the cage door, hosed it out, then emptied a five-ounce bag of Sojourner Farms Dog Food into Rufus's bowl. A high-fiber vegetable blend of grains, nuts and sea grasses.

"Happiness is a balanced meal," said Jerry as he pulled a wet feather from Rufus's ear. He gave him a pat, and Rufus went for the chow. Then he took his Evian back into the kitchen, cut himself a slice of seven-grain bread, spread some hummus on it and sat down at the table. While he ate he studied the photo.

"Took your secret with you, lady," he said aloud.

And with the black felt-tip he drew an X through Maria Terranova's face.

Maybe Chubs in the beard will see reason.

CHAPTER

17

It was a little before noon the next day when Mitch Tojian called with Matty's blood analysis.

Terry held the phone so hard, her hand was a white claw. The good news was that there were no signs of any drugs in Matty's system, and he had been screened for most trafficked substances. However, as expected, his blood revealed an elevation of several hormones.

What bothered Tojian was the high levels of gonadotropic hormones, male sex steroids. Boys of twelve usually had, he said, mean plasma testosterone levels of around 250. Matty's was nearly 2,000 —more than twice that of a male adult. He said it was not clear what was causing the overproduction—whether it was a problem with Matty's adrenal glands or his brain. The high numbers indicated that the pituitary gland might be triggering the excess, accounting for the enlarged genitalia and general hirsutism. That might also explain the rage. As for the cause? Well, they would need more tests. He wanted Matty brought in Saturday for a physical. He had also arranged for an MRI at the Emerson Hospital that same day. When Terry asked what the MRI was for, Tojian explained it was the standard procedure for detecting tumors.

tumors.

The word jabbed Terry's being.

While Mitch assured her that pituitary tumors could be treated, she knew as she hung up that the life they had been living was forever changed. This was the turning point from which they would forever mark the calendar. What certitude about the future they had shared as a family was gone like morning dew. No longer would they measure their lives in Little League standings, math tests and piano lessons, but in the mortal scores of magnetic resonance imaging, mean hormone values and Tanner grades. Suddenly she had something in common with the mothers of cancer-ridden Coburn.

Calvin arrived home shortly before Matty. Her summary of Dr. Tojian's report left him shaken, more than she had expected. More than just fear for Matty, all his dreams of starting a new life in upstate New York had suddenly been shattered.

"There's just no way we can think about moving. Even if his condition is reversible, I don't like the idea of hauling him off to some Podunk place with strange doctors."

"It's not like we're moving to Borneo," Calvin said. "Albany is less than an hour's ride."

"And Boston's in our backyard. Besides, I want Mitch Tojian on his case. He's known Matty all his life."

"He isn't the only pediatrician in the universe."

Her eyes flared at him. "How could you even think of moving?"

"I'm saying let's not just write it off yet."

"I haven't," she said, "but if he gets through this okay, maybe they can put a hold on the job until next year."

Next year? That wasn't how it worked. If he didn't accept the position now, it would be offered to the next name on their list. Priest had all but said that. It was now or never. Frustration tightened his chest. She was right, of course. Yet he felt the promise of his lifetime slip from his fingers. For the past several days Argyle-on-the-Hudson had become in his mind a place of healing, where they would move to and be whole again. "Well, let's not be hasty," he said feebly. "Just wait a few days."

Terry said nothing.

"I better call Beverly."

"I already did," she said.

He nodded. "What did you tell her?"

"That we're putting things on hold."

"You tell her why?"

"Not in any detail. I just said Matty needed some tests. I said we'd know more next week."

"What did she say?"

"She got pissy. Said the woman was putting pressure on her. I told her I understood but this was a priority. If the woman wants it badly enough, she can hold off a few more days."

They were quiet for a minute. Then, as if reading his mind, Terry said, "I'm sorry, Calvin. I know how much you wanted this."

It was around three when Matty came home from school. He said he was hungry and Terry made him a tuna sandwich and warmed up some soup while they both pretended a cheery interest in how school went. He ate quietly, responding only in monosyllables. There was a time when he would go on for hours about what they did in art class and gym or the film they saw on sharks.

Calvin pulled up a chair across from him. He noted a fine black down on the backs of Matty's hands. Calvin tried not to stare and, with as much enthusiasm as he could muster, talked up the game that evening, reminding him that Dr. Tojian was taking the team out for ice cream afterward. Matty showed no interest.

"Matty, there's something we have to talk about."

He took a bite of his sandwich. "Like what?"

"Well," Calvin began, "the other day when you had that blood test of Dr. Tojian's . . . remember? Well, the results are back. He called just a little while ago."

Matty spooned soup into his mouth.

"He said that we're going to have to go back for more tests."

The muscles in Matty's face clenched. "Why?"

"Well, he found something in your blood, something that's throwing off your system, causing changes in you."

Matty looked to his mother and back to Calvin, gauging their complicity. "What changes?"

"Honey," said Terry, "I think you know."

Matty's face darkened, his mouth quivered.

"Matty, this is kind of serious. You've got a medical problem—"

"I don't have a damn medical problem." His chair scraped against the floor as he pushed himself away. He tried to get up but Terry sat him down again. "I don't want to go to the doctor's. I'm not sick."

God, this is so unfair, she thought. "You *are* sick." She felt the urge of tears. "Your body is changing in ways it's not supposed to, not until you're older. And Dr. Tojian wants to stop it from doing that and make you better. You need help, honey, and the only way to cure you is for you to have more tests done . . ."

He brought his fist down so hard, the dishes clattered in place. "He knows? You told him?"

"He's your doctor, Matty. Your blood tests told him you've got a problem—"

"I *don't* have a damn problem."

She put her hand on his shoulder but he recoiled.

"Matty, listen," Calvin said, "the other night I accidentally walked into the bathroom while you were taking a shower . . ."

His face screwed up and his cheeks burned as if slapped.

"Honey, I saw you . . . naked."

His eyes flared. "You were spying on me," he screamed. "That's what you were doing, you goddamn dork. You were spying on me. You didn't have to do that."

"I wasn't spying on you."

"You were. You were. I hate you, Dad. I hate you." Suddenly Matty's whole face seemed to shift—his eyes slitted and his lips pulled back. "You . . ." His voice was full of gravel. "Your ass is grass."

Calvin was too shocked to move. Matty kicked his chair so it skidded across the floor and into Calvin's legs. Calvin picked up the chair holding it in front of him, looking for an absurd moment like a lion tamer. Matty started toward him, still growling, his hands raised, fingers open. When Terry screamed, Matty swiped at her, just missing her face with the back of his hand. Suddenly Calvin slammed down the chair and pushed himself up against Matty.

"You want to hit me, Matthew? Huh? Is that what you want to do?" He put his hands by his sides. "Come on, take a swipe at me. Come on, hit me."

"Calvin, *don't*," Terry pleaded.

Matty suddenly froze. He blinked several times as if coming to. He looked at Terry, then back to Calvin as if wondering why she was crying and why his father was standing there in the middle of the kitchen challenging him to hit him. A moment later he walked out of the kitchen and up the stairs to his room. The door closed quietly behind him.

In the grim silence Calvin cleaned up the spilled soup while Terry stood against the sink, her eyes fixed on one of Matty's art-class drawings magneted to the refrigerator. It was a male figure with a huge body and too-small head, the face distorted, mouth dripping blood. Underneath, like a caption, was written, MATMAN BEWARE.

Minutes later Terry heard Matty's door open. "Mom, could you come here?" His voice sounded normal.

"Sure," she said, and went up, leaving Calvin staring blankly out the window at a solitary crow in the backyard by the pool.

Matty was sitting on his bed. He was still dressed in his turtleneck and jeans. Next to him was a large red photo album containing hundreds of pictures Terry had taken of him from infancy to three. Four more albums, from three to the present, sat in his bookcase. Matty liked to go through them. Sometimes Terry would join him, and Matty would laugh and tease her: "Mom, you're so embarrassing. You always tear up when you look at these." And she would laugh and wipe her eyes and say it was because she was a sentimental sap.

She sat next to him on the bed now. Again she was aware of that cumin-like odor. Like Calvin after a workout. In Matty's lap was a small hand-carved teak jewelry box. In it were all of his baby teeth sitting on the red velvet cushion like so many irregular pearls.

"Remember when I used to believe in the Tooth Fairy?"

"Yes, sure do."

"That was pretty dumb."

"No, it wasn't dumb."

"I still have the last one." From inside his shirt he pulled out a small diamond-shaped gold-chained locket that had been Calvin's as a kid. Inside the hinged compartment was a small tooth—his first.

"Remember when I found these?"

"Yes, I do."

"You forgot to hide it. You were pretty upset, weren't you?"

"Only with myself."

Matty smiled faintly. "You cried."

"You know me," she said, then became silent for a moment. "I cried because . . ."

Because it was the night the fairies died.

No, the night I killed them.

". . . you knew then that it was Dad and I who left the money under the pillow."

"I think about that night once in a while," he said, and twined his finger in the chain.

It had happened two years ago. He had just turned ten—a time for all the big questions—sex, ghosts, vampires, God, heaven and death. It started with the Tooth Fairy. He had found the jewelry box in his mother's closet and began the interrogation. Without stopping, he pursued the logical consequences of his discovery, pumping Terry until she had a full-fledged massacre on her hands. The Easter Bunny fell next when Matty demanded to know if it was Terry and Calvin who hid the colored eggs around the backyard and who left the big basket filled with all sorts of wonderful trinkets and sugared delights. In the dark of his room, lying beside him on the bed, Terry confessed, that it was Mom and Dad. And, yes, all those presents under the Christmas tree, too. "But what about the glass of milk and the chocolate chip cookies and the carrots for the reindeer? And how about the footprints around the fireplace? Those, too."

Those, too. And in a wink all the magic had turned to stone.

In the dark, Matty had asked, "Mom, are you crying?"

She had been torn between letting him go on believing or accepting gray truth. What had finally pushed her to blow out the magic was the thought that at ten he might be a target for ridicule by friends, most of whom were older and scornful of childish make-believe. What tormented Terry still was the realization that Matty could take such pleasure in pretending, that he did not want to let go. He had cried himself to sleep that night . . .

"I wasn't mad or anything. Nobody else believed anyway."

Silence fell between them as she stroked the back of his head.

"Mom," he said softly after a few moments. "Am I going to die?"

The question made her stiffen. "What? No, of course not. Why do you even ask that?"

"Because I'm a freak."

"You're *not* a freak. You just have a problem we're going to fix."

"I've got hair down there like Daddy," he said. "And I'm big. Next year in junior high we're gonna have to take showers for swimming. Everybody will laugh at me. Matty with the gorilla dick." He dropped his eyes to the teeth in the box again. "How come it happened to me?"

Terry was struggling to sound composed. "I don't know, but it happens to other boys, too, and they get fixed. That's why you have to have more tests. We'll go together Saturday."

"What are they going to do to me?"

"You're going to have a physical."

"Will I have to take my clothes off?"

"It's the only way he can examine you."

Matty continued to stare into the box of teeth.

"Then they're going to take X-rays to see where the problem is. It won't hurt and you can keep your clothes on. I promise, and I'll be right by your side. Okay?"

He nodded again. Terry put her arm around him, and when he didn't push her away, she felt a rush of relief. For a minute or so they just sat there quietly, then, in a soft voice, Matty said, "Mom, would you get mad if I used Dad's razor?"

"A razor? What for?" But even as she said it, she noticed the dark shadow of sideburns begin to make a line down the sides of his face. Also, wispy hairs were beginning to define a mustache.

Matty stood up, and before she knew it, he had pulled off his turtleneck. "This is why."

Terry had to bite her tongue from gasping. His chest was a mat of black hair.

"See? I'm a freak." Tears filled his eyes. "*Say* it," he shouted. "Say I'm a freak."

"You're not a freak, damn it. Your hormones are out of balance. It happens to other kids, too."

"Not like this," he said. His tears were flowing now. "Not like this. I belong in a damn zoo."

"Matty, stop it," she said. She could hear the ripple of panic in her voice. "I'm telling you what Dr. Tojian said. It's a condition lots of boys have. You can be cured. You have to believe that."

And he looked at her with a frightening intensity. "Freak," he said. And for a hideous moment, before she could stop him, Terry sat paralyzed in horror as Matty ripped out fistful after fistful of hair in rhythm to his chant. "Freak . . . Freak . . . Freak . . ."

CHAPTER

18

Chubs was Marcus Wiley. The third face in the photo.

Jerry Mars wondered what the jungle would look like in his eyes.

He had studied Wiley's movements for several days. The man lived on Boston's Mount Vernon Street, a quaint and elegant road that climbed Beacon Hill. Unlike the others, he was retired. His wife was dead and he lived with his daughter, Margaret, a cripple. Jerry had watched him push her in a wheelchair through the Public Garden and Common.

As with the other assignments, this was to be an accident. According to Roman, Wiley was a smoker, even though he was being treated for emphysema. Jerry's plan was a nice, innocent house fire. In his briefcase he had duct tape, handcuffs, a half dozen dead C-batteries, cotton and chloroform. It wouldn't bring him the predatory thrill of a one-on-one kill, but it would earn him another $35,000.

The night was warm and starry. Around seven-thirty, just as the sun had declined over the Charles River, Jerry strolled up Charles Street past the fancy cafes and antique shops. It was a neighborhood that could have been designed by Charles Dickens—red-brick structures, big windows with ripply glass, quaint little shops, glass lampposts and brick sidewalks where people strolled arm in arm. The place made him think of Christmas.

At the old meeting house he turned up Mount Vernon Street to number sixty-seven. The lace of the basement window blocked the view of the daughter in her apartment, but he could hear her at the piano.

In the glass side panel Jerry smoothed down his hair and adjusted his tie, which he had bought that afternoon from the Brothers Brooks on Newbury Street just for the occasion. A maroon number with white pigs. WASP-elegant. He rang the bell.

A round white-haired man with a shiny red face and bushy gray eyebrows came to the door. "Dr. Marcus Wiley?"

"Yes?" The beard was gone. He looked like an aged cherub.

Jerry handed Wiley his business card. "My name is Jerry Mars. I'm a private investigator and I'm wondering if we could talk a short while."

Wiley took the card and held it in the light. "Concerning what, if I may ask?" He handed the card back to Jerry but made no move to let him inside.

"Well, sir, it's rather confidential," Jerry said smiling. "It has to do with your association with BiOmega Labs."

"BiOmega? Lord, I haven't heard that name for twenty years." Wiley's expression was unreadable.

Jerry smiled. The man was surprisingly open. "Then it might be a trip down memory lane for you. I have some news about some of your past colleagues you might find interesting . . . if I may?" Jerry indicated that he'd prefer to talk inside.

Wiley opened the door wide. "Sure, come on in. What did you say your name was?"

They shook hands. "Mars. Jerry Mars." He stepped in with his briefcase. There was a smoke alarm just overhead on the wall.

"Mars," Wiley said, closing the door behind them. "Like the planet."

"It used to be Gianmarsiano."

"Irish kid, huh?"

"Yes, like Maria Terranova."

Wiley gave Jerry a startled glance. Was it possible he did not know of her death?

"Nice lady," Jerry said. "And speaking of nice," he continued without missing a beat, "this is a wonderful room."

The room was full of antiques. A large crystal chandelier hung overhead. On the walls were original oil paintings of people in formal eighteenth-century garb. Wiley ancestors, Jerry guessed. He looked Mayflower.

"Thank you," Wiley said. "Mostly my daughter's doing."

"Your daughter?" He pretended ignorance.

"That's her," Wiley said. The sound of piano wafted up from below.

"Lovely."

"*Moonlight Sonata,*" Wiley said. "But I'm sure you didn't come to talk Beethoven."

Wiley indicated an upholstered armchair beside the fireplace. Jerry sat.

"Can I get you a drink?" Wiley moved to a table of crystal decanters and glasses.

"No, thank you, but please go right ahead."

Wiley poured himself some old ruby port, then sat in the facing armchair. He took a sip and lit up a cigarette from a gold case. "You know Maria Terranova?"

"I met her in passing, you might say."

Wiley nodded. "I haven't seen her in years. How is she?"

"Dead. Like Stefan Karsky."

Wiley's glass froze at his lips.

"Karsky drowned and Maria was attacked by a dog. But I have reason to believe their deaths were not accidental, that they had to do with the work that you and they were conducting at BiOmega Labs twenty-some years ago." Wiley's eyes were widening. "I'm terribly sorry to be the bearer of sad news." From the briefcase he pulled photostats of the obituaries. "Here are the reports of their deaths."

Wiley put his glass down and looked at the obits. A photograph of Wiley and his daughter as a teenager sat on the table near his glass. The girl was in a wheelchair.

"Who are you?" Wiley asked.

"I'm an independent investigator, Dr. Wiley."

Wiley studied him for a moment—from his cordovan tassels up his gray slacks to the blue blazer, pinstriped shirt and pig tie.

"And just what do you want?"

"More than anything else, to warn you that your own life might be in danger." Night swarmed behind Wiley's eyes. They were so beautiful, Jerry nearly gasped. "Yes," Jerry went on. His heart was pounding. "But it would help considerably if you tell me the nature of your research project."

Wiley's chest heaved to take in air, making a calliope wheeze. Emphysema from a gold case. "What research project?"

"Black Flag."

"Who sent you?"

"I'm sorry, Dr. Wiley," he said in a measured voice, "but I can't tell you who I'm working for. As you can imagine, it's all very confidential. Nonetheless, if we are going to get to the bottom of things, we'll need your full cooperation."

The delicate plinkings of the Beethoven floated up through the floorboards.

"I'm not going to say anything unless I know who I'm talking to."

"But you've seen my card." It simply said MARS INVESTIGATIVE SERVICES. CONFIDENTIALITY GUARANTEED. No address or telephone number.

"That tells me nothing," Wiley said. "Who are your clients?"

"If I name my clients, then where's confidentiality?"

Wiley started to get up. "I think I've heard enough."

"Very well," Jerry said. He unzipped the briefcase and pulled out the Glock 9, silencer in place. He held it at arm's length as if reading a calling card. "It says, Have gun, will travel."

Wiley made a kind of wheezy hiccup sound in his throat. "My God, you killed them . . ."

The midnight storm broke in Wiley's eyes. Sending electric ripples through Jerry's groin. "Yes," he said. "They chose not to cooperate. Silly of them." Suddenly he slipped to his knees, holding the gun on Wiley. He snatched the photographs off the table. "But you're not so silly, Dr. Wiley, now are you?"

"You son of a bitch—"

"Something like that." Jerry rammed the gun into the pink folds of Wiley's throat. The man's eyes were so radiant that Jerry felt an urge to kiss him. Wiley nodded. For several seconds Jerry felt he was swimming in Wiley's eyes. They were grayish green and flecked with yellow like exotic flowers, and at the center, huge black pearls. "Talk," Jerry whispered.

"Please don't hurt my daughter. I beg you."

Jerry glanced at the eyes of the girl in the photo. He wondered what color they were. "Only if you tell me everything."

"I will, I promise."

Jerry pulled back to his chair. He rested the gun in his lap.

Wiley took a few deep, wheezy breaths. "It was a project funded by the US Army. It was top secret and only a handful of people worked on it." His voice was trembling. He glanced at the photograph. "*Please* don't hurt her . . ."

"She won't be hurt."

"Please, I want your word."

"I will not touch her."

Wiley let out his breath, and his large belly looked like a balloon deflating. For the next several minutes he outlined the nature of Project Black Flag. "The Vietnam war was raging without an end in sight. Some people were concerned that even if the war ended, the conflict would go on for generations, the way it had for the previous two generations. The Communists had been battling different Vietnamese regimes since the forties. There were worries that a war of attrition would go on into the next century. And that's where the idea of Black Flag came from, out of the need to put an end to the hostilities. At the time, I'm afraid I didn't care much about moral implications. Nor did the others. One man's boy was tortured and killed by the VCs. He was nineteen. We were too outraged not to go along with it."

"With what?"

"A genocide virus."

"A genocide virus." Jerry's mouth made an O of comprehension. "Thus, Black Flag."

Wiley nodded. "Horrible code."

"I like it."

Wiley glared at him, then dropped his eyes to the glass of port. "It was designed to sterilize the male population of North Vietnam. Or any future enemy, I suppose. The idea was to administer it through the water supply. Without any noticeable side-effects, it would target spermatozoon cells and reverse the transcriptive of the genetic information. At least that was the plan. Coincidentally, the project was a major breakthrough in genetic engineering."

"Visions of a gook-free future."

Wiley rubbed a spot on his forehead, partly shading his eyes. "Not the way I'd put it," he said softly.

"Or wop-free, Jew-free, Arab-free, even WASP-free. The mind boggles with possibilities." Wiley stared at him in rigid silence. "How many people knew?"

"I don't know, maybe half a dozen. Four of us and two intelligence officers."

"Your own little Manhattan Project," Jerry said. "Who's the man standing next to you?"

Wiley looked at the photo. "Jack Perry." Wiley said he did not know Perry's whereabouts. If he was still alive, Roman might know. If not, Jerry would try his own network.

"What went wrong?" Jerry asked.

"Wrong? What do you mean?"

"We lost the war."

Wiley closed his eyes a moment to collect himself. "The substance chemically known as omnimycinol was made from a mold. We discovered that in its pure white crystalline form the substance was a steroid that generated remarkable pharmacological effects, including the destruction of the spermatozoa cells." Wiley finished the rest of his port in a single swallow. "Unfortunately, when administered to lab animals, we also noticed peculiar activity." Wiley stopped to light up another cigarette. His fifth. The smoke was beginning to get to Jerry but he said nothing. He liked seeing the ashtray fill up.

"Famous geneticist found dead in charred remains of house. Smoking in bed blamed."

"Such as what?"

Wiley inhaled and began a phlegmy hacking. "Hyperaggressive behavior," he said. "Animals began killing each other. Crazy thing, it was the males only. They sexually savaged the females."

The word "savaged" bloomed in Jerry's mind like a rose. He smiled. "What kind of animals?"

"Mice, rabbits, rhesus monkeys. They went crazy, brutalized their mates."

"Tell me what happened."

"Nothing happened," Wiley said. "We could not find a way to curb the aggressions, so we shut it down."

"Shut it down?"

"Yes."

"You mean, that was it? You mean the animals went nuts and no more Black Flag?"

"Yes. It was abandoned."

Jerry's heart sank. "Then why didn't Dr. Terranova want to talk about it?"

"Conscience . . ."

"Conscience?" Jerry said.

"We were toying with the science of extermination. It was *wrong*. It also violated the Geneva Convention, but we let ourselves get down into it by the intellectual challenge of gene-splicing and, I suppose, the political pressure. Fortunately, the project failed."

Jerry studied Wiley's face. There was nothing in it that suggested he was not telling the truth.

"Why, after all these years, do they want you all dead?"

The skin of Wiley's face tightened.

"Any guesses?"

"Please don't kill me . . . my daughter . . ."

Jerry raised the gun toward Wiley's face. "Think hard."

"No, God, please don't. I don't know. *I don't know*. I've told you everything—"

"Even if somebody leaked, the project was a flop, no?"

"Yes. There's no advantage in killing anybody." Wiley was squirming in his chair. He wiped his face again. The skin under his eyes was shiny puffs.

Jerry felt the excitement again. He wanted to shoot him. He wanted to ram the barrel into his mouth and drink from his eyes as he pulled the trigger. But that wasn't the plan.

"I asked if you had any guesses."

"No, no. I don't have a clue."

"When was the last time you talked with Maria Terranova or Stefan Karsky?"

His voice was a high, thin treble. "Maria, I saw maybe five, six years ago at a conference in Washington. Karsky, I haven't seen since the early seventies."

"What about the others?"

"The same. Maria was the only one I saw."

"Stand up and turn around."

"What?"

"I said stand."

Slowly Wiley stood up. "Please, don't. I beg you . . ."

"If you move, I'll shoot."

It was a voice behind Jerry. A woman's voice. He hadn't noticed that the piano had long stopped. He had gotten carried away.

On the wall near where Wiley had refilled his glass, Jerry spotted the intercom box. The small red light was on. Wiley dropped his arms. "Margaret, thank God." She had heard everything. "He was going to kill me."

What happened next took place in a flash. Jerry corkscrewed to the floor. Behind him was a woman dressed in red, sitting in a wheelchair. In her hand she held a small pistol aimed at Jerry. He recorded the white thin face, shoulder-length sandy hair and large eyes. Very large and dark. Even in that lightning glimpse, those eyes would stay with him.

Before they could blink again, he shot her above the left brow. The force snapped back her head, causing the chair to roll into the hall.

Even before Wiley could move, a long thin warble escaped from his lungs. Cat-quick, Jerry threw himself onto Wiley, pressing him into the chairback. Straddling him, Jerry rammed the end of the silencer through the O of his mouth and locked onto Wiley's eyes. Such eyes.

"Plan B," Jerry said, and squeezed the trigger.

CHAPTER

19

Frank DeVoe poured himself a second cup of coffee from the room-service pot. He dumped in some nondairy powder and a packet of Sweet 'n Low, then stirred the contents with his finger, not appearing to mind the heat.

"What do you mean, she won't sell? I thought it was all settled."

"She called this morning and said they had to put it off." Claire Manning sat beside her husband, Julius Wick, in their suite in the Hay Adams across from Lafayette Park, overlooking the White House. Diagonally across the street was the Old Senate Building, where in two days Julius, under his presidential appointment, would set up his commission of biotechnology.

"What do you mean, put it off? There's no putting off. She holding out for more money?"

"No, it's something about her son," Claire said. "She claims he's got a medical condition."

DeVoe's eyes went flat. "Such as what?"

"I don't know. She didn't specify, nor would I expect her to. He looked like a normal, healthy kid."

DeVoe nodded and downed half his coffee. "I don't like it," he said. "If he's got a problem, people are going to want to know why."

"Aren't you being a little paranoid, Frank?" Julius asked.

"Probably, but that's what I'm paid for."

That was also the reason they were meeting in Julius's hotel room and not in Frank DeVoe's own office. DeVoe served as special counsel to the White House. For nine years before that appointment, he worked in the legal office of the Department of Defense. On the wall behind his desk hung a commendation for his DOD service. On the same wall was a photographic collage of DeVoe and President Morgan Reese: on the seventeenth tee of Pebble Beach; bone fishing off the Keys on Reese's boat; shaking hands at a New Orleans campaign fundraiser; locked head-to-head in conference in the Oval Office. Next year DeVoe would head up the president's reelection campaign, a task that, if successful, would all but guarantee his appointment as White House chief of staff.

"She might simply be looking for an excuse," Julius suggested. He got up and walked across the room to the window overlooking the park.

DeVoe followed him with his eyes. "Julius, what kind of mother does that—makes up a story that her kid's sick? And what's she need an excuse for? You offered six hundred grand for a four hundred-thousand-dollar house and bought him a cushy chair at three times his salary."

Of his many appointments over the years, Julius once served as chair for the department of biology at New York Polytechnic Institute and built it into a world-class research center. Though it had been years since retiring from teaching to take over Walden Research, he maintained ties with the school in the form of a donation of two million dollars ten years ago to help develop the genetics component of NYPI's research labs—a gift that earned him a seat on its board of directors. So there was little problem in creating a position for Calvin Hazzard. The only requirement was money, and they had an abundance of that. Enough to buy the Hazzard's house from under them while generously endowing a chair in the English department to relocate. According to Robin Priest, Hazzard had all but accepted.

"Even if he's got some kind of problem," Julius said, "who says it's related?"

DeVoe pulled a copy of the *Patriot Chronicle* from his briefcase and dropped it in Julius's lap. "The wildlife's become headline news."

On the front page above the right-hand column it read: STRANGE ANIMAL BEHAVIOR IN MAGOG—RABIES DISCOUNTED. Julius slipped on his glasses. "Your point?"

"Paragraph four." DeVoe finished his coffee while Julius continued.

" 'Animal Inspector Helen Burdick speculates that the higher-than-usual reports of odd animal behavior might be attributable to media scare. None of the animals in question has tested positive for the disease. When asked what natural explanation she could offer for verifiably odd animal behavior, if not rabies, Burdick suggested "distemper or larval migraine worms or any number of microbes that attack the central nervous system. My best guess," she added "is spring fever." ' " Julius refolded the paper. "I don't see a problem."

DeVoe pushed a stick of gum in his mouth. It was what he did since giving up cigarettes. "You don't see a problem," he said. He snapped the paper away. "It's not spring fever or any of the other shit. It's your omni-whatchamacallit. It's all over the goddamn neighborhood." From a folder he pulled out a two-page computer printout. They were chemical analyses of the ground water DeVoe's men had sampled from and around the Hazzard home.

"It's in their water, Julius."

For a minute Julius studied the figures, then slowly removed his glasses. "Frank, the standard toxin screening cannot detect the omnimycinol molecule. It's almost identical to human hormone structures. And nobody ever screens water for hormones, even in expanded profiles. Even if they did, they'd need highly sophisticated analyses to show it's artificial."

"Julius, if the kid starts to turn funny, they'll be screening for fairy piss," DeVoe said, chewing furiously. "The concentration is twenty parts per million, ten times what it was the last time. I don't know how many containers you people buried, but your average dump truck weighs three tons empty. You drive that a few times over a bunch of barrels five feet down and you're going to have a lot of stuff leech into the aquifer. And that's what happened when they built that pool. Just count your blessings they didn't build the pool on the containers, or we'd be playing slapjack in prison."

Julius returned to his chair and sat quietly for a moment. "So what are you suggesting we do?"

As if in a strange ritual dance, DeVoe got up and walked to the window, blew a large pink bubble and fixed his eye on the White House. "Whatever it takes to get in and neutralize it," he said. "All you need is a rainy summer and it'll be in half the wells in the western suburbs."

"That would be a problem."

DeVoe's gum snapped. "Among your other talents, Julius, you've a genius for understatement. Let me remind you, in case the events of the week have colored your vision. We're sitting on a goddamn time bomb."

DeVoe's plan was to make the Hazzards an offer they couldn't refuse. Once the property was acquired by the Wicks, DeVoe's men would neutralize the substance that had leaked into the ground. The seclusion of the place was in their favor. Nobody, they figured, would notice the pumping equipment secreted in the backyard. Superheated system and a detoxifying compound would be injected into the aquifer and the residue filtered out, the whole process taking no more than a week. As for the disposal barrels, they could be removed under the guise of redesigning the backyard, even removing the swimming pool. Fortunately, the place drew its water from its own well. And because the house was perched up on a lens of clay, the basin of underground water was small, isolated and easily containable. The Hazzard house alone drew from the contaminated water, the surrounding homes from still-clean contiguous wells. What bothered DeVoe was the instability of that polluted basin. Even if the animal problems were not related, a small flood, subsidence or even construction elsewhere in the neighborhood could open the contaminated water to public supplies.

"We offered an outrageous price for their house, we bought her husband a prestigious post at the institute," Julius said. "But we can't force them to sell."

"We may not have an option not to," DeVoe said. "If they don't accept the bait, we'll have to get in the hard way."

Julius's face tightened.

"I agree," Claire Manning said quietly.

Julius looked at her for an explanation. "The hard way?"

"Julius, you know better than I that we're not dealing with ordinary toxic waste. It attacks the rage centers of the brain. I've seen it turn an aquarium goldfish into a piranha. It's left dead animals all over Magog Woods. Need we speculate on the consequences should it spread to the human population?"

"No, but that still doesn't explain how we're going to force our way in there without being noticed."

"Julius, you're the director of the president's commission on biotechnology. You're at the top of your life's accomplishment. My point is that if omnimycinol is discovered, they'll tear up the backyard and find the containers. How long do you think it would take to trace them to BiOmega Labs? There are records about, archives, whatever. They'll find you. They'll find *us*."

"And in case you've forgotten," DeVoe added, "Morgan Reese, your president and mine, was the chief budget officer for Black Flag. Need I tell you what hay his political enemies would make if word got out that the ecology president twenty-some years ago oversaw the funding of a genocide germ that's festering in the ground water of a major American suburb? This isn't Love Canal with a bunch of poor slob factory workers. We're talking Carleton, Massachusetts, an affluent and politically influential community in the state. Doctors, lawyers, corporate CEOs and more Saabs and Volvos per square inch than Stockholm. They make a noise and it's heard 'round the world. It would be like Watergate and Whitewater rolled into one, with special prosecutors, hearings and talk-show sleazefests. And so much for next year's election." He nodded his head outside. "And if he goes down, we *all* go with him."

Julius listened solemnly. "You know, of course, your efforts to eradicate all the ties between the president and Black Flag can only fail."

DeVoe seemed to freeze. "How so?"

"Because there were others who worked on the project. How can we be certain they won't come forward on a spur of conscience?" He glanced at Claire for confirmation, but she was studying her hands.

"No chance of that," Frank said. "They're dead."

"They are?" Julius said. "How do you know that? I haven't heard—"

"Because, Julius, we saw to it."

"God in heaven, Frank, we agreed that was only a last resort, if even then. They wouldn't have said anything—"

"That is not something you would know for *sure* until too late, and then what?" DeVoe said. "Now we're certain. There's much at stake—"

"You had no *right* to take it that far. I pay you. I did *not* sanction any killings . . ."

DeVoe shrugged and blew his gum, his eyes drifting to Claire over the pink bubble.

"Julius, we had no choice," she said.

"Wonderful, now we've got blood on our hands. In two days I move across the street, commissioner of biotechnology *and* accomplice to murder."

"And two days ago," Claire said evenly, "we shared a lunch with the president and the first lady of the United States. Doesn't that mean something to you?"

"Good Lord, not enough to kill for—"

"I doubt you'd say that if one of them had decided to go public on Black Flag."

"Or worse," DeVoe put in. "This week you went from a brilliant, if relatively unknown, microbiologist to a famous person. A VIP. You're big time now, Julius—a national political figure and close personal friend of the chief executive. All you'd need is for one of those little worms to turn on their TV, see you up there smiling with the president's arm around you, tooling about the nation's capital in a limo . . . and feeling a tad disgruntled, they think, Why that son of a bitch! Julius, do you know what a little blackmail note out of your past can do to your sense of well-being, not to mention your bank account? Well, we've prevented all that."

Julius's voice was just above a whisper. "What did you do to them?"

"What difference does it make?"

"I want to know, damn it."

DeVoe shrugged. "We've got a guy named Roman who brokers people who do that kind of work. I'm not sure who did the actual hit. That's Roman's end, but he's got the best. We used him before when I did some jobs for ATF. Trust me, it's all neat, clean. No footprints. Nothing traceable, nothing to worry about. They were made to look like accidents—drowning—or suicide . . . like that."

Julius took a deep breath. "*All* of them?"

DeVoe chewed noisily as he squinted at a note pad. "Karsky, Terranova, Wiley . . ." he read.

Julius closed his eyes. "They were *friends* of mine."

"And now Morgan Reese is."

"What does he know?"

DeVoe laughed. "Nothing, of course, nor should he. But that means nothing, because today he's the biggest political target in the universe, and two days ago you became his biggest liability. This way, you're both covered. Call it national security if it makes you feel any better."

"How . . . how did you know where to find them?"

"It's not important," DeVoe said. "It's why we pay these people so well. In fact, there's one still left. Can't seem to run him down but I'm sure they will." DeVoe checked his list again. "Fellow named Perry. John Perry."

Julius nodded. "Frankenstein's Folly."

"Beg pardon?"

"It's what he called the project. Frankenstein's Folly. Jack said it would come back to haunt us, and he was right."

"Not if we can help it," DeVoe said.

"He was the only one who had the moral fortitude to oppose it from the start. The rest of us, me included, were too caught up in the quest to look up and wonder about the consequences. We were too lost in the madness and hatred—"

"Whatever, we'll get him."

Julius continued as if Frank had not spoken. "He insisted we neutralize everything before we buried it. But by then we were too anxious to wash our hands and clear out."

"Don't make him out to be a hero, for God's sake," Claire said. "He was a little worm."

"Because he questioned the morality of it?"

"No, because he was so goddamn self-righteous," Claire said. "*He* didn't lose a son to those bastards. I *did*."

"Case in point," Frank DeVoe said. "He's a dangerous loose cannon."

"Is that what you plan for this family, too?" Julius asked.

"Not yet," DeVoe said. "First we wait to see if the kid's problem is connected."

"I told the woman I'd call her again next week," Claire said.

"What for?"

"To see how he is. If he's okay, we'll see what she says and put some pressure on."

Julius nodded. "And what if he's not okay?"

DeVoe took the question. "You mean if the kid's got a Black Flag problem?"

"Yes."

"We put Roman's man on overtime, then move in when the house goes on the block."

"You've got it all worked out."

"Clearing tracks," DeVoe said. "For you and me."

"Clearing tracks," Julius repeated. He turned his head to Claire. "I hate this, it's—"

DeVoe snapped his gum. "You'd hate it more in prison."

CHAPTER

20

Matty caught the scent of Gretchen before he heard her. Her doggie tang laced the night air.

She was the Starkeys' German shepherd on Hutchinson Road that angled off from Jason on the other side of Magog Woods. They always put her out at this time of night. Because the woods were quiet, her barking carried like gunfire. And it would continue until they pulled her in at ten-thirty when the news was over. Then, at the crack of dawn, she'd be out again, barking her brains out.

Matty knew his father hated that dog. He said he didn't understand how the Starkeys could be so "bloody inconsiderate."

Matty didn't like Gretchen either, but not because of the barking. She was mean. He was glad they kept her chained to a tree because she growled and tried to get at him whenever he walked by. Not the other kids. Just him.

Matty walked up the driveway from the street. Dr. Tojian had given him a ride home. Every night after a game he would select four of five kids and work on their fielding or hitting for maybe a half-hour. Then, before driving them home, he'd take them to the center for ice cream. Tonight, under the lights, he worked with Matty on his swing. He said it was strong but wild. He didn't have to try to kill the ball every time.

It was a little before nine when Matty was dropped off. With his glove and water bottle, he headed in the dark toward the house. He wasn't thinking about Mitch or baseball or the physical exam or the magnetic whatever tests he had to undergo. He was thinking about Gretchen . . . more than thinking, like he was *feeling* her.

He went around the back of the house and waited until Dr. Tojian pulled away. Then, instead of going inside, he cut into the backyard. His parents were home, because both cars were in the garage. Though light from inside cast an amber glow, the backyard was a black hole to ordinary eyes.

But Matty's eyes were more than ordinary. He could make out features of objects as if the sun were at seven o'clock—the lawn furniture, the logs lying crisscross on the woodpile, his red striped trampoline, the half-dying flowers in the pots around the pool, night bugs, the large male raccoon cowering under a bush. They all stood out in an infrared-like clarity.

He drifted across the lawn toward the pool. It was still not filled to the top. Memorial Day weekend, his father said. (Except now they were threatening to move. Not if he could help it.) He could smell the water. He could smell lots of things. He could smell the raccoon's fear. He thought he could hear its heart as it bolted into the black.

He could hear insects, and not just the crickets. Tiny things in the ground and in the tree bark and under rocks—chittering like static electricity. Nothing he had ever experienced before.

The wind seemed to shift by the time he reached the edge of the woods. The sky was cloudy and there was a pale moon.

He looked back. The stained-glass lamp in the study window was on. He could make out the glow of the computer screen. His father was working on his book. He was always working on his book. Something about a bullfighting story. Through the lace curtains of the nearby window of the master bathroom, he could see his mother. It was her shower time. He could see a flash of her pink nakedness.

For several minutes Matty watched her, experiencing a funny sensation within his belly. Not unpleasant. He had seen his mother naked before—getting out of showers, changing her clothes. He never really thought much about it, nor did he stare. But somehow this was different. He felt no embarrassment. Instead, his heart pounded as he watched her shave her legs over the sink. She was pink and white. Then she stepped into the shower and was gone from view.

Matty laid down his glove and bottle and took off his clothes. He was hairy and big . . . he seemed to have changed overnight. He left his clothes in a scattered heap.

The warm night air seemed to accelerate him. He dashed into the woods, barely aware of twigs gouging his feet or branches whipping his face. Guided by a radar keenness, he made sharp turns around trees, leaping over scrub. He did not slow down for footing; he could see his way clearly. Night vision, Dr. Tojian called it.

The wind at his back rustled the treetops. He stopped for a moment. The place hummed with creature life. Insects, moles, toads, bats. And larger, musty things. Rabbits. Possums, Skunks. They hid but he could feel them, and like the raccoon, he could smell their fear. He thought about finding them but decided to move on.

He was slick with sweat when he reached TopTree, and the noise in his head was now a roar. Hand over hand he went up the tree. He lay flat out on the pillow listening to the blood music in his head. He could not remember such crazy urges taking him over like this. Or his own vague fright. He closed his eyes and tried to control his breathing, hoping the fog would clear.

In time the slick of perspiration cooled like skin tightening. He had no idea how long since he had gone through the woods or lain here. Ten minutes, twenty, an hour. He had no sense of time, nor recollection of why he had come. But he knew he should head back, that he should put his clothes on and go home. His mother was expecting him. She was probably worried and calling around. He really should.

He opened his eyes and through the little cutout could see stars in the leaves, bright pinpricks. He reached over and found Daisy Too. It was musty damp. He thought about Daisy One—the way she curled around his feet in the morning when he fed her; the way she kneaded his belly with her paws; how rough her tongue felt on his face. And then he thought about how she was scared of him . . . and how he liked her being scared of him.

Someplace voices murmured.

Someplace a dog barked.

Through the trees he saw the light; and he remembered, and the red fog was back. But now the fear had given way to a rampant excitement.

He got up. His body was pulsing again. His eyes fixed on the tiny yellow light flickering through the branches. She was up there, in the bedroom. He sensed her.

Gina.

The next moment he was shimmying down the tree.

" 'Wicked weird. Everybody says so,' " he whispered as he touched bottom.

The lights flickered like strobes through the trees as he cut through them with a remarkable grace.

Gina's backyard abutted the woods like the Starkeys' next door. Because of Gina's baby brother, her father had put up a chain-link fence at the edge of the woods. Matty looked to the light of her room. The window was open halfway and the curtains were parted, the shade up. He couldn't see her but he knew she was lying on her bed.

He stopped himself at the edge of the trees.

But the other, stranger part of him turned his attention to the light in that bedroom window. And the garage—it was the same height as Gina's room. With the side window and molding, he could scale it in seconds.

The light from the Starkeys' house spilled out onto the backyard. The blue light of the television pulsed in the front room. With the wind making a pressure at his back, he stepped from the trees into the open of the Starkeys' yard, his mind fixed on that yellow light of the second floor corner room in the next house.

Gina's house. Gina's room. Gina on her bed.

Gina with thick brown hair. Gina who had laughed when Bobby Gorawlski pushed him down. Gina who once giggled to Lisa that Matty's dinky fell off from the cold.

Wicked weird

He felt the coil of anger. He would show her.

He took another step when the barking stopped him.

Gretchen.

She had appeared from nowhere just three feet behind him, her white teeth flashing as she barked. She would have been at him were it not for the rope.

His first impulse was to run. But a counterimpulse flared and he backed into the shadows. Gretchen's hackles made a Mohawk down her back. Her barking was furious, but it drew nobody away from the TV. They were used to her carrying on over some night critter. What they could not hear was the terror trebling her voice.

She pulled hard against her rope to get at him.

Matty crouched and glared into her eyes five feet away. He could smell her fear. Excitement shot through him. "Bad girl," he said in a low voice. "Bad, bad Gretchen."

She stopped barking and backed up a little, making a low, deep-throated growl. Her eyes had turned stark with fear. She kept looking back to the house, hoping that somebody would come out. She was beginning to make funny sounds, yelps and barking sing-whines.

"Gretchen, stop," Matty muttered in a ragged voice. "Now."

The animal fell silent. Her backward shuffle ceased and her legs collapsed; her ears went back and she began licking at her nose. Matty moved closer to her, eyes locked on her eyes. His gaze was like a funnel through which his will flowed.

Gretchen began to whine softly, submissively. "Good doggie," he whispered. "Come to me."

Gretchen looked over her shoulder at the lights from the house. She emitted a bleating whine, then snuffled down on her paws and scraped along the ground toward him.

Matty rose and watched her inch her way to his bare feet. "Good girl."

He could feel her hot breath on his toes. His fingers hummed to touch her, to dig into her fur. But he didn't want to startle her, so he kept himself just inches from her snout.

While she pressed herself onto the ground, she kept up a strange kind of whimpering that sounded to him a little like the yodel-talking that Claudia, the deaf girl in his school, made. "That-a-girl . . ."

She looked up at Matty hanging over her, then rolled over on her back, opening her legs.

"Good Gretchen," he whispered. He looked at her white belly. He wanted to feel the downy fur.

As his hand got closer, Gretchen's whimpers became soft yelps. She was also panting so that her tongue seemed to obstruct her breathing. Matty's fingers stopped just at the tips of the hairs on her belly. He held his fingers there, trying to make sense of the unspeakable urges flickering inside him. Yelping, panting, Gretchen lay there, struggling to keep her legs apart.

The tips of his fingers pressed into the soft fur, and suddenly Gretchen let out a high-pitched yowl.

In the next instant she was up and going pell-mell toward the back door, howling all the way. But she never made it. The rope stopped her in midair with a savage snap.

Matty went over to her.

She lay on the grass just short of the steps, her eyes opened wide, her head at a crazy angle.

Inside the house, sounds of somebody coming. Matty ran back into the woods.

From someplace deep within the black, he heard Mrs. Starkey cry out.

"Gretchen? Gretchen! Oh my God!"

CHAPTER

21

Terry was furry with sleep as she stumbled for the telephone.

The clock said eight-ten, yet there was no barking. Rain or shine, Gretchen was out at six-thirty. If the Starkeys were out of town, they had left pretty early, because Terry heard the dog last night while waiting for Matty.

"Hello?" She caught it before Calvin woke up.

No response.

"Hello?"

Nothing, but she could hear the electronic hush of an open line.

"Who is it?"

More gaping silence, then *click* and the dial tone.

"Jerk," she mumbled, and hung up. Maybe Gretchen had graduated to telephones.

"Who was it?" Calvin's head rose from the covers.

"Hung up."

It was the third time in the last two days. Her first thought was, Claire Manning was calling to put the pressure on. She had called yesterday after Beverly gave her the message that the sale was on hold. She asked about the nature of Matty's medical problems out of what sounded like genuine interest, but Terry politely refused to go into details. Before she hung up, Mrs. Manning again expressed great interest in the house and slipped in how they hoped things worked out with her son so that they could close matters as soon as possible.

Too awake to go back to sleep, she got out of bed. Matty's door was closed. He was deep asleep, no doubt. There was a time not long ago when she would hear the soulless ditty of Nintendo float up

137

from the downstairs TV. It was what Matty did on Saturday mornings—steal down as soon as Gretchen woke him and get in an hour before she and Calvin came down. Now he just slept.

Terry washed and removed her nightgown. She studied herself in the mirror. There was a time she liked looking at her body, when it still held the athletic shapeliness of her twenties. But now it looked dated. Across her lower abdomen was that red zipper of a scar from the Caesarean last fall. That and ten pounds of extra fat was all she had to show for that ordeal. She needed to get back to aerobic classes. Her waist had thickened, and her thighs had that incipient doughy look. No wonder Calvin had lost his sexual appetite.

She took a gargle of mouthwash and headed back to bed. Naked, she crawled beside him. "Hi there, big fella. Come here often?" She ran her hand down his thigh and kissed him.

He looked startled. "What brought this on?"

"Don't look a gift cow in the mouth."

She pulled his face to her breasts. He did not protest, but seemed to respond guardedly—probably shock. Terry stroked his head, determined to make this one good. She felt genuinely aroused, and sought the escape, the relief, only sex could provide her. But more than that, she wanted to break the ramparts of ice that had swelled between them. It had been weeks since they last made love.

"Damage control," she whispered as she threw back the covers and straddled him.

Calvin started to say something but she cut him off with a kiss. "I love you," she whispered.

"Haven't heard that for a long time."

"Sorry," she said. "But I really do."

"I love you, too. Very much."

For several minutes they kissed, and she took Calvin's hand and closed it over her pubis and urged him into motion. She reached down only to discover that he was not the least bit aroused. (The fifth time in a month!)

She tried different strategies, things she didn't ordinarily do. She flicked her tongue in his ear. It didn't help. She rubbed her breasts across his chest. He did not respond.

Why couldn't he get it up? She raised herself and let Calvin probe her with his mouth. He responded, squirming in place, but he was still limp. She slid down his body and took him in her mouth. It was not an act she often initiated, though once into it, she took real pleasure.

Suddenly she was desperate to satisfy him. "What's the problem?"

Calvin shook his head. "I don't know, I—"

"Is it me? Am I doing something wrong?" She felt frantic.

"No, you're fine. I'm just . . ."

Before he could finish, she said, "Try." She could feel him strain, but nothing happened.

Damn it, it's *me*. I've killed his interest in me, I've killed our sex . . . She took him in her hand. "I want you in me," she said stroking him. "I want you to come in me. I want you to come in me, Calvin."

"Terry, calm down."

"I want to make love." She felt wild. Tears were blinding her. "We have to. Please get hard, please, I want you in me."

He made a stupid grin. "I'm trying, honey, I just can't—"

"You've *got* to, Calvin." She felt ready to snap any minute. The buildup of all the anxiety of the last weeks was threatening to pull her under.

"Please, Terry, get hold of yourself."

"Calvin, make *love* to me." Her voice was shattering. Her tears fell on him.

"Honey, I want to, I just can't—"

"What's *wrong*? What's happening? What's happening to us?"

"Terry, it's not *you*. I'm just a little tired . . ." His voice seemed to come from some faraway place.

"PLEASE!" she cried at the ceiling.

"Terry, control yourself."

Her head was spinning. Everything in the room took on a fluid unreality. Nothing was solid. Nothing made sense. She felt disoriented, as if loosed from the fabric of things—as if gravity itself were failing. What she feared was yielding to a consuming fit that she would not be able to come out of.

"Quiet! It's Matty!"

Outside, Matty opened his door and padded into the hall bathroom. Calvin pulled on his top and yanked the covers over them.

Terry lay back and pressed the blanket to her eyes. She was shaking. Sobbing spasms wracked her insides.

A moment later the door opened. "Mom . . . Mom?"

His voice was like the flick of a switch. She sat upright, her mind cleared. "Matty, what happened?"

But he didn't hear her. He pushed his way into the room, his arms tight across his chest as if to protect himself. "Mommy," he cried, "he's coming."

"Who? Who's coming?"

Matty's eyes were open but he seemed locked in a trance.

"My God, what's wrong with him?" Terry grabbed him by the shoulders and shook him. "Matty. Matty! Wake up."

Calvin sat him down on the bed. "Matty, you're dreaming. Wake up."

Matty's face was contorted, as if he were in awful pain or fear or both. "Don't do that! Leave me alone . . ."

Terry was frantic. "Calvin, *do* something." The next moment she reached over for the glass of water on the nighttable and splashed the contents in Matty's face. The effect was instant. Matty blinked in disbelief. "You were sleepwalking," she said, and pulled him to her. "We couldn't wake you up."

Calvin dabbed him dry with the blanket and for a long moment Terry held him against her while he calmed down.

"You were in a bad dream, hon," Calvin said gently. "You're okay now."

"Mom?" Matty's voice was barely audible.

"Yes," she said, pressing him to her.

"I'm going to die."

"Matty, don't say that. You're *not* going to die."

"Yes, I am. I dream it every night."

"What do you dream?" Calvin asked him, but Matty buried his face against Terry's nightgown to say he didn't want to tell in front of him.

Calvin nodded to Terry. "I'll get breakfast ready," he said, and slipped out.

Terry propped up the pillows and pulled the covers over him, then turned on the lamp. "No. Turn it off," he said abruptly, and clapped his hands to his eyes.

She quickly snapped off the lamp. He was light-sensitive, too. The sunglasses. That's why he'd been wearing them for the last month. Not because it was cool or what the other kids were doing. Because the light of day hurt him. She held his hand as he composed himself enough to tell her about the dream.

"Do you remember where the dream takes place?"

"In the woods."

"Are you alone?"

He shook his head. "Somebody's chasing me."

"Do you know who it is?"

He shook his head.

"What does he look like?"

"I couldn't see his face."

"But he's chasing you."

He nodded. "Yes." His eyes filled with tears as he went on. "His face is dark, so I can't see it, and I'm running home through the trees but he's right behind me, I can feel him, and I know he wants to kill me, tear me apart with his fingers and teeth, like some wild animal, and he chases me into the backyard. You and dad are inside and I try to get into the house, but the backyard is like a swamp, all mushy and soft, so I can't run. I fall beside the pool and then I'm crawling toward the edge, and I'm just about to go over the edge into the pool when I see the . . . the thing in the water. I see his face . . ."

"You mean he's under the water?"

"No, the reflection," Matty said in a choked voice. "He's *ME*."

"Oh, God . . . no, honey, he can't be you. It's *not* you. It's just a *nightmare*—"

"It's *me*."

She pulled him against her and for a long while just held him quietly, rocking in place until he fell asleep.

It sickened her to think that he was so mortified by the changes in himself that he subconsciously perceived himself as a monster of some sort. There were fresh self-inflicted scratches on his arm. God, this was so unfair. She would call Tojian for the name of a good child psychologist.

The phone rang again, and she caught it before Matty woke up.

"Mrs. Hazzard?"

"Yes?" She carried the phone to the bathroom.

"Mrs. Hazzard, my name is Jack Perry. You don't know me, but I have some information that might be of vital importance to you. I'm wondering if we can find some time to talk . . ."

She knew the sound of the voice, the nasal timbre of a salesman on the prowl for some poor sap to lay out her money. She got at least one a week, usually during supper. But here was a new pitch, nine o'clock on a Saturday morning. A revolutionary new family protection plan from the good folks at OKAY Insurance Co.; a higher credit line on her VISA; just-built, must-see condos on Lake Winnipesaukee.

"You haven't got a goddamn *clue* what's important to me," she said, and slammed down the phone.

The words rang in his ear. The woman sounded irrational. Maybe he'd show up in person.

Jack Perry lit another cigarette. What about him? Was *he* being irrational? Was there a problem or was he projecting his own paranoia? He had become increasingly worried the last couple of weeks, since his old colleagues began showing up on the obituary page. But to rush up there on impulse would mean exposing himself to strangers. Of course, he'd have to spell out the sordid details to maintain credibility. They would have questions and raise a fuss and call the authorities. Which was where the danger lay. Besides, it could all be for nothing. All he had were a couple of visits to the doctor. That could be anything. Kids were always picking things up. And the father seemed to be in good health. (But how could you tell from two cars back?)

He poured more bourbon into his cup as his mind drifted back twenty-four years to when he was a young technician at BiOmega Labs. Like flash cards he saw the rhesus and chimps in their cages behaving like nothing intended by genetic design. Little faces distorted with lightning rage as they raced around the cages beating their heads with fists. He could still see Waldo, a young male chimp, on his first injection, leap to his ceiling perch and press his face into the bars so hard his nose bled. When his mother, Martha, was released in the cage, she hid in the corner with her hands to her eyes. The transformation did not take long. From his height Waldo watched her press herself into the corner. Suddenly, in one movement he screeched down on her and attacked with such force that Martha died before Jack could dart him with a tranquilizer. In seconds Waldo had broken most of her ribs, fractured her skull and ruptured her internal organs. But what killed her was the loss of blood. Her carotid artery had been severed from the hole he had bitten in her neck.

In those final months Jack Perry knew he had witnessed an obscene violation of nature. Obscene was the word for it. Otherwise docile animals turned into vicious killers, their biology tortured into something unrecognizable, all in the name of national defense, for God's sake. And not just primates. Male rabbits became carnivorous, eating their young; ordinary mallards pounded chicks to death with their feet; even ground squirrels ripped apart their mates. He also witnessed dogs and cats in their sexual heat gnaw at their genitals until they bled to death. The intent was to create a virus that deadened hormonal urges; instead, it had produced a substance that turned normal male sexual aggression into something of a Frankenstein monster.

From the onset of Black Flag, Jack Perry had sensed that it was inherently wrong. He hadn't gotten as caught up in the anti-Commie mania as the others. Nor, like the Wicks, had he lost a son to the Viet Cong. Even as he went about his work designing laboratory hardware, he questioned the moral wisdom of developing a virus designed to destroy the reproductive capabilities in males, no matter who the enemy was. That was a form of genocide. Something Hitler would go for.

It wasn't until he saw what the omnimycinol virus did to test animals that his moral conscience was finally overwhelmed and he spoke out. Only Maria Terranova had sympathized to a degree with his outrage. She had had good cause. It happened one afternoon while they were in the lab and she was routinely retrieving blood from a rhesus named Burt. Apparently feigning sleep, the animal suddenly flew at her when she nudged open the cage. If he hadn't been quick with the morphine dart, Maria would have been blinded. As it was, she wore a scar to the end of her life. And yet she did nothing to put an end to the project. The attack she blamed on her own carelessness. As for Black Flag, it was a military contract funded by the Department of Defense, she said, and that made it bigger than all of them and their concerns. If they didn't do the job, somebody else would, and she needed the work . . .

Jack did not know where the science had gone wrong, but the virus attacked the rage centers of male brains. While the biologists squabbled over causes, Jack's role as lab assistant was to terminate and dispose of hundreds of test animals and test serums, cultures and viral wastes. In those days most organic disposables were dumped into plastic drums and buried at the edge of Magog Woods in nearby Carleton—a site owned by Julius Wick. When Jack questioned the safety of the dump, he was told to just do his job. Plastic lasted forever.

Two weeks later Jack found a memo on his desk informing him that his position had been eliminated. He had one week's notice. He knew the reasons. He also knew who was behind the firing. Claire Manning Wick. She did not work on the project, but she was the force behind Julius. He was a brilliant scientist, a man of scientific insights but dim visions. He was also weak. It was Claire whose sights turned upward, and she directed his career like the mother of a stage prodigy, pushing their way to the top.

Jack Perry had met her on a number of occasions and never much cared for her. She had an open-visitor's permit to enter the lab, even though the project was highly classified. The security guard looked the other way, and nobody inside dared raise protocol since she was the wife of the director and the money behind Bi-Omega. She once cornered Jack about his concerns, listening with chilled silence. Like Lady Macbeth from off-stage, she made sure that Jack was out before he subverted team solidarity. There was no room for ambivalence in the lab where her husband was establishing himself as a pioneer in biological warfare.

Two months later the project was closed down, and BiOmega disappeared and everybody with it. Nobody knew what the effects of the virus would be on humans. What Jack did know was that, at the end, the substance had mutated unpredictably, uncontrollably. And for over two decades it lay in containers five feet below the backyard of the Hazzard family home.

He had not thought about those containers until he noticed scattered news reports of bizarre animal behavior in the Magog Woods. At first he bought the anomalies explanation. Maybe even distemper or rabies. But then came stories of unexplained mutilations in common woodland creatures. What weighed on his mind was that the containers had for some reason leaked, and that the virus was seeping into the ground water and making its way into the food chain. The potential was nightmarish.

But was potential enough to blow the whistle?

He gulped more bourbon. The morning headlines told him somebody else had the same thoughts.

BEACON HILL SHOCKED BY BRUTAL DOUBLE MURDER OF FAMED SCIENTIST AND DAUGHTER.

The two photos had a common caption: "Dr. Marcus P. Wiley, noted biologist, and his paraplegic daughter Margaret were found murdered in their Beacon Hill apartment yesterday morning. Although no motive has yet been established, police suspect they were shot in a burglary attempt."

What burglary attempt? It was the third death in a week. These were not accidents, nor random acts of violence. He was sure the Wicks were eliminating all ties to Black Flag.

He was also sure he was next.

CHAPTER

22

"Why the hell did you bang them?"

"I had no choice."

It was a little after eight, and Jerry Mars was at a pay phone in the parking lot of Bagel Bonanza on the northbound side of Route 1 about four miles south of the 95 interchange.

"It was supposed to be an *accident*, not the Saint Valentine's Day massacre."

"The girl surprised me."

"*Surprised* you? We pay you not to be surprised," said Roman.

Jerry said nothing. Roman would pick at it like a scab.

"She was a crip in a wheelchair, for Chrissakes. You didn't have to blow her head off."

"She had a piece."

"I don't care if she had a bazooka. It was sloppy work. You're trigger-happy, and my people don't like it."

His instinct was to tell Roman he could crank his people through a meat grinder. Instead, he said, "It was the best I could do under the circumstances."

"Listen, Jerry, maybe it was, maybe it wasn't. Maybe she was Annie Oakley on wheels. Personally, I couldn't care less. I'm just reporting the news, *capice*? All's I'm saying is that my clients didn't like it. They wanted minimum attention, and you gave them the front page."

"So, where's that leave us?" Jerry asked.

"You're being riffed. It's only temporary, until things blow over."

"Uh-huh. Well, there's the matter of thirty-two thousand dollars."

"That's right, and it woulda been yours if you fulfilled the terms of the contract. *capice?*"

"Yeah."

"For good measure, my clients say you can keep the five grand advance as kill fee. Pretty generous, if you ask me."

He was right, of course, Jerry knew. Plan B violated the contract. The Wileys were supposed to die in a house fire while they slept. Under the circumstances Roman could have announced he was being retired from Black Flag without a kill fee. But he knew too much: names, connections, details that could compromise Roman's people. Instinct told him that the government would be very unhappy if he went public. It was what he didn't know that fired his interest even more now.

There was one more name on the list, one more face in the photo. Who could tell what he might find under it? His advantage was that Roman's people did not know what information he had managed to glean from the first two assignments. They could not retire him without risking his doubling back, which left them only two choices: putting him on hold as Roman said, or putting a bullet through his voice box.

"Roman?"

"Yeah?"

"Something for your people."

"I'm listening."

"Anything happens to me, my insurance man has instructions to send copies of my will to *20/20.*"

"What's that mean?" Roman had no idea what the hell *20/20* was.

"*Means* if anybody comes popping at me, you're gonna see Black Flag on Barbara Walters. *Capice?*"

He'd heard of her. "Well, I'll pass that on."

"You do that," Jerry said, and hung up.

The Topsfield turnoff was another six miles up. It was nearly eight-fifteen. Doors closed at nine, no exception. He had already missed inspections, which meant he'd be betting blind. The traffic was on his side.

He drove to the turnoff onto one dark country road after another until he got to the Fig's driveway. Two men at the gate sprayed a light on his face, then let him pass. Maybe three hundred yards through high pines, he came to the big farmhouse with a large red converted barn in back. Behind the barn was an open field that seemed to go on forever. Aside from the house and barn, no other lights were visible.

In the crowded lot he spotted the white Eldorado belonging to the man he was looking for, Muzzy Mozzicato. The bumper sticker read: I BRAKE FOR PAWS. Muzzy humor.

The barn was lit up. There might be sixty guys inside, but you'd never know it. The place had been meticulously sound-proofed for the events. Once a month and on special occasions. Tonight was a special night.

This was not your typical pit-bull convention. No grubby little back room of an abandoned silo in some rundown Ohio farm town full of guys in grease jeans and shit-kicker boots and a pocket full of tens. Two doormen in Armani suits greeted him by name and let him enter a brightly lit arena flanked by a full wet bar and tables spread with food. It was the Caesar's Palace for dogfights. On a good night you could walk away with fifty grand.

The place buzzed. The air was laced with cigar smoke and beer and food smells, but nothing suggested animal husbandry. Except for event dogs, the barn had never known four legs. Its sole function was these conventions.

Jerry Mars nodded at familiar faces as he made his way past the tables. As usual, they were laid out with sliced meats and cheeses, a huge bowl of cooked shrimp on ice, meatballs floating in oily sauce, sausages, lasagna and egg rolls. The only thing on the tables that wouldn't clog your arteries was the melon balls. He speared a few with a toothpick.

At the bar stood several men in noisy sport coats. Jerry was dressed in black jeans, a thin black leather jacket and black silk T-shirt. Jerry's look.

The bartender handed him his mineral water with a twist of lime. He took a sip and scanned the crowd. Most of the guys he knew from sight—goombas who had come from all over the Northeast, who liked the dogs and who laid down serious dough.

On the opposite side of the room were rows of chairs and two three-tiered grandstands facing each other across an opening squared off with ropes. Overhead was a cluster of spotlights hanging from the rafters. Below sat the ten-foot-square pit.

Saul "Muzzy" Mozzicato was talking to another man Jerry knew only as Mooch. On the bar between them was a dish piled high with cuts of blue cheese and coins of pepperoni that Muzzy was eating one after the other, no crackers. In his other hand he held a rum and Coke, the thought of which made Jerry's teeth hum.

"Hey, hey," Muzzy sang out. He made a wide, clubby handshake. "Now here's a guy with a *dog*. I mean, Jaws with paws." He made a wheezy laugh that came from his upper chest. "Name's Rufus—you know, Roof-roof, 'cept he don't bark, just grins and bites your leg off. The mutt's the balls is all." He pumped Jerry's hand.

Muzzy was about five-seven, 280 pounds of hard fat. He wore a white shirt open at the neck, around which hung a chain with a gold pepper. When he laughed, his eyes disappeared into folds of fat, a sole benefit of which was that he did not look like his fifty-two years. What would have been wrinkles in a leaner man was flesh plumped out to a shiny smoothness, now slick with perspiration and pink from years of rum and Cokes and cholesterol canapes.

"Why don't you have a real drink, for Chrissakes? I mean, what kind of a time is that health-water shit?"

"Good for the bowels," Jerry said.

Muzzy looked nonplussed at Mooch. "Good for the bowels," he echoed. "*Madone*, all you got in there's yogurt and that cracked wheat shit. Your poor bowels, they're probably screaming for ribs and fries."

Jerry smiled warmly.

"You know Mooch."

"Mooch." Jerry nodded and shook hands. From what Jerry recalled, Mooch was a bookie from Springfield and one of Muzzy's distant cousins.

"Pit bull?" Mooch asked.

"A quarter Rottweiler," Jerry said.

"What the cops in South Africa used against the blacks. Nice combo."

"Yeah, but he ain't no ordinary crossbreed," Muzzy said. "Got fucking lion's blood in his veins."

"Got a couple bulls myself."

"Chopper and Muffin," Muzzy said. "Shoulda seen Chopper two weeks ago. For warmup they threw him a dachshund. The thing lasted two minutes. Put him away like a Fenway frank." Muzzy wheeze-laughed. "Umbelievable. You would of loved it. Then he finished off French DeRoche's Buzzsaw in twenty minutes. Umbelievable. Be a great match against Rufus." He popped another wedge of cheese into his mouth. "When you gonna match him, huh? I mean, you got a natural champion and you keep him locked up."

For months they had been after Jerry to pit Rufus. Jerry kept him finely conditioned, but he knew the fate of convention dogs. Unlike the hundreds of other dogfights taking place any weekend across the country, these were not fight-to-first-yip contests. The animals pitted here fought to the death. Even the winners themselves got so badly chewed up, they ended up in the dumpster out back with a bullet in the head. The men in this building raised fighters, not pets. It was costly, but they could afford to maintain the purity of genetic intention. Decades of selective breeding had produced beasts engineered for mortal combat. If they were humans, they'd be modern-day Samurai.

Rufus, though, was for business, not sport. "I tell you, the gun's not for hire."

Muzzy shook his head. "You're gonna turn that dog into a fucking pansy, the way you treat him. Feeds him health food, so help me God, Mooch. I mean, the dog won't even look at Alpo. Doesn't know what steak is." Muzzy popped another hunk of cheese in his mouth. "Umbelievable." He chewed, licking his fingers. "Plays him classical music records, gets a bath and rubdown once a week. Lives a better life than I do, for Chrissakes."

"Also better looking," Jerry said.

Muzzy let out another wheezy laugh, his eyes pressing to black slits. "*Madone*, the tongue on this guy. I fucking love him." He threw his arm around Jerry's shoulder and kissed him on the cheek.

Jerry hated that—the implied intimacy—and that disgusting stinkhole of a mouth on his face. But Jerry bit the bullet, he needed this pig of a man.

Muzzy Mozzicato was a regional capo who had given Jerry his first break when he came home from Vietnam wild and hurting for work. Over the years Muzzy had set him up with Family when Jerry needed freelancing. He had even procured the phony detective ID. Jerry was obliged to him. But more importantly, Muzzy had recently moved his business into the space age so that he could lay those fat little sausages on information Jerry needed.

"You hear what's on tonight?" Muzzy asked.

"I got here late."

"Your kind of thing." Muzzy beamed. "Jackals."

"Jackals?"

Though most of the matches were pit bulls, for kicks they would pit other breeds—Dobermans, chows, German shepherds and Rottweilers. Sometimes they would hold "Mixy-Matchies."

"How did they get jackals into the country?"

"They were already here." Muzzy said. "The Fig got 'em from a zoo in Atlanta."

Muzzy sent Mooch to save their seats, then took Jerry out back to the two cages separated from the rest.

The lights were low but Jerry could make out the creatures. They looked like dogs Satan might keep—lean, snouty things with long, pointed ears, vicious teeth and hot eyes. As Jerry bent closer to one cage, the dog let out a savage growl. It laid its ears back and bared its teeth. Jerry felt a ripple of excitement.

" 'Black-backed male jackal—*Canis mesomelas,* or whatever the fuck. Three-year-old male, from Kenya,' " Muzzy said. He was reading from a card on top of the cage. "They're the biggest of the jackals, and the meanest. Feed on antelopes. Name's Carlos." He laughed. "Pretty good, huh? The other guy's Joe. Joe Jackal."

He punched the cage, and the animal let out a volley of sharp, high-pitched barks.

"Fucking dogs from hell, is all."

The animal's ears flattened back, its hackles stood up, and maroon eyes blazed at Jerry with savage cunning. Deep, jungle eyes that buzzed to get at the fat man's flesh. For a moment Jerry lost himself in them. He wanted to put his face against that sharp little muzzle to take in that hot Serengeti breath. "Beautiful," he whispered.

The last-call bells went off, sending them to their seats.

"The next time, the Fig says, he's gonna try to get a couple wolves. He's got a guy in Springfield says he can cop 'em from Forest Park. That'll be something, hah? Maybe we should think about spreading out in the animal kingdom, you know, some big cats or something. Maybe pit a couple panthers? No fucking end to the possibilities, hah?"

"No."

When they took their seats, Jerry leaned over to the fat man's ear. "I need a favor."

Muzzy nodded. "Name it."

"Somebody fell into the cracks I gotta find."

Muzzy nodded again. "He from the state?"

"Yeah."

"He drive a car? Own a house? Shop with MasterCard and VISA?"

"Probably all of that."

"Then we'll find him."

The bell rang again. From overhead speakers the voice of Mike "the Fig" Mangiafico welcomed everybody and announced the night's docket, which included six pit-bull fights of three different weight classes. The fighting weights were strictly agreed upon, and during the cocktail hour the dogs were closely weighed. If a dog was over his agreed-upon weight class, the owner would automatically concede the fight and compensate the opponent with his $5,000 entry fee. The Fig announced the odds, then the special event: two Kenyan jackals. Carlos was favored three to one, although nobody was certain jackals could fight. It was an exotic sideshow that would turn out to be a dud—a lot of barking and posturing but no blood.

"Your friend."

"Yeah?"

"You gonna whack him?"

"Going to talk first."

The referee in a blue blazer stood up with a portable microphone and called out, "Gentlemen, face your dogs."

Below, the handlers entered the pit at opposite ends of the square and positioned their dogs, holding them firmly by the flesh of their necks. Though the dogs tugged a little to get at the opponents, there was no growling, no barking, no baring of incisors, no hackles standing up. These animals were so singularly programmed to fight that all display had been bred out of them. In fact, there was an eerie absence of clues that the pit, in a matter of moments, would be a spectacle of fury.

The referee waited for the handlers to square off the dogs.

"What's his name?" Muzzy asked.

But before Jerry could answer, the referee called out, "Gentlemen, release your dogs."

The dogs flew at each other, meeting head-on near the center of the pit. Mouths open, they balanced against each other on hind legs and tried to clamp down on an exposed jaw or nose. There was a lot of movement and snapping but little noise from the dogs. It always amazed Jerry how such primitive ferocity could be so quiet. Not once during the half-hour match did a dog let out anything more than a snarl.

The crowd, however, kept up a constant cheering, reaching crescendo when Max caught Boomer by the right haunch and took out a chunk of flesh. In a split-second reflex, Boomer tried to lick it, but Max caught him on the other hind leg. With bloody jaws locked, Max then shook his head as if to tear it off. But in his enthusiasm he got his head too close, and Boomer caught him by the left ear and tore off the tip.

The place went wild. Muzzy's face was like a giant tomato. He elbowed Jerry. "It don't get much better than this, hah?"

Jerry said nothing, but his concentration was shattered. There were times when he'd fix so intensely on the animals that he fought the match inside his own body—his movements and instincts indistinguishable from those of the animals.

Soon both dogs were covered with blood. As Boomer turned to his right, Max flew at him, catching his neck. With a furious thrust of his hind legs, he drove Boomer into the corner to keep him from rolling out of the hold.

"Smart move," Muzzy shouted. He was on his feet with the others.

Boomer raised his front leg to fend off Max's jaw, a fatal mistake. Max chomped it with that industrial-strength vice, breaking the leg short of the elbow. As Boomer rolled against the pain, Max went at the other leg, snapping that one with the same savage thrashing of his head. Boomer rolled onto his stomach and tried to crawl toward

Max on his two broken legs. He made little distance before Max caught him by the throat and threw him onto his back.

In less than three minutes it was over. When Max was sure Boomer was dead, he ripped a hole in his throat. Before he could make more of a mess, the owner pulled him back, and Boomer's owner dragged out his carcass by the ruined back leg for the dumpster out back.

Muzzy had made $4,000 on the fight.

When he settled down, he pulled out a pen and notepad. "This guy you're gonna whack. What's his name?"

"John Victor Perry. Calls himself Jack."

Muzzy wrote it down. "If your Jack's got a pulse, we'll find him."

CHAPTER

23

Calvin left the house at about three on Friday. He had another stack of senior finals to finish, and grades were due Monday. Terry didn't mind his going, in a way it was a relief after that awful night of frustration. She also had plenty of busy work to keep her mind off things. "If I can get through the day on just my brainstem," she said before he left, "I'll be grateful."

But Calvin did not go to his office. Instead, he headed for the Wilson Library in Carleton center.

He began with the computerized indices for the *Patriot Chronicle*, looking for cross-references on a number of key terms related to Carleton: Magog Woods, chemical dumping, disposal, pollution, hazardous wastes, commercial usage, toxins, toxic materials. From 1970 he found fourteen items which cross-referenced with Carleton. Most had to do with Carleton's long-range fight with the commonwealth's efforts to use land on the other side of town for a disposal site. After a seven-year battle Carleton won, and the state moved its efforts elsewhere.

Of the remaining stories, one snagged Calvin's interest. TOWN BUYS MAGOG ACREAGE FROM RESEARCH FIRM. The author was Sally Forand; the date April 11, 1973. He jotted down the date, then tapped in the author's name. A list of other articles: WHAT'S BURIED IN MAGOG? (May 7, 1973), A QUESTION OF CONTAMINATION. (May 23, 1973).

All *Patriot Chronicle* articles were on microfilm, located in drawers in the reference room. He found the right section and drawer for the year, only to discover that three boxes covering April, May, and June, 1973, were missing. He checked with the librarian, who went

155

through the other drawers to see if they had been misplaced. They hadn't. They were missing, the only ones that were, apparently.

He proceeded down Center Street to the offices of the *Chronicle*, only to be told that their holdings did not go back beyond three years, that the library was the only place with past copies on micro. He asked about Sally Forand and the secretary managed to find an old address and telephone number. She picked up her phone and called someone, and a few moments later a tall thin man in his forties came out from the back room. He had wire-rimmed glasses and thinning hair, and introduced himself as Dennis Waite.

When Calvin told him his name, Waite's eyes lit up. "Any relation to Terry Hazzard?"

"My wife."

"She's submitted some strong op-ed pieces to us. She's a good writer."

"Thank you. I'll pass that on to her."

He led Calvin into a back office where they could be private. "Donna said you asked about Sally Forand?"

"Yes, I've been trying to track down some articles by her."

He studied Calvin for a moment. "Such as?"

Calvin pulled out his notes and tore off a page with the titles and handed it to him.

Waite raised his glasses to read the titles.

"The microfilms containing these are missing from Wilson Library, and I'm told you people don't keep back issues."

"Unfortunately, that's true."

"It's a long shot but I was hoping someone might remember the stories."

"May I ask what your interest is?"

"Well, the titles seem part of a series about Magog land being used as a toxic dump."

Waite made a noncommittal nod.

"Was that the case?"

"That depends on the reasons for your interest."

It wasn't an answer he expected. Nor was Waite's apparent protectiveness. "I'm concerned that my house might be sitting on it."

"What makes you think that?"

"Several reasons," Calvin said, "not the least of which is all this strange animal behavior you people have been reporting on." Calvin saw no reason to mention Matty.

"And you think there's an environmental cause."

"Yes," Calvin said, "and possibly related to what Sally Forand was investigating."

"I see." Waite rocked back and put the tips of his fingers together as if holding an invisible ball. "If I recall, Sally never reported anything about strange animal behavior."

"Love Canal didn't happen overnight either," Calvin said.

"And you think you're living on your own Love Canal."

"That's what I'm asking you."

Waite nodded and crossed the room to a file cabinet, where he stooped down and pulled out a bottom drawer. From in back he extracted a manila file, came back to the desk, opened the folder and pulled from it a five-by-seven black-and-white photo that he handed to Calvin.

It showed an attractive young woman with blond hair pulled back, grinning happily, and beside her, a younger, long-haired Dennis Waite. They were holding a newspaper open to a page with portraits of women too small to make out. FEBRUARY, 1973 was penned on the bottom white margin.

"We were going to be married that June," Dennis Waite said. "She was killed in a car crash on Memorial Day weekend. It was a hit-and-run. She died instantly."

"I'm sorry."

Waite nodded. "They found the other car about half a mile from hers. It had rolled over a couple times down a bank. Some blood but no driver. I had the impression it was staged."

"Staged?" Calvin said. "You mean, you suspected she'd been murdered?"

"At the time," Waite said. "Remember, it was the era of political assassinations and conspiracy theories. And I was a young reporter caught up in Watergate fever, so I was full of suspicions. Her death was my grassy knoll."

"Was there an investigation?"

"Yeah, but it turned up nothing."

"What made you suspect she'd been murdered?"

"She'd gotten a lot of anonymous phone threats and letters. About the articles."

"Who'd you suspect?"

He shrugged. "At the time, everybody," he said. "But mostly the developers. They bought the land from the town for peanuts, so they had the most to lose if somebody found contaminants in the ground."

"Did they?"

"No."

"The titles suggest she'd been angling on those who sold the land."

"Yes, but she got nowhere."

"No evidence?"

"No evidence, and the fact that the people who used the land disappeared. Overnight the place was stripped clean, and no names."

"What was it?"

"A small research lab in Adamsville, the middle of nowhere. She didn't let on much, but she once said she thought they did some kind of government work. What it was, she never learned, or never told."

"But she suspected they were using Magog as a dumpsite?"

He nodded.

"Do you know exactly *which* parcel of land?"

He shook his head. "The town bought something like forty acres. I'm sure it's recorded someplace."

"Any idea what they might have dumped?"

"No," he said, "or even if they did dump."

"You don't believe there was a dump."

"What I believe is irrelevant. There's just no evidence."

"Then what were her leads?"

Waite smiled faintly. "Funny thing about Sally. We were engaged to be married, but she never talked about her stories. My guess is, she had her own Deep Throat who whispered in her ear."

"Did anybody ever excavate?"

"Not on private property," he said. "Even if she had evidence, you'd need the Army Corps of Engineers to dig it up. Forty acres is a major part of Carleton's map. Besides, the developer had already built on it. Including your house, in fact."

Calvin nodded. "Do the names Joseph and Anna Samborsky mean anything to you?"

"No," he said. "Should they?"

"They were the original owners. They moved in in '74."

Waite shook his head. "Sally was already dead," he said, "and nobody was willing to follow up."

"Do you have any copies of her stories?"

"Not after twenty-three years."

Calvin nodded.

"I wouldn't work myself up too much," he said before Calvin left. "She was a good reporter but she only had rumors. When they began to develop the land, nobody found anything suspicious."

"How do you know that?"

"Because I watched them excavate," he said. "Three houses on your street, including yours. I had a vested interest."

"Of course," Calvin said. "Nonetheless, you'd say she really had nothing."

"With all due respect to her memory, yes," Waite said. "Just a lot of false leads."

"One final question: Do you recall the name of the research outfit?"

Without missing a beat Waite said, "BiOmega."

"After all these years."

"It's not a name one forgets." He wrote out the name. "The O in 'omega' was spelled with the Greek letter. It used to be located on Franklin Street near mile marker 23. I think there's a condo complex there now."

Calvin thanked him and left. In a few minutes he was on Route 2 heading east. In half an hour he reached the Adamsville exit. Franklin Street was a wooded country road, infrequently relieved by houses. Waite was right. At mile marker 23 sat a large condominium complex called Sherwood Forest Estates, built into the woods. The gateway entrance was surrounded by mature trees that looked older than the condos. A long asphalt road led to the first of three mock-Tudor buildings set around a parking area. If BiOmega Labs had been built over one or more of them, it must have been well hidden from the road.

Calvin drove up and down Franklin hoping to find a sandwich shop, gas station, store—anything that looked as if it predated Sherwood Estates, where somebody might remember BiOmega Labs. Adamsville center was located where Franklin crossed Route 113. No library, police station or country-store wooden Indian. Just a clutch of small homes, a hardware and video rental, a Global Gas, with convenience store and a small luncheonette called Dotty's Kitchen.

At the Global station was a lone kid who wouldn't have been born in 1973. The hardware looked as if it could have been around that long, so did the proprietor. But when Calvin asked, the man said he was from Virginia and bought the place just twelve years ago. He suggested asking at Dotty's because the woman who owned it was born and raised in Adamsville. "She's like the town historian," he said.

Calvin thanked him and headed for Dotty's. The interior was black and the small sign on the window said the place closed at three on Saturdays. It was nearly six.

He walked across the street to his car and drove out of town, thinking that Dennis Waite was right. Just a lot of false leads.

He drove to Boston and spent the next four hours in his office doing grades. There was a message on his answering machine from Terry that Public Works called to say that the DPW toxicity tests on their water and soil came up negative. None of the known industrial wastes the state tested for turned up in the screening. That still did not explain the raccoon rapine or the stunted flowers, but it got Calvin off the hook for his lawn chemicals.

And maybe BiOmega.

CHAPTER

24

By the time Calvin arrived home, sometime after eleven, he had all but purged himself of BiOmega. Waite said nobody had found anything when they built their house; and the DPW had given their well a clean bill of health. Case closed. It was a twenty-three-year-old false alarm. Whatever was affecting Matty's system, thank God, didn't have Calvin's name on it. Nor did the dogwood and tulips. Maybe Terry was right about the ozone holes.

He pulled up the driveway. The only light in the house came from the kitchen. Matty's room, which hung over the driveway, was black. So was their bedroom. Terry had probably crashed before it got dark.

Calvin took his briefcase and got out of the car, feeling as if cement were flowing through his veins. He wanted to sleep for a week. He pressed the door button and the garage door rolled down with a rusted groan. The backyard and pool lay before him, as Matthew Arnold said, like a "land of dreams/So various, so beautiful, so new."

The night was idyllic. Not even the barking of that jerk Gretchen. (Funny, he hadn't heard her for a few days. Maybe they were out of town.) The only sound was the cozy racket of crickets. He dragged himself toward the back steps, guided by the light from the kitchen windows.

It was the acrid feral odor that hit him first.

The ground by the back steps was covered with blood and scraps of flesh and viscera. There wasn't anything big enough to identify— just scattered lumps of meat and fur, all so small and matted with blood that he couldn't tell if it were a raccoon or skunk or something else. All that was identifiable were strings of intestines. It looked like the remains of an animal that had exploded on the asphalt.

Rabid Rocky strikes again, he thought.

Terry and Matty must not see this. Calvin unraveled the hose under the kitchen window. Could one raccoon do this? Maybe it was a pack attack on some hapless creature. Like that story the other day about domestic dogs wilding on the cape. Killed some woman scientist.

He hosed the scraps down the asphalt driveway and into the sewer just feet from his property. He washed the backyard until he was certain nothing was left. By the time he had finished, his shoes and pants were wet from the spray. They would be dry by morning, and Terry would never know.

He pulled himself up the steps and into the house. The place was dead still. The green glow of the micro clock said eleven twenty-seven. He drank two glasses of bottled water, then headed upstairs. Before he went to bed, he ducked into Matty's room, guided by the light from the outside bathroom.

Matty was sleeping deeply, a raspy snoring sound coming from his chest. Calvin bent over and pulled the covers around his shoulders. He could make out the length of his body in the bed, and it shocked him how big Matty seemed. He felt a rush of love for the boy. He remembered how he used to lie down with him and tell him stories before going to sleep. How long ago that seemed.

Suddenly he felt a rush of sorrow and guilt. He had been so self-absorbed that he hadn't noticed him growing up. It was like looking at a stranger asleep in Matty's bed. *You're a lousy father,* Calvin told himself. Your son's suffering a condition that's tearing him up. He needs the comfort and consolation of his dad. He's frightened and he needs you. Well, he would start doing things with him, take him to Canobie Lake Park, fishing, catch a few movies, go bowling. Take him to the field to play some catch. He couldn't lose touch with him. In a couple years, he won't want to be seen dead with you . . .

He kissed the boy on his forehead. *We'll get better. I promise. I promise.* He left then and crawled into bed. Terry was sleeping soundly on her side with her back to him.

It usually took him less than three minutes to fall asleep, but his heart kept up a high, tympanic rhythm in his ears. He lay there concentrating on his heartbeat, the blood throbbing through his body. Finally he blanked his mind and in a few minutes sleep took him over. No more thoughts. And, please, no dreams.

At 3:48 he woke with a start.

At first he could not determine the disturbance, put together the sounds. Terry was in the same position on her side, still in a deep sleep.

From the hall, a strip of light under their bedroom door. Matty was in the bathroom.

There were muffled sounds, then the toilet flushing. The light was out and Matty was back in bed. The only sound was the quiet flow of water in the pipes refilling the bank.

But by now he was fairly sure that the sounds he had heard were Matty being sick, throwing up.

He thought about getting up and checking on Matty, but he just could not exert himself. Sleep had begun to reform around him like a cocoon. He nearly slipped away when another voice reminded him that he had drunk two glasses of water before he came up and that he might as well pee, since in a hour his bladder would wake him up. He jerked himself out of bed.

Terry rolled onto her back but remained asleep. Before turning into the hall bathroom, he stuck his head into Matty's bedroom. The room was black except for the phosphorescent glow of the plastic skull on Matty's nighttable. Calvin had bought it for him one Halloween. He could hear Matty's breathing—it was louder and wet-sounding. The heaviness of the sound was startling. If he hadn't known his twelve-year-old son was in there, Calvin would have thought the bed was occupied by a grown man. Maybe he had picked up one of those twenty-four-hour flus.

Calvin shuffled into the bathroom. He flicked on the light and squinted into the mirror. He looked like hell. His face was pale and puffy.

He pulled himself out of his pants and lifted the lid of the toilet.

A thin gasp squeezed out of his throat. Like a plastic toy that defied flushing, something lay at the bottom of the bowl.

Calvin looked closely. *Sweet Jesus.*

Was he in some grotesque dream state . . . ? Or did he see what he saw? That Matty had vomited up the paw of an animal.

Daisy's?

CHAPTER

25

"Daisy?"

"Our cat," Terry said.

"What about her?"

"I said, did you let her out?"

"Out? No . . . I mean, yes."

Terry's eyebrow shot up like a polygraph needle. "Which is it?" She was at the stove cooking pancakes for Matty's breakfast.

"I forgot. I let her out when I got up." He had gotten out of bed about five-thirty, before the sun. His eyelids were lined with sandpaper and his head throbbed.

"Did you feed her?"

"She wasn't hungry."

"She's been acting strange lately. I've got to take her to the vet." Then she glanced his way. "You don't look so good yourself. Sleep all right?"

"Little trouble dozing off."

He hadn't slept a moment since 3:48. He had rolled around the entire night trying to blot out the image . . . trying to convince himself that his son had not done the unspeakable. Convince himself that the cat had been ravaged by some night creatures—maybe that sick raccoon; that he found the paw and kept it as a pathetic memento but was so sickened with grief that he dropped it into the toilet, then threw up.

"Finish your grades?" Terry slipped the pancakes.

"All done."

"Calvin, you okay?"

Sure. Our son ate the family cat.

165

"I'm fine." It was grist for a very sick joke . . . *Sure, I'll tell you about my kid—bright, healthy, strong, does well in school, easy to get along with, plays piano, hits a mean ball. Ate the family cat the other night but, hey, nobody's perfect, right?* "Just a little tired."

"What time'd you get in?"

"Eleven."

She glanced at the clock. "It's almost eight. You better wake him." They had a nine o'clock appointment with Mitch Tojian at Emerson.

He tried again to latch onto the explanation that it was really all a freak nightmare—a conspiracy of anxiety and guilt. A dream so wretchedly vivid that he could not distinguish imaginary sensory input from the real thing. On rare occasions he had had such dreams, though none so awful. Dreams in which even the test pinch hurts; dreams you'd bet your life were real; dreams without that nice little aisle where you stand and watch, knowing it's just a movie playing on the inside of your skull. Maybe last night was one of those . . .

please, God

Anything but this unbearable awakeness.

Or maybe he had dream-walked the whole scene, including the toilet—gone through the motions of cleaning up the backyard while totally asleep. He had read about such things, some kind of autohypnosis pressed into action by psychic stress. He'd unraveled the hose and washed away imagined carnage. And right now Daisy was out there in Magog stalking moles.

When he reached the landing, he looked at the photo of the toddler in the milk mustache and tried to let the image fill the dread swelling in him.

He peaked through the keyhole. Black. The venetian blinds were down, the curtain drawn. He turned the knob gently, pushed open the door.

His first awareness was the high-pitched electronic beeping of Matty's alarm clock. He always set it for seven-thirty and never slept through it.

Second, was the inert hump under the spread.

Matty did not stir as Calvin moved into the room. Nor had he moved from the position he was in eight hours ago. And still breathing that deep-throated, wet snoring . . .

Freddy Krueger flashed a little wave as Calvin turned off the alarm. He took in a huge lungful of air. What if I pull back the blanket and some jack-in-the-box demon pops up, with hellfire eyes and incisors humming to tear out your throat?

Come on, this isn't some chiller-thriller flick. It's your son. Calvin pulled back the spread.

Matty lay in a fetal curl. A wave of relief washed through Calvin as he took in the boy. The light caught the sweet profile, the lightly freckled nose, the red full lips, the thick rich canopy of hair with its little tail inching down the back of his neck. As often, the baby finger of his left hand was partway in his mouth, like a pacifier. For a flickering moment Calvin beheld the toddler in his crib, a menagerie of downy stuffed critters snuggling around his head. Calvin's heart ached.

God, don't let it be so.

The boy stirred, a small sigh escaping his throat. Calvin could smell his breath. A sharp odor. Sleep breath, he told himself.

Calvin drew the curtains and pulled up the blinds. Daylight flooded the room. From this angle Calvin could see no signs of the night drama. No scratches or blood. He pulled back the sheet. Matty was dressed in a Red Sox T-shirt and underpants. No telltale signs. (He was still startled, though, at all the hair on his legs and arms.) He stretched the sheet back over him.

He patted his shoulder. "Matty. Time to get up."

He didn't move. Calvin shook him gently, no response. Finally, after a full minute or more, Matty frowned and opened his eyes. He blinked, rolled his head around, squinting up at Calvin as though without recognition. He squeezed his eyes against the light.

Calvin swallowed. "G'morning, champ. Eight o'clock. You overslept." His face was clean. There was dirt under his fingernails, but there usually was. He was a boy, after all. "Whyn't you clean up?"

Matty nodded and got up, his hands shielding his eyes from the sunlight. Without a word, he padded out of his room and into the bathroom, the oversize shirt hanging on him like a sack.

It was a scene so unextraordinary, so altogether homey that Calvin felt stunned he had ever entertained such horrendous suspicions. He rolled back the sheets. The bed was clean. Matty's black Nikes were under the bed side by side. His pants in their usual ball by the hamper. A dirty sock on top. He inspected the clothes. A missing sock, but no tears, no blotches of dried blood. A couple of books on the floor near the bookcase. Nothing out of the ordinary. Even Freddy looked half-benign. It was a clean, well-lighted place. Calvin looked out the window and wondered what was real.

Matty's shower water made a soft hush through the pipes in the wall. Was it possible that none of it took place? Just a slice-and-dice dream?

Through the window sunlight poured in. The backyard was fresh after the midnight rain. The only thing moving was the pool's surface in the breeze. And the crows. Three big ones strutting across the asphalt like the Fates. One of them found something in the grass and began picking on it. The others joined it.

Back down in the kitchen, Terry asked, "Why's he taking a shower? He took one last night."

"He did?" He took morning or evening showers, not both. But that meant nothing. He had a doctor's appointment coming up.

Terry put Matty's plate of pancakes in the micro.

"What did you do last night?"

"Went to an early movie. Read a little when I got back. Must have dozed off about ten."

Calvin didn't say anything. He heard the shower turn off and Matty go into his room.

"You two eat," Terry said, and went up to get dressed.

Matty came down dressed in clean jeans and a long-sleeve pullover. He sat down and began to eat the pancakes. From the other side of the table, Calvin sipped his coffee and fixed his eyes on his son. "I saved you some time."

"You did?"

"I fed Daisy."

Without breaking the rhythm of his chewing, without the slightest betrayal of expression, Matty said, "Thanks."

"I let her out." Calvin added.

Matty nodded and put a wedge of pancake into his mouth. "We going to the hospital today?"

"Yes. Does that bother you?"

Matty shrugged.

Calvin's insides felt as if they'd been wrung out and stretched to dry. Matty had always been a bad liar. Even with his best effort, some slight change in expression gave him away. Calvin saw no hint of it now.

While Matty ate, Calvin stepped outside, his heart pounding that he'd spot something that would make it all real.

It was a newborn spring morning. The sun was warm, the grass sparkling. The asphalt was clean. He walked down the driveway to the street. Just a few leaves and pebbles. He returned to the back-yard. The crows fluttered off as he approached. Matty's pitching net stood near the pool, beside it, a bucket of hardballs. Something white at the pool's edge caught his eye. A white tube sock with blue stripes at the top. Matty's. It probably blew off the line. The pool water was green with algae.

At the far end of the pool, something floated in the bright scum. He walked around the edge to the far side. The usual backyard flotsam—beetles, twigs, leaves and an old hardball from when Matty overthrew the pitching net. Calvin picked up the long-handled net and scooped it out.

A moment's numbness as recognition settled in. No hardball. Daisy's head. One eye missing, the other frozen in fright.

"Hey, Dad, we're going to be late." Terry and Matty were getting in the car.

Calvin would never be able to understand how he managed to affect casualness, to keep from screaming—maybe some kind of autopilot kicking in when the mind shut down. But in one motion he flung the net like a lacrosse stick, sending the cat's head into the Magog Woods.

"Dad?"

"I'll be right there."

Matty sat in the back. He wore sunglasses. "What were you doing back there?"

"Looking for Daisy."

Matty didn't respond.

Calvin glanced at him in the rearview mirror. Twin circles of black stared at him.

"We better step on it," Terry said. "It's quarter of."

Calvin started the car.

Before they pulled away, Matty said in a barely perceptible voice, "Daisy's around."

CHAPTER

26

Mitch Tojian was waiting for them in the lobby of Emerson Hospital.

Terry looked worried, as expected. Calvin was a wreck. His voice had a high, strained quality, as if he couldn't get enough air. When Mitch led them into a private conference room, Calvin could not sit still. By contrast, Matty was in a state of subdued resignation.

Mitch reviewed the magnetic resonance imaging procedure. Matty would be given an injection of radioactive gadolinium, then be put on a table where he had to lie still for twenty minutes while the machine took pictures of his brain from different angles. Except for the needle, there would be no discomfort. All Matty had to concentrate on was lying still for the imaging. Before they got to that, Mitch said he wanted to talk privately with Matty and give him a quick visual exam. The boy looked reluctant but it was clear he had no choice.

Mitch led him to an adjoining room, closed the door, then asked Matty to sit on the examining table and remove his shirt. Because of Terry's call yesterday, Mitch was prepared, so he did not show the slightest reaction to Matty's chest, a patchwork of black hair and scabby blotches where he had torn out clumps.

"You want to tell me about it?"

Matty looked away and shrugged.

"The hair really bothers you."

"Kind of."

"A razor would've been less messy."

Matty made a flat smile. "I guess."

"Could also use what's known as a depilatory, which is a cream

171

you just rub on, wait a minute, then wipe away the hair. Your mom can get it in any pharmacy."

"It would only grow back."

"True, but you can keep using it until the medicine takes over. I'm giving you a prescription for something that will stop it from the inside. In the meantime, use the depilatory so you can wear T-shirts again. We've got a long hot summer ahead of us, and I don't want you passing out on second from the heat, okay?"

Matty nodded.

"Just a few questions." Mitch opened the file folder. "Can you tell me when you first noticed the chest hair?"

Matty let the question sit in the air for a while. He didn't seem to want to talk about it.

Mitch coaxed him. "Two years ago? A year?"

"I guess around Christmas."

"About five months ago," Mitch said. The growth had come on fast. "What did you think when you saw it start to come in?"

"I guess I got scared."

"Why did you get scared?"

"I thought I was turning into a freak."

"A freak? Why did you think that?"

"You know," he said. "You saw me."

"You mean your privates."

He nodded.

"Matty, I know this is hard, but it will help," Tojian said. "And when did you notice the changes there?"

"About the same time, I guess."

"So it happened kind of fast."

"Mmm."

"I know you're not going to like it, but I'd like to take a quick look," Mitch said.

Matty looked away for a moment, then, without a word, he slipped off the table, unbuttoned his pants and lowered his undershorts. Mitch quickly examined him and said he could pull his pants up.

Even though he had been prepared and had had cases of precocious puberty before, the sight was startling. Framed by a twelve-year-old's narrow thighs were the testes and penis of an adult male.

The scrotal skin was dark like an adult's, and the pubic hair was adult in quantity, type and distribution.

A Tanner level of five, the highest—the final level of puberty. For all practical purposes, he was fully developed.

Over the next several minutes Mitch questioned him about other changes he had experienced: headaches, loss of sleep, lack of appetite, the sensitivity of his eyes, periods of restlessness, and of anger. Matty's answers were sparse, mostly nods or shakes of the head. When Mitch asked him about feeling angry, Matty did open up. He admitted to getting mad, to doing bad things but hardly remembering them.

"What kinds of things?"

"Fighting."

"Your mother mentioned having a run-in with three other kids. Want to tell me about that?"

He shrugged.

"Did you attack them?"

"I guess."

"One boy, Bobby Gorawlski, was pretty badly messed up—facial scratches. Do you remember doing that?"

Matty shook his head. "I just remember animals."

"Animals?" Tojian said. "What kind of animals?"

More shrugs. "I don't know, there's a lot of voices and screaming but it's all blurry and red. I can't remember too well."

"So while you and Bobby are going at it, in your mind you thought you were being attacked by animals. Is that right?"

"I guess."

"Has this happened before?"

"Mmm."

"What kind of animals?"

"Dogs and cats. Sometimes bigger animals. I don't know, it's hard to remember, I can't see them too well. But it was like they were attacking me."

"Can you describe anything about the fights, what actually happens?"

He shook his head. "They attack me and I fight them off. But it's hard to remember. It's like it's all red smoke when it happens."

"Anything else?"

He shook his head again. "Just a lot of noise."

"Such as?"

"Screaming and growling."

Matty put his shirt back on and they headed back out to the lobby. Tojian explained that he and Matty had had a good talk, that he had examined him and taken another blood sample. Then he led them down the hall to the elevators and up to the fifth floor, where the MRI would be done. They were met by an endocrinologist with whom Mitch would consult and the radiologist and nurse who would administer the imaging.

Terry kissed Matty as he was led into the MRI room. Through the window they could see the huge machine and the table where Matty would lie and have his head inserted in the small opening. Mitch had asked for a full workup of Matty's brain and adrenal glands. The procedure would take about half an hour.

Nobody was allowed in the imaging room with patients, so Terry stayed in the viewing antechamber just to reassure Matty that she was nearby.

Mitch would have remained with her, but Calvin whispered that he wanted to speak to him privately. As an excuse, he told her he would bring back coffees for all of them. They headed down the hall and back to the conference room.

When Mitch closed the door, Calvin said, "I think Matty killed our cat."

Mitch listened grimly as Calvin described the backyard the previous night and finding the paw in the toilet.

"And you don't think it was wild animals."

He shook his head. "Her head was in the pool, as if it had been thrown there. Animals can't do that."

"And you really think Matty . . . threw it up."

"I *heard* him, throwing up . . ."

"But that doesn't prove that he killed her and". . . struggling for the right words. . . "ate her. It's conceivable that he found what you did and brought in her paw. Tried unsuccessfully to flush it down the toilet, threw up at the horror of it all."

"That's something I'd like to believe, Mitch."

Tojian nodded. "Does Terry know?"

"No."

"You might think about telling her."

Mitch then pulled his pad off the desk and wrote out a full pre-scription for lithium. "It's a standard, midlevel repressant," Tojian said. "For aggression."

"What about the game tomorrow night?"

"It's important that he show up even if he spends it on the bench. I'll watch him. If he seems okay, I'll put him in. It won't dull his reflexes. But he should be there, so he won't feel he's some kind of pariah."

Calvin nodded. On the way out he asked, "Could his condition be . . . environmental?"

Mitch eyed him. "If you're still worried about lawn chemicals, I doubt it."

"I mean something in the air or water?"

"Why do you ask?"

Calvin shook his head to say it was nothing.

"If you're concerned, you can have your soil and water tested."

"We did, and it turned up negative."

"Well, there you are."

"Right. There we are."

CHAPTER

27

Jerry Mars was right about the jackals. They weren't made for the pit. He had guessed that even before they were taken out of the cages. Wild dogs rarely fought each other. They just made a lot of noise and gestures with no payoff. Carlos and Joe were too spooked by the crowd to do anything more than hunker down in their corners with their ears flat and whimper. A couple minutes of that, and the ref had them hauled back to their cages. Everybody booed and hissed, and the Fig promised he'd make it up to them by squaring off a couple of timber wolves. He couldn't get it through his skull that the pit bull was the finest fighting beast in creation. All those other animals were exotic wimps.

Jerry was also right about Muzzy. Two days after the convention he called with an address for Jack Perry, traced through associates working at the Massachusetts Registry of Motor Vehicles with a cross-check of contacts who worked the computers at the Department of Revenue. There were fifty-seven John Perrys driving cars in the commonwealth, but only one with Victor for a middle name.

Apparently the life of a retired assistant microbiologist was not bountiful. No fancy Beacon Hill pad or seaside spread on Cape Cod. Jack Perry hung his hat in a Winnebago in a beat up South Shore trailer camp about thirty miles below Boston.

After three days of surveillance Jerry got a good look at the last guy in the photo. Though, at first, it was through a pair of binoculars. Jerry was struck by how Jack Perry had aged—more than the twenty years. It didn't look like the same guy. His hair was gray and thin and cropped close to his scalp. But it was what the years had done to his face. While most people fleshed out by their sixties,

Perry had gone the other way. His face looked like beef jerky, dark and shriveled up with deep lines. He looked like one of those guys you saw with several coats on, sleeping in a refrigerator box. Killing him would be an act of mercy—put the poor bastard out of his misery.

Toward that end, Jerry carried his briefcase. But he had no intention of putting a hit on Jack Perry, at least not yet. Technically, he was still on hold with Roman's clients, and he wasn't about to do them a freebie. Besides, his gut instinct told him that Jack Perry was worth a lot more to him while he still had breath.

Jerry traveled in a different rental vehicle every day, staking out Jack Perry's trailer and following him on local errands. The guy drove around in a black Chevy van with a bad muffler pipe hanging from wires. During those three days he never had a guest and never visited anybody. When he wasn't in his trailer or conducting affairs about town—stops at the banks, the laundry, the post office—he would take excursions to a small town west of Boston.

Twice Jerry followed him up a dead end with no street sign, circle back, then park in front of number 12—a white colonial, where he'd sit for ten or fifteen minutes as if waiting for someone. But nobody came out to meet him, and he never left the van. He'd just sit and watch the house. Then he'd drive off, sometimes stopping by a school down the street, where he would again sit and watch the kids at recess. Yesterday he broke the pattern and got out. He stood by the chain-link fence around the field, apparently interested in one particular kid. A boy about eleven or twelve. It might have been his kid from a broken marriage.

Jerry was not sure what he was after, but he knew that he had only a few days to find out before the guy would be taken out. Muzzy named the trailer park—Rumson's Mobile Homes—but not which of the three hundred rigs was Jack Perry's. It was the manager in the park's office who directed him to the Winnebago. In passing, he told Jerry that if he was a bill collector, he had come none too soon, because Perry had just paid his last week's rental. On Saturday he was pulling up stakes and heading to Tucumcari, New Mexico, for good. He had had it with New England winters, he'd said.

That was bullshit, of course. Jack Perry knew that his number was up. He had heard about the other hits and was running scared. Which raised a problem for Jerry, because by the time Roman's people put him back on payroll, Jack Perry would be tumbling around the sagebrush. As far as Jerry knew, Perry was the last of Black Flag. Which meant that Jack Perry had information that only Jack Perry could provide—why the contracts on the scientists, why after twenty years the sudden scramble to bury an experiment? Every instinct in Jerry told him that information was eminently and lucratively salable.

At about four o'clock Wednesday afternoon, Jack Perry left his trailer and got into the van. Instead of heading into town or one of the nearby malls, he drove to the highway taking the northbound lane. All too accustomed to the trail, Jerry fell a few cars back. They headed up Route 3 for a half-hour, then onto 128 for fifteen minutes, off the highway and onto back roads cutting through several small backwater towns. They were going back to Carleton, probably to mooch around another playground. Maybe the guy was some kind of pervert who finally worked up the nerve to flash a whole field when the teachers were gone.

But instead of heading to the Butler Elementary, Jack Perry cut to the other side of town to a baseball field.

None of it made sense. For a man on the run from his own execution, what the hell was he doing hanging around the playground of an elementary school and going to Little League games.

And who was that kid in the red number 11 T-shirt he was watching?

CHAPTER

28

The red number 11 T-shirt filled Terry's rearview mirror as she drove them to the game.

Under it Matty wore a long-sleeve white turtleneck. She had bought him a jar of scent-free depilatory, but he had refused to use it. If he showed up smooth as a newborn, the other kids would know he'd shaved or, worse, used his mom's Nair. He didn't seem bothered that it was warm. He didn't, in fact, seem bothered by anything. Terry was certain it was the effect of the lithium—he had none of the brooding spells or angry outbursts during the last day. He also did not complain of headaches.

For these small favors, Terry was grateful. However, anticipation of tomorrow's MRI results scratched at her all day. Calvin's reaction didn't help. For the last two days he had been edgy and aloof. So much so, that she wondered if he were withholding some awful news. Twice he had approached her as if to confess something, then pulled back with "it's going to be fine" or "I'll be glad when the results are back." She even called Mitch to see if he had told him something she didn't know, but he reassured here there was nothing. The MRI results would be in tomorrow and no sooner.

But Terry resolved that for the next three hours she was going to bottle up all that. It was baseball night. And Matty was playing second and determined to smash a few. It was a tight match because the Devil Dogs were tied with the Cardinals for first place. Unfortunately, the Cards had five twelve-year-olds, while the Dogs had only two, counting Matty. Worse still, they had six rookies under ten. It was their first match and the Cards were strongly favored.

She eyed Matty in the mirror. "Honey, did you take your medication?"

"Hnn."

"That yes or no?"

"Yes," Matty said.

"All of it?"

"Hnn." He sat in the back, quietly picking at the rawhide on his glove.

When he gave his head a shake, she asked, "You okay?"

"Just a little headache."

"I have some aspirin," Terry said, and handed Calvin her bag to dig them out. "If they don't help, we'll head home."

Matty swallowed the aspirin with the water from his squeeze bottle. "I'm all right."

"Just remember, keep your eye on the ball and swing easy," Calvin threw out for something to say. "Don't try to kill it. The secret is control." Then he added, "You're not playing for blood, okay, champ?"

Matty grunted.

"If it doesn't go away," Terry said, "tell Dr. Tojian. You don't have to play."

"It's only a headache."

Only a headache. How about brain tumor . . .

Please, dear God, not my son.

For the rest of the ride, nobody said anything. She parked the car in the field lot, and Matty sauntered off to the home team's bench with his glove and squeeze bottle, occasionally giving his head a snap to shake away the pain.

Terry and Calvin headed for the home-team grandstand behind the screen. Terry was too distracted by Matty's change to notice the black Chevy van pulled up behind her car.

But Jerry Mars noticed. Hard not to, with that muffler pipe. He had tailed him for the last hour.

He pulled past the van to an empty spot where he had an open view of Jack Perry.

The man did not immediately get out of the van but waited while the lot filled up with cars. Most were parents with kids in uniforms. Jerry could see Jack Perry's attention taken by the same boy in red. The adults he did not recognize, but the kid he could not mistake.

The parents sat themselves in the grandstand and the kid took to the home bench. It was then Jack Perry got out of his van, looked around cautiously, then headed for the fence separating a small gallery of fans from the Devil Dogs. Just behind number 11.

Jerry moved to the other side of the diamond, under a tree in the shadows. Watching.

Matty did not start, because all fourteen kids had shown up. He would sit out until the fourth-inning changeover.

The game began disastrously with the Cardinals scoring seven runs in the first inning, mostly on walks and Devil Dogs errors. But that was Little League. A grounder to first could end up a homer.

During the second inning, Terry took Calvin's hand. "Calm down." His left leg was bouncing.

"I'm okay."

"You're making me nervous," she said. "Is there something you want to tell me?"

"No. Nothing. I just want him to do well." His voice was thin. "I just want him to be okay, you know?"

Terry nodded. She glanced down at his hand in hers, at the thin sprout of hair on the backs, the shape of the fingers, the way the nails grew. She knew everything about Calvin's body. It nonetheless amazed her that you could live with a person, recognize him down to the hair on his fingers, yet could never be sure of the interior landscape. There were always those blind ravines, those alien sanctuaries. Yes, he was worried sick. They both were, yet she had a disturbing sense of barely felt signals of deception, vague disparities between things he said and what he was feeling.

He's hiding something, she told herself, and tried to bury the thought.

For the first two innings Matty sat by himself at the end of the bench, fidgeting with his glove. He did not engage in conversation with the other kids, nor did he pay particular attention to the game.

Some man behind the fence near the bench was chatting with him, but Matty did not appear interested.

In the visitors' grandstand Terry spotted Betty Gorawlski. Her son was a backup pitcher for the Cardinals, sitting on the opposite bench waiting for the fourth-inning shift. Beside him were the other Bully Boys—Mikey Rizzo and Jackie Stoneburner. And snuffling up to them were the wannabes. Occasionally they would leer at Matty and make jokes. The little shits.

Halfway through the second inning, she spotted Beverly Otis hustling across the parking lot. Beverly was a short, squat woman of sixty, but she moved through the rows of cars as if motorized. Hanging from a shoulder strap was a fat briefcase that struck Terry as odd baggage for a Little League game. When she reached the field, she stopped to survey the grandstands, then spotted Terry and Calvin and jostled over. Calvin made a motion to get some drinks but Terry pulled him back.

Beverly's face glowed from exertion. "Thought you'd be here," she panted, and flopped beside them. She pressed against Terry. "I just got off the phone with Claire Manning. She's been trying to get hold of you all afternoon."

There were two messages on Terry's machine but she hadn't called back. "We've been out."

She pressed her head close to both of them. "You're not going to believe it." She put her hand on Terry's arm and lowered her voice to a conspiratorial whisper so people around them couldn't hear. *"They bumped it another hundred."*

"Come again?"

"They upped the offer to seven hundred thousand."

"Jesus!" Calvin said.

"That's ridiculous," Terry said. "I'm starting to get suspicious something else is going on."

Beverly shook her head. "What can I say?" Beverly said. "They're nuts about it—I think it's the woods. But they want an answer, like right now."

"There are other places on Magog," Terry said.

"But not for sale," Beverly said. She pressed a card in Terry's hand. An out-of-town number was penned on the back. "She's waiting. I've got a phone in the car. I'll call, and while you're enjoying the game, I can draw up the papers and have them ready before it's over." She slapped her briefcase. "And by ten tomorrow you can have your check." Her eyes were fairly popping.

"Beverly, it's an incredible offer but we have to put it on hold. I told you that."

"Terry, hon, you don't put that kind of money on hold."

"I explained to you that Matty's got a medical problem." How she hated putting it into words.

Beverly squinted at the Devil Dogs bench. "He looks perfectly fine to me. I mean, he's playing ball. What's the problem?"

"That's frankly not your business," Terry said. She couldn't believe her tone.

"Look, you're right, I'm sorry. But she's been pushing me like you wouldn't believe."

"I understand, but my son's health comes first. We'll give you a definite answer tomorrow."

"Tomorrow," she echoed.

"But it's entirely possible we may not move for a few months."

"A few months?" Angry disbelief flitted across Beverly's eyes but she nodded it away. "Look, hon, I understand. I'm sorry to hear. I hope he's going to be okay. But you can do both. Sell your house and take a temporary place nearby while Matty gets his treatment. There are plenty of places for rent all around here. Meanwhile, put the money in a CD, and when everything blows over, move someplace else."

Terry glowered at Calvin. "Feel free to contribute," she said.

"Can't we talk about this some other time? It's my kid's game," he said.

"It's just that she's not the kind of woman you put off."

"Maybe not, but we're not living according to her time clock." Then to soften the edge, he added, "We're getting some test results tomorrow. We'll know better then."

"Okay," Beverly said. "Tomorrow." Then, as if she couldn't help herself, she said, "Tonight, if you hear something . . . anytime, forget about waking me. Believe me, you don't want to lose this offer. It's a once-in-a-lifetime thing. What can I say?"

As she was leaving, she turned to Calvin. "By the way, I checked on that thing we were talking about the other day. It was a small scientific lab. I mean, like it wasn't Dow Chemical or something. Nothing to worry about."

Calvin glared at her to shut up.

Beverly caught his look. "Gotta go. Scotty's almost up." Her nephew in the yellow number 3 was on deck. She flung her brief-case across her shoulder. "Who's ahead anyway?"

"You are." Terry watched her leave.

Calvin left to get drinks.

He came back with two Diet Sprites just as the fourth inning began. It was nearly seven. The third inning had taken nearly thirty min-utes, during which the Cardinals pushed the score to a nine-to-seven lead.

"We can still catch them," Calvin said. He sipped his drink and began to settle into the game when Terry turned to him.

"What was that about a small scientific lab?"

"Oh, nothing. I'd just called her about something . . ."

They were silent for a moment. "Like what?"

He made an exaggerated dismissal gesture. "Something about the deed."

"The deed? What about it?"

"It's not important."

Terry nodded to the opposite grandstand. "I can ask her myself if you prefer."

"Jesus, Ter, it was nothing. I just had some questions about the background."

"Calvin, you're a lousy liar."

"Christ," he began but didn't seem to know where to take it. "All the talk about moving to New York, and all. That's all."

"What's the deed have to do with it?"

"If we were going to sell, there would have to be a title search."

"Suddenly you're a real estate attorney? She said it was a small scientific lab, not Dow Chemical, nothing to worry about. *What* was she talking about?"

Calvin shot to his feet.

A Cardinal hit a grounder to the right of second, directly toward Matty. The grandstand moaned as it went through his legs and into right field. It was his second error and he punched his glove. The outfielder snapped up the ball and hurled it to Matty. He caught it cleanly but overthrew to third, allowing a runner an easy trot home.

Matty was mortified. He pulled the cap over his eyes and pounded his stomach with his fist. Other kids on the team shouted at him. And from the Cardinals bench Bobby Gorawlski yelled, "Way to go, Hazzard."

"The little bastard," Terry muttered. But her anger turned inward. Why were they putting Matty through this? It was unnatural. He wasn't out there having fun. He was a wreck, crying into his hat and hitting himself. The next batter hit an infield fly to the pitcher and retired the side.

Terry turned back to Calvin. "You were saying?"

"Huh?"

She was growing weary of playing games.

"Where's he going?" he asked.

Terry looked. Matty was heading into the woods. "Probably has to pee," she said, then lowered her voice. "Stop trying to change the subject. What was that between you and Beverly?"

He turned to her, took a deep breath, let it out slowly. They were sitting at the end of the top row, so nobody was behind them or to their right. Nonetheless, he kept his voice low. "I was going to tell you later. It's nothing."

His manner had changed so abruptly that she became frightened.

"Our house didn't always sit on residential property. Back in the seventies the zoning laws were different. It was leased by a research place called BiOmega Labs."

For the next several minutes, while Matty was in the woods, Calvin explained how their house sat on a site where BiOmega had buried waste. It was the reason he got the place at a bargain price. Looking back, it was impulsive, but on his salary it was the only shot they'd have at a dream house. Yes, there was a small liability, but he had seen no need to tell her, especially in light of her sensitivity to environmental causes. "It was dumb not to mention it, but you might have disapproved and we would have lost the place."

By the time he finished, Terry's throat was constricted. For ten years they'd been living on a chemical dump. "What made you call her now?" Her voice was low and rough.

"All that talk about dead trees and chemicals. But it's not a problem," he said. "I mean, the water and soil tests turned up nothing.
Everything's okay."

Her anger swelled into the silence. "How could you have taken
the chance?"

"It was stupid, okay? I admit it—it was stupid. But on a lousy
twenty thousand dollars, it was an option we'd never have again. You
could understand that."

"No, I can't." Her voice was scathing. "Why didn't you check what
the liability was, who did the dumping, what they buried and how
much. For all you know, they could have buried a truckload of radioactive plutonium."

"I felt that if I didn't put down a deposit, we would have lost it."

Terry looked away in disbelief.

"In any case, like I said, it's clean. We have no problem."

Matty emerged from the woods. Terry watched him cross to the
bench and put on a red helmet. He moved to the plate and took a
couple of practice swings. A man dressed all in black stood on the
sidelines nearby, watching him.

"What if they missed something?"

But Calvin didn't hear her.

In his red cap and blue shirt, Jack Perry looked like just another
Little League dad standing along the fence behind the visitor's
bench giving batting tips to his kid. Nobody would have suspected
that he was studying every move of the kid in number 11, as he had
for the last week.

Jack wasn't certain what the signs would be. Many kids had funny
little tics that surfaced under stress. Some blinked too much, some
spit every five seconds, some chewed the inside of their cheeks,
some did queer things with their mouths. But this kid was a wad of
raw nerve-endings. He looked possessed. Every few seconds he
would give his head a shake, as if trying to displace a migraine. But
the giveaway was his hands. He couldn't seem to control them. They
were in constant motion, like a couple of birds trying to take flight.
He sat on them, but they kept pulling free, rubbing his face or
secretly knuckling his forehead. At one point the coach asked if he

was okay. He nodded and went back to sitting on his hands, then began pawing the dirt with his feet. In minutes he had dug a small ditch.

For three innings the boy sat out the game. At the end of the third, Jack watched him walk off to the nearby woods, where the boys went to relieve themselves. Jack followed him. The kid had fallen to the shadows behind the gallery and moved into the dark shade of the oaks. Jack sauntered toward the opening where he had disappeared and waited until he was certain nobody had followed. Then he slipped into the woods.

What Jack Perry saw froze his blood. The kid was standing in front of a thick tree pounding his head against the trunk, as if trying to crush his skull.

No, as if trying to pound back something inside of it.

What Alphonse had done before ten ccs of·sodium penthelate ended his freak-house existence.

Suddenly the green wall of trees fell away, and Jack Perry was back in the fluorescent chambers of BiOmega, thick with the close smell of animal feces and urine and disinfectant. He could hear the rhesus chatter cut by the shrieking of a three-year-old male chimp with the red, raw head fighting the restraints to hammer his head against the grate of his cage. The harness had been a last-ditch effort to save him from the fate of the others, including another chimp that in a lunatic frenzy had battered his head against the bars.

The boy snapped his head at Jack. It was a look that chilled him.

Mother of God, thought Perry. The same feral eyes. He tried to say something to deflect the intensity, but they held him and in a split second he felt the kid drill his way through. The kid was in his head.

The moment passed when some boys outside the trees called Matty back to the field. He brushed past Jack Perry and out of the woods, leaving him stunned in his tracks and wondering in the aftermath of the kid's withdrawal if he knew that he, Jack Perry, had helped conjure the demon raging in his skull.

From the third-base line Jerry Mars watched the boy in red number 11 run out of the trees and return to the bench. Then he saw Jack

Perry come staggering out a minute later. He appeared drunk, his face colorless in the night lights. No, not drunk. More like he was dazed. Like he'd seen something unspeakable.

Jack Perry was still trembling as he made his way back to the gallery.

The kid had gotten a bat and moved on deck. The bill of his hat stuck out from his helmet, pulled so low his eyes were lost. But Jack thought he could feel them fingering his mind.

As he moved back to the fence, he glanced at the kid's parents in the grandstand, thinking that they had no idea what lay ahead of them.

CHAPTER

29

Matty's brain felt too small for his skull.

This wasn't a typical headache behind his eyebrows. This was a hot, throbbing presence at the core of his brain, fuzzing his vision and filling his ears with raucous noises.

It had hatched late that afternoon and steadily grew throughout the game. By the end of the third inning, it was nearly impossible to keep a thought from fragmenting under the crush. Worse still, he could not sit still on the bench or keep his hands from jumping around. That was when he took off for the woods and that guy had followed him, the one who had been spying on him for days. Who was he, what did he want?

Matty had had bad headaches of late, but this was the worst. Including the other night when Daisy came at him in the backyard. Of that he remembered very little because he had blacked out. All he recalled was her claws—so big—and the noise. And then his father waking him up in his bed the next morning. Everything else was a blank. His fear was that he would suddenly pass out again. He considered dropping out of the game, telling his coach that his head hurt, but that would upset his parents, especially his mother, who was already worried about his condition. Worse, the Bully Boys would consider it a wimp-out, that he couldn't face Bobby Gorawlski on the mound. Also, it was bottom of the fifth and he had not yet been to bat. With a runner on second, the ten-year-olds were counting on him to even the score.

It didn't help his head that Bobby glowered at him from the pitcher's mound. When his turn came, he selected his favorite bat, a heavy black metal number, and took a few practice swings. Bobby watched him, his eyes reflecting the meanness of years of being knocked around by a father with a hair-trigger temper.

Before Matty moved to the plate, Mitch called for a timeout. He went over to Matty and hung his arms loosely on his shoulder.

"Everything okay?"

"Yeah."

Mitch looked at him carefully. "You sure? You look a little jumpy."

"I'm okay."

"Listen, he's fast but he's sloppy. His pitches are all over the place."

Matty nodded and looked up. A secret grin twisted on Bobby's face. He spit in Matty's direction and ground the ball into his glove. He had pitched two no-hitter innings, not because he beamed them down the strike zone, but because the ten-year-olds were spooked by the sixty-mile-an-hour speed. "I'll be okay," Matty said.

"You're a hitter, Matty," Mitch said. "But make sure it's got your name on it. Otherwise, let it go. Let him walk you. We can score on balls and steals, okay?"

Matty nodded. God, his head hurt.

Mitch adjusted Matty's stance. He lowered the bat, raised his back elbow and pushed his feet closer. He also had him choke up.

The first two pitches were fast but high and outside, and Matty let them go by. "Good eye, Matty. Good eye. Make him work," Mitch shouted.

Matty's body was humming. He felt that if something didn't happen soon, he'd explode. The next pitch was low. Matty saw it was, yet he took a huge swing just to relieve the pressure. He missed, and the crowd groaned.

But the next pitch did not go by. He connected with a loud crack that sounded like gunfire. Half the grandstand shot to its feet. "Jesus!" somebody shouted. The ball bulletted high into the sky but sliced into the woods. "Weren't for the trees, that woulda ended up in the next mail zone."

"Straighten it out, Matty," Mitch shouted.

The next pitch was fast and high. With all his might Matty swung, but missed. And Bobby flashed him his best shit-eating grin.

For a brief moment Matty took hold of that grin. He knew that, if he chose, he could do something to that grin—something bad. But he let it go. He tapped his shoe; but before he set his stance, the next pitch came at him—so fast he barely knew he had been hit until he was rolling in the dirt with a sharp pain between his shoulder blades.

Mitch was quickly at his side, helping him up. Tears pressed from Matty's eyes, and through them he could see Bobby beaming with delight. Had his reflexes been a fraction duller, Matty knew he would have caught the pitch in his face.

The crowd applauded as he slogged down the base line. He took the bag, and before the next batter, Bobby cast an eye on him. Matty caught it fast and held him long enough for Bobby to feel the exchange. No wild pitch. Bobby had aimed and fired before his guard was up.

The next two batters struck out wildly, leaving Matty on first. He got his glove and headed to the infield. It was the top of the sixth, the last inning, with the Cardinals now one run up and raring to take home another victory.

Matty positioned himself between second and first. The sun had dipped over the treeline, casting blue spikes across the field. He could not wait for the game to be over. The clamor in his head was getting louder by the minute. Worse, there was that weird, tingling sensation in his legs and hands—a kind of warm giddiness that rapidly spread from his fingers up his arms and neck and across his scalp. He opened and closed his hands. They were humming to do bad stuff.

He looked toward the Magog Woods. He would give anything to be in there now. In the cool dark shadows, running to put out the wildfire coursing through his veins. Running as fast as he could "to sweat the poisons out," as his dad would say.

To sweat the poisons out.

To clear the madness jamming his head. His brain felt like a radio playing every station at once, the volume on max. He could hear the bright chittering of the things swarming around the night lights on the poles. He prayed the game would end fast. He prayed that he would not be involved in a play, because he'd fumble around and blow it. He could barely focus enough to stand still.

Mercifully, the first batter popped up to right field. The second batter was walked. That was bad, because it meant he would be pulled into play if the next batter connected.

Matty heard the chant before it registered. "Bobby, Bobby, Bobby."

The big, lumbering twelve-year-old approached the plate. He fanned the bat and spit a few hawkers. Matty barely processed him. It could have been anybody. Bobby was big and strong, and maybe he'd smash one and end the game.

The first pitch was outside. The second was high and Bobby went for it without contact. Before Matty knew it, the kid on first stole second. Matty was glad nobody tried to stop him. The runner looked at him, and Matty pulled back. His breathing was now an audible rasp.

Matty didn't see the next pitch, but he heard the loud, metal clank of a line drive. Movement was blurry. A roar from the crowd, and the kid on second whipped past him, rounded third and was heading home before Craig DeMaris in center field winged the ball toward Matty. Miraculously, he caught it on the base line just as another roar went up to announce the tie-breaking run.

The next moment Matty sensed before it actually arrived. He turned just in time to see Bobby bearing down on him. The victory run had been scored and the game was over, but Bobby still plowed into him, his elbow ramming his chest and catapulting him ten feet backward onto the dirt. His head hit with a solid thud.

For one stunning moment Matty slipped into a black hole void of the fugue of shrieks and smells that had afflicted his brain. He closed his eyes and squeezed onto the moment, somehow knowing it would all be back with a vengeance.

And it was.

When he opened his eyes again, his head was a rush of shrieking monkeys. But it did not distract him. The universe had been reduced to Bobby Gorawlski's chipped-tooth grin and the wad of watermelon bubble gum he worked furiously in his jaws as he glared down on him.

It was the one moment of shuddering clarity Matty would know that night.

He did not actually feel himself go through the air. It was only some vague time later that he put the pieces together. One moment he was on the ground, his breath coming wet and raspy from a half-crushed windpipe; the next, he was on top of Bobby, with his teeth sunk into the wedge of his tormentor's chin. A deep-bellied growl filled his ears. He was only half-aware that the sound rose from his own throat. All he could process was the urge to tear the flesh off Bobby Gorawlski's face.

Blows rained down on the sides of his head as Bobby tried to get away. But by now Matty was lost in that thick red fog. He heard Bobby scream. It came with such jagged-edged violence, for an instant Matty froze, his teeth clamped on Bobby's chin bone, warm blood filing his mouth.

Voices and bodies swirled around him. Hands pulled at his shirt, his arms, his head. Fingers dug into his throat.

"MATTY, STOP!"

His mother's scream.

Before she reached him, the crowd had pulled him off the boy. A wall of bodies had contracted around him. They were yelling and grabbing at him.

Behind him he saw the woods—the cool tangle of night.

He looked at the faces, then tore himself free of their grip and was off to the trees, his weird howl stopping the others in their tracks.

Had he looked back, he would have seen a frieze of faces, all pale with horror. All but one, that is—a tall, thin man in black, smiling as though at a kindred spirit.

CHAPTER

30

It all happened so fast that Terry could not remember pushing her way out of the grandstand or even stumbling over Betty Gorawlski. Nor was she aware of Calvin chasing after her into the infield. The moment had been broken into shards: Bobby plowing elbow first into Matty . . . Matty's body flying backward, his head smacking the ground . . . Matty shooting up from the ground, on top of Bobby, mouth fixed on the bully's fat pink face . . . Matty howling like a . . . like God knew what.

She went after him into the woods, leaving a knot of people around Bobby, who lay on the ground with a bloody towel against his face.

Voices swirled around her. Somebody said to get an ambulance. Another said he would need stitches. Another said something about drugs. Suddenly Betty Gorawlski's face filled her vision. "YOUR KID'S A GODDAMN ANIMAL," she screamed. "HE SHOULD BE PUT AWAY."

The words clanged in Terry's head as she pushed out of the crowd. Her son had shot into Magog Woods, and people were chasing after him.

When she got to the trees, she turned to Calvin. "Keep them back."

"What?"

"Don't let them go after him."

She ran toward the woods behind the others. "Don't you touch him," she yelled to them. "I'm his mother . . ."

One man in black stopped and turned toward her. In the light she caught the lean, sharp face and the wide razor-slash of a grin. She wondered how he could possibly find pleasure in this.

But the moment passed and she cut into the woods, leaving Calvin behind to keep back the others.

A few feet in, and the place was dense with nightfall. She could barely see the trees in front of her, having to keep her arms up to prevent impaling her face on branches.

She had no sense of direction and found no path through the underbrush. In the distance she could hear others who had gone after Matty. She called Matty's name. No response—nothing but the cicadas.

Several times she felt a rush of panic that she would stumble around until daybreak without finding him. Or that others would find him first.

He should be put away . . .

Or, that he would come out the other side and not stop . . . until he got to a highway to Boston or New York and become just another street kid.

She was not certain how long she had groped around in the woods. Maybe ten minutes, maybe thirty. The place had no time-space continuum. And she could not read the face of her watch. She was also not sure if she were cutting a path through the woods or stumbling around in circles. She was without direction until she heard a cry—the kind she imagined an animal would make when wounded and treed by baying hounds. Not a sound like any animal from these woods. But it was a beacon to her in the dark and she followed it with just enough ambient light to spare her from crashing into trees.

After some time she came to a clearing—or what she sensed was an opening in the canopy of oaktops. In the filtered moonlight her eyes took in something that nearly stopped her heart. Some huge creature was rearing up before her. Massive and round like a cave bear. Before the scream could dislodge from her throat, the creature took the familiar form of the granite outcropping—Druid Rock.

The next moment she was running past it, her feet now moving as if guided by radar. She knew the way.

TopTree.

Calvin had built it thirty feet from the ground in a four-pronged crotch of sturdy branches. Together they had pounded two-by-four rungs all the way up the tree. The underside of the base made a flat void against the sky. She could hear no sound coming from it. In fact, she could hear no sounds at all anymore. Not even the cicadas. It was as if somebody had suddenly switched off the nightwood audio. Maybe it was her presence.

Suddenly she could hear breathing. A raspy scraping. As she looked up the tree into the black, she said a silent prayer that at the end of this penny-dreadful nightmare she would not find her son dying of brain hemorrhage from whatever hideous condition had taken him over.

"Matty? Matty? It's me. Mom."

Nothing.

"Matty, I'm coming up."

Still nothing.

Her hand found a rung, she pulled herself onto it. Matty could climb to the top in less than ten seconds. They would stand at the bottom with his stop watch and laugh until her sides ached as Matty played monkey and shimmied up the tree. "Zero to TopTree in nine-point-four seconds," he would announce. "Another Guinness World Book record for Matthew Adam Hazzard."

She struggled to the top.

Matty was there, and he was not dead.

The sound of rough breathing came from the far corner. She pulled herself onto the platform. A shaft of moonlight fell onto a dark form on the floor opposite her. Because of the canopy she could only sense the lower part of his body. He appeared to be squatting in the corner facing her.

"Matty?"

A momentary ruffle in his breathing.

"Matty?"

She crawled to the left on hands and knees. Although she had not been up here for weeks, she knew the layout. Her old rattan clothes trunk was against the side rail beside a waterproof futon that Matty would sprawl out on and read. She opened the trunk and felt around and pulled out the battery-operated lantern they had given him last Christmas. (She could still smell the kerosene lamp he had picked up at a yard sale. Why hadn't he gotten rid of that, like she told him to? The thing was a fire hazard.)

She flicked on the light, half expecting that Matty would order her to turn it out. He said nothing. She turned the beam toward him. He was sitting in the far corner, asleep with Daisy Too, the stuffed cat, clutched in his arm. His face was scratched and bruised. There were bloodstains on his chin and turtleneck.

She put her hand on his shoulder. "Matty, Matty. It's Mom. Wake up."

He stirred. Gently she shook him. "Matty, it's okay. Wake up." In the light she saw his eyes slit open. "Honey, it's me, Mom."

His eyes widened. They locked on her, and for one moment she felt she was looking into eyes that did not belong to her son, but to a thing that would spring at her the way it had at Bobby Gorawlski.

But Matty did not spring at her. He groaned and pressed his face into the stuffed cat. Terry's heart ached as she stroked his arm. In the distance she could hear others coming for them.

"Mom?" he whispered. "I did something bad, didn't I?"

"You don't remember?"

He shook his head, puzzled, then looked down at his shirt and pants. "We had a game," he said, trying to recall the night. "I was playing second . . ."

"That's right."

Slowly he began to rub his brow. "And I had a wicked headache. Then, I think I fell. Then I was up here." He stopped and looked at her. "How did I get up here?"

"You don't remember anything else?"

"No."

There was no sign of dissembling or pretense. "You don't remember Bobby Gorawlski running into you? Or you jumping on him?"

"Bobby . . ." He trailed off as he tried to put it together. "Kind of," he said. "But not really. Did I hurt him?"

Terry nodded. The lithium had failed miserably.

"Bad?"

"I think he'll need stitches."

"What did I do?"

"You really don't remember?"

"No."

"You . . . you bit him in the face."

"Oh God . . . that's why there's blood on me. What's going to happen to me?" His voice was small.

"You're going to need medical help, hon. You're having some kind of spells that are causing you to . . . lose control. We'll talk to Dr. Tojian. But you're going to have to have help. You're going to have to cooperate so that we can make you better."

He looked at the stuffed animal with the foolish, big-toothed grin. "I miss Daisy."

She had been gone for the last three days. "She'll be back, I'm sure," Terry said, although she was convinced that the cat had gotten run over someplace.

"No, she won't," he said, his voice cracking. "She used to come up here and lick my face and sleep with me." He closed his eyes again and the tears ran down his cheeks. "She'll never come back."

"She might have gotten lost."

"Cats don't get lost."

"If she doesn't come back, we'll get another one."

A moment of silence, then in a trembly voice he said, "Mom, I don't want to be bad, I don't want to do these things . . ."

"Matty, you're *not* bad."

He shook his head. "I'm weird. I'm a sicko. Everybody says so, that's why she's gone. She's afraid of me. Everybody is. I do these bad things—"

"Matty, stop saying that. You have a medical problem we're going to take care of."

She made an effort to pull him toward her, but suddenly he stiffened and sat up. "I can feel them." He was staring into the black.

"Who?"

"The animals. Raccoons, squirrels, dogs. It's like I can tell what they're feeling, when they're afraid . . . I can smell them, inside my head . . ."

"Matty, what are you *talking* about?"

"I mean, I can get inside them, *their* heads, and . . . and I know they know it." He was still staring off into the black trees. "It's like sometimes I think I'm like them, one of them . . ."

Terry was nearly giddy with fright. "No, you're *not*, Matthew, and stop talking that way."

"How did I get this way?"

"I don't know, but you're going to be okay. Hear me? Now let's go home—"

Suddenly he pushed her away, perched himself on his hands and knees and, incredibly, seemed to test the air with his nose. He moved to the edge and peered down.

"What? What is it . . . ?"

"A man."

"Who? What man?"

Terry moved to his side with the light. She aimed it down. Nothing but the empty rungs leading up and the black woods.

Matty looked out into the jumble of black trees. "He's watching us," he said in a voice barely audible.

"Who?"

"Smells like smoke."

"Smoke? Who does? What are you talking about?" Before her words were out, there was a rustling in the bushes. Feet on dry twigs and leaves. "Who's there?" Terry called out.

A flickering of lights through the brush. "Terry?"

"Calvin," Terry cried in relief. "It's only Dad," she said to Matty.

"No," Matty whispered. "Somebody else."

But his words slipped by her. A moment later Calvin and Mitch Tojian pushed their way to the base of TopTree. With them were two policemen.

"He's all right," Terry said. "He's fine. We're coming down."

The police stepped back from the tree. Whatever had distracted Matty in the woods had apparently passed. He swung onto the trunk and shimmied down. Calvin caught him at the bottom and hugged him.

Matty looked at the police. "Am I going to jail?"

"Of course not," Calvin said.

Dr. Tojian put his arm around Matty's shoulder. "You feeling okay?"

Matthew nodded.

"Good, because I thought it might be a good idea if you came with me."

"To your house?"

"No, a hospital."

CHAPTER

31

They drove Matty to the children's psychiatric unit of McLean Hospital in Belmont. Terry rode with Matty in the rear of a police cruiser, Calvin and Mitch Tojian tailing their cars. Matty slept against his mother's shoulder all the way.

Because of the severity of the attack, Matty was released in custody of Dr. Tojian, who assured the investigating officers that Matty needed immediate professional attention. Meantime, Bobby Gorawlski was taken by ambulance to Emerson emergency, his mother screaming that she would press charges, sue the Hazzards' asses off for damage. At the moment that was the least of their worries.

McLean looked nothing like a hospital and everything like a New England college campus. Located on hundreds of rolling green acres twelve miles west of Boston, the place consisted of a dozen or more huge Victorian and colonial homes originally designed for wealthy mental patients. The one exception was the children's center—a squat, cubical structure with plastic bubble-light ports on the roof. The unit housed, schooled and treated a few dozen children, many of whom had suffered some form of sexual, physical and/or drug abuse. They ranged in age from five to seventeen; they were racially diverse; they came from all over. And they shared one fundamental characteristic: rage. It was where they checked Matty in for four days of observation and testing.

After he was medicated and put to bed, a resident pediatric psychiatrist, Dr. Don Givens, reviewed possible procedures Matty might be put through, depending on their observations. Rage in some children, he explained, was one manifestation of aggressive behavior intended to establish control, dominance or superiority over others. It could also be strictly pathological—the results of birth injuries, fetal drug or alcohol syndrome, cranial trauma, encephalitis, early seizures or a variety of neurological disorders. Or, in absence of such, prolonged abuse.

Although Matty's attack of Bobby Gorawlski was not unprovoked, and though there was a history of animosity between the boys, the ferocity of Matty's attack was seen as out of proportion to the provocation. One guess was that Matty had experienced some kind of seizure. But in light of the elevated androgynes in his blood and symptoms of precocious puberty, it seemed more likely that he was suffering some kind of neurological disorder. Which meant a variety of tests—from psychiatric profiles to neurological and chemical workups: electro-encephalograms and SPECT (single photon emission computerized tomography) imaging.

Calvin asked most of the questions during the conference, while Terry sat in numbed silence. On the way out Mitch assured them that he would stay on Matty's case as primary physician, while Dr. Givens would head up the psychiatric testing. His expertise was children of violent behavior.

children of violent behavior

All the way home, the phrase echoed and reechoed in Terry's brain.

"He's got it."

"How do you know?"

"The real estate agent," Claire Manning Wick said. "Her nephew's on the Little League team that played his team last night. She said somebody knocked him down with a pitch and he went nuts. He attacked the kid like an animal. She said if they hadn't pulled him off, he would have bitten him to death. The kid needed sixty stitches."

"What about the Hazzard kid?" DeVoe asked.

"He ran off into the woods," she said. "Howling, or some such."

"They find him?"

Claire nodded.

"Great," DeVoe said. "We've gone public."

They were in Julius Wick's new office, outfitted in a claret-and-blue Bijar and a robust mahogany desk, at which Julius sat facing his wife and DeVoe. He said nothing.

"What's in our favor is the rumor going around," Claire said. "They're saying he's got a drug problem. The agent says he's got a reputation for being aloof and a little unpredictable in his behavior, sometimes violent. She says people are speculating he's been experimenting with cocaine or LSD."

"Until they start sampling his body fluids," DeVoe said. "Where's he now?"

"A private hospital in Belmont."

"What else did she say?"

Claire shook her head. "She carried on about the house being off the market."

DeVoe leaned back in his chair. "Time to call Roman."

Julius snapped his head around. "Christ, no, Frank."

"You got a better suggestion?"

"We're *not* in the business of killing children—"

"Oh? What the hell were you doing with Black Flag?"

"That's not the same thing."

"Did you think your designer virus was partial only to Viet Cong guerillas over twenty-one? Give me a break, he's got to be taken out."

"Can't you people ever come up with any other options? Does it always mean . . . eliminating someone in the way? And now a child?"

"In a way it's a humane option," DeVoe said. "We do nothing and the country watched a twelve-year-old boy turn into an animal because of a secret government project with the president's *and* your name on it."

"So we're doing him a *favor* by killing him?"

"Actually, him and maybe a lot more people," DeVoe said. "Ever consider the possibility that he might be contagious? I'm no scientist, but what if he's now the carrier of a whole new kind of plague that attacks the rage centers and is spread on contact? Ever think of *that*, Julius? It would make AIDS look like chicken pox."

"That's ridiculous," Julius said. "It's not communicative."

DeVoe leaned forward. "You don't know that, Julius. You only tested it on rabbits and monkeys, then you buried it in the ground twenty-three years ago and ran off."

Julius said nothing.

"If the boy dies," his wife said, "the first thing the mother'll want is to move out. When it's done and all blown over, we get the agent to resurface the offer and get in there and neutralize the stuff before it spreads."

"And I suppose you'll get Roman's guy to make it look like another accident."

"That was a mistake," DeVoe said.

"He shot Marcus Wiley *and* his daughter," Julius said.

"Roman said he didn't have a chance. We'll make sure he does it right this time."

"And how do we do that?" Julius asked. "The guy's a hired killer without a name or face. If he screws up again . . ." He shook his head, as though disgusted with himself for even talking this way.

"He's only in it for the fee, which, you'll recall, is contingent upon performance. Like it or not, it's the only leverage we've got."

Claire gave Julius a shut-up look, then said to DeVoe, "It's going to have to be soon. Once they start testing him, they're going to connect the ends."

DeVoe nodded. His hope was that the kid's condition was so anomalous that nobody would think of environmental testing until they ran out of other possibilities. The virus would mask itself as a hormonal disorder that could even be deduced as genetic. The last place they'd check to look was the tap water.

"If the virus has entered his system," Julius said, trying to come to grips with reality and forestall the solution of DeVoe, "it will probably prove fatal. Why not . . . let it run its course? We can still take the place over—"

"Too risky and too unpredictable. The longer he hangs on, the more they know about his condition. Look, I don't like it either. He's a kid, but the reality is, it's him or us. President Morgan Reese is the closest thing to an actual Greenpeacer without the Birkenstocks. If he's linked to the leakage of a genocidal hormone festering in the public-water supply, we're dead, all of us."

"But nobody's going to trace it to Morgan Reese?"

"It's public record: he worked in the Defense Department as budget officer when you and your pals were doing Dr. Strangelove experiments. All it'll take is one snoopy reporter pressing the freedom-of-information button and the proverbial cat will be out of the proverbial bag," DeVoe said.

"How would anybody think to look that up?"

"That's not the question. It's what if somebody does. Morgan Reese is one of forty-odd men in history who've held his office. He's the consequences of all he has ever been—that's the weight of the office. He was the financial overseer of genocidal warfare, which just happened to get dumped in the local water supply? If you don't think this will fly in his face, think of the number of AGs or Supreme Court nominees who got rolled because they smoked a joint at a party thirty years ago or didn't pay taxes on their cleaning ladies. Or think about Watergate and Irangate and Whitewater and the sexual claims against Bill Clinton. And speaking of that, let me tell you why JFK lasted as long as he did: because there were people like me who kept the smoke machines going while he was jumping up and down on Marilyn Monroe."

"It's not the president you're concerned about," Julius said.

DeVoe nodded. "That's right," he said. "Ultimately, it's our own hides."

Julius looked at his wife and shook his head.

For a long moment she closed her eyes. When she opened them, they were small blue beads. "Call Roman," she said to DeVoe.

CHAPTER

32

With a yellow highlighter Jack Perry had traced his route on the map the AAA had given him. He would take the Mass. Pike to 84 straight across Connecticut through the New York Interstate, across Pennsylvania to Hagerstown, Maryland, where he would lay up. Then on through West Virginia and Virginia to 40 and straight across all the way to Tucumcari, New Mexico. The trip would take him five days. If he left by noon, he'd make Hagerstown Holiday Inn by nine that night. The rest of the nights, he'd sleep in the trailer on the Interstate. He could not wait to get out of the state.

Earlier that morning he had shopped for food and supplies and filled the van with gas. Only two matters were left before he disappeared. First, to finish putting on the new muffler pipe. Then, a final stop before he dropped off the face of the earth for good.

The French had a saying: "The softest pillow is a clear conscience." He could not sleep knowing the Hazzard kid had been infected by a virus that only he could identify. Nor could he just disappear while it spread throughout the community with Doomsday vengeance. It was morally imperative that he do something, if not just to save lives, to atone for having helped developed this horror. For days he had agonized over how best to unburden himself. But the murders of Marcus Wiley and his daughter reduced his options to one.

He would not go to the parents, after all. They had enough on their hands with their kid. Besides, he did not want to face their reaction, their interrogation, their blame. Nor did he want to be prime witness in the case once the authorities were summoned to investigate. Overnight he would be at the eye of maybe the biggest

205

scandal since Watergate. And with his face splashed all over the media, just how long would he last until somebody put a bullet through his head? Even if he was put in a witness protection program, they'd still get him. If he had to go underground, the last people he'd want to know was the government. The only option was the boy's doctor.

Earlier he had called the man to say he had information about Matthew Hazzard's condition. He did not specify, nor did he identify himself. The doctor tried to press him for information, but he said he'd be in at eleven o'clock, then hung up. It would be a short visit during which he would unload all he could recall of Project Black Flag, the science, the monstrous consequences, the wanton disposal and, now, a deadly coverup. He'd name names, show him the obituaries, even his old project notes. And the warning that this was a high-level coverup that might extend to the Hazzard family. Once he'd done all that, he would disappear forever.

It was a little after ten and he was lying on his back under the van held up in the rear by the wheeljack. It would take him only a few minutes to clamp up the new tailpipe. He was just fitting the bolts in place when he heard a car approach. He rolled back out. A maroon sedan with Rhode Island plates had pulled up, and a tall, thin-faced man in a powder blue sport coat approached.

"John Victor Perry?"

Jack stiffened. He lowered his hand so that it rested against the snub-nosed .38 that filled his right pocket. "Who wants to know?"

The man handed him a card. There were only three fingers on his hand. But no scars of shiny skin to indicate an accident or burn. "My name is Jerry Mars. I'm a private investigator."

The man's face was vaguely familiar. "What can I do for you?"

"Well . . ." he said, looking around to say it was private, "my business is rather confidential."

"This'll have to do," Jack said, meaning the tar-top driveway.

The man made an exaggerated nod of conciliation. "No problem."

Except for the cars rolling by, nobody was in sight. The man removed a newspaper and held it up. The photo of Marcus Wiley stared at Jerry. "You might have seen the article." He reached into his briefcase, but before he could remove what he was going for, Jack had out his gun.

"Put your hands over your head. Now!"

Jerry Mars looked more amused than frightened. "Do you always greet visitors this way?"

"I said put your hands on your head." Jerry did, and Jack patted him down. He was not carrying a weapon. And his briefcase was full of papers, including a group photo of Stefan Karsky, Maria Terranova, Marcus Wiley and himself. They were closing in.

"Where did you get this?"

"It was sent to my office anonymously, Mr. Perry, and that's what I want to talk to you about. Do I have to keep my hands like this? You can see for yourself that I'm not armed."

Jack let him lower his hands but did not take the gun off him. If this guy was a private detective, how come he didn't carry a gun?

"I'll be straight with you. I have been hired to investigate these deaths because it's believed they are related to and part of a coverup of activities involving a scientific project you and they worked on at BiOmega Laboratories."

How did it get out? Who was left? Jack looked at the photo. He remembered posing for it, must have been in 1972. Maria Terranova had taken it with her camera set on a time release. She wanted a shot of everybody in the lab. Except somebody was missing. The photo had been cropped just to the right of Wiley. But in the slant of the sun the shadow of the cropped figure fell across Wiley's white shirt. Julius Wick.

The man's card said Mars Investigative Services, with a Boston address and telephone number. "Who are you working for?" Jack asked.

Mars nodded to say that it was a reasonable question. "As I said, sir, I'm a private investigator, and I do my best to uphold the confidentiality of my clients."

Jack raised the gun to the center of Jerry Mars's chest. "Who sent you?"

The man stared at him, a mirthless grin spreading across his face. Jack couldn't tell if it came from a perverse kind of pleasure or if he was taunting him. Or if it was just a macho display of arrogance.

"Mr. Perry, believe me, I have no intention of dying for professional ethics." As he said it, Mars simply stared at Jack as if watching a movie in his eyes.

"I said, who sent you?"

"Does the name Matthew Hazzard mean anything to you?"

Jack felt his stomach twist but said nothing.

Mars made a little nod. "Okay, then. Matthew Hazzard is a twelve-year-old boy who is in considerable danger, and I have reason to believe that you know what I am talking about."

Jack badly wanted to believe this guy, to open up to him, but he also realized he should fight the impulse.

"Maybe you figure wrong."

"Then why the gun?"

Jack wanted a smart comeback, but all he could come up with was: "Because I don't like people probing into my business." He could see the guy was not impressed.

"Mr. Perry, I'm investigating the possibility that your former associates were murdered. In a sense I'm working for you, too."

The guy knew so much, but how? "I don't need your protection."

"I think you do, and it's because of what you know. It would make sense if you simply answered a few questions."

"Julius Wick . . ." The man just slipped out of his thoughts. God-damn . . . he was losing it . . .

"Who?"

The son of a bitch, it had to be him. Otherwise, why was he razored out of the photo?

"Mr. Perry, I don't know who Julius Wick is, but I do know that a young boy's life is in danger. And every minute we play twenty questions, the more the danger increases. If you are not going to cooperate, then please let me leave."

Jack looked at the business card, then waved the gun at him. "Put your hands back on your head and lie face down on the ground."

"I beg your pardon?"

"You heard me." He had to get it back, let this guy know he knew what was going on.

"Just what do you have in mind, sir?" Jerry Mars did not smile as he lay down as told while Jack went into the trailer and came back out with a portable phone.

"If you're calling the police, you'll only bring attention to yourself."

He was right about that. Jack punched the number on the card. It rang four times, an answering machine kicked on and a pleasant female voice said, "You have reached the office of Mars Investigative Services. Mr. Mars and his associates are out of the office at the moment, but if you have a message, you may leave it at the sound of the beep."

Jack put the phone back and returned. He put the gun into his pocket and reached down to help Mars to his feet. "I'm sorry about this."

The man got up, brushing himself off. "I understand. In fact, you're wise to be cautious."

Jack still felt uneasy, even though he now believed Mars, partly because he so much needed to. It was lonely out in the cold. During the next several minutes he listened as Mars rattled off details about the Black Flag project that, to his knowledge, remained classified information. He mentioned things that only those intimate with the project could have known or passed on to him. "The missing piece is what it all has to do with Matthew Hazzard."

"Mr. Mars, I don't know Matthew Hazzard, at least not personally."

"But you know who he is."

He could hear that small voice telling him not to let on so much, but it was fading. "Yes."

Jerry Mars nodded emphatically. "Good." And then as if to reassure Jack, Mars went on, "His father is an English professor and his mother is a housewife, so professionally they don't appear to have been linked with BiOmega. In fact, they seem to be innocents in all this, wouldn't you say?"

"Yes."

"Then we're back to the question of connection. Can you help us?"

Jack wanted to get it out, but a gnawing instinct still held him back.

Jerry Mars, sensing his conflict, reached into his coat pocket and pulled out a newspaper clipping that he handed to Jack. It was a photo from the Middlesex *Ledger* of the year's Devil Dogs Little League team. Jerry pointed to Matthew in the lineup. "He plays second base and I hear he's very good."

Jack looked at the picture. "I think he's been infected with the virus," Jack heard himself say. "His house is where we disposed of the stuff and the dead test animals. It was just a bunch of trees in the woods at the time. We hired a backhoe and dug a hole and laid out the containers and covered them up. I guess there was a leak, because the boy's sick."

Jerry's eyes focused like a cat on a bird. "And somebody doesn't want anyone to know?"

"Yes."

"A coverup."

"I guess."

"And you think it might be this Julius Wick."

Jack shrugged a maybe.

"Do you have any idea where Mr. Wick might be found?"

". . . the White House."

"No kidding." Mars' face lit up.

Jack then told about the news coverage he had followed of Julius Wick's new post. Jerry Mars listened with great interest.

"Do you have any idea about the kind of effect the virus might have on Matthew?"

"Rage . . ."

"Rage?"

And Jack described what he remembered of the lab animals and the awful fits of violence. When he got through, he felt less relieved than drained. He had gotten it out, but somehow the actual articulation of all the sordid details left him feeling hollow, sullied. Before Jerry Mars left, Jack asked him if he would be called as a witness.

Mars shook his head. "I'm a private investigator, not a law-enforcement officer. I cannot issue arrest warrants. It's possible I might drop back, in case I've got a few more questions, but your identity and this conversation will remain completely confidential. I can promise you that," he said, and held out his hand. "I can't thank you enough. You can rest assured that you may have helped save Matthew Hazzard's life."

"Hope so."

"You have my card, in case you think of anything else."

Jack nodded and watched him get back into his car and drive off. He walked out to the road, which was empty in both directions.

Back inside the trailer, he drank a glass of milk, felt better, and rolled back under his van. Relief began to loosen the knot in his gut. It was out and in the hands of a private investigator with experience and the law on his side. He was working for the family, he'd know where to turn about the boy's problem. No need now for him to go to Dr. Tojian. The investigator, Mars, would pass that on, he told himself.

While Jack worked on the muffler clamp, he let his thoughts wander, and for the first time in some twenty minutes he could think more clearly and begin to wonder about the specific nature of the threat to Matthew Hazzard. Who, for example, had notified the Hazzard family? Had they received a tip-off? An anonymous call? If so, why were they out there at the baseball game last night? And a call from whom? The only one left was Julius Wick, but why was his face cut out of the photo? He should have asked Mars where he'd gotten the photo. He thought about other possibilities—government connections, but they wouldn't put out contracts on a boy . . . would they? And even if so, how would a private investigator get hold of it?

As he was able to consider the possibilities, he began to wish he had asked this Mars more questions, wished he had been more circumspect, more cautious . . .

And suddenly a chilling thought emerged. What if this Jerry Mars, Private Investigator, was not what his card said, that he was somebody working for whoever (Julius and Claire Manning Wick?) was behind the killings of Marcus Wiley and the others? A crazy notion? The product of an imagination tenderized by paranoia? Well, some paranoia makes sense . . .

This all happened just about the time Julius Wick was tapped by the president to head up the Agency of Biotechnology. A position that did not allow for skeletons in the closet. And, God knew, the iron maiden, Claire, would see to that, yes, even if it meant . . .

And if this Jerry Mars was their hired killer . . . if he had murdered the others . . . Jack Perry was the odd man out. Of course, the son of a bitch looked familiar. He had seen him the other night at that Little League game. That guy all in black. He wasn't guarding the kid—he was stalking Jack Perry.

He should have stuck with his resolve to talk to the doctor. His mother's favorite adage was: "Your first thought is always your best thought." She was right, and he may have put his life on the line not acting on it.

His heart pounded wildly, and his hands could barely work the wrench on the last two bolts. The raspiness of his breath magnified under the close ceiling of the van. Then, as if in a half-glimpsed premonition, he heard the sound of traffic, and a side effect . . . too close for the usual road noise.

He looked down the length of his body to see the light blue car turn sharply onto the asphalt and head straight for his van's rear. It slammed into the van, knocking it off the tirejack and crushing the last breath in John Victor Perry's chest.

CHAPTER

33

He stands about five feet, slender. No ear studs or rings like the others. His hair is greasy; he looks dirty. He's maybe twelve or thirteen, but looks older in the black jacket and tight jeans. A cigarette is stuck behind an ear. The pack over his left shoulder probably contains all his earthly possessions. It is the hunger in his eyes that identifies him as one of the street kids who hustle the train stations and bus terminals at night, who roam the subways and back streets in packs for handouts, leasing their bodies for food and dope.

The man with the narrow face strikes up a conversation with the boy, who says his name is Brendon. It's a nice name, the man tells him. The boy offers a flat smile. He's still new to the scene. Nervous. Recent runaway.

A few people eye the tall man in black and the boy hunched together. They could be father and son, or social worker and client, or a lay priest and returnee. Or partners in commerce. It was not unusual for men to cruise the station for boys.

The man says something, the kid sniggers and mutters something back. The man nods and names a price. The boy agrees, makes a high sign to his mates to say he's off.

He struts his way through the small crowd of travelers toward the side-street exit. The man is a step behind him. He estimates the boy's body. Tight, athletic. Will do just fine.

They step outside the station. The night is loud and cool. Buses pull out in caravans from the bays.

They walk to the car. The boy removes the cigarette from his ear and lights up. The man waits until the boy finishes his butt before he unlocks the door. He sucks a last drag and flicks it away like a movie tough. The man lets him inside.

"Stuff's bad for your health."

They drive.

In the outer pocket of his jacket is the set of handcuffs. In the inside breast pocket is the hypodermic needle. He reaches in and taps the protective cap with his finger. He has never used one on humans. Only dogs. Should work fine, he thinks as he drives them to the motel.

CHAPTER

34

The only explanation they offered for Matty's absence was "medical reasons." Of course, word of the attack spread across town like a firestorm, and with it rumors that Matty had been on drugs and was being treated at some detox center for adolescents.

The Hazzards could not care less what stories circulated. They were too beset by fears that their son was suffering an inoperable brain tumor. They talked briefly with him over the phone during his four days at McLean's but could not visit because tests were ongoing day and night. On the morning of the third day, Mitch Tojian called to say that the staff was ready to review the results of their assays. The meeting was set for ten.

They arrived at nine-thirty and met Mitch in the lobby. Matty was downstairs having a late breakfast. They could visit after the consultation. He led them down a corridor to a conference room. Waiting for them were Dr. Givens and a woman introduced as Dr. Jean Hagan, a pediatric psychiatrist. On the table were folders, fat with papers.

Terry felt her heart gulp for blood. Nobody in the room was smiling, and Mitch's face was stretched. He spoke with a flat voice. "Let me begin by saying that we think we've located the source of Matty's problem, which is half the battle." His eyes moved from Terry's face to Calvin's. "To give you a picture of what's been going on, we thought it best to review the diagnostic stages of his condition."

Mitch opened the folder and put on his half-glasses. "Two weeks ago Matty came into my office on the pretext of fitting him for his Little League uniform. That's when I first noticed his unusual musculature and strength. It was also when I got a glimpse of his enlarged genitals and pubic hair, which explained his extreme modesty. On a routine check of his eyes with an ophthalmoscope, I noticed something unusual about their anatomy. The pigment epithelium on the back surfaces glistened like that of a newborn's. Not only could he read the bottom lines on the eye chart, he could do it in the dark. In short, he has night vision significantly beyond the normal range. My first concern was that perhaps a tumor had developed in the pituitary region of his brain and was affecting the optic nerves.

"Last week, before he entered the hospital, I conducted a more thorough visual exam of Matty, and it was clear from the size and dark pigmentation of his testes and penis and the amount and distribution of pubic and axial hair that he was a grade five on the Tanner scale of puberty. Likewise, his blood workup showed very high readings of testosterone and other hormones, all supporting the suspicion of a tumor in the region of the pituitary gland, which secretes hormones. What had bothered me then was the elevation of several different hormones. A pituitary adenoma usually secretes a single hormone. We then called for an MRI the same day to look for any brain tissue changes." Mitch then opened a large envelope and took out photographic emulsions. "The results came back the day after we checked Matty into McLean's." He held the emulsions up to the light of the window. There were colored images of Matty's brain shot from different angles, but Terry could barely focus.

Mitch's pencil now pointed to a yellow blotch at the center of one image. "Compared to normal brain anatomy, there appear to be structural changes in the amygdala, the almond-shaped structure here that regulates hypothalamic activity and can bring on sudden violent behavior when stimulated or damaged."

"Are you saying there's no damage there?" Calvin asked.

"Not so much damage as hypertrophy," said Dr. Givens. "The amygdala is unusually large for a boy of Matty's age."

"Meaning what?" said Terry, afraid to ask and afraid not to.

"Well, we're not so sure," Dr. Givens said. "But we're certain there was no tumor, as first expected." He put his hand on another pile of envelopes. "Two days ago Dr. Hagan and I did an electrical study, an EEG, and a SPECT, which allows picturing of the metabolic activity. What we found were clear hot spots of brain activity in the area of the pituitary and amygdala, which would account for his explosive behavior at the game."

Next he removed from one of the folders a long strip of EEG scrawlings. "Although Matty has no history of seizures nor any signs while he'd been here, the electrical profile shows eleptiform spike waves deep in the temporal lobes, bilaterally, characteristic of epileptic seizures. What all this means is that there is remarkable electrical activity in those areas associated with violent behavior and the secretion of male steroids and other hormones." Mitch took off his glasses. "However, there are *no* signs of tumors or seizures, and except for the enlarged amygdala, no other unusual brain physiology."

"So, what's causing it?" Calvin asked.

Dr. Givens nodded to Dr. Hagan. "Well, that was our question, because the results are random and unusual," she said. "Twelve years of Dr. Tojian's records on Matty show no early signs of neurological disorders—seizures, headaches, lack of attentiveness, trouble sleeping, dizzy spells. That's when we began to suspect something else was going on."

She stopped for a moment and looked to Dr. Givens. "Two days ago we did a lumbar puncture—a spinal tap. We extracted some cerebral spinal fluid and sent it off for an elaborate analysis." She penned the folder on her lap to a packet of pale green computer printouts covered with a long list of figures. "They were quite thorough," she said as she fanned through the sheets. She stopped at the last page. "There appears to be a strange substance in Matty's CSF."

"Strange substance?" Calvin asked.

"Well, there's an unlabeled chemical in high concentration in the neurological fluid that has the signature of a hormone that is chemically similar to human gonadotropins but isn't something naturally produced by the body. And yet it appears to have caused the hypertrophy of the amygdala, as well as a surge of gonadotropins that accounts for his sudden outbursts."

Terry's voice was unsteady. "What the hell are you saying?"

Mitch made a gesture to the others. "Terry, Dr. Hagan is saying that some kind of synthetic compound has gotten into Matty's system and is throwing it off. Whatever it is, it's the culprit behind all the changes he's experienced, including his rage."

"Synthetic compounds? Where did it come from?"

Mitch shook his head. "My first thought was that Matty had gotten hold of some anabolic steroids, but the molecular structure of the stuff didn't match any of the synthetic steroids going around. And after talking to him, I was convinced he hadn't taken any. He also swore he'd never experimented with drugs, although he confessed sampling marijuana once and hating it. I have no reason to believe that he wasn't telling the truth. Besides," he added, "no drug I know of would have the effect this stuff has on his vision. As I said, he can see in the dark."

"I'm no chemist," Dr. Hagan said, "but the substance is bizarrely elusive. It's a lipophilic substance, which means it can cross the blood-brain barrier. What's strange is that it appears to do contrary things . . . drops the production of sexual hormones while at the same time activating them. I think its effect depends on the concentration. Whatever, it appears to be something that was purposefully manufactured."

"Over the last few days," Dr. Givens added, "we tried to establish a time-line. We talked to Matty to determine when he started noticing the changes in his body—the hair growth, the headaches, his night-sensitivity, his rage. From what we can tell, it all started late last year, before Christmas—which jibes with when you started noticing his mood swings. Does that seem about right to you?"

"Yes," said Calvin " . . . when we had the pool built."

"The pool?" Dr. Givens said.

"The backyard was all torn up." Calvin's voice was flat.

Givens looked at the others. "I'm afraid I'm not following you, Mr. Hazzard."

"Our backyard was once used as a dump for a biological research lab. It's possible, with all the digging and heavy equipment, that containers could have been ruptured," he said. "Our well water lies under our backyard."

"I see."

Terry gave him a look, hearing this for the first time.

"I take it you've had EPA out to monitor it."

"We had the water tested last week," Calvin said, avoiding Terry's stare.

"Last week." Dr. Givens frowned. "How long have you known about the dump?"

"Since I bought the place," Calvin said uneasily. "Ten years—"

"Ten years?"

"Terry didn't know . . ."

There was a moment of crackling tension. "I see."

"I was told when I saw the place how the land had been used, but that there had been no reports of health problems with the previous tenants," Calvin hurried on. "I didn't tell you, hon, you wouldn't have approved. And at the price it seemed too good an opportunity to pass up . . ."

Terry turned away toward the window.

Tojian broke the tension. "Do you know the nature of the research firm?"

"No," Calvin said. "And I think it folded some twenty years ago."

"Well," Dr. Tojian said, "there may or may not be a connection. But it makes sense that we take another look at your water before we draw any conclusions or file a report with any authorities. I have a friend whose lab is equipped to screen water for microbiology."

"How do we treat him?" Calvin asked.

"We're hoping that the standard treatment for precocious puberty and the related behavioral problems will check the progress. For the last twenty-four hours we've had him on antihypertensives and anticonvulsants, as well as L-dopa to reverse the hirsutism. We've also put him on propranolol to counter hormone stimulation."

"Propranolol," Terry repeated. "Isn't that what they use on rapists?"

"It's a widely used antiandrogenic agent to counter hormonal stimulation. At the extreme end of the spectrum, it is used to treat sexual offenders. It's commonly used for Cushing's Syndrome."

"When can he come home?" Calvin asked.

"Tomorrow. We still want to monitor his reaction to the different medication. So far it's working well."

"Then what?" Terry asked.

"He'll be sedated some," Dr. Hagan said, "but he can function almost as normal. However, we recommend that he take the next week off from school until his body adjusts to the medications. If all goes well, he can resume a normal routine the week after. However, it might be a good idea to take him out of Little League."

Terry nodded.

"Also, I'll want to have periodic checkups," Mitch said. "In fact, I've scheduled one for Friday. Just be sure he stays on the medication and keep an eye on him. If he has any problems or reports anxiety or headaches, whatever, give me a call. Night or day."

Terry began to fill up again, and Mitch put his hand on her arm. "I know this is very difficult for you, but I do think we can turn things around."

Terry nodded. "What happens if the medication fails?"

"It shouldn't," Dr. Hagan said. "And if it does, we've a lot of backup weapons. The important thing is that he not go off the medication and that he be checked periodically."

Terry nodded. "But he's stubborn."

"We've already impressed upon him the importance of his treatment."

"And if he goes off?"

Dr. Hagan looked at her for a moment, then said, "I'm not sure, but I would guess that at some point his condition may not be reversible."

Mitch quickly looked at his watch. "We can get Matty now, but before that, I'd like to take a blood sample from both of you, if you don't mind."

Calvin and Terry agreed. The other doctors left and Mitch extracted a few ccs of blood from the Hazzards. They then followed him down the hall to the entrance lobby.

Matty was waiting for them in a chair by the window. A male aide was sitting quietly with him. Terry had prepped herself not to cry when she saw him, telling herself that a breakdown was the last thing Matty needed. But when she saw him in that chair, looking so fragile, she felt the tears come again.

The medication had worked its sedative effect. Matty's shoulders were drooped and his eyes were like spent fuses. What shocked her was how dark his face was. In the three days a beard had begun to form like a film on his face.

Terry wiped her eyes and sat beside him. "Hi, honey."

Matty looked at her, then looked back through the window.

"How do you feel?"

"All right."

"Did they explain what they're doing?"

He nodded.

"You're going to be fine."

"We'll be coming for you tomorrow," Calvin said. "Just one more day."

Matty said nothing, just continued to stare out the window at the playground. He looked lobotomized.

Calvin took Terry's arm as they left the building for their car. "I'm sorry," he said. "But there may not be any connection . . ."

Terry did not respond. It was a bright, warm May morning, but she could barely focus. She was functioning on autopilot, walking to the parking area by mechanical reflexes.

In the car Calvin asked if she wanted to stop someplace for a coffee. She shook her head. She just wanted to go home, to fall into unconsciousness.

She stared blankly out the window as the car pulled past the children's unit. Matty was still sitting by the window, his eyes fixed beyond the playground. She waved and Calvin flapped his hand through the sunroof. Matty did not notice. He seemed fixed on something in the playground.

As they rolled by, Terry noticed a tall, thin man in black sitting on a bench at the far side of the sandpit. She thought that he looked familiar, that she had seen him recently, but at the moment recollection was not worth the effort.

CHAPTER

35

They brought Matty home late Friday morning.

Because of the medication, he was subdued. He ate very little and spent most of the day in his room with the curtains drawn, napping on and off.

For reasons the doctors could not explain, one side effect of his condition was heightened sensitivity to natural light. Whatever the neurophysiological cause, included in the batch of prescriptions was medication they hoped would reduce the discomfort.

Nonetheless, he stayed inside for the next three days, mostly in his room, where Calvin had moved a portable television.

By Tuesday morning the effects of the medication were evident. His eyes were less sensitive, and the week of counterhormone therapy had all but eliminated his facial hair, although the axial hair was fading more slowly.

More importantly, the psychoactive prescriptions, while making him drowsy, had checked all signs of aggressiveness. Not once since leaving the hospital did Matty experience anything approaching rage. To the profound gratitude of his parents, there were none of those awful scenes—the swearing fits, the tearing up of his room, the self-pummeling.

Their hope was that in a week or so Matty would feel comfortable having tutors come to the house to help him complete the school year. Consulting with his teachers, they had decided it best for him to stay out of school the rest of the year. In the fall he would start again at a private middle school, where his history would not dog him.

In spite of turnaround signs, it was not until Tuesday morning that Terry let Matty leave the house. He had said he wanted to take a little walk by himself, that he felt calm and anxiety-free. He just wanted some fresh air. It had been a week, after all.

Terry agreed he could go, but only for twenty minutes, and he had to stick to the sidewalks and stay out of the woods. He had a checkup appointment at noon with Dr. Tojian, she reminded him.

The morning was overcast, but Matty still wore sunglasses. Perhaps out of habit, he put on a white long-sleeve-shirt, but it was the first open-neck shirt he had worn in months. And through it Terry noticed the gold neck chain with the little locket containing his first baby tooth. Affixed to the chain was a medical emergency tag.

Before he left, she handed him two capsules and some water. He popped them in his mouth and told her he'd be back by eleven-thirty.

What Matty did not tell her was that for two days he had not swallowed any of his medication. Nor had he let on how he hated all that stuff they had pumped into him. It had dulled him. He missed his mind opening up to hear the thoughts of the woodland creatures. For those days in McLean's—the el dopey days, he now called them—his brain felt congealed. That was no cure—just the opposite. Before they had hauled him off and numbed him, he had never felt more alive. Whatever had gotten into him, he craved more of it. Now after two days reprieve, he felt his old self come back. As he made his way to Jason, he wondered just how far it could go.

The streets were deserted because of school. As he strolled down the sidewalk, Magog tugged at him like some huge green magnet. His mother had said explicitly not to go in there, that he was to stick to the street. He had sworn he'd keep away. He felt her eyes at his back as she watched from the window while he strolled down the drive and turned down Jason. But once out of sight, he spit out the capsules she'd given him and cut into the woods.

In a moment the cool, green air closed around him. The place was alive with winged things and the hum of furry minds. His fear was that all the medication had permanently damaged his sensitivity, cut him off from the wild symphony. But it hadn't. It was all back—the wordless needs and hungers and fears.

I'm back.

He pranced through the woods. In minutes he was at the base of TopTree. He had run much of the way with his eyes closed, maneuvering around the trees and over hummocks and deadfalls as if following a light-up map on the inside of his forehead. He had once seen a show about whales and other migrating animals who would return thousands of miles to their breeding grounds. Maybe he had developed a similar kind of power.

He shimmied up the tree. Because of the thick shade and overcast sky, the air was cool and dim. He removed the futon from its waterproof bag and spread it out on the floorboards. The dry planks creaked as he stretched himself out on it. Above him, new leaves made a dappled canopy in green and white. He could taste the greenness on his tongue. And the wet earth . . . the cardamom scent of flowers . . . licorice barks and musky fungus . . . and under it all, like bad thought, the smell . . . of kerosene that filled the Coleman lamp.

In the dayroom of McLean's there was a fat brown rabbit in a small mesh cage on a windowsill. Its name was Jazzy and it spent most of its time plopped on shredded newspaper in a corner by a bowl of green food pellets. The other kids didn't pay it much attention, its novelty having worn off after a day or two. Besides, the animal didn't do anything but eat and sleep. It wasn't allowed out of its cage for fear it might get loose in the building or be attacked by one of the more fit-prone residents.

One afternoon during a break from the battery of tests, Matty made friends with Jazzy, but not in the ordinary sense. It happened on the second day during a medication changeover that left his mind less anesthetized than usual. He was sitting in the playroom reading a Clive Barker "Nightbreed" comic when he had an overpowering sense of being watched. Except for an aide lost in his newspaper at the other end, the dayroom was completely empty. It was a little after lunch, and all the other kids were in class downstairs. But even before he looked across the room, Matty knew the source. Jazzy's face was up against the mesh, one huge pink eye glaring at him.

Matty turned his head and all his awareness funneled down onto that pink ball of jelly. In an instant he locked onto it, feeling himself pass down its beam like signals across a high-power line. Suddenly he was inside the animal's head, resonating with its primitive instincts of desire, fear, hunger. In a few seconds he held himself there, probing the strange scintillations. But what astounded him was how through the sheer flex of his will he could manipulate those instincts, blow on them, cross them, twist them as he chose— making Jazzy rise from his squat to munch his pellets, standing him on his hind quarters like a circus-act dog, turning him round and round and round until he had the animal racing in circles, kicking up scraps of paper, pellets and droppings until the floor was littered and the animal flopped over, panting.

Matty wasn't sure how he did that or if it could work on all animals. Maybe he was psychic, like those people on *Unsolved Mysteries*. He couldn't read people's minds, just the urges of animals. The doctors had asked him lots of questions—any strange dreams, hallucinations or odd mental experiences? They asked about his sense of smell, putting him through a mess of tests. He had apparently impressed them, because they remarked on his "extraordinary olfactory sense"—how, as they explained it, he had highly developed powers of smell, the ability to "read pheromones" beyond the normal human range. Then there were the vision experiments that got them even more worked up, because he could see things in the dark where other people were blind. About these powers he was upfront, admitting he could find his way through a blackened room even blindfolded or make his way through the woods in the dark. He did not mind that they knew. But about the psychic stuff—his animal telepathy—getting into Jazzy's mind—he was mum. He knew it was part of his "condition," that he should have fessed up. But he held firm. This was his special secret, and there was just no way he was going to let that out. No way were they going to kill that.

He stretched out on the futon, yawned and opened his mind to the symphony.

Creatures—large and small, winged and furred—they were all around him by the hundreds, quietly letting him finger their awareness. But, odd: he sensed a low-grade edginess in their music, a subtle, cautious treble. Maybe because he had been away. Maybe they had to get used to him again, learn to accept him as an old friend who'd been away a little while. It was a nice thought, and he closed his eyes against it and let their minds play softly across his like wind chimes.

Soon he felt himself grow sleepy. If he dozed off, his mother would get upset. He did not want to go to Dr. Tojian's . . . that meant a blood test that would show he had gone off his medication. That would be a problem.

He rolled on his side and let his mind drift back to the night Daisy had attacked him. He couldn't remember exactly what had happened. Just her hissing and clawing, then those dreamlike images of her dead and mangled, as if a truck had gone over her . . . but his hands were wet with blood. And she had not been back since then. If he had hurt her, he didn't remember, just as he didn't remember attacking Bobby G. Some kind of selective amnesia, the doctors had called it. But it wasn't his fault, because they had said some bad microbe had gotten into his system—whatever a microbe was. Some kind of bug that made him lose control, forget things, see things that weren't there. Had to be some kind of wild bug, and he tried to imagine what it looked like, if it had legs and antennae. He wondered where it was in him, and if it had made him do something bad to Daisy.

His mind continued to drift.

And now he was walking through Magog, noisy with critters. And preternaturally green—as if each tree leaf and shrub were glowing with an inner light. While he moved through the neon forest, he happened to look down at his feet. They were large and hairy, like some kind of Halloween-monster feet with long clawlike toes and thick black hair. Odder still, they were not touching the ground. He was floating through the woods as if filled with helium. Instead of worrying, he decided to go along for the ride. Shortly he spotted Daisy sitting in a small elm, smiling absurdly like the Cheshire cat in Alice in Wonderland. *As he approached, her grin gave way to an awful fright. Her ears flattened back and she hissed at him, showing the white needles of teeth. Suddenly she exploded, her head flying off like a deflating balloon . . . He floated on until Bobby Gorawlski emerged from a large rock like a pop-up. His face was a bright pink ball with stitches crisscrossing his face in a big* X. *But the* X *did not hold its shape for long, spreading almost at once into a huge dark spot in the green. Suddenly Bobby was gone and the spot sphinctered, opened up like a hole in the woods. Matty tried to pull it back but he couldn't control his feet. The thing came toward him, sucking in the green light like a black funnel. For some reason his feet had grown so absurdly big that they were hopelessly entangled in branches and underbrush. Desperate to get away, he tried to pull himself out of its way by grasping onto tree limbs. But that was useless. The lower half of his body had swelled to unmanageable proportions, and the funnel got closer and closer. A large opaque sinkhole in the green closing on him. Closer. He could smell its malevolent musk—*

His eyes snapped open.

Creaking sounds.

TreeTop was swaying.

He rolled off the futon and looked behind him. "You," Matty whispered, his heightened senses picking up the man's odor.

"You," said the man in black.

Matty twisted to get out of range but the gun went off, making a surprisingly dull popping sound—more like a toy than a movie gun. But it was no toy that sent the spike of lightning into his chest and threw him against the rail.

At the center of his shirt was a small blot of red.

Given the piercing sensation, he thought there would have been more blood. He raised his hands to the terrible burning, but his arms were too heavy, as if his blood were hardening. In seconds his breathing became almost too great an effort. As he lay there nearly paralyzed, he fought to keep his eyes open, to see the man who did this to him.

A dark thin face. Eyes of black ice. A thin, crescent grin that showed small white teeth.

How come? Why did he shoot me? Maybe God had sent the devil to punish him for being so bad.

Matty tried to keep his mind open. He tried to call his mom.

Through the dark mist, he saw her at the back door calling his name. "Mom . . . I'm here."

"Matteee."

He should have kept his promise. Just a walk around the block.

Sorry, Mom.

"Matteee."

Mom, I don't want to die . . .

But the words never reached his lips.

Before blackness closed in, his head filled with kerosene and air, crackling with terrible heat.

CHAPTER

36

Terry's eyes fixed on the single white lily. Like a baby's cheek, the petals.

She had smelled the smoke before the sirens began to wail. Though it was always a membrane away from her conscious mind, the thought never occurred to her that this time they were wailing for her. It wasn't until she saw the faint glow reflecting in the clouds above the trees that the night loom of her mind began to weave together the vague strands that, over the course of one mad hour, brought to inexorable completion a tapestry of horror culminating in that single white lily resting on the casket of her son Matthew Adam Hazzard.

For the second time in a week, she had run into the woods to rescue him. But this time police and firemen stopped her before she reached the smoldering remains of TopTree. What there was of Matty had already been taken to the morgue.

Terry had fainted on the spot when the police sergeant told her that her son had apparently fallen asleep when the Coleman lamp tipped over, and had died when the tree house went up in flames. Later, when it no longer mattered any more, she would learn how firefighters had to resort to portable extinguishers because truck hoses couldn't reach so far into the woods. Because of the recent dry spell and the kerosene, the tree house was engulfed in flames in seconds. Matty had been burned beyond recognition.

When she regained consciousness, she was on her own bed, and for a moment it all seemed just a hideous dream, but as she focused on Calvin, his face red and swollen, it all came back. Hysterical, she pounded Calvin's chest to tell her it wasn't true.

Later Mitch gave her a shot that put her under. She woke up in the middle of the night, and when she mindlessly stumbled into Matty's bedroom, she collapsed on his bed and cried herself into unconsciousness.

The next two days had passed in a gray haze. Calvin made the funeral arrangements and selected the casket. Considering Terry's brittle state, he had suggested that they cremate Matty's remains and hold a memorial service at the Unitarian Church. She strongly resisted. She could not go through with that, even given the coroner's report.

They waked Matty in a closed casket for an afternoon and evening only. Any longer would have been madness. Terry could not have survived it. Nor was it fair to dope her up for two days so she could sit like a zombie in front of the casket while a blur of people cried in her face and told her Matty was now with God.

The casket sat amid flowers at the Palmer Funeral Home in Carleton center. Calvin and Terry were positioned along the wall to the left: Terry sat in a numb trance while Calvin stood beside her to receive consolations. On the other side of Terry sat Mitch Tojian, her sister Alice and some distant relatives.

Hundreds of people with wet faces shuffled up to the coffin to kneel and bow their heads and tell Calvin and Terry how terribly sorry they were. To keep from screaming, Calvin tried to clutter his mind with minutiae. He focused on people's shoes when they knelt. Three had holes in the soles. Because of all the kids, he counted a dozen gray Nikes like Matty's. (They, too, had been burned beyond recognition.)

He tried to lose himself in the flower arrangements. On a stand to his immediate left was a springtime bouquet from the Middlesex English department. On the floor was a large pot of gladiolas in reds and yellows. The card said: WHITEHEAD FAMILY. Cards from other neighbors and friends flagged arrangements down the line. On a pedestal beside the head of the casket was a huge display of yellow roses. Calvin had to lean over to read the card. It said: WITH SYMPATHY, CLAIRE MANNING. The name was vaguely familiar, and it took him a while to place it.

The afternoon passed into evening, and the flow of faces kept up. Calvin guessed that nearly all the kids and their parents from Butler came by, including the Gorawlskis. Many kids cried openly. Dozens of teachers and staff also visited, as did several of Calvin's colleagues and people they barely knew. Beverly Otis and her nephew Scott paid respects. Beverly embraced Calvin and cried against his shoulder. Dennis Waite shook his hand and expressed his condolences. It was later Calvin remembered him from the *Patriot Chronicle* and how over the last few days he had meant to contact him.

In the forty-eight hours since it happened, Terry tortured herself with blame. She should never have let him go out while he was on medication. She knew that the lithium caused drowsiness. He had probably grown tired halfway through his walk and headed to the tree house for a nap. She should have guessed he'd go in there. He loved the woods. She should have known. She should have remembered the kerosene lamp and gotten it out of there a long time ago. One of the fire officials investigating the accident said that he had probably knocked it over in his sleep.

But a darker possibility had wormed its way into her mind: that he had done it on purpose because he could no longer endure the agony of his affliction. The thought that he had committed suicide was nearly unbearable for her. But no less so than the realization that she could have prevented it.

In the days following Matty's death, she did not eat or talk.

The only relief from the curse of consciousness was whatever Mitch Tojian gave her to swallow. Even then, her sleep was fitful as the sedative wore off. Calvin helped her dress for the funeral. When she wasn't lost in wracking sobs, she just stared through red sunken eyes at the wall. She craved sleep so desperately that Calvin was afraid she would take her own life. So was Mitch, who left tabs of tranquilizers with Calvin to dole out.

Terry's mind was a fugue of agony and disbelief. On a few occasions Calvin would discover her suddenly buoyed up by denial and jabbering broken thoughts about Matty getting his Greek report done and having to enroll him in summer camp and whether the Devil Dogs would make the playoffs. The night before the funeral she had a dream that Matty had come to her bed as he sometimes did, crawled in with her and slept by her side. The dream had been so real that it had preempted the reality of his death.

And then she woke that morning only to lose him again.

Most of Matty's clothes they gave to Goodwill. Others—baby sun-suit clothes, his first shoes, his baseball uniform and his favorite sweatshirt—Terry could not part with, and the sight of them broke her down. Nor could she enter his room. Calvin had to go in to retrieve things. She kept the door closed and even avoided the central staircase, taking the rear steps. But on the evening of the funeral, she wandered in and slept in his bed. Had her mind been clear to analyze her behavior, she would have understood that she was trying to get on top of her grief, to accept the reality of his loss. The next morning she woke up desperate to leave the house.

Her earlier apprehension had been confirmed. The place was a malignant entity that had claimed all of her children. While to some that might seem a purely irrational reflex fashioned in the fragility of her state, Terry Hazzard could not shake the feeling. Nor could she wait to get out.

Matthew Adam Hazzard was buried on Thursday, May 28, Memorial Day weekend.

The next morning Terry flew to her sister's place in Maine.

And Calvin called Robin Priest at New York Polytechnic Institute, then Beverly Otis at her real estate office.

CHAPTER

37

The slanting sun cast Washington in a glorious incandescent glow. At about 3,000 feet over the bay, the pilot banked the eight-passenger Learjet to the right, giving Julius Wick a full view. From that height the Mall could have been Pierre L'Enfant's visionary model board.

"So it's done," Julius said, without taking his face from the window.

"Yes," Frank DeVoe said. "No complications."

Sitting beside DeVoe was Dan McDermott in seats that faced those occupied by Julius and his wife Claire. McDermott and DeVoe had known each other since the late seventies when they both attended Boston University Law School. McDermott was now an attorney at the Treasury Department. Because of his lack of visibility, DeVoe had asked him to be acting counsel at the transfer of the Hazzard property tomorrow morning. He was qualified because he had passed the bar in Massachusetts and had practiced there for four years before moving to Washington and into a variety of federal positions. But more than that, he was a good point man with an instinct for expedience—for taking the path of least resistance, ruthlessly if necessary. At the Treasury he had masterminded covert operations for the ATF that had resulted in the permanent disappearance of drug-operation informants who were no longer useful to the government but were definite liabilities while they walked the street. He received promotions. But he quietly kept his eyes on the true prize. Next year he would assist Frank DeVoe, who was slated to run the reelection campaign of President Morgan Reese. The success of that campaign promised McDermott wonderful possibilities, including appointment to the coveted post of White House aide. It was where he wanted to be—the inner circle embracing Morgan Reese.

As Julius had requested, the pilot tipped the wing so he could get an unobstructed view of the White House. It sat like a piece of jewelry in the setting sun.

Two years had passed since Julius Wick had retired from his post as CEO of Walden Industries and had sold all his interests in the company, thereby avoiding any potential conflict-of-interest claims in his post as biotech czar. But he had not relinquished the Learjet. The plane was particularly handy when they wanted to get someplace without leaving a trail. For Julius and Claire, this was a round-trip. But DeVoe and McDermott were being dropped off in Boston, where they would oversee the passing of papers and the setup of the pumping operation when the Hazzard property became theirs.

Julius's eye took in a line from the White House to the newly restored Old Senate Office Building, which housed the offices of his own Biotechnology Commission. He could just make out the west turret on the eighth floor and the bow of his office windows. He had been at his new post for less than a week, but his briefcase bulged with the red leather folder containing pending legislation regarding the patenting of new life forms. His review of the impact was his first major assignment.

"No complications?" Julius said, echoing Frank DeVoe. "You mean we got away with murder again."

Frank glanced at McDermott. "He made it look like an accident, Julius."

"An *accident*. We killed a twelve-year-old boy and call it an accident."

Frank DeVoe said nothing. He was tiring of all the self-righteous remorse, of Julius's pot-calling-the-kettle-black. If it weren't for him and his genocide geniuses, they wouldn't be in this mess. But it was Julius's plane, so he bit back the words.

"If it's any consolation, there weren't any innocent bystanders, as with the Wileys," offered McDermott.

"Some consolation," Julius said. "He set the boy on fire in his tree house. Your man's an animal."

DeVoe shrugged. "I didn't like it either. None of us did, but we've been through this already," he said. "It was a him-or-us situation. We're lucky we got him when we did. They worked him over in the hospital for almost a week, probably gave him every test known to medical science."

"You should know," McDermott added, "that he was already far gone. There's no telling where his condition would have led. Chances are, it would have been a slow, miserable demise—like your lab animals. So it's better for everybody in the long run. Now we just do what we have to do."

Julius looked at him, then turned back to the window. " 'The best lack all conviction, while the worst/Are full of passionate intensity.' "

"Come again?" Frank said.

Claire shook her head. "It's a line of poetry."

"William Butler Yeats," McDermott said. "But it ends, 'And what rough beast, its hour come round at last,/Slouches towards Bethlehem to be born?' Do we really want that?"

Julius did not answer.

"Of course not." McDermott took a sip of his Pepsi. "Tomorrow we pass papers which, of course, we'll take care of," he said to them. "According to the agreement we've drawn, they and their belongings will be out by Sunday. The agent reports that the wife is planning to leave town and that the husband has already taken a hotel room. That means we can move our people in to begin neutralizing the water."

"Memorial Day."

"Yes," McDermott said with a brightness that paled Julius's sarcasm. He put his hands together in a silent applause. "You might be interested to know that our man in the Boston EPA quashed a report of contaminated water at number 12 Jason Road." McDermott looked through his half-glasses at the memo. "A Dr. Mitchell Tojian had filed a 714–C toxic-substance complaint, specifying an artificial hormonelike compound." McDermott looked up and smiled. "The report, as they say, was cut off at the pass."

"Then they know it's in the water."

"Calm down," DeVoe said. "In four, five days we'll have it neutralized. There'll be nothing to substantiate the claim even if it's issued again. Next week at this time, you can put that water in Evian bottles."

Julius shook his head. "You've thought of everything."

"It's how we clear the tracks," Frank said.

"One more week and it'll all be behind us," McDermott said.

Julius winced but said nothing.

"Think of it this way, Dr. Wick," McDermott said. "While you're in your office reviewing legislation on new life forms, our men will be working around the clock to clear any signs of your past, ah . . . transgressions. And when it's over, we go our way and you get a cleaned-up little *pied-à-terre* just west of Boston."

Julius looked at him. "Your sense of irony is lost on me, Mr. McDermott."

McDermott smiled. "Why should you be any different?" he said, and finished off his Pepsi.

The Lear landed a little before nine and taxied to the private hangar where a Lincoln Town Car waited for them. The chauffeur greeted Julius and Claire, took DeVoe and McDermott's bags and placed them in the trunk. They said goodbye to Claire and Julius, who were continuing in the Lear to New York State for the long holiday weekend.

Fifteen minutes later the Lincoln was heading up Dartmouth Street in midtown Boston to drop off DeVoe and McDermott at the Westin Hotel. It was where they would stay until the neutralizing process was underway. They would keep Julius and Claire posted by phone.

They took separate rooms on the eleventh floor with a view of Back Bay and the Charles River. About nine-forty-five they strolled into the piano bar on the second floor. The place was a large, open room with stuffed chairs and love seats hunched around glass tables. At the center was a glossy white grand piano. Because it was the holiday weekend, the place was nearly empty. They took a seat out of the way and ordered beer.

"They've got a nice fish restaurant downstairs. Great chowder," Danny McDermott said. "You're hungry, aren't you?"

Frank DeVoe shook his head and took a large swig of beer. "But I'll join you."

"Forget it," McDermott said, and waved over the waitress, who returned with two plates of hot hors d'oeuvres. When she was gone, he said, "You want to talk or continue with your Mount Rushmore impersonation?"

DeVoe took a sip of beer. "He's weak."

"Who?"

"Julius Wick. Someday he's going to have a fit of conscience and say something."

"You worry too much. When it's over, he'll settle. He's too much of an egomaniac to slip. And if he does, he brings his own roof down."

Frank DeVoe listened, then stuck his fork into a meatball. "What worries me is that it's our roof, too."

Early Saturday morning Calvin woke up to the sound of crying, and for a crazy moment, thought it was Matty lying beside him in the dark—that he was six or seven and had crawled into their bed because of a bad dream. He kissed the top of his head and put his arms around him—

But it wasn't Matty, of course. Terry rolled toward him and buried her face in his chest. He could feel her body quake as she let it out. He put his arms around her and tried to comfort her, but broke down himself. He knew he should have shown more strength but he couldn't summon it. And for a while they cried against each other.

Later he got up, leaving Terry in her pillow. He took a shower and got dressed and headed downstairs, grateful for the mindless task of making coffee. He ground the beans and boiled the water and poured it through the filter. He made a cup for Terry and brought it upstairs, but her eyes were closed and she lay still. He glanced at the night table. The small vial of Valium sat beside an empty glass. He picked it up, and the rattle of pills relieved him that she had merely cried herself to sleep again. For a long moment he studied Terry. Her thick brown hair pooled around her shoulders, her beautiful Acropolis profile made a pallid cast against the blue pillow.

A short time later Terry came down. She had dressed in jeans and a baggy pullover. Her face was drawn and colorless, her hair roughly brushed. He felt the dumb, obligatory question *are you okay?* form in his mind but he knew the answer. She was scooped out. And there was no name for how he felt.

He made her some toast and poured her a second cup of coffee. She did not touch the toast but sipped the coffee. Then in a soft voice she said that she'd better get packed for her sister's. Alice, who had returned the day before, was expecting her.

Calvin said he wished she could stay but he understood. Terry could not bear another day in the house. Besides, the moving men would be in and out all day.

In a zombielike trance she put a few things in the suitcase, then around nine-thirty, Calvin put her on the plane to Portland.

At eleven, on schedule, Calvin walked into the office of Beverly Otis to give her the papers on his house.

The only others present were Beverly and an attorney, Daniel McDermott, representing Claire Manning.

McDermott offered his condolences for the death of Calvin's son. Calvin thanked him. The papers were signed in Claire Manning's name, as was the bank check for over $450,000 made out to Calvin and Terry Hazzard—less Beverly's commission.

The whole transaction took less than twenty minutes. When it was over, Calvin shook McDermott's hand. Beverly said goodbye and gave him a hug. There were tears in her eyes. She wished them luck in their move to New York State and the new job. Calvin thanked her.

He walked across Center Street to the Carleton Savings Bank at the corner of Standish. A week ago the check would have made him levitate with joy. Today it was a piece of paper with numbers. With it they would purchase a house in Argyle-on-the-Hudson. What was left over would be put in a bank. They had no plans beyond the moment. The move was no longer the start of a new life but a strategy for surviving the old.

When he got home, the moving men were stacking boxes into the long Mayflower van in the driveway. Most of the downstairs rooms had been emptied. The furniture would be driven to a warehouse in Roseville, New York, about ten miles from Argyle, to be stored until they found a house.

The upstairs office still had his desk and a single lamp. The rest had been cleared out. Boxes of books filled the floor. The red light on the answering machine said that there were three calls. He hit the play button. Robin Priest said that the college's personnel office had located a few nice places Calvin and his wife might want to look at. He gave details that escaped Calvin. If they could come up this weekend or next week, he could arrange a visit. The next call was from Terry's sister to say that Terry had arrived and was resting.

The third call was from Mitch Tojian. "Calvin, sorry to bother you, but I found something I think you should know about. Come in anytime. I'll be here until six-thirty." He left his number.

It was not quite noon. Calvin punched the number and looked out the window at the front. The men were moving Matty's bureau into the rear of the truck.

When Calvin identified himself, the secretary immediately switched him to Mitch's office. "Can you meet me in half an hour?"

"Yes." Tojian's office was ten minutes away.

"Good, but not here. At the Emerson."

"The Emerson?"

"I'll meet you in the lobby."

Calvin did not ask why. There was little anybody could say to involve his interest. But he would meet with Tojian, it would be something to do. Like calling the gas and electric companies to turn off service. Returning library books. Dropping off Matty's bike at the Home for Little Wanderers.

When he hung up, Calvin just stood by the big push-out window. The sky was a blue steel bowl. A flock of starlings sat on the telephone wires like notes on a staff. Below, the lawn made a gaudy green mat to the gray asphalt.

What held his mind was the dogwood. It rose out of the grass like a charred claw.

CHAPTER

38

Tojian was in the Emerson lobby when Calvin arrived. In one hand was a folder. "How're you doing, Calvin?"

"Getting by."

Tojian nodded. "I'm sorry to get you in here, but there's something I think you should know."

Calvin followed him to the elevators and they rode in silence to the sixth floor. They walked down a white corridor to a small sitting room with stuffed vinyl chairs and a coffee table. Calvin took a seat and Mitch sat beside him and put the folder on the tabletop.

"I know how painful it is, but I'd like to talk to you . . . about Matty."

"Aren't we a little late?"

"For Matty, yes." Tojian opened the folder. "I think we've found the source of his condition."

Calvin looked at him blankly. Why would Tojian think he cared anymore? They had buried Matty two days ago. He was steeped in his grief, holding onto the bare threads of defense. The last thing he needed was to feign intellectual interest in the metabolic culprit of precocious puberty.

"It's your water."

For a moment Calvin did not react, then the words penetrated. "But we had that checked. Terry sent a sample in two weeks ago. It turned up negative."

"Yes, I know, but what caused the changes was a hormonelike substance that standard screening could never have picked up. I took a water sample to a friend in the department of microbiology at MIT and asked him to test for certain families of organic com-

240

pounds with the molecular structure of human hormones." Tojian
put on his half-glasses and opened his file to some computer printouts. "He found a high concentration of the same lookalike hormone
we found in Matty's spinal fluids. And it's man-made."

"Oh . . . so it's official, I bought my son's death."

"That's not a conclusion I would draw, Calvin."

"He committed suicide out of self-loathing and despair."

"There's no proof it wasn't an accident," Tojian said. "And recrimi-
nation is not why I called. I'm concerned that the substance
will spread to the public water supply. Your and Terry's blood readings are clean. And none of the physicians in the area have reports
of hormonal abnormalities. That means it's still localized to your
well."

"So you want my permission for the authorities to come out and
tear the place up."

"Yes."

"Once again we're a little late," Calvin said. "I sold the place two
hours ago."

"I see," Tojian said. "Well then, you'll have to tell the new owners."

"Otherwise I'll be liable. Nice irony," he said. "What goes around
comes around." Calvin got up and walked to the door. Tojian did not
move from his desk. When Calvin glanced back, Tojian was staring
at him with a strange intensity.

"Before you go, I'd like you to see something."

Tojian then opened the door and led Calvin down the corridor to a
set of swinging double doors. Above them was a sign: SPECIMEN
PATHOLOGY RESEARCH—AUTHORIZED PERSONNEL ONLY

The swinging doors did not swing open. With a key Mitch
unlocked the door, which relocked when it closed behind them.
The corridor was a bright white tube with occasional doors to the
right and left. They walked nearly to the end, then turned right.
With another key Mitch unlocked a windowless door labeled
ROOM 666.

They went inside and a distinct chemical odor struck Calvin. It
was a scent out of his past. Of high school biology labs. Formalin.

Along both walls were steel cases containing large jars of human
fetuses. All deformed. Some had short stumps instead of arms and

legs. Others had none at all, or had limbs growing where they shouldn't be. In one jar he spotted a Janus-like specimen with two shrunken faces growing out of either side of a single oversized head. As he followed Tojian down the aisle of the fetal monstrosities, a sense of inevitability swelled up in him. By the time Mitch Tojian reached his destination, Calvin knew.

At the end of one shelf at eye level was a two-gallon jar. Filling the inside was something with clawlike hands and feet. Its back was twisted and rough with the scaly protrusions of some throwback creature uncertainly poised between reptile and mammal. But what nearly made his heart stop was the face. Though bloated from the formalin, it was smooth and white. Its eyes were large and slitted and to the sides of the head rather than in front. And beneath them was a prognathous jaw that swept forward. Against the side of the glass a milky gray eye stared out at Mitch, as though in accusation.

"It was what they took out of Terry last Thanksgiving. You can understand why we never told her," Mitch said. "Or you."

Calvin said nothing. He was too transfixed on that eye. All they had said was that the fetus was deformed.

"Calvin, I lied to you," Tojian said. "It wasn't a stillbirth. That . . . it was born live."

"Why in God's name are you showing me this?"

"Because I had a tissue analysis done yesterday. It contains the same substance that's in your water," Tojian said. "It scrambled the genetic codes."

Calvin's breath was coming short. "There's no end to the punishment."

"That's not my intention," Tojian said.

"What is?"

"I want you to know how bad the stuff is."

"How bad? It killed my family."

"Calvin, I feel terrible, but you have to know. You've been exposed to the stuff for ten years. You might even want to have more children someday. I had to tell you."

Before he left, Tojian asked him, "Do you know anything about this BiOmega outfit?"

"No."

*   *   *

Calvin left the hospital at about one-thirty. But he did not drive back
to Carleton. Instead, he pulled onto the highway and drove to
Adamsville, the home of the late, unlamented BiOmega Laboratory.

CHAPTER

39

"*Madone*," Muzzy gasped. "You got yourself a goddamn werewolf."

The kid was naked and filthy, his face and body covered with coarse black hair, even the thick-knobbed hands. He looked at Muzzy and growled, his white teeth flashing against red gums, his eyes mostly pupils. The sight took Muzzy's breath away.

"I think he's beautiful," Jerry said.

"Beautiful? I think *you're* nuts," Muzzy said. He looked back at the kid. "I mean, what *is* it?"

"Name's Matthew. He's twelve."

A week had passed since that day in the woods when he had fired the dope-laden dart into the kid and replaced him with the body of that street hustler from the train station. What startled Jerry was how fast Matty was changing.

"You steal him from Barnum and Bailey or something? I mean, look at it. It's a freak." Muzzy stepped back from the cage.

Jerry grinned. "He's got an unusual medical problem."

"Unusual medical problem? I'll say. Gives me the goddam creeps."

Matty hunched over to the bucket of water on the floor. He raised it with his hands and guzzled it noisily. When he had emptied it, he banged it against the floor.

"Wants a refill," Jerry said with a smile.

Muzzy muttered, "Where you get it?"

"Around."

"Around? What do you mean, around? I mean, somebody's missing a twelve-year-old caveman or whatever the fuck it is. Where'd he come from, all's I want to know?"

"You know the old saying, 'Ask me no questions and I tell you no lies'?"

Matty banged the pail again.

"Whaddya feed him besides water?"

"Steak," Jerry said. "On the rare side."

Muzzy looked back at the thing sitting in the middle of the cage banging the pail. "Least is, you can tell me what you're gonna do with the thing."

"Meet the mother of all pit dogs," Jerry said, straight-faced.

"You mean you're gonna conference him? Gonna put that in the pit?"

"Among other options. I bet he could pull twenty-to-one odds against anything on four legs. Minimum fifty grand upfront."

"Fifty grand's a lotta ante, is all." Muzzy tried to look away but kept glancing at the cage. The kid crouched in the far corner. "Besides, who's gonna wanna see that thing fight?"

"Connoisseurs."

If it came to that, Jerry would get the Fig to come up with a select list of players, by special invitation. Only "the most discriminating." It was one thing to watch dogs tear each other apart, but some of the regulars with families might have a problem with a kid and bulls going at it. Even though he was, as Muzzy said, a freak, and apparently getting freakier by the day, behind the jungle glare, the hair and jumbo wang, he was still a twelve-year-old boy. Jerry could not risk any ethical dilemmas—bettors going weak-kneed on him during the main event. He had in mind guys with cast-iron guts who didn't have children or, if they did, who saw their own as insulated from the dark pleasures of their fathers. The kind of guys who were morally anesthetized to their grade—goombas who dealt in kiddie prostitution, chicken flicks and snuff movies, whose cocaine operations stretched from schoolyards to video arcades. A designer clientele.

"Whaddya gonna match him with, Dracula?"

Jerry's grin was mirthless. "At the moment, nothing."

Muzzy looked puzzled. "I don't follow." Matty threw the bucket with a loud clang against the cage where they were standing. "Can't he talk?"

Jerry shook his head.

"Some kind of retard or something," Muzzy said. "Or one of those artistics. I saw a thing on TV 'bout these kids who don't talk for years, in their own world, or something. 'Cept this one's part gorilla with a King-Kong swantz."

Jerry moved to a utility table with a video camera and opened a drawer. "He drinks about two gallons a day."

"How come you keep him naked?"

"Tears clothes to shreds."

"He's got some kinda thing around his neck."

"Just a pendant on a chain," Jerry said. He came back with a thick pistol in his hand, opened the side chamber and slipped in a tranquilizer dart.

"What's that for?"

"It's how we keep things reasonable."

Jerry unlocked the door. When Matty spotted the gun, he let out a deep rumble and slunk back into his corner.

Jerry waved the gun at him as he entered the cage, picked up the bucket and slipped out of the cage. He then filled the bucket from the hose but, instead of placing it near Matty, he set it against the bars next to where Muzzy was standing.

He locked the door and picked up a small wall mirror from the utility table. He held it by his side and waited. Matty came over to the bucket, dropped on his knees and began slurping the water.

Jerry squatted until he was head-high with Matty through the cage. "Hey, kid."

Matty looked up and Jerry pressed the mirror against the bars at eye level.

"Mirror, mirror on the wall."

For a blank moment Matty glared at his reflection. Slowly he raised his hand to finger the mat of long hair at the side of his head and the thick black beard. When it sank in that it was his own face, he raised himself up and let out a howl neither human nor animal— a hybrid noise that filled the air with its anguish.

Muzzy jumped back to the wall as Matty punched his hand through the cage to get at the mirror. Jerry pulled back just in time and tossed the mirror onto the table. From nowhere he produced a metal pan and noisily rapped the bars. Matty pulled back into his corner, cradling a bloodied hand.

"*Madone!*"

"He's getting worse," Jerry said.

"What do you mean?"

"Getting more like an animal by the day. A week ago there wasn't a hair on his face. He's changing and he can't believe it."

"What's doing it?"

Jerry didn't answer. "But the thing is, the mirror's like priming the pump. Might come in handy at a conference."

"Where you *get* that thing?"

"That's the third time you asked me."

"And you still haven't answered me."

"You're catching on."

"But you owe me, for locating that Perry guy."

"True," Jerry said. "But this isn't a need to know."

Muzzy conceded with a shrug. "You fight him yet?"

"No. But you should see him spar."

Jerry left the room and came back carrying a stray mutt he had picked up a few streets away. It was a good size, looking as if it might contain some Lab. Jerry had fitted it with leg tethers and a muzzle. As soon as it entered the room, it began to kick and yowl through its clenched teeth. Jerry untied its legs and whipped off the muzzle, then threw it into the cage through the trap.

The dog slammed itself into the corner opposite Matty, crouching in on itself. When it saw Matty rise at him, he tried to ward him off with confused gestures of aggression and submission. It scraped itself along the floor, rolling on its back. But as Matty closed in, the dog shot to its feet, baring its teeth in a last-ditch effort. When it leapt for his face, Matty caught it by the head and slammed it down. The first blow knocked the wind out of the animal. The second ruptured its insides. While Matty ripped at its innards, Jerry grinned like a proud father. " 'What doesn't kill us makes us strong,' " he said quietly.

"Enough," said Muzzy, heading up the stairs. "I seen enough. The fucking thing's from hell, is all."

"That's what you said about the jackals."

"Yeah, but this is real," Muzzy said with his hand on the doorknob. "I mean, the Fig's gonna cream when he sees it."

As Muzzy opened the door to the kitchen, Rufus dashed by him, nearly throwing the fat man off his feet. The dog shot by him to the cage. It was the second time Rufus had laid eyes on Matty since he'd arrived. The first time, he slammed into the bars to get in. To keep him from injuring himself, Jerry had quarantined him to the interior of the house.

Now Jerry made a move to collar him, but the dog had come to a dead stop just two feet from the cage, frozen at the bars, looking like a pointer stalking a thrush. Across the cage Matty sat in a crouch. His eyes were wide and motionless as he took in the dog. For a minute the two stared at each other like in a still life—Rufus arrowing without sound or movement except the rise and fall of his chest; Matty hugging his knees with his chin squared on them, his eyes locked onto the dog.

While Jerry and Muzzy waited in fascination for the stare-down to break, Matty worked his mind on Rufus, holding him in stunned embrace while he probed.

Suddenly and without warning, Rufus licked his nose, turned around, and slowly click-clacked back into the house.

CHAPTER

40

It was just after two when Calvin reached the center of Adamsville. From the car he could see a few late lunchers at the counter. The place closed at three on Saturdays.

He parked the car and went in. Two people sat at the far end of the counter. Stacking cups behind it was an amiable-looking black woman wearing an apron over her dress. A Red Sox baseball cap sat on her head. She looked to be in her fifties.

"Are you Dotty?"

"Only if you want the meatloaf special."

"No way to sell a man a meal." A black man stuck his head out the service window. He was wearing a green A's hat.

Dotty scowled. "Put your face away, Paul, nobody's asked your opinion." To Calvin: "Ain't nothin' wrong with it. Just that it's the last piece and I hate to see it wasted."

"No woman your size can be accused of wasting food," Paul chimed in. The customers at the other end of the counter chuckled. The Paul-and-Dotty act.

"You keep it up, and I'm gonna be wasting you." She winked at Calvin.

"I'll take the meatloaf," Calvin said.

In a few minutes Dotty was placing in front of him a large plate with meatloaf, mashed potatoes and asparagus spears. He had no appetite but forced himself to eat. Soon the other counter customers cleared out, but there was one couple at a front table. Paul was cleaning up in the kitchen, and Dotty was busying herself at the counter putting condiments into refrigerator jars. They were closing for the weekend.

249

When she moved close to his end of the counter, Calvin said, "I'm told you're something of the town historian."

"Only because I've been here longer than most everybody else."

He took a bite of meatloaf. "Then maybe you can help me."

"Give it a swing."

"BiOmega."

She straightened up. "Bio what?"

"BiOmega Laboratory. It was a small research place located on Franklin the early seventies."

"Oh yeah . . . where they put up the Sherwood."

"That's right."

"So, what do you want to know?"

"Whatever you remember. The people who worked there probably came in here for lunch, you might have overheard something."

"Like what?"

"Like what kind of research they were doing. Names of folks who worked there. How long they were here . . . whatever."

She glared at him for a moment, removed his dishes and put them into a bin, then wiped off the counter. "You want dessert?"

"Just coffee."

"Milk or cream?"

"Neither . . . look, it was a research lab of some kind."

"If you say so." She poured a cup of coffee. "I remember it as just a quiet little building tucked in the trees."

"Is there anything you can tell me? Something you heard about what they were doing there?"

"Unh-uh. Not much noise outta them. They kept pretty much to themselves."

"But you remember them?"

She slid the sugar dispenser to him. "Why are you so interested in a place that's been gone twenty years?"

"It's too long a story," he said. "I'm just curious about the kind of research they conducted."

"How do I know you're not some kind of spy or other?"

Just then the man in the A's hat came out of the kitchen with an empty dish bin. Probably her husband, Calvin thought. He looked her age and was wearing a wedding band. "Whyn't you tell the man what he wants to know?" he said, and shoved the empty bin under the counter.

"Whyn't you mind your own business?" she said.

The man wiped his hand on a towel and extended his hand over the counter to Calvin. "Paul Fellows, her old man," he said, and smiled. "Spending too much time with Robert Ludlum." Then with mock formality: "The ladies at number four would like a coffee refill, *if* you please."

Dotty took the pot and huffed off, mumbling under her breath.

"With all due respect, even if you were a spy, there's nothing we could tell you would be of any use."

"How so?"

"Like Dotty said, they were pretty close-mouthed when it came to shoptalk. You a reporter or something?"

Calvin shook his head.

"Cop?"

"Nothing like that," Calvin said. "The land where they used to dump their wastes ended up as my backyard. I just want to know what they put in the ground."

"Beats me."

"The name suggests some kind of biological research."

"Hey, your guess is as good as mine."

"How about the names of people who worked there?"

Fellows shook his head. When Dotty returned, he asked, "What was the name of that big tall guy with gap teeth used to work there?"

"How'm I supposed to remember?" she said, and pushed her way into the kitchen. A moment later she pushed the door open with her foot a crack. "Jack something-or-other." Then the door closed.

"Jack. Yeah, that's it. Nice fella."

He poured more coffee into Calvin's cup. "You know, I'm not so sure they used their real names."

"Why do you think that?"

"Well, it's been almost twenty-five years, a few times they called some lunch orders when they didn't have time to come out. Remember once we got a call from, say, Bob. When I called back to say we were out of whatever it was, the guy who answered said there was no Bob working there, I had the wrong number. When I called back a second and third time, he must have caught on it was a code name or something. Suddenly a Bob comes to the phone, the same one who placed the order. I guess that says something."

"Like what?"

Fellows shrugged. "Like whatever they were making up there, and whoever was making it, didn't have names attached."

Calvin nodded.

"Maybe it was some kind of top-secret stuff they were doing. Or maybe, being scientists, they were too good for us mortals."

"Any idea how many worked there?"

"Few times, when they were too busy to come out, I delivered. Maybe a half-dozen, judging from the orders and cars in the lot."

"Anybody else in town who might know any of them?"

Paul shook his head, then remembering, " 'Cept that once."

"Once what?"

"When they called a delivery for about fifteen people," he said. "They wanted party platters with all the trimmings. Remember taking it up there in the wagon. Lots of military brass and limos outside. Yeah, I never got past the gate. Coupla second looies met me to carry in the eats. Remember thinking they had something cooking in there that the Almighty didn't even know about."

Calvin thanked the man and left.

The Registry of Deeds closed at five, so at four-thirty, when Calvin arrived, it was virtually empty except for the staff preparing to leave.

But this time he knew exactly where to look. GRANTORS AND GRANT-EES aisle number 11, volume 13664. He turned to page 486, surprised at his recall. At the bottom of the third page he found what he was looking for. Under the schematic diagrams of the property was the footnote reference to Plot 5, recorded in Book 9238, page 235. He jotted those figures down and found the volume.

On page 235 he found the deed and plan drawing for Plot 5. According to the description, the four acres which would eventually hold his house originally had been part of Magog Woods and designated as underdeveloped property. But it had been clearly and precisely sectored off from the rest of the town-owned conservation land and sold to a private party. The deed, which comprised the next two pages, had been recorded on September 28, 1968. The ownership designated: Julius B. Wick.

The ride back to Middlesex University took only twenty minutes in the light traffic. Calvin parked his car in the faculty lot.

School was out and the place was a ghost campus. The library still kept regular hours. It must have struck the few staffers as odd that, two days after his son's funeral, Prof. Calvin Hazzard was in the periodical room doing research. Perhaps throwing himself back into scholarship was a means of grappling with his sorrow. So might it have been, had that name Wick not rung like a buoy in a fogbound sea.

On the reference terminal he tapped in the letters, finding no entry. He then checked three different *WHO'S WHO*'s including *WHO'S WHO IN THE EAST, IN THE MIDWEST, IN THE WEST,* where he found no entries. But in *WHO'S WHO IN SCIENCE* he found an entry that made his heart skip wildly:

Wick, Julius Benton
    Adminr. Environ Protection Agency, Washington D.C.; b. Tacoma, Wash. Jan. 21, 1928. Education: A.B. (cum Laude), Princeton U., 1950; Ph.D., U. Wisconsin, 1960; Post doctoral, Mass. Inst. Tech., 1960-62; founder & director Biomega Research Labs, 1965-72; Dept. of Defen., 1966-72; prof & researcher NY Poly. Tech., 1973-83; founder & pres. Walden Research; bd. of directors, NY Poly. Tech., 1980–; Chm. 1989–. Member Biotechnic Inst.; pres. 1986-89. *Honors & Awards*: fellow, Amer. Inst. of Science 1986; fellow, Amer. Acad. Science 1989; President's Award 1992; Presidential advisor on biotech, 1993. Married 1953 to Claire C. Manning.

Calvin read the entry twice to be certain. He made a photocopy of it, then checked the last two years' indices of the New York *Times*, which were only current as of last December. There were no entries for Julius Benton Wick—which meant that the paper had published no articles by him or about him. Calvin then hurried upstairs to the periodicals room, where for the next hour he scoured the current year's copies of *Newsweek, Time* and *U.S. News and World Report.*

It was in the May 2 issue of *Newsweek* that he found a small piece entitled "Reese's New Biotech Czar." It described the past week's ceremonious appointment of Julius Benton Wick to be head of the president's new commission on biotechnology. Beside the article was a photo of the president shaking hands with Wick. He did not recognize the man. A similar story and photo were found in *Time*. In *U.S. News and World Report* there was a side shot of Wick with the president, but because of the angle, the woman sitting behind him and smiling had not been cropped out. The caption identified her as his wife Claire. What caught Calvin's eye was the strawberry birthmark under her right eye—just as Terry had mentioned about Claire Manning.

Calvin tore the page out of the magazine and left.

What was going on? Why had Claire Manning not identified herself as the wife of Julius Wick nor as the original owner of the property during the seventies? And most of all, why out of the blue come back bearing $700,000 to buy back the place, especially if they lived in New York State and would spend most of their time there or in Washington? What sent a rash of gooseflesh up his back was the entry: *Chm. bd. of directors, NY Poly. Tech.*

Chairman of the board of directors of New York Polytechnic Institute. *Sweet Jesus.*

He felt he'd been used. Felt used, and scared.

He did not go back to the hotel. Instead, he drove back to Carleton center.

Beverly Otis was not in the office when he walked into Otis Realty.

Another agent, whom he recognized, said that she was out of town for the holiday weekend and wouldn't be back until Tuesday. It was clear from the tone of her voice and solicitous manner that she knew about Matty.

"Is there something I can help you with, Mr. Hazzard?"

"Yes," he said unfolding the *Newsweek* page. "You remember the woman who purchased my house?"

"Mrs. Manning? Of course."

"Is this she?"

The woman took one look at the picture and lit up. "Goodness, she's with President Reese."

"Claire Manning?"

"Yes, that's her. How . . . ?"

Calvin folded the picture.

"Thank you," he said, and quickly left.

CHAPTER

41

Dennis Waite was in his backyard attaching a basketball hoop to his garage when Calvin pulled into the driveway. His son of eight waited patiently on the back stoop with a ball.

Waite climbed down from the ladder and shook Calvin's hand, again expressing his condolences.

Calvin nodded. "That's kind of why I'm here."

Waite didn't understand but could see Calvin wanted to talk. He went over to his son and said something in his ear. The boy protested but reluctantly headed into the house.

Waite pointed Calvin to a wrought-iron lawn table and chairs under some trees in back. "Will a beer go with it?"

"Thanks," Calvin said, and took a chair while Waite went in and got a couple of bottles of Sam Adams.

Waite sat down opposite Calvin, eyeing him speculatively. "There are no right words," Waite began. "What happened was a bitch."

Calvin gestured with his hand that he hadn't come to spill over. He took a swig of beer and leaned forward. "Dennis, I think my son's death is connected to the death of Sally Forand."

"What?"

"I think she was killed to cover up what it was that destroyed Matty."

While Dennis Waite listened in disbelief, Calvin reeled out the details of the last few weeks—Matty's condition, the fight in the woods, the battery of medical exams and tests, his attack on Bobby G., the McLean findings, the mock-hormone substance in the water, that grotesque thing floating in a jar of formaldehyde, the sale of their house to Julius and Claire Manning Wick, the death of their

256

son. Twice Calvin Hazzard caught himself filling up, but he held tight.

Calvin did not mention that for ten years he had bottled up the "minor liability" that eventually claimed the lives of his children.

Waite's eyes were on the *Newsweek* photo and write-up of Julius Wick. "So you're saying Wick rigged the job offer at NYPI and made an offer on the house you couldn't refuse?"

"Yes."

"And you think it's all connected to Sally?"

"Because of the story she was doing on the toxic dump in Magog Woods. The last time we talked, you said yourself you never believed the official story of her death, that it looked as if it had been staged."

"I said I was suspicious but I got over it—"

"Well, I think you might have been dead right, because, according to the locals, BiOmega Labs was engaged in military research. Everything about the place was top secret. Nobody was even sure how many worked there—maybe just a handful—and they never let on about their work."

"But you couldn't expect them to, if it was classified."

"True, but they said they didn't even use their real names outside the labs."

"What the hell were they up to?"

"I don't know, but whatever it was, they didn't want their names on it. When rumors began to spread that somebody was using Carleton conservation land to bury their waste, your Sally came along threatening to blow their cover."

"So they ran her off the road," Waite said. "Like Karen Silkwood . . ."

"And with the same results: her death, and no way to prove it was murder."

"All in the name of national security."

"Or to cover up something that went dirty. Very dirty."

"Any idea what they were making?"

"No, but my guess is some kind of biochemical warfare material. Maybe with a genetic component. Tojian said the stuff is an artificial human hormone that apparently works havoc on human DNA.

Whatever, they dumped the stuff into the ground and killed two babies and my son. And maybe your fiancée."

Waite was weighing Calvin's words against old suspicions. "Have you told anybody else?"

"Terry's with her sister in Maine. She's not in any state to handle it."

"Anybody else?"

"No."

"Good, because if what you say is true, one of our president's men is up to his hiney in a coverup that could knock him out of the White House."

"Trouble is, there's no hard proof linking the stuff to Wick and BiOmega."

"Which means you can't blow the whistle until you have more. Otherwise, you may end up like Sally."

"I'm aware of that," Calvin said.

"Also, even if you did go to the authorities, they couldn't connect the stuff to BiOmega because what they did was classified and Wick has all the records, if they even exist . . . What the hell were they doing? Maybe something to do with the Vietnam War . . . considering when it was . . . But why buy the place after two decades?"

"Maybe they know the stuff's leaked out."

"Based on what?"

"Stories about strange animal behavior."

Waite shook his head. "They'd need something more substantive."

Suddenly a small rent in Calvin's memory. "My God," he said. "I remember Terry saying something about DPW guys drilling the streets around our place."

"So?"

"The town had no record of them, no permits, town or state. And one of them came to the house one day for a drink. She offered him bottled water but he insisted on taking it from the tap."

"Bingo."

"God, they were part of it," Calvin said. "They were working for Wick and found it in the water. The bastards knew for weeks, which is why they invited me to NYPI to set up the job offer. Then his wife shows up with a fat check to buy us out. They wouldn't take no for

an answer. The son of a bitch. It was all rigged to clear the way."
The pieces were falling into place with dizzying, scary logic. "My
God, they've been directing our lives for weeks. All to get us out
before anybody caught on."

"The problem is, the stuff is still in your well. It'll need to be
decontaminated or drained or something. When are you officially
out of there?"

"Tomorrow."

"And when do they move in?"

"Monday."

"Did they give any indication of their plans?"

"They didn't even show up for the exchange of closing papers.
Just some lawyer."

Waite took a long swig of beer and leaned back as the implications
sank in, a small-town reporter trying to grapple with a dream scoop.

"Dennis, I'm telling you all this because of Sally. Also because I'm
alone with something bigger than me and I don't know what the hell
to do. And I *don't* want to drag my wife into it. She's barely coping as
it is."

"I understand," Waite said. "And I'll do what I can to help. Before
we go to any authorities, we need some hard facts. And with the
holiday weekend, there's nothing we can do until next week. Meanwhile, I'd like to call a few people in Washington."

"Sure, but what we are waiting for?"

"The problem with the EPA is that they do their own water tests,
which means Dr. Tojian's friend isn't official. Which means we'd
need permission from Julius Wick himself, since it's now his well.
Nice irony, huh?"

"There are other ways."

"And all illegal or dangerous. But let me poke around first, make
some calls. Hey, a story of lethal environmental contamination, potential homicide, wrongful deaths and a coverup involving a mem-
ber of the presidential cabinet could have repercussions up the
yingyang. You know, I think it'd be a good idea if I put your story on
tape."

"In case anything happens to me?"

"That, too."

*   *   *

Terry woke with a start Sunday morning. She had had that dream again. The second time since Matty's death . . .

She was at the kitchen window when she saw Matty walking out of the woods across the back lawn behind the pool. She burst out the door and ran toward him. His face was dark, his clothes tattered and fire-blackened. But he was alive and standing on the other side of the pool motioning for her to come. The pool water was swampy black. With every step the pool swelled out in that direction, creating a barrier to her advance. When she tried the other way, the same thing happened— the flank bulging out to block her. She tried to talk to him—ask how he was, if he was hurt, how she could reach him. But he appeared to have lost the power of speech. He just made those beckoning gestures with dark hands and some queer animal-like sounds. Crazy with frustration, she threw herself into the foul soup and swam, her eyes on the gold locket around his neck. But with every stroke the opposite side receded, keeping Matty perpetually out of reach . . .

The first morning she woke up empty and crying.

This morning she was unable to shake the feeling that her son was alive, that somehow he had survived the fire. That it wasn't Matty's body they'd found. She *felt* it, and almost believed it.

On the phone Calvin said it was denial, maybe a self-protective survival reflex. But she wasn't convinced—no matter what he said, no matter that her rational mind told her Matty was dead and buried in Rose Hill cemetery.

It was not even six when Terry got up. Her sister was still asleep. She went down and made some coffee and sat on the porch. On the back lawn among the tulips sat the ceramic statue of a grinning leprechaun Alice had put out there when Matty was three. He loved to visit it.

Her attention fixed on the statue. She thought about the dream.

Maybe this was the madness. Maybe she was so broken by grief that she had actually lost her mind—nothing dramatic: no gibbering hysterical fits; just a snapless segue from sanity to dementia.

She sipped her coffee. Shortly after seven a boy dropped off the Sunday newspaper. Terry watched him walk back down the drive-way pushing a cart full of papers. He was wearing a baseball cap with the visor curled the way Matty did his. He looked about the same age, same size . . .

She sipped her coffee and glanced over the front page, grateful she had something to keep her distracted. But her mind could not hold any of it. There was an article about a Middle East terrorist attack. A big parade was planned for Portland tomorrow. On the bottom left were the headlines: NEW BIOTECH CZAR TO REVIEW PENDING GENE LEGISLATION. There was a picture of the man . . . he had a high forehead and a lean face, lidded, intelligent eyes. She thought about reading it but decided it meant nothing to her. None of it did. The world did not touch her life.

Up the street the paperboy was pushing his cart.

And then she remembered . . . Matty was wearing the locket the day he died, and the stainless steel emergency tag the doctors insisted he wear. Along with his remains they had found charred scraps of his shoes and clothes, the buckle of his belt, a few coins, and his Swiss pocket knife. *But no chain, no pendant, no tag.* And they had gone over the place with a metal detector . . .

Terry went into the house and called the airline. The only available seat was on the evening flight. She called Calvin at his hotel and told him to meet her at Logan Airport at eight-thirty. When he asked her why, she didn't say. All she knew . . . *felt* . . . was the urge to go back home, even if it made no sense.

Calvin tried to talk her out of it but finally gave up. After all, what difference did it make? She had nothing left to lose.

CHAPTER

42

Julius was at his desk staring at the blank screen of the huge Sony console when DeVoe and McDermott showed up.

He let them in and locked the door. The expression on his face was grimmer than usual. Which didn't make sense, since a few hours ago they had returned from Boston with news of how smoothly the transfer went. DeVoe had also reported that his men were all set to begin neutralizing the well.

Julius nodded to the leather armchairs facing the television. "I want you to see something," he said.

DeVoe and McDermott crossed the room to the chairs and Julius returned to his desk. Through the window just behind him glowed the west wing of the White House. He glanced at it through the curtains before he closed them.

"About an hour ago a courier dropped this off," he said.

DeVoe stared at him. "Dropped what off?"

Julius picked up the remote control and hit the "play" button. There was a slight whir of the VCR as the lights went on and the television lit up. At first the screen was a silent blur of browns, blacks and grays. But slowly as the lens pulled back, the image came into focus.

"God," DeVoe said.

Ferocious black eyes glared out of an inhuman face covered with hair. Like some kind of Halloween mask. But quickly it became evident that what filled the screen was no rubber mask, no slick makeup job. It was real. And the only certain sign that it might be human was the flatness of the face. Yet dark hair with the gloss of pelt covered the skin to the eyes.

Then a voice came on. "My name is Matthew Hazzard, and I've got a secret." It was obviously not the boy's voice.

The camera pulled back to reveal the boy crouched in a cage with his legs pulled up and his face resting on his knees. He was naked, and his body was covered with thick black down. He looked like one of those prehuman models in glass-front dioramas of natural history museums. Except this model breathed.

From someplace in the unseen background came the sharp clanging of metal on metal. The effect was immediate. The boy hissed open-mouthed. He pulled himself up and slouched toward one side of the cage, hands pendant like a primate.

"Matthew used to play second base on Little League," the voice continued in a tone of fatuous amusement. "Number 11, for the Devil Dogs." A chuckle, then: "You scientists have such foresight."

Matthew slid down the bars into a squat, estimating the camera.

"The fact is, he used to be a normal, healthy all-American boy. Lived at number 12 Jason Street in Carleton, Massachusetts—"

The boy let out a sharp cry.

"See, Dr. Julius Wick, he remembers," the voice said. "But in case you don't, it's where you and your colleagues at BiOmega Research labs a long time ago buried your dirty little secret called Black Flag. That nasty little genocide germ for use in Vietnam or wherever national security called. Just ask your colleagues Stefan Karsky, Maria Terranova, Marcus Wiley, and Jack Perry. Oh, I forgot. They're no longer with us. Gone to the great white petri dish upstairs. Which means there's only you. And Matthew here. As you can see, he's very much alive."

The boy growled at something off-camera.

"Where the hell did you get this?" DeVoe said.

"*Your* hired gun," Julius told him.

God . . . then who did they bury? DeVoe looked at McDermott. But McDermott did not take his eyes from the screen.

"Like all boys," the voice continued, "he loves dogs."

Something off-camera snapped Matthew's head around. He slipped to his knees, letting out a rumble. It was answered by frantic whimpers. The camera swung left to a large brown mongrel cowering at the gate. "And this is Buster."

Buster was clearly terrified. His ears were flat and his head scraped low, as if to be whipped. He whimpered, then scampered to the opposite side of the cage. Matty slowly straightened up, his eyes stalking the dog.

"Isn't he something?" the narrator said. There was no irony in the voice this time. "Look at those eyes."

The camera zoomed in. They blazed with excitement.

"Word is," the voice continued, "he got this way because a little Black Flag leaked into his water well. Kind of a pity, because it messed up his Little League plans. Not to mention what it could do to the Office of Biotechnology."

"There's more," Julius said.

The dog did a little jig of panic. Matty closed in, his mouth slack and stringed with drool. When he got to within a few feet, the dog bolted to the opposite side of the cage and slammed itself into the bars. Matty still came, and in a reflex the dog lunged at Matty, who caught him in midair by the neck. The next instant the dog went sailing across the cage into the bars. For a stunned moment he looked around, then terror-charged rage sent him at Matty, catching him by the ankle. Matt chopped the dog's head with his hand, the dog's grip went slack. The next moment Matty was on him.

The camera rolled for only another twenty seconds, just long enough to show Matty red-mouthed at the dog's throat. Then the picture went blank.

"Christ Almighty," DeVoe muttered.

"In case you're wondering," the voice resumed, "Buster was removed with a mop. The good news is that we won't have to feed Matty for a couple of days. As you can see from this demonstration, Matthew is quite adept at handling himself. Of course, his usual meal consists of smaller competition. We can't risk having damaged goods, can we, Dr. Wick? Which brings up the purpose of this greeting."

When the picture came on again, they were looking at a magazine photograph of Julius Wick shaking hands with President Morgan Reese.

"Need I remind you what a shame it would be if word got out about Matty and Black Flag? But that need not happen."

With the camera still trained on the *Newsweek* photo, the voice went on to the ransom. "At an agreed time and place, Matty and all copies of this video will be released to you on the condition that you deposit two million dollars in a specified bank account. The details will be spelled out to you on Monday. Have a nice weekend."

The screen went to snow.

Julius pulled the cassette out.

Frank was on his feet. "How the hell did he get the kid?"

"You dropped him in his lap when you hired him to *clear tracks*," Julius told DeVoe.

"I don't need that, Julius," Frank said.

Julius looked at him. "I'm the one whose head is on the block. You can walk away from this right now. I told you it wasn't necessary to spill blood. They wouldn't have said anything—"

"You don't know that—"

Julius slammed his fist on the desk. "Could it be worse than *that*?" He nodded toward the television. "Now we've got to deal with a hit man turned blackmailer."

"We did what we thought best to protect our interests, our own president's," Frank said feebly.

"And now it's come back on us. No, on *me*."

Frank turned toward Julius. His face was red. "Julius, I'm getting very tired—"

McDermott cut him off. "Cool it. He's right, it backfired. What's important now is where we go from here."

"Straight to prison," Julius said.

"Not if we play along."

"So it's going to cost two million dollars."

"It beats the alternative," McDermott said.

"What's to guarantee he'll deliver the boy?" Julius asked. "Or maybe save a backup tape for when he needs another two million?"

"We have no guarantee," McDermott said. "But if he wants his money, he'll have to deliver the boy and the tapes first. Once we have the boy, the tapes will be practically useless. In two or three days the well will be neutralized. After that, there's no case against us. It'll be the word of a presidential appointee against the claims of some anonymous crazy on a crude video—just one more ransom attempt that gets trashed every day in this town."

Julius was not convinced. "What about your contact man, Roman? Why not get your men to locate the hit man through him?"

McDermott shook his head. "Roman knows nothing about him, including his name."

"Well, how the hell does he pay him?"

"Electronically and anonymously," McDermott explained. "The fee was deposited by computer into a different anonymous bank account every time. He hasn't a clue where the guy lives or what his name is."

"My God," Julius said. "At first I thought we were dealing with a mindless killer. Bad enough. But the guy's a Machiavellian genius. While we were wiring him tens of thousands of dollars to clear our tracks, he's quietly setting us up for blackmail."

"He's not exactly in the loyalty business."

"And we are."

McDermott looked at Julius. There was no challenge in his eyes this time. "Yes, we are."

"One of them must have talked," Frank DeVoe said.

"Or he got it out of him, then," McDermott said. "It makes no difference now." He got up and pulled the cassette out of the VCR. Along the spine was a piece of masking tape, across which in black pen were the words: SON OF BLACK FLAG. The son of a bitch was taunting them. He looked at Julius. "Did any of your people know about Morgan Reese's link to Black Flag?"

"I was the only one."

"You're absolutely sure?"

"Yes," Julius said. "And Claire, of course."

McDermott nodded. "Then there's no way he could have linked Black Flag to Morgan Reese."

"No way I can think of."

McDermott nodded and glanced at DeVoe.

"So what do we do?" Julius asked.

"We pay him his two million," McDermott said. "He's too smart to telephone you here, he knows it can be traced. Unfortunately you'll have to make arrangements to transfer the money. But the stipulation is that we get the boy first."

"And what if he doesn't comply?"

"If he wants his money, he has no choice."

Julius got up and looked out the window. "He can bring us all down, and we don't even know his name."

"He won't," McDermott said. "Transfer the money on Monday and this will all be behind us." His tone was soothing.

"You keep saying 'us' but I keep hearing *me*,'" Julius said.

"Julius, we're in this together."

"One for all and all for one, right?"

McDermott got up and came over to him. "Yes."

"But on my two million dollars."

"I'm afraid so, Julius. But it could be worse."

Julius turned from the window to face him. "You'd have to prove that to me."

McDermott said nothing.

While McDermott and DeVoe went out for dinner, Julius made the necessary arrangements with his lawyer to transfer money on Monday morning when the instructions came through.

Two hours later DeVoe and McDermott returned to Julius's office. They drove him to the airport, where Claire had cabbed in from the house they had bought in Vienna. For the remainder of the weekend they were taking the Lear to their place near Argyle-on-the-Hudson, where Julius would continue reviewing the pending legislation for the president.

They loaded the suitcases into the storage area of the jet and secured it closed.

"It'll be behind us by the middle of the week," McDermott said. "I guarantee it."

Julius acknowledged with a nod.

"Have a good flight."

They shook Julius's hand and each gave Claire a hug.

A few minutes later they watched the Lear streak into the violet afterglow of the sun.

At ten-seventeen the jet cut northeast toward the New Jersey coast. At a point some eleven miles southwest of Newark, the pilot noticed the fuel gauge begin to drop. At first he thought the readout was faulty. But the auxiliary gauge gave the same indication that fuel was pouring out of the tanks. A moment later an emergency warning light went on, with an accompanying buzz. They were losing fuel and fast. Given their position and altitude, they could, the pilot figured, just make it to Newark airport. On the emergency frequency he called in the request to land.

In the cabin Julius Wick sat with his face in the window, staring down into the black, plasticine surface of the Atlantic. Claire reclined beside him, her eyes closed and her head against the head-rest. A half-empty glass of Lillet sat in the holder of her tray. She had just dined on a prepared meal of lobster tail, sautéed fiddle-heads and boiled new potatoes, kept warm by the on-board micro. Julius had no appetite and was halfway through a glass of red wine.

On his tray table sat the red leatherbound legislation package. He and President Morgan Reese were scheduled to meet at five on Monday to discuss whether the president should sign. The review was Julius's first major order of business as biotech czar, and his insights were critical to the president. From what he had read, the legislation would essentially liberalize restrictions on the biochemi-cal industry. While the president was reluctant to sign on to such measures, he managed to attach a tagalong condition for the protec-tion of the ozone layer. It was a trade-off with congressional opposi-tion: increasing industry-wide restrictions on atmospheric pollutants while relaxing those on land-and-water dumping for biotech firms. As the president told him, such trade-offs happened all the time: one giant step forward, a half step backward.

But Julius could not concentrate enough to open the package. That video kept getting in the way.

Ever since its arrival, he had on some wordless level of conscious-ness felt a terrible vulnerability. No, not just the obvious vulnerabil-ity to blackmail, which was bad enough. Something more . . .

We're all in this together, McDermott had said.

But were they? Somehow McDermott's words did not generate much reassurance. It was his two million. More, it was his reputa-tion and his post. Suppose their enterprising hit man refused to deliver the boy until payment was received? They were not in a leverage position to demand the boy be turned over first. Of course, the risk to them—no, to him—was that unfulfilled payment could go on until he was drained. And still they might not get the boy *or* the videos. And suppose word of the boy was made public? That would be the end of him. *And* the president himself by association.

Guilt by association.

Take us all down.

As Julius's eyes trained on the moon rippling across the water, a chilling thought surfaced.

What if something happened to me? And Claire? We're the only ones that link the president to Black Flag. Even if word of the boy and Black Flag gets out, there's *nobody* who knows Morgan Reese was part of the project, that he oversaw the financial operations and so was also culpable. Nobody, that is, except McDermott and DeVoe . . .

Julius Wick felt the jet go into premature descent. He had no hint of the urgency in the cockpit—not until he became aware of an oddly sweet odor. Jet fuel.

At first it barely registered on his consciousness. It wasn't until he noticed the orangey glow reflected off the wings that the moment telescoped his horror. His first thought was exterior lights or reflections from cities below. But there was too much flickering for that. Something else.

Suddenly the smell filled his head. Flames were fluttering beneath the wing.

"Oh, God . . ."

He had to alert the pilot. As his hand released the tongue of his seat belt, Claire opened her eyes. "What's wrong?"

"We're on fire."

"What?"

"Lousy bastards!" he pushed to his feet.

But he never reached the cockpit door. And the last thought that bloomed in his mind was . . . "clearing track."

The next moment exploded into a concussion of light.

CHAPTER

43

Jerry Mars arrived at the Fig's at eight. He had an hour.

Through the back door he brought in Matty, who was draped in a black hooded robe and with leg irons, handcuffs and a muzzle.

Jerry led him to a back stall and bound him to a steel support beam. The tranquilizer had nearly worn off and the boy thrashed violently.

Jerry had had no intention of fighting him. At least not until he saw the news last night about Julius Benton Wick and his wife killed in a plane crash. Now it made no difference, because there was nobody to bargain with. He had eliminated two-thirds of the Bi-Omega connection, and a leaky fuel line took care of the rest. There were no next of kin, and nobody to press for hush money. If the kid was going to make him some fast cash, Jerry decided he would have to do it soon, before the boy dropped dead from his own adrenalin.

Given the short notice, the Fig outdid himself. Since Jerry's call he had contacted each of the regulars with the news: that the annual Memorial Day conference would be an event to mark the calendar from. One beyond their wildest dreams. But they would need strong stomachs. He did not explain, only said that the main event would be a blind match—meaning that they would not know the star contestant until event time. But he promised a match to beat all matches; and if they wanted in, they would have to bring their best dogs and minimum antes of twenty-five grand.

Understandably, there were protests about all the mystery and the antes; and half the takers turned down the invitation. But twenty-seven men did arrive that Sunday night, cash in hand, more than a dozen with dogs. They had not seen the video of Matty taking apart a junkyard dog, as the Fig had. But from the new configuration of the pit, they knew something big was planned. The old four-foot-high plywood walls had been replaced by a quarter-inch steel bar cage ten-feet square and seven-feet high. The review area told them nothing. Just their own dogs in a row of cages. A couple throwaways for warmup. But rumor buzzed that the Fig had gotten hold of timber wolves or maybe some big zoo cats.

The first four events took less than an hour and a half. Muzzy watched Chopper against French DeRoche's two-year-old bull named Arnie. Chopper lost most of his left ear and Arnie had to be dragged off with a rope. Of the six other bulls, two were so badly mauled that they ended up in the dumpster.

The main event was scheduled to begin immediately after the last dogs. But the Fig kept them waiting until nearly ten. He had read someplace that Harry Houdini always showed up late to peak the audience's anticipation, so that when he finally walked out on stage, the place went wild. By ten the twenty-seven men around the cage were more than ready. They hollered and stamped their feet. When it appeared that he could no longer contain them, the Fig, with a love for drama, suddenly killed the lights from the switch at the rear door. A grumbling dismay charged the audience.

"Hey, Fig," someone yelled, "this better be good or I'm going in there with you."

Which broke the place up.

The noise was suddenly cut by Fig's voice over the PA. "Gentlemen, I give you Kid Kong."

The lights went on and Matthew stood hunched in the middle of the cage, naked and furred. When he saw the men, he roared and shook the cage with his hands.

Somebody called out, "What *is* it?"

The question of the moment.

Jerry stood outside the cage door, beaming.

Over the PA the Fig announced that Kid Kong was being conferenced with his own prize Rottweiler, Jake, 110 pounds of compact fury that had never lost a match. The winner would take on Jerry Mars's Rufus.

The odds on each were announced and the betting slips were

passed out. Minimum bet was $25,000. Jerry pushed a bucket of water into the cage, and Matty lowered his head to drink, then slouched to a corner and waited.

There was a hush, somebody in back hooted. Down the aisle came the Fig being pulled toward the cage by Jake, a muscle-wadded brown-and-white black berserker that knew no fear. The Fig had to struggle against the choke chain as Jake fought to get to Matty, thrashed his head to get the muzzle off.

When he got to the door, Jerry took hold of Jake, so Muzzy could talk through the hand mike. "Gentlemen, as usual, it's a fight to the finish."

Applause. They were getting their money's worth. So was Jerry. Even if Matty did not survive the night, he'd walk away with a minimum of $400,000. And if he survived, maybe twice that. Who needed Julius Wick?

The Fig unlocked the cage and led Jake in, still fighting against the chain. With a tug he heeled the dog and released the muzzle. Matty tried to probe his brain but it was too scrambled. An impenetrable mass.

The Fig removed the choke collar. At the same time Matty got to his feet and let out a deep-throated sound that for an instant seemed to startle Jake. The animal licked its nose and looked over its shoulder at Fig, who was locking the cage door. Matty flailed his hands at Jake. The dog lowered its head like a blunderbuss, eyes slitted.

With a crack of his palms the Fig ordered "GO," and Jake shot toward Matty as though spring-released. In a twirling motion Matty forearmed the dog by the side of the head, deflecting him to the sawdust.

Jake made another pass, this time clamping onto Matty's ankle. Matty let out a yell and fell backward to the ground. Jake thrashed against the joint while Matty fought to reach his head. But Jake was smart, pulling Matty by the foot across the cage so that it was impossible to gain a hold. Matty grabbed the bars to stop them, the spike vise pierced to the bone. With a fist Matty pounded Jake on the nose. The blow released the jaws but Jake then went at Matty's face. In reflex Matty threw up his bad arm, only to catch the dog's jaws on the wrist. The weight of the animal was startling. So was the pain. They struggled until, in a sudden thrust of his legs, Matty pushed Jake onto his back, the dog's jaws still locked on his wrist. With his left hand Matty caught the right front paw and twisted it halfway around. Instantly Jake released Matty's hand, and Matty swiftly latched onto the other paw.

In the three years the Fig had owned Jake, he had never heard the dog make a sound. Never a bark, never a whimper—nothing more than a thin, involuntary whine of anticipation as the Fig dangled him a snack cat. But the sound that now came from Jake cut to the quick of the Fig's brain. Matty had straddled Jake, and with a paw in each hand spread-eagled the dog. The howl from the dog was punctuated by two sharp cracks of the shoulder joints, and Jake lay there, hind legs absurdly trying to walk in the air, front legs twitching limp adieus.

It was supposed to be a fight to the finish but the Fig wouldn't allow it. Disregarding the crowd's demands, he unlocked the cage, gun in hand, and pulled Jake out by the hindquarters. The dog's jaws were working to catch its breath against the blood flow. Mooch helped haul the animal out back. There were two muffled shots, and Jake was in the dumpster.

When the crowd caught its breath, some at ringside began the Rufus chant that quickly spread. "ROOF-US, ROOF-US."

Another bucket of water for Matty. Then Rufus.

Slowly Jerry walked him down the aisle as if he were a legendary martial artist—sleek and implacable. He moved him toward the cage—muzzle quietly in place, stride unbroken and measured, eyes fixed and purposeful.

From the mat of sawdust Matty rubbed his ankle. The flesh had been torn to the bone but his eyes were on Rufus as he was promenaded to the cage.

Though Rufus had never been fought, breeding and conditioning had left his instincts sharp. For most of a week Jerry would not feed the dog; then, when he was nearly mad from hunger, he would toss Rufus an animal to heighten the craving for blood. For endurance he would tie Rufus to a tree limb by his muzzle strap for as long as twenty minutes, his life spared by the sheer strength of his neck muscles and his will to live. In an upstairs room Jerry kept a treadmill rigged with a harness that gave Rufus only one option—to run in place while Jerry cranked up the speed and incline. Once he kept

Rufus in motion for two hours. If during any of the conditioning Rufus made a sound, Jerry would jab him with an electric prod. For not yelping he was rewarded with a chicken or cat. So Rufus no longer showed pain. After three years of such premium tuning he was the finest conditioned killing machine on four legs.

While the Fig made the announcements, Jerry undid the muzzle. Rufus pressed his face against the bars and waited patiently for the door to open. His mouth was closed. No flash of teeth. No growl. No hard breathing. His heartbeat was not elevated. And yet, in an instant, he could become a berserker.

Matty, in his state, sensed what lay just beneath the placid surface. Cunning crossed with intelligence and power. Rufus was death.

The cage opened and the dog moved inside.

Matty pushed himself to his feet and limped to the bars to steady himself. Blood trailed his foot and matted the hair of his arm. Rufus, expressionless, stood in place, watched. Matty edged his way along the bars, the men pulling back as he approached.

For a minute Matty and Rufus made slow, deliberate circles around each other, moving as if in liquid crystal, held in a soundless bond of the eyes. A boy-beast and his dog, engaged in a weird ritual courtship before the kill.

"Hey, what the hell's the story?" somebody said. Others were muttering.

But Jerry knew. Matty and Rufus were coursing each other, alert for the precise angle of attack.

Jerry's grin widened as Matty dipped into a crouch, arms spread. Jerry pressed himself to the bars just inches from Matty.

"Beautiful," he said to himself.

Then, like the crack of a whip, Jerry said, "Rufus, kill."

The change was instant. Rufus reared back on his haunches, his mouth glittering, his lips stretched tight across his teeth.

But it was Matty who made the first move. He grabbed the bars, and before Jerry could react, Matty had stretched open a wide hole, so wide that he pulled Jerry into the cage, then pressed himself out, squeezing closed the bars behind him.

People pulled back as Matty staggered up the aisle. A few started after him, but he made it to the back-door switch and plunged the place into darkness. Panic filled the black. After a minute of scrambling, somebody turned on the lights again.

Matty was gone.

In the cage, however, Rufus was gaping at Jerry.

They tried to shout him down. Somebody even shot in the air. But it did not stop Rufus. He had been trained not to be startled by sharp sounds, including gunshots. Jerry Mars had been very thorough.

It did not take long. And Jerry did not cry out. His eyes were wide with terror—and something else—a kind of ecstasy. In the brief, hushed reprieve, Jerry dove into the night water of Rufus's eyes and swam until the green flash of his own life flicked out.

Then a gunshot found its mark, and Rufus died with his master's neck in his jaws.

Amid the noisy confusion someone did spot Matty at the rear of the hall. Guns came out. But in the darkness Matty had unbolted the twelve cages, and before the men could take aim, Matty had unleashed the dogs' minds as well as their bodies and sent them down on the men. In the melée he found the light switch by the rear door and once again threw the barn into darkness, then crashed through the door and into the night.

Across the blackened fields he hobbled, his hand and arm half-mangled, his ankle nearly crushed, pushed on by the savage howls of dogs and men.

CHAPTER

44

Calvin met Terry's plane at 8:30 P.M.

Her call that morning had taken him by surprise. When he had put her on the plane yesterday, her sole intent was to get out of Carleton. And her sister's place was the necessary sanctuary. The plan had been that Calvin would drive up Monday. When he announced that he might be held up until Tuesday or Wednesday, she agreed, seeing the delay as that much more private healing time. Then, out of the blue, she announced her return. He tried to convince her to stay, but conceded when his protests somehow became suspect.

Terry arrived with only a carry-on bag. She wore jeans and a blue denim shirt. She looked tired but in control. Maybe she had taken the Valium Mitch had given her.

When she emerged from the secured area, they embraced for a long moment. "I love you very much," he whispered. And as he held her, he thought how their love was the ballast of his sanity. That now she was the central condition of his life.

Yet as they drove in silence, guilt roared inside him.

"Is something wrong?" Terry asked.

"No, I'm fine. You know . . ."

"You seem somewhere else."

"I'm just dead tired," he said, and turned on the radio.

Since the morning, he had unreeled his plan to tell her how he had bought Matty's death. In the hotel, with some wine to soften the blow. He would be straight with her: that he had laid down the deposit in a careless rush at a good buy, all but dismissing the liability. Yes, he should have checked it out. Especially after the second miscarriage. He had done wrong, and it would eat at him until his death.

He would tell Terry what he'd learned about BiOmega and the machinations of Julius Wick and his wife. They couldn't offset his own guilt, but at least they could put the whole awful business in some perspective, maybe redirect her outrage. For what *that* was worth . . .

As they rode to the hotel, Calvin wondered where it would all end. He recalled reading someplace that seventy-five percent of the marriages in which a child died eventually ended in divorce. He suspected that his confession tonight would raise those odds.

They arrived at the hotel at nine-thirty. Terry unpacked her things, then stretched out on one of the twin beds.

Calvin poured her a glass of wine. She took a sip and relaxed against the pillow. She closed her eyes and let out a deep breath. He moved to the foot of her bed.

"Terry, I have something more to tell you . . . A couple of weeks ago I told you about how a research lab had buried some waste in the backyard."

The look in her eyes asked why he was bringing this up again.

"The water tests you had done turned up negative. Well, Mitch Tojian did a more comprehensive analysis and . . . they found something. An artificial hormone made in a lab back in the early seventies . . . the same chemical that they found in Matty."

Terry's hand moved involuntarily, spilling some wine on her wrist.

He took a deep breath.

"It was also found in the miscarried fetuses."

There was a long hush. Then Terry made an inarticulate sound, as if trying to formulate words. Calvin rushed on as she pressed her face into the pillows. He told her the details of the dump and the cover-up. He showed her photocopies of their deed and the *Newsweek* story on Julius Wick.

"He was hand-picked for a prestigious job by the president just a few weeks ago. I believe they wanted to buy our place before word got out that this . . . stuff was in the water. Which explains the inflated offer. And the suddenly-endowed job at twice my salary. It was all a setup. Vile, vicious conspiracy and setup . . ."

Her mouth worked without words. Finally she got it out. "I don't *care* if it was a conspiracy or who it was. My babies are *dead*. And, Calvin, you let it happen, you let it happen."

"I didn't know—"

"You knew from the beginning, you said so. You could have stopped it. Matty would still be alive . . ."

"I didn't know what it was, Terry. I didn't know it was dangerous," he said, hating the feebleness of his defense. "They said it was nothing to worry about—"

"Who did?"

"Beverly."

"*Beverly*? Of course, she'd say not to worry. She was making a sale. Why didn't you check it out yourself?"

It was the question that would always haunt him. "I'm sorry," he whispered. It was futile to say more.

"Sorry? Why the hell did you even tell me about my babies?"

"Guilt, I guess. Also maybe to divert your grief—"

"Divert to *what*?"

"To exposing the bastards behind it all."

She swung her feet off the bed and ran into the bathroom.

For a long moment Calvin just stared at his image in the dresser mirror thinking *I've killed us all* when the telephone rang.

Calvin looked at it. Its persistence made him want to tear it out of the wall but he answered it.

"Calvin, Dennis Waite. Sorry to bother you at this hour, but I've got to see you."

"I can't."

"Well, it's important. I'm downstairs here in the lobby."

"Terry's here."

A pause. "I see. The lobby's a mob scene. A busload of tourists just returned. I know it's awkward, but can I come up? It'll just take a minute."

Calvin sighed. "Okay," he said, and hung up.

He told Terry that Dennis Waite was on his way up. She said nothing and sat in a chair staring out the window. When Waite arrived, there were awkward introductions. Terry's eyes were dry but red, and Waite immediately picked up the tension.

"I'll be quick," he said. "I take it, you haven't seen the news."

"What news?" Calvin said, his voice wooden.

"Julius Wick and Claire Manning are dead."

For a moment Calvin couldn't process the significance of the news. "How . . . ?"

"They were killed last night when their jet caught fire over the Jersey coast. It's in the news. They're saying it was a faulty fuel line or ruptured tank."

Calvin listened, still not clear about the significance of this news.

"There's more," Waite said. He unfolded a sheet of paper from his jacket pocket. "I've got a good friend at the Washington *Post*. After we talked yesterday, I called her. I told her I needed background on the new biotech czar. Deep background that might mean prying things open with the Freedom of Information Act. Of course, all Washington is closed down for the weekend, but bureaucrats are bureaucrats, and some even work on Christmas Day. I told her it was red alert and I needed stuff now. She owed me a favor and, to make a long story short, she found somebody at the National Security Archives who was burning the midnight oil. She just faxed me this." He handed the memo to Calvin.

"BiOmega Research Laboratory, Adamsville, MA. From 1968–1972. Involved in a military contract financed by the Department of Defense and the US Air Force. The project was classified Top Secret and went under the code name of Black Flag." Some contract numbers were listed. "The project was intended to develop a viral compound that could be passed through the food chain or water supply and would result in the sterilization of human males." He handed it back to Waite. Terry gave them a vacant look.

"Given the dates," Waite said, "it could only mean they had targeted future generations of Viet Cong. In other words, biochemical genocide. Evidently they scrapped the project in '72. And according to Jane, BiOmega was dissolved even before the war ended, maybe because it was winding down. Or maybe because it wasn't working right."

"It worked." Terry's voice was barely audible.

Waite thought he understood what she meant, but realized that was beyond anything he could say or do. He turned back to Calvin. "What's critical now is that the stuff's still in the water and has to be dealt with. What's certain is that nobody can get at the well until the lawyers hash out legal ownership, with the Wicks dead. And until then we'd have to get a restraining order to show cause to test the well. Hell could break loose while the goddamn red tape holds it up."

While Waite talked, Terry looked blankly out the window. She had receded into a private place from where, Calvin feared, he might never bring her back. She surely didn't need this.

"Which means sometime next week—"

Calvin cut him off. "Dennis, thanks for the information, but I think we should talk another time." He didn't care anymore. Not about the well or the conspiracy or coverup. He just wanted his wife back. She was all he had left. All that mattered now.

Waite looked up at him, then at Terry. He nodded. "Sorry." He opened the door. "I'll call tomorrow."

When he left, Calvin turned to his wife. "Anything I can get you?"

She shook her head, then mechanically removed her clothes and dropped them on the floor and pulled up the covers, her back to Calvin.

He undressed, got into his twin bed and turned out the light. He stared into the dark. He felt no connectedness to the bed or the room. He felt no connectedness to the world. He wished he could vaporize into the black.

Calvin was asleep when the lights snapped on. Through fuzzy slits he saw Terry getting dressed.

"What are you doing?"

"Going out."

"Out? It's one-thirty."

She continued to dress.

"Terry."

"I'm having bad dreams."

"There's no place to walk around here."

"I'll take the car."

He watched her pull on her jeans. Her bare back faced him. He studied the fine definition of her shoulders. He wanted to massage her the way she liked. He wondered if she'd ever let him touch her again.

"You want company?"

"I don't care."

He grabbed at that and got dressed.

In minutes they were pulling out of the parking lot. They drove through Harvard Square in silence. Except for a few late stragglers, the streets were deserted.

They cut behind the square into Mass. Ave. and headed west. "Where do you want to go?"

"No place." Her voice was flat, lifeless.

He let the silence settle, then said, "Terry, will you ever forgive me?"

No answer.

He did not repeat the question. He'd been stupid to ask. What did he expect?

The car moved down Mass. Ave. through Porter Square. The farther they got from Harvard, the more barren the streets. When they reached the intersection at Alewife before crossing into Arlington, Terry said, "I want to go home."

"Okay." He slowed the car down to make a U-turn.

"Not the hotel. Home."

"Why? Why in God's name go back there?"

She did not answer. In the dim light she just stared out of the window, her face a blank.

Maybe it was a last-ditch effort to reconcile with the past. Maybe a kind of ritual leavetaking. Or maybe it was something else. Whatever, he didn't understand. And he wasn't certain that she did. It was the last place he would have imagined her wanting to go this night. She hated the house, all it had become. But he drove her there.

As expected, at 2:00 A.M. the neighborhood was pitch dark. He resented the coziness of the other homes—families in bed, mornings full of life. He rounded the corner of Jason and was about to drive by and turn around at the top when Terry said, "No, pull in."

He cut the wheel and slowly drove up the driveway.

The house, of course, was black, but somehow it was still unsettling. No matter how late it was when he'd return, there was always some sign of life—an outside light, the kitchen lamp, even the green glow of the digital clock on the micro. But this was more than the absence of a light. In the headlights the windows seemed to gape like sightless eyes, stripped of curtains and blinds. And within, naked walls. The place looked like it had died.

Calvin did not drive around back but stopped at the front wall. He got out, still not clear why they were here.

There was no sound but the static charge of crickets. The light of a full moon white-washed the front lawn.

Terry headed up the walk with a kind of slow deliberation. She stopped once to take in the dead dogwood. In the cold moonlight it looked like an X-ray.

"Terry, let's not torture ourselves." He took her arm. "Come on, let's go—"

But she pulled away and dug into her pockets for the key. She looked driven. Obsessed.

She unlocked the front door and he followed her through.

It was as if he had entered a vacuum. The emptiness sucked his breath. Nothing stirred. Nothing broke the blankness.

Calvin made a move to turn on the dining room chandelier—the only remaining fixture—but Terry stopped him. The moonlight seepage would guide her.

She moved through the downstairs rooms with her arms wrapped tightly to her chest. The only sound was of their feet across the oak floorboards.

In the family room Calvin said, "Terry, why are we here? What's the point?"

Her eyes were wide. "I don't know . . ." And there was nothing in her face to say she did.

He followed her upstairs, trying to fight back the memories . . . Matty diapered and climbing the stairs for the first time, Matty bounding down on Christmas morning, his feet stuffed in Kermit-the-Frog slippers, Matty sitting on the bottom step trying to teach Daisy to talk . . .

At the top Terry turned into his room. Calvin again caught her arm. "Don't do this to yourself."

Again she pulled away, not with anger but an iron determination.

The room was like a vacant cube. All the gaudy monsters had

been ripped off the walls. The only sign that it had once belonged to their son was Terry's mural on the west wall, a goofy Cheshire-cat caricature of Daisy grinning out at the world from a leafy tree house. That and the hole Matty had punched in the wall.

Calvin stepped outside to the landing. He wanted to go. "Terry . . ."

She did not answer. She was at the window peering into the back-yard.

"Terry, enough. This is sick."

But she remained frozen, her eyes fixed on something below.

"Are you all right?"

She walked by him and down the stairs. He followed.

But instead of heading back to the car, she turned left and walked around to the rear.

The backyard was a still-life canvas except for a wrinkled moon that floated on the black slick of the pool. And the white noise of crickets—thousands of insect legs scraping against each other. Someplace an air conditioner hummed.

Still without a word, Terry moved across the grass toward the pool. Calvin followed a few steps behind. She came to a stop at the dead end, near the diving board, and stared into the dense shadows of the woods.

"Terry, what is it?"

It was as if his words never reached her. After a moment she lowered her face to the water—

"*No*," he said, and before she could step off the edge, he grabbed her. "What are you doing?"

He turned her around. Her eyes appeared sightless. He pulled her against his chest, put his arms around her. Finally he felt her relax against him. "I love you," he whispered. "Terry, we still have each other. Please, let's not lose that." Did he feel her nod, ever so slightly?

For several minutes they held each other by the pool's edge with-out speaking. Calvin closed his eyes and caressed her back. He tried to make his mind blank. Still, the rumble of the air conditioner. The Starkeys'. He had heard it earlier but in the moment hadn't thought about it. The woods carried sound . . . But this was too close, and it didn't have that fanlike purr of air conditioners. More a kind of resonating thrum.

"You hear that?"

"What?" Terry said.

"A motor. Like a pump." He picked up its direction. "Over there."

He took her hand and walked them past the pool and toward the far corner where their property ended and Magog Woods began.

Some kind of machine. Deep in the shadows of the trees.

Calvin wished he had kept a flashlight in the car. The garage was empty, of course, and the spare flashlight was long gone.

What struck him first was the odd structure. Sitting at the wood's edge was a shed, maybe seven feet high. Like one of those prefab sheds for storing tools.

"What is it?" Terry asked.

Somebody had constructed a housing over their well pump. The persistent thrumming came from a generator, the exhaust of which passed through the roof. Whoever put it up had worked at muffling the sound, because Calvin could feel heavy vibrations under his feet. He could also feel waves of heat from inside. Running through scrub and high grass behind the structure were thick rubber pipes carrying water. Also heavy orange extension wires that seemed to stretch toward the garage.

"They're pumping out the well," he said.

"Who?"

Who, indeed. Dr. Tojian had said it would be at least a week for the authorities to take notice.

They followed the wires from the housing down the edge of the lawn and across the rear flank of the pool around the flower bed and into the rear window of the garage.

Calvin picked up the faint banana odor of spray paint.

All the garage windows had been blackened, which explained why they hadn't noticed the light when they'd pulled up. But at the rear was one small half-broken pane. Through it they saw two large vans backed up inside. The far one was closed and dark, but the vehicle at the window had its rear door open, and inside he could make out the green glow of computer monitors and the blinkings of some other electronics. At one screen sat a man with headphones.

"What . . . ?" Terry never finished her question.

"You can see better inside."

A tall blond man was standing behind them. In his hand was a pistol.

"You?" Terry said.

"That's right." He pointed the gun at them. "Inside."

The man moved them around to the front. He hit the garage door button, and the door rose with a familiar rusty squeal. The interior light went on. The man was wearing a navy blue sweatshirt, jeans and a safari vest. He had a hard, pale face. With his fist he pounded the closed van. "Company."

The side door slid back and two other men emerged, each holding a short-barrel revolver. They were in their shorts, one barechested, the other in a Raiders red T-shirt. The man monitoring the equipment stepped around his van. He was wearing a shoulder holster and gun. "Who are they?"

"Used to live here," said the blond.

"What do they want?" he asked, looking at Calvin and Terry.

"Who knows? Snooping, I guess."

"This is the same one?" Calvin asked Terry.

"Yes."

The phantom DPW crew. The BiOmega backstage, but how were they connected? "Who are you protecting?" Calvin demanded. "Your bosses are dead."

The one in the Raiders shirt moved up to Calvin. He was about Calvin's height and muscular. "You keep that up and I'm gonna have to shut your mouth."

The blond nudged him back. "What bosses would that be?"

"Julius Wick and his wife." Calvin wished he hadn't said it, the minute it was out of his mouth.

Raiders glanced at the others as if he didn't recognize the names. But the blond did not take his eyes off Calvin. "What the hell are you doing here? It's the middle of the night, this place no longer belongs to you."

"We saw the vans."

"When did you see the vans?"

"An hour before I notified the FBI."

"He's jerking you around," Raiders said. "He saw shit."

The blond pressed on. "And when exactly was that?"

"Last night." It seemed plausible, he hoped.

The man's expression did not change. "And what did you tell the FBI?"

"That you people were setting up a clandestine pumping operation to drain the well of any traces of the poison that killed my son." No point holding back now.

Raiders mumbled something to the man from the high-tech van.

"Then why are you two good citizens here alone?" the blond said.

"What makes you think we're alone?"

He stared at Calvin, then from a vest pocket removed a round length of metal. With deliberate turns he attached the silencer to the end of his gun barrel.

The blond nodded toward the door. Raiders and the others returned to the van, came out in shoes and pants and ran outside to check, their guns held close to their chests.

"Stupid to come here," the blond said.

Calvin looked at the silencer. So this is how it would end. Some nameless stranger in his own backyard . . .

Calvin nodded at the electronics van. "You're doing more than pumping the well."

"You got it. We're . . . neutralizing it," the blond said, figuring there was no need to hold back.

Which explained to Calvin the size of the shed and the heat. They were somehow sterilizing out the poisonous organics. There was probably a holding tank and some kind of filter in there, too. They must have been at it for the last thirty-six hours, from the moment he had moved into the hotel yesterday. "Who's paying you?"

When the blond didn't answer, Calvin said, "What's the difference? We're not leaving here."

"Guy's name's Roman," the blond man said.

"Who's he?"

"A voice on the phone."

"What's your connection with BiOmega?"

"You tell me."

Unless he was leading him on, it appeared they were freelancing.

And the gun made clear the man had no need to lead him on. "Do you *know* what you're neutralizing?"

The guy shrugged. "It gets to the right level, we pack up and move on."

Calvin stared at the stolid eye of the silencer. "You mean you dig up streets and drain wells and kill people and don't ask why?"

"Something like that."

During the exchange Terry stood in numbed silence. But suddenly all the grief-nurtured outrage that had been dammed up burst out of her. "You rotten bastards . . ." and she lunged at the man, who swiped her with his free hand, sending her against the van.

Calvin made a move toward him, but a chop to his neck from behind dropped him to his knees. The others were back.

"Nobody out there," Raiders said.

"Good." The blond nodded, then handed the pistol to Raiders. "Take them out back."

The pain in Calvin's neck was near blinding. He pulled himself up against the van and helped Terry to her feet.

Raiders prodded him with a gun to turn around.

With a plastic cord they bound Calvin's hands behind him, then Terry's.

"Calvin—"

The blond cut her off. "Dig a hole," he said to the other one. "A nice one just for two."

They put duct tape across their mouths and pushed them out back.

The blond and the monitor held their guns on Calvin and Terry, the other two led the way toward the woods. The one in red carried a shovel in each hand, the other a pick.

They crossed the lawn. Calvin looked at Terry. Matty's death seemed to have leeched her will to live. She did not struggle against the gunman, did not make a sound. These men were executing the inevitable.

As they made their way across the lawn, Calvin could only think he had brought this on, not Terry.

NOT HER.

They were halfway up the diving-board end of the pool when

Calvin felt his body shift to its own command. He bent at the waist and bulldozed the blond with his right shoulder, catching him mid-section and driving him sideways into the black water.

Calvin mouthed against the tape for Terry to run. She began to stumble across the lawn, but the man with the shovel threw her onto the grass.

A muffled *thwup*, and Calvin felt a burning flash in his right side. He stumbled to the concrete apron of the pool. A bullet had gone through his side. Someplace across the lawn, he heard Terry cry out.

Calvin's hands were behind him, so he couldn't feel where he had taken the round. Never mind, he was more concerned with not moving, of playing dead. Out of the corner of his eye he saw the men rush to the pool.

The blond had surfaced and was flapping his arms and spitting up foul water. "Help me, goddammit, I can't swim . . ."

Two of them crouched at the edge but the blond had surfaced out of reach. One stretched the shovel handle to him, but he was too panicked and went under.

Raiders kicked off his shoes and lowered himself in. Still holding the shovel, the monitor eyed Calvin.

Across the lawn Terry picked herself up under the gun of the fourth man.

The two men at the pool worked to pull in the blond. When Calvin saw Raiders grab for the shovel to be towed in, he pushed himself up and staggered into the woods. The monitor was too preoccupied to take aim.

"Get him," Raiders shouted.

"I can't see him . . ."

Calvin cut deep into the trees, trying not to blind himself on branches or stumble. His footfall was noisy. So was the man's behind him.

He risked ducking down and listening. No footsteps behind. When he was fairly certain the man had gotten lost or given up, he made his way back to the rear of the garage.

The light was out, so he had to feel blindly for the jagged glass. He backed up to it and sawed away at the bonds, the glass lacerating his fingers.

Someplace a dog growled at the commotion. The Starkeys' new shepherd? He could go there for help—but in the time it would take, they would kill Terry. One of them was pushing her into the open, a hand knotted in her hair.

Calvin finally freed his hands, sticky now with blood. He ducked into the shadows again. His adrenalin was pumping, so strong he could scarcely feel his wound.

He cut along the edge of the woods, just inside them. The blond was at the side of the pool gasping for air. Raiders was on his knees holding him up, his back to Calvin. He could see Terry on her knees in the middle of the lawn, her head pushed to the side by the force of the man's grip. The sound from her escalated Calvin's fury. But that was their purpose—to draw him out. They figured he wouldn't leave her behind.

"I know you're in there," the man said. "Come out or I'm going to take pieces off her while you watch." He turned so Calvin could see the knife held to Terry's face.

Calvin stepped out of the woods. From behind him the fourth man punched him, hard, in the kidneys.

"Take them out," ordered the blond from the pool's edge. "Right goddamn *now*."

Raiders tossed the silenced automatic to the other, who pulled Terry by the hair into the woods, Calvin forced to watch the black swallow her.

Calvin then looked back. The man's gun had no silencer. If he shot him, the woods would rock.

Calvin started to walk, but just as he passed the blond pulling himself up, he turned and, hard as he could manage, kicked him in the face. The blond's head snapped backward and he went under.

Calvin turned around to catch the barrel across the back of the head, and pancaked onto the grass, just as from inside the woods he heard a muffled gunshot.

Terry . . .

Another shot. Two more. No way Terry could have escaped, tied up as she was . . .

Calvin felt himself jerked to his feet. A hand clamped his mouth, a cold gun barrel pressed into the soft pocket at the base of his skull. There was commotion at the pool, trying to find the blond guy in the muck. He did not resist as he was hustled into the woods—and heard what sounded like a strangled cry coming from there. He could barely see through his pain, but from somewhere just ahead a black form splintered into the moonlight. The man who had shot Terry. He was moving in a stumpy shuffle. His right arm was raised halfway from his side, the gun with the silencer still in one hand. At first Calvin couldn't take in what was odd about his appearance. Until the man collapsed to his knees just feet away.

His left arm was missing.

"Jesus Christ!" Raiders rushed over to the guy.

Suddenly the grip on Calvin broke, and everything went surreal. As Calvin turned around, the gunman appeared to be driven headlong into the trunk of a huge oak. Calvin could hear the sickening crack of his skull. There was a vague movement in the black shadows where he fell. Then a low, grating, animal-like sound. Something dark receded into the trees. There were two muffled shots at the retreating figure, then Raiders took off after it into the trees. Calvin tried to get to his feet but was dazed from blood loss. He turned, just in time to see the monitor lower his gun to finish him off. Calvin rolled back his head to receive the bullet straight on. "Get it over with—"

The moment was fractured by a shriek. Raider's.

From the other side of the pool, a shape rushed across the moonlit lawn. There were two bursts of gunfire from the monitor but the figure still came, and in a flash Calvin saw it swipe at the man's head, saw him fold backward on his legs, his head at a broken angle.

The figure staggered into the woods.

And a nightmare afterimage filled Calvin's mind.

As if through a mist of unreality, Calvin saw Terry step into the moonlight from the woods.

Her voice scated chillingly, "Matteeee . . ."

EPILOGUE

They found him at the base of the charred remains of TopTree, bleeding and unconscious. He had been shot twice—in the thigh and upper chest. He was barely recognizable with all the hair on his body and face. But Terry knew at once, even in the darkness. And the locket around his neck was confirmation.

They rushed him and Calvin to Emerson Hospital, where two ER teams worked on them. Although Calvin had lost a good deal of blood, the round that caught him in the side had passed through his left beer-wing, missing his kidney by an inch. His collarbone was fractured and his left arm broken. The bullet to Matty's chest had shattered a rib and was removed, as was the one lodged in his left thigh.

Under Mitch Tojian's supervision the staff put Matty in a private room of the intensive care unit, where he remained for six days. He was then transferred to a private room in a pediatric wing of Children's Hospital in Boston, where he was intravenously treated with a battery of neuropharmacological compounds, targeting the elevated hormones in his system. By the end of the third week MRI and SPECT analyses showed a marked reduction of the size of his amygdala and electrical activity in those brain sectors associated with violent behavior. The blood tests indicated normalized hormonal levels, which, with medication, would be kept in check until his body had stabilized. By the end of June nearly all signs of hirsutism had vanished. The only outward sign of his terrible ordeal was the limp in his left leg. Dr. Tojian predicted that in a matter of months he would be walking normally again.

As for his disappearance, Matty could provide authorities with little solid information. Apparently he had been kidnapped by an unknown party or parties and another boy's body had been substituted at TopTree. Matty spoke only vaguely of some real, far-out stuff . . . fighting dogs and being locked in a cage. Wild imaginings, and no details. Police assumed that most or all of what he said had to be delusional. The forensic examination of the exhumed remains had not, so far, revealed an identity that checked with any known missing youth. Whatever had happened to Matty in the nine days he had been missing and presumed dead would forever remain a mystery.

As for the four men who had attacked Calvin and Terry, three were dead, including the blond, who was pulled from the bottom of the pool. The fourth had lost an arm. The identities of two revealed previous records for armed assault in New York and warrants for arrest in connection with gangland slayings in Pennsylvania. The third had no record. The one-armed survivor, who was indicted on various charges, including conspiracy and attempted murder, was uncooperative when asked who had hired him, leaving investigators to assume it had been the late Julius Wick.

Of course, the media jumped on the story of Wick's connection to BiOmega, the genocide virus, and the murky world of hired guns. The president publicly expressed his shock at the revelations. He and Wick had been friends for years, and he had always regarded him as a man of the highest moral integrity who apparently had tried to cover some past mistakes, or what appeared to be mistakes, taken out of their time and place. Yet some called for investigations of the government's role in BiOmega, citing the genocidal objectives of Black Flag as flagrant violations of the Geneva Convention.

Responding, the attorney general set up a team of investigators to examine improprieties committed by BiOmega. Those investigative efforts, the media reported, were headed up by an attorney for the Treasury Department and, according to President Morgan Reese, "a man with an impeccable record." Daniel McDermott. The following week the president found a replacement for the post of biotech czar. Because of the time lapse, the lack of records and the unfortunate, accidental death of Julius Wick, the investigative efforts were eventually dropped, with no new revelations. In time the story of Matthew Hazzard and BiOmega faded from the public consciousness. And to the pleasure of the president and his aides, the pending legislation that he had supported successfully passed both houses of Congress.

While Matty was recovering, Charlie Cobb visited Calvin in the hospital and offered him his old job back with a $5,000 increase. To Charlie's dismay, Calvin accepted. He had called Robin Priest at NYPI and withdrawn his acceptance of the endowed post. He could not accept a job engineered by Julius Wick. Priest denied knowing anything about the circumstances; in fact, he told Calvin that, no insult intended, his department had protested the usurpation of their selection powers by the anonymous director. "Well," Calvin told him, "I guess it works out for us all." Priest could pass the offer on to his own choice of candidates, Matty would not be forced to move away, and Calvin was back at Middlesex pulling down his age plus four.

Financially, Calvin's family still fared well, since they had over $600,000 of the Wicks' money in their bank account. For a few weeks, while living out of their hotel, Calvin and Terry looked at houses. By mid-July they had found a place in Wellesley. Meanwhile, the backyard of their old place had been torn up. Some twenty-seven containers of various sizes had been removed and destroyed by the EPA, while the aquifer was decontaminated using Wick's own apparatus. Water tests showed that the Black Flag substance had not leached into the main wells that served Carleton and the surrounding towns.

The morning of Matty's release from Children's Hospital was a glorious June day.

Matty was in a chair watching television when Calvin and Terry arrived, holding hands. Terry had forgiven Calvin, grateful Matty was alive and they were whole again. Calvin's lapse of sexual interest was clearly related to the hormonal substance in the water. The excess in his case had apparently created antigens that reduced his testosterone level and thereby, his potency. By the Fourth of July he was his own best firecracker.

Dr. Mitch Tojian showed up at eleven and presented the family with four tickets to box seats behind the Red Sox's dugout on the first-base line for the next weekend. It would be only the third time Matty had been to Fenway, and the first in a box seat.

Checkout was on the second floor in the business office. Mitch would head down with them; it was moments such as this when the profession felt good, when the dark backroom door faded from view. He handed Terry prescriptions for Matty's medication.

When his mother and father were a little ahead of them, Matty asked the doctor in a low voice, "Do I still have to take all that?"

Dr. Tojian put his hand on the boy's shoulder. "Guess you've had it with the medicines, right?"

"Yeah," Matty said. "Makes me feel kinda dead."

"Dead? In what way?"

Matty shrugged. "I'm weaker, and I don't feel as much."

"As much as what?"

"The way I used to. You know, when I was the other way . . ."

For a moment they stopped while his parents moved down the hall. "You *liked* the way you felt?"

"Yes . . ." A darkening in his eyes.

Dr. Tojian could only guess at what lay behind them. Some residue of heightened awareness? Besides his extraordinary strength and agility, his senses had been inordinately acute—night vision, canine olfaction, hearing acuity of a bat. It still boggled the mind how, in the middle of the night, he had managed to find his way home over some thirty miles with a chewed-up hand and foot. Some terrified dogs, they figured, must have attacked him on his way home. They were, of course, closer than they knew, or than Matty could tell them. Police surmised Matty had been taken someplace on the North Shore, since he was first spotted running across Route 1 in Danvers and moving southwest to Carleton. It was easy to trace his route, since all that night police from towns along the way had received frantic calls from people claiming to have seen a gorilla or yeti running through their yards.

"But you're back to normal again," Mitch said. "Isn't that a lot better?"

Matty said nothing.

"You can go out in the day again, play ball, go to school, wear T-shirts."

"I suppose."

Well, what could you expect, Tojian thought. For weeks the boy's blood had buzzed with adrenalin, gonadotropins and other visceral stimulants.

"I'm afraid we'll have to keep you on the medicines for a few weeks more," Tojian said. "Just until your body's defenses take over." He added, "You'll feel better, Matty, once you get back into the swing of things. Believe me."

They continued down the corridor toward the elevators when Mitch heard his name on the PA system and left Matty with his parents. "I'll be right with you," he told them, and took the call at the nurse's station across from where they waited for him.

The duty nurse handed him the receiver. "Dr. Rosenblum."

On Mitch's urging a few months earlier, Larry Rosenblum had taken up golf and was now fanatical about the game. Whenever he saw a four-hour window in his schedule, he would call Mitch to join him for a game. It made no difference whether he was at home, in the office or making rounds. He was a golf junkie.

"Only if we can quit at a hundred or nine holes, whichever comes first," Mitch said into the receiver.

But now there was no equivalent tone of banter in Larry's voice. "Mitch, we've got us a problem."

"I'm listening."

"It's related to the Hazzard case."

"He's being released as we speak." Mitch gave Matty a wink.

Matty looked back and smiled.

"I know," Dr. Rosenblum said. "He's not alone . . ."

"I don't follow."

"I just got a call from epidemiology. Another case has been reported."

"Another case of what?"

"Explosive behavior. A young male, eleven years old, went berserk and mauled some people. One died from bites on the neck and face."

"Oh, God," whispered Tojian. He had to concentrate on keeping his expression neutral, Matty was watching him. He turned a profile to the Hazzards.

"Where?"

"Lexington, west side. He's at the General now."

"That's six, seven miles away. How do you know they're related?"

"Same symptoms—hirsutism, night vision, rage. All of it," Larry said. "Like the Hazzard boy, he was a nice kid—friendly, no record of problems, played soccer, sang in the church choir, your basic kid. Then in a couple weeks . . . It's like the start of an epidemic of lycanthropy, for God's sake . . . All it takes is a few micrograms to insult the system."

Tojian turned his back to the Hazzards.

"There's something else," Rosenblum said, his voice edged. "From Mount Auburn and Beth Israel. Some real bad deliveries, Mitch. I mean, they're talking about genetic monsters."

"I thought we caught it, I thought it didn't seep through . . ."

"We did. It's not in the water. It's apparently communicated through the *air*."

"What?" Tojian looked around. From across the hall Matty was staring at him.

"The stuff's seeped to the surface and into the grass and trees. It's spreading through water vapor in the atmosphere." Rosenblum said. "It's airborne, Mitch. It's contracted by breathing—"

"*Breathing?*" Mitch closed his eyes.

When he opened them again, Matty was still glaring at him, but now with a grin as deep as night.